SMOKE AND MIRRORS

D0488991

Smoke and Mirrors

Short Fiction and Illusions

Neil Gaiman

HEADLINE
FEATURE

Copyright © 1999 Neil Gaiman

The right of Neil Gaiman to be identified as the Author of
the Work has been asserted by him in accordance with
the Copyright, Designs and Patents Act 1988.

First published in 1999
by AVON BOOKS

First published in Great Britain in 1999
by HEADLINE BOOK PUBLISHING

First published in paperback in Great Britain in 2000
by HEADLINE BOOK PUBLISHING

10 9 8 7 6 5 4 3 2 1

All rights reserved. No part of this publication may be reproduced,
stored in a retrieval system, or transmitted, in any form or by any
means without the prior written permission of the publisher, nor be
otherwise circulated in any form of binding or cover other than that
in which it is published and without a similar condition being
imposed on the subsequent purchaser.

All characters in this publication are fictitious and any resemblance
to real persons, living or dead, is purely coincidental.

ISBN 0 7472 6368 X

Typeset by Avon Dataset Ltd, Bidford-on-Avon, Warks

Printed and bound in Great Britain by
Mackays of Chatham plc, Chatham, Kent

HEADLINE BOOK PUBLISHING
A division of the Hodder Headline Group
338 Euston Road
London NW1 3BH

www.headline.co.uk
www.hodderheadline.com

For Ellen Datlow and Steve Jones

Contents

But where there's a monster there's a miracle.

— OGDEN NASH, *DRAGONS ARE TOO SELDOM*

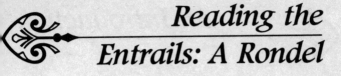

Reading the Entrails: A Rondel

'I mean,' she said, 'that one can't help growing older.'
'*One* can't perhaps,' said Humpty Dumpty, 'but *two* can.
With proper assistance, you might have left off at seven.'
– LEWIS CARROLL, *THROUGH THE LOOKING-GLASS*

They'll call it chance, or luck, or call it Fate –
The cards and stars that tumble as they will.
Tomorrow manifests and brings the bill
For every kiss and kill, the small and great.
You want to know the future, love? Then wait:
I'll answer your impatient questions. Still –
They'll call it chance, or luck, or call it Fate,
The cards and stars that tumble as they will.

I'll come to you tonight, dear, when it's late,
You will not see me; you may feel a chill.
I'll wait until you sleep, then take my fill,
And that will be your future on a plate.
They'll call it chance, or luck, or call it Fate.

An Introduction

Writing is flying in dreams.
When you remember. When you can. When it works.
It's that easy.

— AUTHOR'S NOTEBOOK, FEBRUARY 1992

*T*hey do it with mirrors. It's a cliché, of course, but it's also true. Magicians have been using mirrors, usually set at a forty-five-degree angle, ever since the Victorians began to manufacture reliable, clear mirrors in quantity, well over a hundred years ago. John Nevil Maskelyne began it, in 1862, with a wardrobe that, thanks to a cunningly placed mirror, concealed more than it revealed.

Mirrors are wonderful things. They appear to tell the truth, to reflect life back out at us; but set a mirror correctly and it will lie so convincingly you'll believe that something has vanished into thin air, that a box filled with doves and flags and spiders is actually empty, that people hidden in the wings or the pit are floating ghosts upon the stage. Angle it right and a mirror becomes a magic casement; it can show you anything you can imagine and maybe a few things you can't.

(The smoke blurs the edges of things.)

Stories are, in one way or another, mirrors. We use them to explain to ourselves how the world works or how it doesn't work. Like mirrors, stories prepare us for the day to come. They distract us from the things in the darkness.

Fantasy – and all fiction is fantasy of one kind or another – is a mirror. A distorting mirror, to be sure, and a concealing mirror, set at forty-five degrees to reality, but it's a mirror nonetheless, which we can use to tell ourselves things we might not otherwise see. (Fairy tales, as G. K. Chesterton once said, are more than true. Not because they tell us that dragons exist, but because they tell us that dragons can be defeated.)

Winter started today. The sky turned grey and the snow began to fall and it did not stop falling until well after dark. I sat in the darkness and watched the snow falling, and the flakes glistened and glimmered as they spun into the light and out again, and I wondered about where stories came from.

This is the kind of thing that you wonder about when you make things up for a living. I remain unconvinced that it is the kind of activity that is a fit occupation for an adult, but it's too late now: I seem to have a career that I enjoy which doesn't involve getting up too early in the morning. (When I was a child, adults would tell me not to make things up, warning me of what would happen if I did. As far as I can tell so far it seems to involve lots of foreign travel and not having to get up too early in the morning.)

Most of the stories in this book were written to entertain the various editors who had asked me for tales for specific anthologies ('It's for an anthology of stories about the Holy Grail,' '. . . about sex,' '. . . of fairy stories retold for adults,' '. . . about sex and horror,' '. . . of revenge stories,' '. . . about superstition,' '. . . about more sex'). A few of them were written to amuse myself or, more precisely, to get an idea or an image out of my head and pinned safely down on paper; which is as good a reason for writing as I know: releasing demons, letting them fly. Some of the stories began in idleness: fancies and curiosities that got out of hand.

I once made up a story as a wedding present for some friends. It was about a couple who were given a story as a wedding present. It was not a reassuring story. Having made up the story, I decided that they'd probably prefer a toaster, so I got them a toaster, and to this day have not written the story down. It sits in the back of my head to this day, waiting for someone to get married who would appreciate it.

It occurs to me now (writing this introduction in blue-black fountain pen ink in a black-bound notebook, in case you were wondering) that, although one way or another most of the stories in this book are about love in some form or another, there aren't enough happy stories, stories of properly requited love to balance out all the other kinds you'll find in this book; and indeed, that there are people who don't read introductions. For that matter, some of you out there may be having weddings one day, after all. So for all of you who *do* read introductions, here is the story I did not write. (And if I don't like the story once it's written, I can always cross out this paragraph, and you'll never know that I stopped writing the introduction to start writing a story instead.)

The Wedding Present

After all the joys and the headaches of the wedding, after the madness and the magic of it all (not to mention the embarrassment of Belinda's father's after-dinner speech, complete with family slide show), after the honeymoon was literally (although not yet meta-phorically) over and before their new suntans had a chance to fade in the English autumn, Belinda and Gordon got down to the business of unwrapping the wedding presents and writing their thank you letters – thank yous enough for every towel and every toaster, for the juicer and the breadmaker, for the cutlery and the crockery and the teasmade and the curtains.

'Right,' said Gordon. 'That's the large objects thank-you'd. What've we got left?'

'Things in envelopes,' said Belinda. 'Cheques, I hope.'

There were several cheques, a number of gift tokens, and even a £10 book token from Gordon's Aunt Marie, who was poor as a church mouse, Gordon told Belinda, but a dear, and who had sent him a book token every birthday as long as he could remember. And then, at the very bottom of the pile, there was a large brown businesslike envelope.

'What is it?' asked Belinda.

Gordon opened the flap and pulled out a sheet of paper the colour of two-day-old cream, ragged at top and bottom, with typing on one side. The words had been typed with a manual typewriter, something Gordon had not seen in some years. He read the page slowly.

'What is it?' asked Belinda. 'Who's it from?'

'I don't know,' said Gordon. 'Someone who still owns a typewriter. It's not signed.'

'Is it a letter?'

'Not exactly,' he said, and he scratched the side of his nose and read it again.

'Well,' she said in an exasperated voice (but she was not really exasperated; she was happy. She would wake in the morning and check to see if she were still as happy as she had been when she went to sleep the night before, or when Gordon had woken her in the night by brushing up against her, or when she had woken him. And she was). 'Well, what is it?'

'It appears to be a description of our wedding,' he said. 'It's very nicely written. Here,' and he passed it to her.

She looked it over.

It was a crisp day in early October when Gordon Robert Johnson and Belinda Karen Abingdon swore that they would love each other, would support and honour each other as long as they both should live. The bride was radiant and lovely, the groom was nervous, but obviously proud and just as obviously pleased.

That was how it began. It went on to describe the service and the reception clearly, simply, and amusingly.

'How sweet,' she said. 'What does it say on the envelope?'

' "Gordon and Belinda's Wedding",' he read.

'No name? Nothing to indicate who sent it?'

'Uh-uh.'

'Well, it's very sweet, and it's very thoughtful,' she said. 'Whoever it's from.'

She looked inside the envelope to see if there was something else inside that they had overlooked, a note from whichever one of her friends (or his, or theirs) had written it, but there wasn't, so, vaguely relieved that there was one less thank you note to write, she placed the cream sheet of paper back in its envelope, which she placed in a box file, along with a copy of the wedding banquet menu, and the invitations, and the contact sheets for the wedding photographs, and one white rose from the bridal bouquet.

Gordon was an architect, and Belinda was a vet. For each of them what they did was a vocation, not a job. They were in their early twenties. Neither of them had been married before, nor even seriously involved with anyone. They met when Gordon brought his thirteen-year-old golden retriever, Goldie, gray-muzzled and half-paralyzed, to Belinda's surgery to be put down. He had had the dog since he was a boy and insisted on being with her at the end. Belinda held his hand as he cried, and then, suddenly and unprofessionally, she hugged him, tightly, as if she could squeeze away the pain and the loss and the grief. One of them asked the other if they could meet that evening in the local pub for a drink, and afterward neither of them was sure which of them had proposed it.

The most important thing to know about the first two years of their marriage was this: they were pretty happy. From time to time they would squabble, and every once in a while they would have a blazing row about nothing very much that would end in tearful reconciliations, and they would make love and kiss away the other's tears and whisper heartfelt apologies into each other's ears. At the end of the second year, six months after she came off the pill, Belinda found herself pregnant.

Gordon bought her a bracelet studded with tiny rubies, and he turned the spare bedroom into a nursery, hanging the wallpaper himself. The wallpaper was covered with nursery rhyme characters, with Little Bo Peep, and Humpty Dumpty, and the Dish Running Away with the Spoon, over and over and over again.

Belinda came home from the hospital, with little Melanie in her carry-cot, and Belinda's mother came to stay with them for a week, sleeping on the sofa in the lounge.

It was on the third day that Belinda pulled out the box file to show her wedding souvenirs to her mother and to reminisce. Already their wedding seemed like such a long time ago. They smiled at the dried brown thing that had once been a white rose, and clucked over the menu and the invitation. At the bottom of the box was a large brown envelope.

' "Gordon and Belinda's Marriage",' read Belinda's mother.

'It's a description of our wedding,' said Belinda. 'It's very sweet. It even has a bit in it about Daddy's slide show.'

Belinda opened the envelope and pulled out the sheet of cream paper. She read what was typed upon the paper, and made a face. Then she put it away without saying anything.

'Can't I see it, dear?' asked her mother.

'I think it's Gordon playing a joke,' said Belinda. 'Not in good taste, either.'

Belinda was sitting up in bed that night, breast-feeding Melanie, when she said to Gordon, who was staring at his wife and new daughter with a foolish smile upon his face, 'Darling, why did you write those things?'

'What things?'

'In the letter. That wedding thing. You know.'

'I don't know.'

'It wasn't funny.'

He sighed. 'What are you talking about?'

Belinda pointed to the box file, which she had brought upstairs and placed upon her dressing table. Gordon opened it and took out the envelope. 'Did it always say that on the envelope?' he asked. 'I thought it said something about our wedding.' Then he took out and read the single sheet of ragged-edged paper, and his forehead creased. 'I didn't write this.' He turned the paper over, staring at the blank side as if expecting to see something else written there.

'You didn't write it?' she asked. 'Really you didn't?' Gordon shook his head. Belinda wiped a dribble of milk from the baby's chin. 'I believe you,' she said. 'I thought you wrote it, but you didn't.'

'No.'

'Let me see that again,' she said. He passed the paper to her. 'This is so weird. I mean, it's not funny, and it's not even true.'

Typed upon the paper was a brief description of the previous two years for Gordon and Belinda. It had not been a good two years, according to the typed sheet. Six months after they were married, Belinda had been bitten in the cheek by a Pekingese, so badly that the cheek needed to be stitched back together. It had left a nasty scar. Worse than that, nerves had been damaged, and she had begun to drink, perhaps to numb the pain. She suspected that Gordon was revolted by her face, while the new baby, it said, was a desperate attempt to glue the couple together.

'Why would they say this?' she asked.

'They?'

'Whoever wrote this horrid thing.' She ran a finger across her cheek: it was unblemished and unmarked. She was a very beautiful young woman, although she looked tired and fragile now.

'How do you know it's a "they"?'

'I don't know,' she said, transferring the baby to her left breast. 'It seems a sort of "they"-ish thing to do. To write that and to swap it for the old one and to wait until one of us read it ... Come on, little Melanie, there you go, that's such a fine girl ...'

'Shall I throw it away?'

'Yes. No. I don't know. I think ...' She stroked the baby's forehead. 'Hold on to it,' she said. 'We might need it for evidence. I wonder if it was something Al organised.' Al was Gordon's youngest brother.

Gordon put the paper back into the envelope, and he put the envelope back into the box file, which was pushed under the bed and, more or less, forgotten.

Neither of them got much sleep for the next few months, what with the nightly feeds and the continual crying, for Melanie was a colicky baby. The box file stayed under the bed. And then Gordon was offered a job in Preston, several hundred miles north, and since Belinda was on leave from her job and had no immediate plans to go back to work, she found the idea rather attractive. So they moved.

They found a terraced house on a cobbled street, high and old and deep. Belinda filled in from time to time at a local vet's, seeing small animals and housepets. When Melanie was eighteen months old, Belinda gave birth to a son, whom they called Kevin after Gordon's late grandfather.

Gordon was made a full partner in the firm of architects. When Kevin began to go to nursery, Belinda went back to work.

The box file was never lost. It was in one of the spare rooms at the top of the house, beneath a teetering pile of copies of *The Architect's Journal* and *Architectural Review*. Belinda thought about the box file, and what it contained, from time to time, and, one night when Gordon was in Scotland overnight consulting on the remodelling of an ancestral home, she did more than think.

Both of the children were asleep. Belinda went up the stairs into the undecorated part of the house. She moved the magazines and opened the box, which (where it had not been covered by magazines) was thick with two years of undisturbed dust. The envelope still said *Gordon and Belinda's Marriage* on it, and Belinda honestly did not know if it had ever said anything else.

She took out the paper from the envelope, and she read it. And then she put it away, and sat there, at the top of the house, feeling shaken and sick.

According to the neatly typed message, Kevin, her second child, had not been born; the baby had been miscarried at five months. Since then Belinda had been suffering from frequent attacks of bleak, black depression. Gordon was home rarely, it said, because he was conducting a rather miserable affair with the senior partner in his company, a striking but nervous woman ten years his senior. Belinda was drinking more, and affecting high collars and scarves to hide the spiderweb scar upon her cheek. She and Gordon spoke little, except to argue the small and petty arguments of those who fear the big arguments, knowing that the only things that were left to be said were too huge to be said without destroying both their lives.

Belinda said nothing about the latest version of *Gordon and Belinda's Marriage* to Gordon. However, he read it himself, or something quite like it, several months later, when Belinda's mother fell ill, and Belinda went south for a week to help look after her.

On the sheet of paper that Gordon took out of the envelope was a portrait of a marriage similar to the one that Belinda had read, although, at present, his affair with his boss had ended badly, and his job was now in peril.

Gordon rather liked his boss, but could not imagine himself ever becoming romantically involved with her. He was enjoying his job, although he wanted something that would challenge him more than it did.

Belinda's mother improved, and Belinda came home again within the week. Her husband and children were relieved and delighted to see her.

It was Christmas Eve before Gordon spoke to Belinda about the envelope.

'You've looked at it too, haven't you?' They had crept into the children's bedrooms earlier that evening and filled the hanging Christmas stockings. Gordon had felt euphoric as he had walked through the house, as he stood beside his children's beds, but it was a euphoria tinged with a profound sorrow: the knowledge that such moments of complete happiness could not last; that one could not stop Time.

Belinda knew what he was talking about. 'Yes,' she said, 'I've read it.'

'What do you think?'

'Well,' she said. 'I don't think it's a joke anymore. Not even a sick joke.'

'Mm,' he said. 'Then what is it?'

They sat in the living room at the front of the house with the lights dimmed, and the log burning on the bed of coals cast flickering orange and yellow light about the room.

'I think it really is a wedding present,' she told him. 'It's the marriage that we aren't having. The bad things are happening there, on the page, not here, in our lives. Instead of living it, we are reading it, knowing it could have gone that way and also that it never did.'

'You're saying it's magic, then?' He would not have said it aloud, but it was Christmas Eve, and the lights were down.

'I don't believe in magic,' she said, flatly. 'It's a wedding present. And I think we should make sure it's kept safe.'

On Boxing Day she moved the envelope from the box file to her jewellery drawer, which she kept locked, where it lay flat beneath her necklaces and rings, her bracelets and her brooches.

Spring became summer. Winter became spring.

Gordon was exhausted. By day he worked for clients, designing, and liaising with builders and contractors; by night he would sit up late, working for himself, designing museums and galleries and public buildings for competitions. Sometimes his designs received honourable mentions, and were reproduced in architectural journals.

Belinda was doing more large animal work, which she enjoyed, visiting farmers and inspecting and treating horses, sheep and cows. Sometimes she would bring the children with her on her rounds.

Her mobile phone rang when she was in a paddock trying to examine a pregnant goat who had, it turned out, no desire to be caught, let alone examined. She retired from the battle, leaving the goat glaring at her from across the field, and thumbed the phone open. 'Yes?'

'Guess what?'

'Hello darling. Um. You've won the lottery?'

'Nope. Close, though. My design for the British Heritage Museum has made the short list. I'm up against some pretty stiff contenders, though. But I'm on the short list.'

'That's wonderful!'

'I've spoken to Mrs Fulbright and she's going to have Sonja baby-sit for us tonight. We're celebrating.'

'Terrific. Love you,' she said. 'Now got to get back to the goat.'

They drank too much champagne over a fine celebratory meal. That night in their bedroom as Belinda removed her earrings, she said, 'Shall we see what the wedding present says?'

He looked at her gravely from the bed. He was only wearing his socks. 'No, I don't think so. It's a special night. Why spoil it?'

She placed her earrings in her jewellery drawer, and locked it. Then she removed her stockings. 'I suppose you're right. I can imagine what it says, anyway. I'm drunk and depressed and you're a miserable loser. And meanwhile we're ... well, actually I *am* a bit tiddly, but that's not what I mean. It just sits there at the bottom of the drawer, like the portrait in the attic in *The Picture of Dorian Gray*.'

' "And it was only by his rings that they knew him." Yes. I remember. We read it in school.'

'That's really what I'm scared of,' she said, pulling on a cotton nightdress. 'That the thing on that paper is the real portrait of our marriage at present, and what we've got now is just a pretty picture. That it's real, and we're not. I mean' – she was speaking intently now, with the gravity of the slightly drunk – 'don't you ever think that it's too good to be true?'

He nodded. 'Sometimes. Tonight, certainly.'

She shivered. 'Maybe really I *am* a drunk with a dog bite on my cheek, and you fuck anything that moves and Kevin was never born and – and all that other horrible stuff.'

He stood up, walked over to her, put his arms around her. 'But it isn't true,' he pointed out. 'This is real. You're real. I'm real. That wedding thing is just a story. It's just words.' And he kissed her, and held her tightly, and little more was said that night.

It was a long six months before Gordon's design for the British Heritage Museum was announced as the winning design, although it was derided in *The Times* as being too 'aggressively modern', in various architectural journals as being too old-fashioned, and it was described by one of the judges, in an interview in the *Sunday Telegraph*, as 'a bit of a compromise candidate – everybody's second choice'.

They moved to London, letting their house in Preston to an artist and his family, for Belinda would not let Gordon sell it. Gordon worked intensively, happily, on the museum project. Kevin was six and Melanie was eight. Melanie found London intimidating, but Kevin loved it. Both of the children were initially distressed to have lost their friends and their school. Belinda found a part-time job at a small animal clinic in Camden, working three afternoons a week. She missed her cows.

Days in London became months and then years, and, despite occasional budgetary setbacks, Gordon was increasingly excited. The day approached when the first ground would be broken for the museum.

One night Belinda woke in the small hours, and she stared at her sleeping husband in the sodium-yellow illumination of the streetlamp outside their bedroom window. His hairline was receding, and the hair at the back was thinning. Belinda wondered what it would be like when she was actually married to a bald man. She decided it would be much the same as it always had been. Mostly happy. Mostly good.

She wondered what was happening to the *them* in the envelope. She could feel its presence, dry and brooding, in the corner of their bedroom, safely locked away from all harm. She felt, suddenly, sorry for the Belinda and Gordon trapped in the envelope on their piece of paper, hating each other and everything else.

Gordon began to snore. She kissed him, gently, on the cheek, and said, 'Shhh.' He stirred, and was quiet, but did not wake. She snuggled against him and soon fell back into sleep herself.

After lunch the following day, while in conversation with an importer of Tuscan marble, Gordon looked very surprised and reached a hand up to his chest. He said, 'I'm frightfully sorry about this,' and then his knees gave way, and he fell to the floor. They called an ambulance, but Gordon was dead when it arrived. He was thirty-six years old.

At the inquest the coroner announced that the autopsy showed Gordon's heart to have been congenitally weak. It could have gone at any time.

For the first three days after his death, Belinda felt nothing, a profound and awful nothing. She comforted the children, she spoke to her friends and to Gordon's friends, to her family and to Gordon's family, accepting their condolences gracefully and gently, as one accepts unasked-for gifts. She would listen to people cry for Gordon, which she still had not done. She would say all the right things, and she would feel nothing at all.

Melanie, who was eleven, seemed to be taking it well. Kevin abandoned his books and computer games, and sat in his bedroom, staring out of the window, not wanting to talk.

The day after the funeral her parents went back to the countryside, taking both the children with them. Belinda refused to go. There was, she said, too much to do.

On the fourth day after the funeral she was making the double bed that she and Gordon had shared when she began to cry, and the sobs ripped through her in huge ugly spasms of grief, and tears fell from her face onto the bedspread and clear snot streamed from her nose, and she sat down on the floor suddenly, like a marionette whose strings had been cut, and she cried for the best part of an hour, for she knew that she would never see him again.

She wiped her face. Then she unlocked her jewellery drawer and took out the envelope and opened it. She pulled out the creamcoloured sheet of paper and ran her eyes over the neatly typed words. The Belinda on the paper had crashed their car while drunk and was about to lose her driving licence. She and Gordon had not spoken for days. He had lost his job almost eighteen months earlier and now spent most of his days sitting around their house in Salford. Belinda's job brought in what money they had. Melanie was out of control: Belinda, cleaning Melanie's bedroom, had found a cache of five and ten pound notes. Melanie had offered no explanation for how an eleven-year-old girl had come by the money, had just retreated into her room and glared at them, tight-lipped, when quizzed. Neither Gordon nor Belinda had investigated further, scared of what they might have discovered. The house in Salford was dingy and damp, such that the plaster was coming away from the ceiling in huge crumbling chunks, and all three of them had developed nasty bronchial coughs.

Belinda felt sorry for them.

She put the paper back in the envelope. She wondered what it would be like to hate Gordon, to have him hate her. She wondered what it would be like not to have Kevin in her life, not to see his drawings of airplanes or hear his magnificently tuneless renditions of popular songs. She wondered where Melanie – the other Melanie, not *her* Melanie but the there-but-for-the-grace-of-God Melanie – could have got that money and was relieved that her own Melanie seemed to have few interests beyond ballet and Enid Blyton books.

She missed Gordon so much it felt like something sharp being hammered into her chest, a spike, perhaps, or an icicle, made of cold and loneliness and the knowledge that she would never see him again in this world.

Then she took the envelope downstairs to the lounge, where the coal fire was burning in the grate, because Gordon had loved open fires. He said that a fire gave a room life. She disliked coal fires, but she had lit it this evening out of routine and out of habit, and because not lighting it would have meant admitting to herself, on some absolute level, that he was never coming home.

Belinda stared into the fire for some time, thinking about what she had in her life, and what she had given up; and whether it would be worse to love someone who was no longer there, or not to love someone who was.

And then, at the end, almost casually, she tossed the envelope onto the coals, and she watched it curl and blacken and catch, watched the yellow flames dancing amidst the blue.

Soon the wedding present was nothing but black flakes of ash which danced on the updrafts and were carried away, like a child's letter to Santa Claus, up the chimney and off into the night.

Belinda sat back in her chair, and closed her eyes, and waited for the scar to blossom on her cheek.

* * *

And that is the story I did not write for my friends' wedding. Although, of course, it's *not* the story I did not write or even the story I set out to write when I began it, some pages ago. The story I thought I was setting out to write was much shorter, much more fablelike, and it did not end like that. (I don't know how it did end originally any more. There was some kind of ending, but once the story was underway the real ending became inevitable.)

Most of the stories in this volume have that much in common: The place they arrived at in the end was not the place I was expecting them to go when I set out. Sometimes the only way I would know that a story had finished was when there weren't any more words to be written down.

Reading the Entrails: A Rondel

Editors who ask me for stories about '. . . anything you want. Honest. Anything at all. Just write the story you always wanted to write' rarely get anything at all.

In this case, Lawrence Schimel wrote asking for a poem to introduce his anthology of stories about foretelling the future. He wanted one of the verse forms with repeating lines, like a villanelle or a pantoum, to echo the way we inevitably arrive at our future.

So I wrote him a rondel about the pleasures and perils of fortune-telling and prefaced it with the bleakest joke in *Through the Looking-Glass*. Somehow it seemed a fine starting point for this book.

Chivalry

I'd been having a bad week. The script I was meant to be writing just wasn't happening, and I'd spent days staring at a blank screen, occasionally writing a word like *the* and staring at it for an hour or so and then, slowly, letter by letter, I'd delete it and write *and* or *but* instead. Then I'd exit without saving. Ed Kramer phoned and reminded me that I owed him a story for an anthology of stories about the Holy Grail which he was editing with the ubiquitous Marty Greenberg. And seeing nothing else was happening and that this story was living in the back of my mind, I said sure.

I wrote it in a weekend, a gift from the gods, easy and sweet as anything. Suddenly I was a writer transformed: I laughed in the face of danger and spat on the shoes of writer's block. Then I sat and stared glumly at a blank screen for another week, because the gods have a sense of humour.

Several years ago, on a signing tour, someone gave

me a copy of an academic paper on feminist language theory that compared and contrasted 'Chivalry', Tennyson's 'The Lady of Shalott', and a Madonna song. I hope one day to write a story called 'Mrs Whitaker's Werewolf' and wonder what sort of papers that might provoke.

When I do live readings, I tend to start with this story. It's a very friendly story and I enjoy reading it aloud.

Nicholas Was . . .

Every Christmas I get cards from artists. They paint them themselves or draw them. They are things of beauty, monuments to inspired creativity.

Every Christmas I feel insignificant and embarrassed and talentless.

So I wrote this one year, wrote it early for Christmas. Dave McKean calligraphed it elegantly and I sent it out to everyone I could think of. My card.

It's exactly 100 words long (102, including the title) and first saw print in *Drabble II*, a collection of 100-word-long short stories. I keep meaning to do another Christmas card story, but it's always December 15 before I remember, so I put it off until next year.

The Price

My literary agent, Ms Merrilee Heifetz of New York, is one of the coolest people in the world, and she has only once, to the best of my recollection, ever suggested that I should write a specific book. This was some time ago. 'Listen,' she said, 'angels are big these days, and people always like books about cats, so I thought, "Wouldn't it be cool if someone did a book about a cat who was an angel or an angel who was a cat or something?"'

And I agreed that it was a solid commercial idea and that I would think about it. Unfortunately, by the time I had finally finished thinking about it, books about angels were the-year-before-last-year's thing. Still, the idea was planted, and one day I wrote this story.

(For the curious: Eventually a young lady fell in love with the Black Cat, and he went to live with her, and the last time I saw him he was the size of a very small mountain lion, and for all I know he's growing still. Two weeks after the Black Cat left, a brown tabby arrived and moved onto the porch. As I write this, he's asleep on the back of the sofa a few feet away from me.)

While I think of it, I'd like to take this opportunity to thank my family for letting me put them in this story, and, more importantly, both for leaving me alone to write, and for sometimes insisting I come out to play.

Troll Bridge

This story was nominated for a 1994 World Fantasy Award, although it didn't win. It was written for Ellen Datlow and Terri Windling's *Snow White, Blood Red*, an anthology of retellings of fairy tales for adults. I chose the tale of 'The Three Billy Goats Gruff'. Had Gene Wolfe, one of my favourite writers (and, it occurs to me now, another person who hid a story in an introduction), not taken the title many years earlier, I would have called it 'Trip Trap'.

Don't Ask Jack

Lisa Snellings is a remarkable sculptor. This was written about the first of her sculptures I saw and fell in love with: a demonic jack-in-the-box. She gave me a copy of it and has promised me the original in her will, she says. Each of her sculptures is like a story, frozen in wood or plaster. (There is one on my mantelpiece of a winged girl in a cage offering passersby a feather from her wings while her captor sleeps; I suspect that this one is a novel. We'll see.)

The Goldfish Pool and Other Stories

The mechanics of writing fascinate me. This story was begun in 1991. Three pages were written and then, feeling too close to the material, I abandoned it. Finally, in 1994, I decided to finish it for an anthology to be edited by Janet Berliner and David Copperfield. I wrote it higgledy-piggledy on a battered Atari Portfolio palmtop, on planes and in cars and hotel rooms, all out of order, jotting down conversations and imaginary meetings until I was fairly sure it was all written. Then I put the material I had in order and was astonished and delighted that it worked.

Some of this story is true.

Triptych: 'Eaten (Scenes from a Moving Picture)', The White Road, Queen of Knives

Over a period of several months a few years ago, I wrote three narrative poems. The first, Eaten (Scenes from a Moving Picture), began, somewhere in my head, in May 1993, as a musing on the way people treat other people; and on film, and on the limits and language of film; on pornography and the low standards of pornography; on the language of film treatments and scripts; and on the relationship between food and sex. Or it began one night in 1984, when I had a nightmare in which I was being eaten alive by an elderly witch-woman; I was being kept for food, a zombie, following her around. My left arm and hand were just bone and clinging morsels of chewed flesh. I turned the dream into a story back then, but fragments of it still lingered and began, slowly, to wrap another story around themselves, layers of nacreous image accreting, layering themselves around something I would still rather not have in my head.

When I read scripts, and when I write them, I always pronounce, in my head, 'Int' and 'Ext' as just that, not 'Interior' or 'Exterior'. I was surprised to discover, on showing a few early readers this poem, that other people do not do this. 'Eaten' is a very literal poem, however, and pronounces these words just like I do.

The second was a retelling of a number of old English folktales called 'The White Road'. It was as extreme as the stories it was based on. The last to be written was a tale about my maternal grandparents and about stage magic. It was less extreme, but – I hope – just as disturbing as the two stories that preceded it in the sequence. I was proud of all three of them. The vagaries of publishing meant they were actually published over a period of years, so each of them made it into a best of the year anthology (all three of them were picked up in the American *Year's Best Fantasy and Horror*, one in the British *Year's Best Horror*, and one, somewhat to my surprise, was solicited for an international best erotica collection).

The White Road

There are two stories that have both haunted and disturbed me over the years, stories that have attracted and repelled me ever since I encountered them as a small boy. One of them is the tale of Sweeney Todd, 'the demon barber of Fleet Street'. The other is the tale of Mr Fox – it's a sort of English version of Bluebeard.

The versions in this retelling of the story were inspired by variants on the tale I found in *The Penguin Book of English Folktales*, edited by Neil Philip: 'The Story of Mr Fox' and the notes that follow it and a version of the tale called 'Mr Foster', where I found the image of the white road and the way that the girl's suitor marked the trail down the white road to his gruesome house.

In the story of Mr Fox, the refrain 'It was not so, it is not so, and God forbid it should be so' is repeated as a litany, through the recounting of each horror that Mr Fox's fiancée claims she saw in a dream. At the end she throws down the bloody finger, or the hand, that she took from his house and proves that everything she said was true. And then his story is effectively over.

It's also about all the strange Chinese and Japanese folktales in which, ultimately, everything comes down to Foxes.

Queen of Knives

This, like my graphic novel *Mr Punch*, is close enough to the truth that I have had, on occasion, to explain to some of my relatives that it didn't really happen. Well, not like that, anyway.

The Facts in the Case of the Disappearance of Miss Finch

This began when I was shown a Frank Frazetta painting and asked to write a story to accompany it. I couldn't think of a story, so I told what happened to Miss Finch instead.

Changes

Lisa Tuttle phoned me one day to ask me for a story for an anthology she was editing about gender. I have always loved SF as a medium, and when I was young, I was certain that I would grow up to be a science fiction writer. I never really did. When I first had the idea for this story, almost a decade ago, it was a set of linked short stories that would have formed a novel exploring the world of gender reflection. But I never wrote any of those stories. When Lisa called, it occurred to me that I could take the world I'd imagined and tell its story in the same way that Eduardo Galeano told the history of the Americas in his *Memory of Fire* trilogy.

Once I'd finished the story, I showed it to a friend, who said it read like an outline for a novel. All I could do was congratulate her on her perspicacity. But Lisa Tuttle liked it, and so do I.

The Daughter of Owls

John Aubrey, the seventeenth-century collector and historian, is one of my favourite writers. His writings contain a potent mixture of credulity and erudition, of anecdote, reminiscence and conjecture. Reading Aubrey's work, one gets an immediate sense of a real person talking from the past in a way that transcends the centuries: an enormously likable, interesting person. Also, I like his spelling. I tried writing this story in a couple of different ways, and I was never satisfied with it. Then it occurred to me to write it as by Aubrey.

Shoggoth's Old Peculiar

The overnight train to Glasgow from London is a sleeper that gets in at about five in the morning. When I got off the train, I walked to the station hotel and went inside. I intended to walk down the hall to the reception desk and get a room, then get some more sleep, and then, once everyone was up and about, I planned to spend the next couple of days at the science fiction convention that was being held in the hotel. Officially, I was covering it for a national newspaper. The year was 1985.

On the way down the hall to the reception desk, I passed the bar, empty but for a bemused barman and an English fan named John Jarrold, who, as the Fan Guest of Honour at the convention, had been given an open bar tab, which he was using while others slept.

So I stopped to talk to John and never actually made it to the reception desk. We spent the next forty-eight hours chatting, telling jokes and stories, and enthusiastically massacring all we could remember of *Guys and Dolls* in the small hours of the next morning, when the bar had started to empty out again. At one point in that bar, I had a conversation with the late Richard Evans, an English SF editor, that, six years later, would start to turn into *Neverwhere*.

I no longer remember quite why John and I began talking about Cthulhu in the voices of Peter Cook and Dudley Moore, nor why I decided to start lecturing

John on H. P. Lovecraft's prose style. I suspect it had something to do with lack of sleep.

These days John Jarrold is a respectable editor and a bastion of the British publishing industry. Some of the middle bits of this story began life in that bar, with John and I doing Pete and Dud as creatures out of H. P. Lovecraft. Mike Ashley was the editor who cajoled me into making them a story.

As of October 1999, the story is nominated for a World Fantasy Award as best short story.

Virus

This was written for David Barrett's *Digital Dreams*, a computer fiction anthology. I don't play many computer games anymore. When I did, I noticed they tended to take up areas of my head. Blocks fell or little men ran and jumped behind my eyelids as I went to sleep. Mostly I'd lose, even when playing with my mind. This came from that.

Looking for the Girl

This story was commissioned by *Penthouse* for their twentieth-anniversary issue, January 1985. For the previous couple of years I'd been surviving as a young journalist on the streets of London by interviewing celebrities for *Penthouse* and *Knave*, two English 'skin' magazines – tamer by far than their American equivalents; it was an education, all things considered.

I asked a model once if she felt she was being exploited. 'Me?' she said. Her name was Marie. 'I'm getting well paid for it, love. And it beats working the night shift in a Bradford biscuit factory. But I'll tell you who's being exploited. All those blokes who buy it. Wanking over me every month. They're being exploited.' I think this story began with that conversation.

I was satisfied with this story when I wrote it: It was the first fiction I had written that sounded in any way like me and that didn't read like me doing someone else. I was edging toward a style. To research the story, I sat in the Penthouse U.K. Docklands offices and thumbed through twenty years' worth of bound magazines. In the first *Penthouse* was my friend Dean Smith. Dean did makeup for *Knave*, and, it turned out, she'd been the very first *Penthouse* Pet of the Year in 1965. I stole the 1965 Charlotte blurb directly from Dean's blurb, 'Resurgent individualist' and all. The last I heard, *Penthouse* was hunting for Dean for their twenty-fifth-anniversary celebrations. She'd dropped out of sight. It was in all the newspapers.

It occurred to me, while I was looking at two decades of *Penthouses*, that *Penthouse* and magazines like it had absolutely nothing to do with women and absolutely everything to do with photographs of women. And that was the other place the story began.

Only the End of the World Again

Steve Jones and I have been friends for fifteen years. We even edited a book of nasty poems for kids together. This means that he gets to ring me up and say things like 'I'm doing an anthology of stories set in H. P. Lovecraft's fictional town of Innsmouth. Do me a story.'

This story came from a number of things coming together (that's where we writers Get Our Ideas, in case you were wondering). One of them was the late Roger Zelazny's book *A Night in the Lonesome October*, which has tremendous fun with the various stock characters of horror and fantasy: Roger had given me a copy of his book a few months before I came to write this story, and I'd enjoyed it enormously. At about the same time, I was reading an account of a French werewolf trial held 300 years ago. I realised while reading the testimony of one witness that the account of this trial had been an inspiration for Saki's wonderful story 'Gabriel-Ernest' and also for James Branch Cabell's short novel *The White Robe*, but that both Saki and Cabell had been too well brought up to use the throwing-up of the fingers motif, a key piece of evidence in the trial. Which meant that it was now all up to me.

Larry Talbot was the name of the original Wolfman, the one who met Abbott and Costello.

Bay Wolf

And there was that man Steve Jones again. 'I want you to write one of your story poems for me. It needs to be a detective story, set in the near future. Maybe you could use the Larry Talbot character from "Only the End of the World Again".'

It happened that I had just finished co-writing a screen adaptation of *Beowulf*, the old English narrative poem, and was mildly surprised by the number of people who, mishearing me, seemed to think I had just written an episode of 'Baywatch'. So I began retelling *Beowulf* as a futuristic episode of 'Baywatch' for an anthology of detective stories. It seemed to be the only sensible thing to do.

Look, I don't give you grief over where you get *your* ideas from.

Fifteen Painted Cards from a Vampire Tarot

One day, perhaps, I'll finish the major arcana: seven cards, and seven little stories, still to go. And then there's the minor arcana. You can draw your own pictures.

We Can Get Them for You Wholesale

If the stories in this book were arranged in chronological order, rather than in the strange and haphazard well-it-feels-right sort of order I have put them in, this story would be the first in the book. I dozed off one night in 1983, listening to the radio. When I fell asleep, I was listening to a piece on buying in bulk; when I woke up, they were talking about hired killers. That was where this story came from.

I'd been reading a lot of John Collier short stories before I wrote this. Rereading it several years ago, I realised that it was a John Collier story. Not as good as any good John Collier story, nor written as well as Collier wrote; but it's still a Collier story for all that, and I hadn't noticed that when I was writing it.

One Life, Furnished in Early Moorcock

When I was asked to write a story for an anthology of Michael Moorcock's Elric stories, I chose to write a story about a boy a lot like I was once and his relationship with fiction. I doubted I could say anything about Elric that wasn't pastiche, but when I was twelve, Moorcock's characters were as real to me as anything else in my life and a great deal more real than, well, geography lessons for a start.

'Of all the anthology stories, I liked your story and Tad Williams's the best,' said Michael Moorcock when

I ran into him in New Orleans several months after finishing the story. 'And I liked his better than yours because it had Jimi Hendrix in it.'

The title is stolen from a Harlan Ellison short story.

Cold Colours

I've worked in a number of different media over the years. Sometimes people ask me how I know what medium an idea belongs to. Mostly they turn up as comics or films or poems or prose or novels or short stories or whatever. You know what you're writing ahead of time.

This, on the other hand, was just an idea. I wanted to say something about those infernal machines, computers, and black magic, and something about the London I observed in the late eighties – a period of financial excess and moral bankruptcy. It didn't seem to be a short story or a novel, so I tried it as a poem, and it did just fine.

For *The Time Out Book of London Short Stories* I reformatted it as prose and left a lot of readers very puzzled.

The Sweeper of Dreams

This one began with a Lisa Snellings statue of a man leaning on a broom. He was obviously some kind of janitor. I wondered what kind, and that was where this story came from.

Foreign Parts

This is another early story. I wrote it in 1984, and I did the final draft (a hasty coat of paint and some grouting in the nastiest cracks) in 1989. In 1984 I couldn't sell it (the SF mags didn't like the sex, the sex mags didn't like the disease). In 1987 I was asked if I would sell it to an anthology of sexual SF stories, but I declined. In 1984 I had written a story about a venereal disease. The same story seemed to say different things in 1987. The story itself might not have changed, but the landscape around it had altered mightily: I'm talking about AIDS here, and so, whether I had intended it or not, was the story. If I was going to rewrite the story, I was going to have to take AIDS into account, and I couldn't. It was too big, too unknown, too hard to get a grip on. But by 1989 the cultural landscape had shifted once more, shifted to the point where I felt, if not comfortable, then less uncomfortable about taking the story out of the cabinet, brushing it down, wiping the smudges off its face, and sending it out to meet the nice people. So when editor Steve Niles asked if I had anything unpublished for his anthology *Words Without Pictures*, I gave him this.

I could say that it wasn't a story about AIDS. But I'd be lying, at least in part. And these days AIDS seems to have become, for good or evil, just another disease in Venus's armoury.

Really, I think it's mostly about loneliness, and identity, and, perhaps, it's about the joys of making your own way in the world.

Vampire Sestina

My only successful sestina (a verse form in which the last word of each of the first six lines repeat in ever-changing sequence over the next verses and in one three-line endpiece). First published in *Fantasy Tales* and reprinted in Steve Jones's *Mammoth Book of Vampires*, for years this was my only piece of vampire fiction.

Mouse

This story was written for the Pete Crowther-edited *Touch Wood*, an anthology about superstitions. I'd always wanted to write a Raymond Carver short story; he made it look so easy. Writing this story taught me that it wasn't.

I'm afraid I actually did hear the radio broadcast mentioned in the text.

The Sea Change

I wrote this in the top flat of a tiny mews house in Earls Court. It was inspired by a Lisa Snellings statue and by the memory of the beach at Portsmouth when I was a boy: the dragging rattle that the sea makes as the waves pull back over the pebbles. I was writing the last part of *Sandman* at the time, which was called 'The Tempest', and bits of Shakespeare's play rattle through this as well, just as it rattled through my head back then.

How Do You Think It Feels?

I had agreed to write a story for an anthology of short stories about gargoyles, and, with the deadline rapidly approaching, was feeling rather blank.

Gargoyles, it occurred to me, were placed over churches and cathedrals to protect them. I wondered if a gargoyle could be placed over something else to protect it. Such as, for example, a heart . . .

When We Went to See the End of the World by Dawnie Morningside, age 11¼

Alan Moore (who is one of the finest writers and one of the finest people I know) and I sat down one day in Northampton and began talking about creating a place that we would want to set stories in. This story is set in that place. One day the good burghers and honest townsfolk of Northampton will burn Alan as a warlock, and it will be a great loss to the world.

Desert Wind

One day a cassette tape arrived from Robin Anders, best known as drummer for Boiled in Lead, with a message, telling me that he wanted me to write something about one of the tracks on the tape. It was called 'Desert Wind'. This is what I wrote.

Tastings

This story took me four years to write. Not because I was honing and polishing every adjective, but because I'd get embarrassed. I'd write a paragraph and then I'd leave the story alone until the red flush had faded from my cheeks. And four or five months later I'd go back and write another paragraph. I began writing the story for Ellen Datlow's *Off Limits: Tales of Alien Sex*, an erotic SF anthology. I missed the deadline for that, carried on writing it for the sequel. Managed about another page or so before I missed the deadline for that as well. Somewhere in there I phoned Ellen Datlow up and warned her that, in the event of my untimely death, there was a half-finished pornographic short story on my hard drive in a file called DATLOW and that it was nothing personal. Two more anthology deadlines came and went, and, four years from the first paragraph, I finished it and Ellen Datlow and her partner in crime Terri Windling took it for *Sirens*, their collection of erotic fantasy stories.

Most of this story came about from wondering why people in fiction never seem to talk while making love or even while having sex. I don't think that it's erotic, but once the story was, finally, finished, I stopped finding it embarrassing.

In The End

I was trying to imagine the very last book of the Bible.

And on the subject of naming animals, can I just say how delighted I was recently to discover that the word 'yeti', literally translated, apparently means 'that thing over there'. ('Quick, brave Himalayan Guide – what's that thing over there?'

'Yeti.'

'Gosh, really?')

Babycakes

A fable, written for a publication to benefit People for the Ethical Treatment of Animals (PETA). I think it makes its point. It's the only thing I've ever written that has disturbed me. Last year I came downstairs to find my son Michael listening to *Warning: Contains Language*, my spoken-word CD. 'Babycakes' started as I arrived, and it caught me by surprise when I heard a voice I scarcely recognised as my own reading this aloud.

For the record, I wear a leather jacket and eat meat, but I am quite good with babies.

Murder Mysteries

When I had the idea for this story, it was called 'City of Angels'. But around the time I actually began to write it, a Broadway show with that title appeared, so when the story was finished, I gave it a new name.

'Murder Mysteries' was written for Jessie Horsting at *Midnight Graffiti* magazine for her paperback anthology, also called, coincidentally, *Midnight Graffiti*. Pete Atkins, to whom I faxed draft after draft as I wrote and rewrote it, was invaluable as a sounding board and a paragon of patience and good humour.

I tried to play fair with the detective part of the story. There are clues everywhere. There's even one in the title.

Snow, Glass, Apples

This is another story that began life in Neil Philip's *The Penguin Book of English Folktales*. I was reading it in the bath, and I read a story I must have read a thousand times before. (I still have the illustrated version of the story I owned when I was three.) But that thousand and first reading was the charm, and I started to think about the story, all back to front and wrong way around. It sat in my head for a few weeks and then, on a plane,

I began to write the story in longhand. When the plane landed, the story was three-quarters done, so I checked into my hotel and sat in a chair in a corner of my room and just kept writing until it was done.

It was published by DreamHaven Press in a limited-edition booklet that benefited the Comic Book Legal Defense Fund (an organization that defends the First Amendment rights of comics creators, publishers and retailers). Poppy Z. Brite reprinted it in her anthology *Love in Vein II*.

I like to think of this story as a virus. Once you've read it, you may never be able to read the original story in the same way again.

I'd like to thank Greg Ketter, whose DreamHaven Press published several of these stories in *Angels and Visitations*, a small-press miscellany of fiction, book reviews, journalism, and stuff I'd written, and who published others as two chapbooks to benefit the Comic Book Legal Defense Fund.

I want to thank the multitude of editors who commissioned, accepted and reprinted the various stories in this book, and to all the beta-testers (you know who you are) who put up with my handing them, faxing them or e-mailing them stories, and who read what I sent them and told me, often in no uncertain terms, what needed fixing. To them all, my thanks. Jennifer Hershey shepherded this book from an idea to reality with patience, charm and editorial wisdom. I cannot thank her enough. My thanks also to Doug Young for his patience and help in preparing the Headline edition of this book.

Each of these stories is a reflection of or on something and is no more solid than a breath of smoke. They're messages from Looking-Glass Land and pictures in the shifting clouds: smoke, and mirrors, that's all they are. But I enjoyed writing them, and they, in their turn, I like to imagine, appreciate being read.

Welcome.

Neil Gaiman

Chivalry

*M*rs Whitaker found the Holy Grail; it was under a fur coat.

Every Thursday afternoon Mrs Whitaker walked down to the post office to collect her pension, even though her legs were no longer what they were, and on the way back home she would stop in at the Oxfam Shop and buy herself a little something.

The Oxfam Shop sold old clothes, knick-knacks, oddments, bits and bobs, and large quantities of old paperbacks, all of them donations: secondhand flotsam, often the house clearances of the dead. All the profits went to charity.

The shop was staffed by volunteers. The volunteer on duty this afternoon was Marie, seventeen, slightly overweight, and dressed in a baggy mauve jumper that looked like she had bought it from the shop.

Marie sat by the till with a copy of *Modern Woman* magazine, filling out a 'Reveal Your Hidden Personality' questionnaire. Every now and then, she'd flip to the back of the magazine and check the relative points assigned to an A), B) or C) answer before making up her mind how she'd respond to the question.

Mrs Whitaker puttered around the shop.

They still hadn't sold the stuffed cobra, she noted. It had been there for six months now, gathering dust, glass eyes gazing balefully at the clothes racks and the cabinet filled with chipped porcelain and chewed toys.

Mrs Whitaker patted its head as she went past.

She picked out a couple of Mills & Boon novels from a bookshelf – *Her Thundering Soul* and *Her Turbulent Heart*, a shilling each – and gave careful consideration to the empty bottle of Mateus Rosé with a decorative lampshade on it before deciding she really didn't have anywhere to put it.

She moved a rather threadbare fur coat, which smelled badly of mothballs. Underneath it was a walking stick and a water-stained copy of *Romance and Legend of Chivalry* by A. R. Hope Moncrieff, priced at five pence. Next to the book, on its side, was the Holy Grail. It had a little round paper sticker on the base, and written on it, in felt pen, was the price: 30p.

Mrs Whitaker picked up the dusty silver goblet and appraised it through her thick spectacles.

'This is nice,' she called to Marie.

Marie shrugged.

'It'd look nice on the mantelpiece.'

Marie shrugged again.

Mrs Whitaker gave fifty pence to Marie, who gave her ten pence change and a brown paper bag to put the books and the Holy Grail in. Then she went next door to the butcher's and bought herself a nice piece of liver. Then she went home.

The inside of the goblet was thickly coated with a brownish-red dust. Mrs Whitaker washed it out with great care, then left it to soak for an hour in warm water with a dash of vinegar added.

Then she polished it with metal polish until it gleamed, and she put it on the mantelpiece in her parlour, where it sat between a small soulful china basset hound and a photograph of her late husband, Henry, on the beach at Frinton in 1953.

She had been right: It did look nice.

For dinner that evening she had the liver fried in breadcrumbs with onions. It was very nice.

The next morning was Friday; on alternate Fridays Mrs Whitaker and Mrs Greenberg would visit each other. Today it was Mrs Greenberg's turn to visit Mrs Whitaker. They sat in the parlour and ate macaroons and drank tea. Mrs Whitaker took one sugar in her tea, but Mrs Greenberg took sweetener, which she always carried in her handbag in a small plastic container.

'That's nice,' said Mrs Greenberg, pointing to the Grail. 'What is it?'

'It's the Holy Grail,' said Mrs Whitaker. 'It's the cup that Jesus drunk out of at the Last Supper. Later, at the Crucifixion, it caught His precious blood when the centurion's spear pierced His side.'

Mrs Greenberg sniffed. She was small and Jewish and didn't hold with unsanitary things. 'I wouldn't know about that,' she said, 'but it's very nice. Our Myron got one just like that when he won the swimming tournament, only it's got his name on the side.'

'Is he still with that nice girl? The hairdresser?'

'Bernice? Oh yes. They're thinking of getting engaged,' said Mrs Greenberg.

'That's nice,' said Mrs Whitaker. She took another macaroon.

Mrs Greenberg baked her own macaroons and brought them over every alternate Friday: small sweet light brown biscuits with almonds on top.

They talked about Myron and Bernice, and Mrs Whitaker's nephew Ronald (she had had no children), and about their friend Mrs Perkins who was in hospital with her hip, poor dear.

At midday Mrs Greenberg went home, and Mrs Whitaker made herself cheese on toast for lunch, and after lunch Mrs Whitaker took her pills; the white and the red and two little orange ones.

The doorbell rang.

Mrs Whitaker answered the door. It was a young man with shoulder-length hair so fair it was almost white, wearing gleaming silver armour, with a white surcoat.

'Hello,' he said.

'Hello,' said Mrs Whitaker.

'I'm on a quest,' he said.

'That's nice,' said Mrs Whitaker, noncommittally.

'Can I come in?' he asked.

Mrs Whitaker shook her head. 'I'm sorry, I don't think so,' she said.

'I'm on a quest for the Holy Grail,' the young man said. 'Is it here?'

'Have you got any identification?' Mrs Whitaker asked. She knew that it was unwise to let unidentified strangers into your home when you were elderly and living on your own. Handbags get emptied, and worse than that.

The young man went back down the garden path. His horse, a huge grey charger, big as a shire-horse, its head high and its eyes intelligent, was tethered to Mrs Whitaker's garden gate. The knight fumbled in the saddlebag and returned with a scroll.

It was signed by Arthur, King of All Britons, and

charged all persons of whatever rank or station to know that here was Galaad, Knight of the Table Round, and that he was on a Right High and Noble Quest. There was a drawing of the young man below that. It wasn't a bad likeness.

Mrs Whitaker nodded. She had been expecting a little card with a photograph on it, but this was far more impressive.

'I suppose you had better come in,' she said.

They went into her kitchen. She made Galaad a cup of tea, then she took him into the parlour.

Galaad saw the Grail on her mantelpiece, and dropped to one knee. He put down the teacup carefully on the russet carpet. A shaft of light came through the net curtains and painted his awed face with golden sunlight and turned his hair into a silver halo.

'It is truly the Sangrail,' he said, very quietly. He blinked his pale blue eyes three times, very fast, as if he were blinking back tears.

He lowered his head as if in silent prayer.

Galaad stood up again and turned to Mrs Whitaker. 'Gracious lady, keeper of the Holy of Holies, let me now depart this place with the Blessed Chalice, that my journeyings may be ended and my geas fulfilled.'

'Sorry?' said Mrs Whitaker.

Galaad walked over to her and took her old hands in his. 'My quest is over,' he told her. 'The Sangrail is finally within my reach.'

Mrs Whitaker pursed her lips. 'Can you pick your teacup and saucer up, please?' she said.

Galaad picked up his teacup apologetically.

'No. I don't think so,' said Mrs Whitaker. 'I rather like it there. It's just right, between the dog and the photograph of my Henry.'

'Is it gold you need? Is that it? Lady, I can bring you gold . . .'

'No,' said Mrs Whitaker. 'I don't want any gold thank *you*. I'm simply not interested.'

She ushered Galaad to the front door. 'Nice to meet you,' she said.

His horse was leaning its head over her garden fence, nibbling her gladioli. Several of the neighbourhood children were standing on the pavement, watching it.

Galaad took some sugar lumps from the saddlebag and showed the braver of the children how to feed the horse, their hands held flat. The children giggled. One of the older girls stroked the horse's nose.

Galaad swung himself up onto the horse in one fluid movement. Then the horse and the knight trotted off down Hawthorne Crescent.

Mrs Whitaker watched them until they were out of sight, then sighed and went back inside.

The weekend was quiet.

On Saturday Mrs Whitaker took the bus into Maresfield to visit her nephew Ronald, his wife Euphonia, and their daughters, Clarissa and Dillian. She took them a currant cake she had baked herself.

On Sunday morning Mrs Whitaker went to church. Her local church was St James the Less, which was a little more 'Don't think of this as a church, think of it as a place where like-minded friends hang out and are joyful' than Mrs Whitaker felt entirely comfortable with, but she liked the vicar, the Reverend Bartholomew, when he wasn't actually playing the guitar.

After the service, she thought about mentioning to him that she had the Holy Grail in her front parlour, but decided against it.

On Monday morning Mrs Whitaker was working

in the back garden. She had a small herb garden she was extremely proud of: dill, vervain, mint, rosemary, thyme, and a wild expanse of parsley. She was down on her knees, wearing thick green gardening gloves, weeding, and picking out slugs and putting them in a plastic bag.

Mrs Whitaker was very tenderhearted when it came to slugs. She would take them down to the back of her garden, which bordered on the railway line, and throw them over the fence.

She cut some parsley for the salad. There was a cough behind her. Galaad stood there, tall and beautiful, his armour glinting in the morning sun. In his arms he held a long package, wrapped in oiled leather.

'I'm back,' he said.

'Hello,' said Mrs Whitaker. She stood up, rather slowly, and took off her gardening gloves. 'Well,' she said, 'now you're here, you might as well make yourself useful.'

She gave him the plastic bag full of slugs and told him to tip the slugs out over the back of the fence.

He did.

Then they went into the kitchen.

'Tea? Or lemonade?' she asked.

'Whatever you're having,' Galaad said.

Mrs Whitaker took a jug of her homemade lemonade from the fridge and sent Galaad outside to pick a sprig of mint. She selected two tall glasses. She washed the mint carefully and put a few leaves in each glass, then poured the lemonade.

'Is your horse outside?' she asked.

'Oh yes. His name is Grizzel.'

'And you've come a long way, I suppose.'

'A very long way.'

'I see,' said Mrs Whitaker. She took a blue plastic basin from under the sink and half-filled it with water. Galaad took it out to Grizzel. He waited while the horse drank and brought the empty basin back to Mrs Whitaker.

'Now,' she said, 'I suppose you're still after the Grail.'

'Aye, still do I seek the Sangrail,' he said. He picked up the leather package from the floor, put it down on her tablecloth and unwrapped it. 'For it, I offer you this.'

It was a sword, its blade almost four feet long. There were words and symbols traced elegantly along the length of the blade. The hilt was worked in silver and gold, and a large jewel was set in the pommel.

'It's very nice,' said Mrs Whitaker, doubtfully.

'This,' said Galaad, 'is the sword Balmung, forged by Wayland Smith in the dawn times. Its twin is Flamberge. Who wears it is unconquerable in war, and invincible in battle. Who wears it is incapable of a cowardly act or an ignoble one. Set in its pommel is the sardonynx Bircone, which protects its possessor from poison slipped into wine or ale, and from the treachery of friends.'

Mrs Whitaker peered at the sword. 'It must be very sharp,' she said, after a while.

'It can slice a falling hair in twain. Nay, it could slice a sunbeam,' said Galaad proudly.

'Well, then, maybe you ought to put it away,' said Mrs Whitaker.

'Don't you want it?' Galaad seemed disappointed.

'No, thank you,' said Mrs Whitaker. It occurred to her that her late husband, Henry, would have quite liked it. He would have hung it on the wall in his study next to the stuffed carp he had caught in Scotland, and pointed it out to visitors.

Galaad rewrapped the oiled leather around the sword Balmung and tied it up with white cord.

He sat there, disconsolate.

Mrs Whitaker made him some cream cheese and cucumber sandwiches for the journey back and wrapped them in greaseproof paper. She gave him an apple for Grizzel. He seemed very pleased with both gifts.

She waved them both good-bye.

That afternoon she took the bus down to the hospital to see Mrs Perkins, who was still in with her hip, poor love. Mrs Whitaker took her some homemade fruitcake, although she had left out the walnuts from the recipe, because Mrs Perkins's teeth weren't what they used to be.

She watched a little television that evening, and had an early night.

On Tuesday the postman called. Mrs Whitaker was up in the boxroom at the top of the house, doing a spot of tidying, and, taking each step slowly and carefully, she didn't make it downstairs in time. The postman had left her a message which said that he'd tried to deliver a packet, but no one was home.

Mrs Whitaker sighed.

She put the message into her handbag and went down to the post office.

The package was from her niece Shirelle in Sydney, Australia. It contained photographs of her husband, Wallace, and her two daughters, Dixie and Violet, and a conch shell packed in cotton wool.

Mrs Whitaker had a number of ornamental shells in her bedroom. Her favourite had a view of the Bahamas done on it in enamel. It had been a gift from her sister, Ethel, who had died in 1983.

She put the shell and the photographs in her shopping bag. Then, seeing that she was in the area, she stopped in at the Oxfam Shop on her way home.

'Hullo, Mrs W.,' said Marie.

Mrs Whitaker stared at her. Marie was wearing lipstick (possibly not the best shade for her, nor particularly expertly applied, but, thought Mrs Whitaker, that would come with time) and a rather smart skirt. It was a great improvement.

'Oh. Hello, dear,' said Mrs Whitaker.

'There was a man in here last week, asking about that thing you bought. The little metal cup thing. I told him where to find you. You don't mind, do you?'

'No, dear,' said Mrs Whitaker. 'He found me.'

'He was really dreamy. Really, really dreamy,' sighed Marie wistfully. 'I could of gone for him.

'And he had a big white horse and all,' Marie concluded. She was standing up straighter as well, Mrs Whitaker noted approvingly.

On the bookshelf Mrs Whitaker found a new Mills & Boon novel – *Her Majestic Passion* – although she hadn't yet finished the two she had bought on her last visit.

She picked up the copy of *Romance and Legend of Chivalry* and opened it. It smelled musty. *EX LIBRIS FISHER* was neatly handwritten at the top of the first page in red ink.

She put it down where she had found it.

When she got home, Galaad was waiting for her. He was giving the neighbourhood children rides on Grizzel's back, up and down the street.

'I'm glad you're here,' she said. 'I've got some cases that need moving.'

She showed him up to the boxroom in the top of the house. He moved all the old suitcases for her, so she could get to the cupboard at the back.

It was very dusty up there.

She kept him up there most of the afternoon, moving things around while she dusted.

Galaad had a cut on his cheek, and he held one arm a little stiffly.

They talked a little while she dusted and tidied. Mrs Whitaker told him about her late husband, Henry; and how the life insurance had paid the house off; and how she had all these things, but no one really to leave them to, no one but Ronald really and his wife only liked modern things. She told him how she had met Henry during the war, when he was in the ARP and she hadn't closed the kitchen blackout curtains all the way; and about the sixpenny dances they went to in the town; and how they'd gone to London when the war had ended, and she'd had her first drink of wine.

Galaad told Mrs Whitaker about his mother Elaine, who was flighty and no better than she should have been and something of a witch to boot; and his grandfather, King Pelles, who was well-meaning although at best a little vague; and of his youth in the Castle of Bliant on the Joyous Isle; and his father, whom he knew as 'Le Chevalier Mal Fet', who was more or less completely mad, and was in reality Lancelot du Lac, greatest of knights, in disguise and bereft of his wits; and of Galaad's days as a young squire in Camelot.

At five o'clock Mrs Whitaker surveyed the boxroom and decided that it met with her approval; then she opened the window so the room could air, and they went downstairs to the kitchen, where she put on the kettle.

Galaad sat down at the kitchen table.

He opened the leather purse at his waist and took out a round white stone. It was about the size of a cricket ball.

'My lady,' he said, 'This is for you, an you give me the Sangrail.'

Mrs Whitaker picked up the stone, which was heavier than it looked, and held it up to the light. It was milkily translucent, and deep inside it flecks of silver glittered and glinted in the late-afternoon sunlight. It was warm to the touch.

Then, as she held it, a strange feeling crept over her: Deep inside she felt stillness and a sort of peace. *Serenity*, that was the word for it; she felt serene.

Reluctantly she put the stone back on the table.

'It's very nice,' she said.

'That is the Philosopher's Stone, which our forefather Noah hung in the Ark to give light when there was no light; it can transform base metals into gold; and it has certain other properties,' Galaad told her proudly. 'And that isn't all. There's more. Here.' From the leather bag he took an egg and handed it to her.

It was the size of a goose egg and was a shiny black colour, mottled with scarlet and white. When Mrs Whitaker touched it, the hairs on the back of her neck prickled. Her immediate impression was one of incredible heat and freedom. She heard the crackling of distant fires, and for a fraction of a second she seemed to feel herself far above the world, swooping and diving on wings of flame.

She put the egg down on the table, next to the Philosopher's Stone.

'That is the Egg of the Phoenix,' said Galaad. 'From far Araby it comes. One day it will hatch out into the

Phoenix Bird itself; and when its time comes, the bird will build a nest of flame, lay its egg, and die, to be reborn in flame in a later age of the world.'

'I thought that was what it was,' said Mrs Whitaker.

'And, last of all, lady,' said Galaad, 'I have brought you this.'

He drew it from his pouch, and gave it to her. It was an apple, apparently carved from a single ruby, on an amber stem.

A little nervously, she picked it up. It was soft to the touch – deceptively so: Her fingers bruised it, and ruby-coloured juice from the apple ran down Mrs Whitaker's hand.

The kitchen filled – almost imperceptibly, magically – with the smell of summer fruit, of raspberries and peaches and strawberries and red currants. As if from a great way away she heard distant voices raised in song and far music on the air.

'It is one of the apples of the Hesperides,' said Galaad, quietly. 'One bite from it will heal any illness or wound, no matter how deep; a second bite restores youth and beauty; and a third bite is said to grant eternal life.'

Mrs Whitaker licked the sticky juice from her hand. It tasted like fine wine.

There was a moment, then, when it all came back to her – how it was to be young: to have a firm, slim body that would do whatever she wanted it to do; to run down a country lane for the simple unladylike joy of running; to have men smile at her just because she was herself and happy about it.

Mrs Whitaker looked at Sir Galaad, most comely of all knights, sitting fair and noble in her small kitchen.

She caught her breath.

'And that's all I have brought for you,' said Galaad. 'They weren't easy to get, either.'

Mrs Whitaker put the ruby fruit down on her kitchen table. She looked at the Philosopher's Stone, and the Egg of the Phoenix, and the Apple of Life.

Then she walked into her parlour and looked at the mantelpiece: at the little china basset hound, and the Holy Grail, and the photograph of her late husband Henry, shirtless, smiling and eating an ice cream in black and white, almost forty years away.

She went back into the kitchen. The kettle had begun to whistle. She poured a little steaming water into the teapot, swirled it around, and poured it out. Then she added two spoonfuls of tea and one for the pot and poured in the rest of the water. All this she did in silence.

She turned to Galaad then, and she looked at him.

'Put that apple away,' she told Galaad, firmly. 'You shouldn't offer things like that to old ladies. It isn't proper.'

She paused, then. 'But I'll take the other two,' she continued, after a moment's thought. 'They'll look nice on the mantelpiece. And two for one's fair, or I don't know what is.'

Galaad beamed. He put the ruby apple into his leather pouch. Then he went down on one knee, and kissed Mrs Whitaker's hand.

'Stop that,' said Mrs Whitaker. She poured them both cups of tea, after getting out the very best china, which was only for special occasions.

They sat in silence, drinking their tea.

When they had finished their tea they went into the parlour.

Galaad crossed himself, and picked up the Grail.

Mrs Whitaker arranged the Egg and the Stone where the Grail had been. The Egg kept tipping on one side, and she propped it up against the little china dog.

'They do look very nice,' said Mrs Whitaker.

'Yes,' agreed Galaad. 'They look very nice.'

'Can I give you anything to eat before you go back?' she asked.

He shook his head.

'Some fruitcake,' she said. 'You may not think you want any now, but you'll be glad of it in a few hours' time. And you should probably use the facilities. Now, give me that, and I'll wrap it up for you.'

She directed him to the small toilet at the end of the hall, and went into the kitchen, holding the Grail. She had some old Christmas wrapping paper in the pantry, and she wrapped the Grail in it, and tied the package with twine. Then she cut a large slice of fruitcake and put it in a brown paper bag, along with a banana and a slice of processed cheese in silver foil.

Galaad came back from the toilet. She gave him the paper bag, and the Holy Grail. Then she went up on tiptoes and kissed him on the cheek.

'You're a nice boy,' she said. 'You take care of yourself.'

He hugged her, and she shooed him out of the kitchen, and out of the back door, and she shut the door behind him. She poured herself another cup of tea, and cried quietly into a Kleenex, while the sound of hoofbeats echoed down Hawthorne Crescent.

On Wednesday Mrs Whitaker stayed in all day.

On Thursday she went down to the post office to collect her pension. Then she stopped in at the Oxfam Shop.

The woman on the till was new to her. 'Where's

Marie?' asked Mrs Whitaker.

The woman on the till, who had blue-rinsed gray hair and blue spectacles that went up into diamante points, shook her head and shrugged her shoulders. 'She went off with a young man,' she said. 'On a horse. Tch. I ask you. I'm meant to be down in the Heathfield shop this afternoon. I had to get my Johnny to run me up here, while we find someone else.'

'Oh,' said Mrs Whitaker. 'Well, it's nice that she's found herself a young man.'

'Nice for her, maybe,' said the lady on the till, 'But some of us were meant to be in Heathfield this afternoon.'

On a shelf near the back of the shop Mrs Whitaker found a tarnished old silver container with a long spout. It had been priced at sixty pence, according to the little paper label stuck to the side. It looked a little like a flattened, elongated teapot.

She picked out a Mills & Boon novel she hadn't read before. It was called *Her Singular Love*. She took the book and the silver container up to the woman on the till.

'Sixty-five pee, dear,' said the woman, picking up the silver object, staring at it. 'Funny old thing, isn't it? Came in this morning.' It had writing carved along the side in blocky old Chinese characters and an elegant arching handle. 'Some kind of oil can, I suppose.'

'No, it's not an oil can,' said Mrs Whitaker, who knew exactly what it was. 'It's a lamp.'

There was a small metal finger ring, unornamented, tied to the handle of the lamp with brown twine.

'Actually,' said Mrs Whitaker, 'on second thoughts, I think I'll just have the book.'

She paid her five pence for the novel, and put the

lamp back where she had found it, in the back of the shop. After all, Mrs Whitaker reflected, as she walked home, it wasn't as if she had anywhere to put it.

older than sin, and his beard could grow no whiter. He wanted to die.

The dwarfish natives of the Arctic caverns did not speak his language, but conversed in their own, twittering tongue, conducted incomprehensible rituals, when they were not actually working in the factories.

Once every year they forced him, sobbing and protesting, into Endless Night. During the journey he would stand near every child in the world, leave one of the dwarves' invisible gifts by its bedside. The children slept, frozen into time.

He envied Prometheus and Loki, Sisyphus and Judas. His punishment was harsher.

Ho.

Ho.

Ho.

The Price

*T*ramps and vagabonds have marks they make on gateposts and trees and doors, letting others of their kind know a little about the people who live at the houses and farms they pass on their travels. I think cats must leave similar signs; how else to explain the cats who turn up at our door through the year, hungry and flea-ridden and abandoned?

We take them in. We get rid of the fleas and the ticks, feed them, and take them to the vet. We pay for them to get their shots, and, indignity upon indignity, we have them neutered or spayed.

And they stay with us: for a few months, or for a year, or for ever.

Most of them arrive in summer. We live in the country, just the right distance out of town for the city dwellers to abandon their cats near us.

We never seem to have more than eight cats, rarely have less than three. The cat population of my house is currently as follows: Hermione and Pod, tabby and black respectively, the mad sisters who live in my attic office and do not mingle; Snowflake, the blue-eyed long-haired white cat, who lived wild in the woods for years before she gave up her wild ways for soft sofas and beds; and, last but largest, Furball, Snowflake's cushionlike tortoiseshell long-haired daughter, orange and black and white, whom I discovered as a tiny kitten in our garage one day, strangled and almost dead, her head poked through an old badminton net, and who surprised us all by not dying but instead growing up to be the best-natured cat I have ever encountered.

And then there is the black cat. Who has no other name than the Black Cat and who turned up almost a month ago. We did not realise he was going to be living here at first: he looked too well-fed to be a stray, too old and jaunty to have been abandoned. He looked like a small panther, and he moved like a patch of night.

One day, in the summer, he was lurking about our ramshackle porch: eight or nine years old, at a guess, male, greenish-yellow of eye, very friendly, quite unperturbable. I assumed he belonged to a neighbouring farmer or household.

I went away for a few weeks, to finish writing a book, and when I came home he was still on our porch, living in an old cat bed one of the children had found for him. He was, however, almost unrecognizable. Patches of fur had gone, and there were deep scratches on his grey skin. The tip of one ear was chewed away. There was a gash beneath one eye, a slice gone from one lip. He looked tired and thin.

We took the Black Cat to the vet, where we got him some antibiotics, which we fed him each night, along with soft cat food.

We wondered who he was fighting. Snowflake, our

beautiful white near-feral queen? Raccoons? A rat-tailed, fanged possum?

Each night the scratches would be worse – one night his side would be chewed up; the next it would be his underbelly, raked with claw marks and bloody to the touch.

When it got to that point, I took him down to the basement to recover beside the furnace and the piles of boxes. He was surprisingly heavy, the Black Cat, and I picked him up and carried him down there, with a cat basket, and a litter box, and some food and water. I closed the door behind me. I had to wash the blood from my hands when I left the basement.

He stayed down there for four days. At first he seemed too weak to feed himself: a cut beneath one eye had rendered him almost one-eyed, and he limped and lolled weakly, thick yellow pus oozing from the cut in his lip.

I went down there every morning and every night, and I fed him and gave him antibiotics, which I mixed with his canned food, and I dabbed at the worst of the cuts, and spoke to him. He had diarrhoea, and, although I changed his litter daily, the basement stank evilly.

The four days that the Black Cat lived in the basement were a bad four days in my house: the baby slipped in the bath and banged her head and might have drowned; I learned that a project I had set my heart on – adapting Hope Mirrlees's novel *Lud in the Mist* for the BBC – was no longer going to happen, and I realised that I did not have the energy to begin again from scratch, pitching it to other networks or to other media; my daughter left for summer camp and immediately began to send home a plethora of heart-tearing letters and cards, five or six each day, imploring us to bring her home; my son had some kind of fight with his best friend, to the point that they were no longer on speaking terms; and, returning home one night, my wife hit a deer that ran out in front of the car. The deer was killed, the car was left undriveable, and my wife sustained a small cut over one eye.

By the fourth day, the cat was prowling the basement, walking haltingly but impatiently between the stacks of books and comics, the boxes of mail and cassettes, of pictures and of gifts and of stuff. He mewed at me to let him out and, reluctantly, I did so.

He went back onto the porch and slept there for the rest of the day.

The next morning there were deep new gashes in his flanks, and clumps of black cat hair – his – covered the wooden boards of the porch.

Letters arrived that day from my daughter, telling us that camp was going better and she thought she could survive a few days; my son and his friend sorted out their problem, although what the argument was about – trading cards, computer games, *Star Wars*, or A Girl – I would never learn. The BBC executive who had vetoed *Lud in the Mist* was discovered to have been taking bribes (well, 'questionable loans') from an independent production company and was sent home on permanent leave: his successor, I was delighted to learn when she faxed me, was the woman who had initially proposed the project to me before leaving the BBC.

I thought about returning the Black Cat to the basement, but decided against it. Instead, I resolved to try and discover what kind of animal was coming to our house each night and from there to formulate a plan of action – to trap it, perhaps.

For birthdays and at Christmas, my family gives me gadgets and gizmos, pricy toys which excite my fancy but, ultimately, rarely leave their boxes. There is a food dehydrator and an electric carving knife, a breadmaking machine, and, last year's present, a pair of see-in-the-dark binoculars. On Christmas Day I had put the batteries into the binoculars and had walked about the basement in the dark, too impatient even to wait until nightfall, stalking a flock of imaginary Starlings. (You were warned not to turn it on in the light: that would have damaged the binoculars and quite possibly your eyes as well.) Afterward I had put the device back into its box, and it sat there still, in my office, beside the box of computer cables and forgotten bits and pieces.

Perhaps, I thought, if the creature, dog or cat or raccoon or what-have-you, were to see me sitting on the porch, it would not come, so I took a chair into the box-and-coatroom, little larger than a closet, which overlooks the porch, and, when everyone in the house was asleep, I went out onto the porch and bade the Black Cat goodnight.

That cat, my wife had said, when he first arrived, *is a person*. And there was something very personlike in his huge leonine face: his broad black nose, his greenish-yellow eyes, his fanged but amiable mouth (still leaking amber pus from the right lower lip).

I stroked his head, and scratched him beneath the chin, and wished him well. Then I went inside and turned off the light on the porch.

I sat on my chair in the darkness inside the house with the see-in-the-dark binoculars on my lap. I had switched the binoculars on, and a trickle of greenish light came from the eyepieces.

Time passed, in the darkness.

I experimented with looking at the darkness with the binoculars, learning to focus, to see the world in shades of green. I found myself horrified by the number of swarming insects I could see in the night air: it was as if the night world were some kind of nightmarish soup, swimming with life. Then I lowered the binoculars from my eyes and stared out at the rich blacks and blues of the night, empty and peaceful and calm.

Time passed. I struggled to keep awake, found myself profoundly missing cigarettes and coffee, my two lost addictions. Either of them would have kept my eyes open. But before I had tumbled too far into the world of sleep and dreams, a yowl from the garden jerked me fully awake. I fumbled the binoculars to my eyes and was disappointed to see that it was merely Snowflake, the white cat, streaking across the front garden like a patch of greenish-white light. She vanished into the woodland to the left of the house and was gone.

I was about to settle myself back down when it occurred to me to wonder what exactly had startled Snowflake so, and I began scanning the middle distance with the binoculars, looking for a huge raccoon, a dog, or a vicious possum. And there was indeed something coming down the driveway toward the house. I could see it through the binoculars, clear as day.

It was the Devil.

I had never seen the Devil before, and, although I had written about him in the past, if pressed would have confessed that I had no belief in him, other than as an imaginary figure, tragic and Miltonian. The figure coming up the driveway was not Milton's Lucifer. It was the Devil.

My heart began to pound in my chest, to pound so hard that it hurt. I hoped it could not see me, that, in a dark house, behind window glass, I was hidden.

The figure flickered and changed as it walked up the drive. One moment it was dark, bull-like, minotaurish, the next it was slim and female, and the next it was a cat itself, a scarred, huge gray-green wildcat, its face contorted with hate.

There are steps that lead up to my porch, four white wooden steps in need of a coat of paint (I knew they were white, although they were, like everything else, green through my binoculars). At the bottom of the steps, the Devil stopped and called out something that I could not understand, three, perhaps four words in a whining, howling language that must have been old and forgotten when Babylon was young; and, although I did not understand the words, I felt the hairs rise on the back of my head as it called.

And then I heard, muffled through the glass but still audible, a low growl, a challenge, and – slowly, unsteadily – a black figure walked down the steps of the house, away from me, toward the Devil. These days the Black Cat no longer moved like a panther, instead he stumbled and rocked, like a sailor only recently returned to land.

The Devil was a woman, now. She said something soothing and gentle to the cat, in a tongue that sounded like French, and reached out a hand to him. He sank his teeth into her arm, and her lip curled, and she spat at him.

The woman glanced up at me then, and if I had doubted that she was the Devil before, I was certain of it now: the woman's eyes flashed red fire at me, but you can see no red through the night-vision binoculars, only shades of a green. And the Devil saw me through the window. It saw me. I am in no doubt about that at all.

The Devil twisted and writhed, and now it was some kind of jackal, a flat-faced, huge-headed, bull-necked creature, halfway between a hyena and a dingo. There were maggots squirming in its mangy fur, and it began to walk up the steps.

The Black Cat leapt upon it, and in seconds they became a rolling, writhing thing, moving faster than my eyes could follow.

All this in silence.

And then a low roar – down the country road at the bottom of our drive, in the distance, lumbered a late-night truck, its blazing headlights burning bright as green suns through the binoculars. I lowered them from my eyes and saw only darkness, and the gentle yellow of headlights, and then the red of rear lights as it vanished off again into the nowhere at all.

When I raised the binoculars once more, there was nothing to be seen. Only the Black Cat on the steps, staring up into the air. I trained the binoculars up and saw something flying away – a vulture, perhaps, or an eagle – and then it flew beyond the trees and was gone.

I went out onto the porch, and picked up the Black Cat, and stroked him, and said kind, soothing things to him. He mewled piteously when I first approached him, but, after a while, he went to sleep on my lap, and I put him into his basket, and went upstairs to my bed, to sleep myself. There was dried blood on my T-shirt and jeans, the following morning.

That was a week ago.

The thing that comes to my house does not come every night. But it comes most nights: we know it by the wounds on the cat, and the pain I can see in those leonine eyes. He has lost the use of his front left paw, and his right eye has closed for good.

I wonder what we did to deserve the Black Cat. I wonder who sent him. And, selfish and scared, I wonder how much more he has to give.

 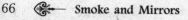

Troll Bridge

*T*hey pulled up most of the railway tracks in the early sixties, when I was three or four. They slashed the train services to ribbons. This meant that there was nowhere to go but London, and the little town where I lived became the end of the line.

My earliest reliable memory: eighteen months old, my mother away in hospital having my sister, and my grandmother walking with me down to a bridge, and lifting me up to watch the train below, panting and steaming like a black iron dragon.

Over the next few years they lost the last of the steam trains, and with them went the network of railways that joined village to village, town to town.

I didn't know that the trains were going. By the time I was seven they were a thing of the past.

We lived in an old house on the outskirts of the town. The fields opposite were empty and fallow. I used to climb the fence and lie in the shade of a small bulrush patch, and read; or if I were feeling more adventurous I'd explore the grounds of the empty manor beyond the fields. It had a weed-clogged ornamental pond, with a low wooden bridge over it. I never saw any groundsmen or caretakers in my forays through the gardens and woods, and I never attempted to enter the manor. That would have been courting disaster, and besides, it was a matter of faith for me that all empty old houses were haunted.

It is not that I was credulous, simply that I believed in all things dark and dangerous. It was part of my young creed that the night was full of ghosts and witches, hungry and flapping and dressed completely in black.

The converse held reassuringly true: daylight was safe. Daylight was always safe.

A ritual: on the last day of the summer school term, walking home from school, I would remove my shoes and socks and, carrying them in my hands, walk down the stony flinty lane on pink and tender feet. During the summer holiday I would put shoes on only under duress. I would revel in my freedom from footwear until the school term began once more in September.

When I was seven I discovered the path through the wood. It was summer, hot and bright, and I wandered a long way from home that day.

I was exploring. I went past the manor, its windows boarded up and blind, across the grounds, and through some unfamiliar woods. I scrambled down a steep bank, and I found myself on a shady path that was new to me and overgrown with trees; the light that penetrated the leaves was stained green and gold, and I thought I was in fairyland.

A little stream trickled down the side of the path, teeming with tiny, transparent shrimps. I picked them up and watched them jerk and spin on my fingertips. Then I put them back.

I wandered down the path. It was perfectly straight,

and overgrown with short grass. From time to time I would find these really terrific rocks: bubbly, melted things, brown and purple and black. If you held them up to the light you could see every colour of the rainbow. I was convinced that they had to be extremely valuable, and stuffed my pockets with them.

I walked and walked down the quiet golden-green corridor, and saw nobody.

I wasn't hungry or thirsty. I just wondered where the path was going. It travelled in a straight line, and was perfectly flat. The path never changed, but the country-side around it did. At first I was walking along the bottom of a ravine, grassy banks climbing steeply on each side of me. Later, the path was above everything, and as I walked I could look down at the treetops below me, and the roofs of occasional distant houses. My path was always flat and straight, and I walked along it through valleys and plateaus, valleys and plateaus. And eventually, in one of the valleys, I came to the bridge.

It was built of clean red brick, a huge curving arch over the path. At the side of the bridge were stone steps cut into the embankment, and, at the top of the steps, a little wooden gate.

I was surprised to see any token of the existence of humanity on my path, which I was by now convinced was a natural formation, like a volcano. And, with a sense more of curiosity than anything else (I had, after all, walked hundreds of miles, or so I was convinced, and might be *anywhere*), I climbed the stone steps, and went through the gate.

I was nowhere.

The top of the bridge was paved with mud. On each side of it was a meadow. The meadow on my side was a wheatfield; the other field was just grass. There were the caked imprints of huge tractor wheels in the dried mud. I walked across the bridge to be sure: no trip-trap, my bare feet were soundless.

Nothing for miles; just fields and wheat and trees.

I picked an ear of wheat, and pulled out the sweet grains, peeling them between my fingers, chewing them meditatively.

I realised then that I was getting hungry, and went back down the steps to the abandoned railway track. It was time to go home. I was not lost; all I needed to do was follow my path home once more.

There was a troll waiting for me, under the bridge.

'I'm a troll,' he said. Then he paused, and added, more or less as an afterthought, 'Fol rol de ol rol.'

He was huge: his head brushed the top of the brick arch. He was more or less translucent: I could see the bricks and trees behind him, dimmed but not lost. He was all my nightmares given flesh. He had huge strong teeth, and rending claws, and strong, hairy hands. His hair was long, like one of my sister's little plastic gonks, and his eyes bulged. He was naked, and his penis hung from the bush of gonk hair between his legs.

'I heard you, Jack,' he whispered in a voice like the wind. 'I heard you trip-trapping over my bridge. And now I'm going to eat your life.'

I was only seven, but it was daylight, and I do not remember being scared. It is good for children to find themselves facing the elements of a fairy tale – they are well equipped to deal with these.

'Don't eat me,' I said to the troll. I was wearing a stripy brown T-shirt, and brown corduroy trousers. My hair also was brown, and I was missing a front tooth. I was learning to whistle between my teeth, but wasn't there yet.

'I'm going to eat your life, Jack,' said the troll.

I stared the troll in the face. 'My big sister is going to be coming down the path soon,' I lied, 'and she's far tastier than me. Eat her instead.'

The troll sniffed the air, and smiled. 'You're all alone,' he said. 'There's nothing else on the path. Nothing at all.' Then he leaned down, and ran his fingers over me: it felt like butterflies were brushing my face – like the touch of a blind person. Then he snuffled his fingers, and shook his huge head. 'You don't have a big sister. You've only a younger sister, and she's at her friend's today.'

'Can you tell all that from smell?' I asked, amazed.

'Trolls cān smell the rainbows, trolls can smell the stars,' it whispered sadly. 'Trolls can smell the dreams you dreamed before you were ever born. Come close to me and I'll eat your life.'

'I've got precious stones in my pocket,' I told the troll. 'Take them, not me. Look.' I showed him the lava jewel rocks I had found earlier.

'Clinker,' said the troll. 'The discarded refuse of steam trains. Of no value to me.'

He opened his mouth wide. Sharp teeth. Breath that smelled of leaf mould and the underneaths of things. 'Eat. Now.'

He became more and more solid to me, more and more real; and the world outside became flatter, began to fade.

'Wait.' I dug my feet into the damp earth beneath the bridge, wiggled my toes, held on tightly to the real world. I stared into his big eyes. 'You don't want to eat my life. Not yet. I – I'm only seven. I haven't *lived* at all yet. There are books I haven't read yet. I've never been on an airplane. I can't whistle yet – not really. Why don't you let me go? When I'm older and bigger and more of a meal I'll come back to you.'

The troll stared at me with eyes like headlamps. Then it nodded.

'When you come back, then,' it said. And it smiled.

I turned around and walked back down the silent straight path where the railway lines had once been.

After a while I began to run.

I pounded down the track in the green light, puffing and blowing, until I felt a stabbing ache beneath my ribcage, the pain of stitch; and, clutching my side, I stumbled home.

The fields started to go, as I grew older. One by one, row by row, houses sprang up with roads named after wildflowers and respectable authors. Our home – an aging, tattered Victorian house – was sold, and torn down; new houses covered the garden.

They built houses everywhere.

I once got lost in the new housing estate that covered two meadows I had once known every inch of. I didn't mind too much that the fields were going, though. The old manor house was bought by a multinational, and the grounds became more houses.

It was eight years before I returned to the old railway line, and when I did, I was not alone.

I was fifteen; I'd changed schools twice in that time. Her name was Louise, and she was my first love.

I loved her grey eyes, and her fine light brown hair, and her gawky way of walking (like a fawn just learning to walk which sounds really dumb, for which I apologize): I saw her chewing gum, when I was thirteen, and I fell for her like a suicide from a bridge.

The main trouble with being in love with Louise

was that we were best friends, and we were both going out with other people.

I'd never told her I loved her, or even that I fancied her. We were buddies.

I'd been at her house that evening: we sat in her room and played *Rattus Norvegicus*, the first Stranglers LP. It was the beginning of punk, and everything seemed so exciting: the possibilities, in music as in everything else, were endless. Eventually it was time for me to go home, and she decided to accompany me. We held hands, innocently, just pals, and we strolled the ten-minute walk to my house.

The moon was bright, and the world was visible and colourless, and the night was warm.

We got to my house. Saw the lights inside, and stood in the driveway, and talked about the band I was starting. We didn't go in.

Then it was decided that I'd walk *her* home. So we walked back to her house.

She told me about the battles she was having with her younger sister, who was stealing her makeup and perfume. Louise suspected that her sister was having sex with boys. Louise was a virgin. We both were.

We stood in the road outside her house, under the sodium yellow streetlight, and we stared at each other's black lips and pale yellow faces.

We grinned at each other.

Then we just walked, picking quiet roads and empty paths. In one of the new housing estates, a path led us into the woodland, and we followed it.

The path was straight and dark, but the lights of distant houses shone like stars on the ground, and the moon gave us enough light to see. Once we were scared, when something snuffled and snorted in front of us.

We pressed close, saw it was a badger, laughed and hugged and kept on walking.

We talked quiet nonsense about what we dreamed and wanted and thought.

And all the time I wanted to kiss her and feel her breasts, and maybe put my hand between her legs.

Finally I saw my chance. There was an old brick bridge over the path, and we stopped beneath it. I pressed up against her. Her mouth opened against mine.

Then she went cold and stiff, and stopped moving.

'Hello,' said the troll.

I let go of Louise. It was dark beneath the bridge, but the shape of the troll filled the darkness.

'I froze her,' said the troll, 'so we can talk. Now: I'm going to eat your life.'

My heart pounded, and I could feel myself trembling.

'No.'

'You said you'd come back to me. And you have. Did you learn to whistle?'

'Yes.'

'That's good. I never could whistle.' It sniffed, and nodded. 'I am pleased. You have grown in life and experience. More to eat. More for me.'

I grabbed Louise, a taut zombie, and pushed her forward. 'Don't take me. I don't want to die. Take *her*. I bet she's much tastier than me. And she's two months older than I am. Why don't you take her?'

The troll was silent.

It sniffed Louise from toe to head, snuffling at her feet and crotch and breasts and hair.

Then it looked at me.

'She's an innocent,' it said. 'You're not. I don't want her. I want you.'

I walked to the opening of the bridge and stared up at the stars in the night.

'But there's so much I've never done,' I said, partly to myself. 'I mean, I've never. Well, I've never had sex. And I've never been to America. I haven't . . .' I paused. 'I haven't *done* anything. Not yet.'

The troll said nothing.

'I could come back to you. When I'm older.'

The troll said nothing.

'I *will* come back. Honest I will.'

'Come back to me?' said Louise. 'Why? Where are you going?'

I turned around. The troll had gone, and the girl I had thought I loved was standing in the shadows beneath the bridge.

'We're going home,' I told her. 'Come on.'

We walked back and never said anything.

She went out with the drummer in the punk band I started, and, much later, married someone else. We met once, on a train, after she was married, and she asked me if I remembered that night.

I said I did.

'I really liked you, that night, Jack,' she told me. 'I thought you were going to kiss me. I thought you were going to ask me out. I would have said yes. If you had.'

'But I didn't.'

'No,' she said. 'You didn't.' Her hair was cut very short. It didn't suit her.

I never saw her again. The trim woman with the taut smile was not the girl I had loved, and talking to her made me feel uncomfortable.

I moved to London, and then, some years later, I moved back again, but the town I returned to was not the town I remembered: there were no fields, no farms, no little flint lanes; and I moved away as soon as I could, to a tiny village ten miles down the road.

I moved with my family – I was married by now, with a toddler – into an old house that had once, many years before, been a railway station. The tracks had been dug up, and the old couple who lived opposite us used it to grow vegetables.

I was getting older. One day I found a grey hair; on another, I heard a recording of myself talking, and I realised I sounded just like my father.

I was working in London, doing A&R for one of the major record companies. I was commuting into London by train most days, coming back some evenings.

I had to keep a small flat in London; it's hard to commute when the bands you're checking out don't even stagger onto the stage until midnight. It also meant that it was fairly easy to get laid, if I wanted to, which I did.

I thought that Eleanora – that was my wife's name; I should have mentioned that before, I suppose – didn't know about the other women; but I got back from a two-week jaunt to New York one winter's day, and when I arrived at the house it was empty and cold.

She had left a letter, not a note. Fifteen pages, neatly typed, and every word of it was true. Including the PS, which read: *You really don't love me. And you never did.*

I put on a heavy coat, and I left the house and just walked, stunned and slightly numb.

There was no snow on the ground, but there was a hard frost, and the leaves crunched under my feet as I walked. The trees were skeletal black against the harsh grey winter sky.

I walked down the side of the road. Cars passed

me, travelling to and from London. Once I tripped on a branch, half-hidden in a heap of brown leaves, ripping my trousers, cutting my leg.

I reached the next village. There was a river at right angles to the road, and a path I'd never seen before beside it, and I walked down the path, and stared at the partly frozen river. It gurgled and plashed and sang.

The path led off through fields; it was straight and grassy.

I found a rock, half-buried, on one side of the path. I picked it up, brushed off the mud. It was a melted lump of purplish stuff, with a strange rainbow sheen to it. I put it into the pocket of my coat and held it in my hand as I walked, its presence warm and reassuring.

The river meandered away across the fields, and I walked on in silence.

I had walked for an hour before I saw houses – new and small and square – on the embankment above me.

And then I saw the bridge, and I knew where I was: I was on the old railway path, and I'd been coming down it from the other direction.

There were graffiti painted on the side of the bridge: FUCK and BARRY LOVES SUSAN and the omnipresent NF of the National Front.

I stood beneath the bridge in the red brick arch, stood among the ice cream wrappers, and the crisp packets and the single, sad, used condom, and watched my breath steam in the cold afternoon air.

The blood had dried into my trousers.

Cars passed over the bridge above me; I could hear a radio playing loudly in one of them.

'Hello?' I said, quietly, feeling embarrassed, feeling foolish. 'Hello?'

There was no answer. The wind rustled the crisp packets and the leaves.

'I came back. I said I would. And I did. Hello?'

Silence.

I began to cry then, stupidly, silently, sobbing under the bridge.

A hand touched my face, and I looked up.

'I didn't think you'd come back,' said the troll.

He was my height now, but otherwise unchanged. His long gonk hair was unkempt and had leaves in it, and his eyes were wide and lonely.

I shrugged, then wiped my face with the sleeve of my coat. 'I came back.'

Three kids passed above us on the bridge, shouting and running.

'I'm a troll,' whispered the troll, in a small, scared voice. 'Fol rol de ol rol.'

He was trembling.

I held out my hand and took his huge clawed paw in mine. I smiled at him. 'It's okay,' I told him. 'Honestly. It's okay.'

The troll nodded.

He pushed me to the ground, onto the leaves and the wrappers and the condom, and lowered himself on top of me. Then he raised his head, and opened his mouth, and ate my life with his strong sharp teeth.

When he was finished, the troll stood up and brushed himself down. He put his hand into the pocket of his coat and pulled out a bubbly, burnt lump of clinker rock.

He held it out to me.

'This is yours,' said the troll.

I looked at him: wearing my life comfortably, easily, as if he'd been wearing it for years. I took the clinker from his hand, and sniffed it. I could smell the train from which it had fallen, so long ago. I gripped it tightly in my hairy hand.

'Thank you,' I said.

'Good luck,' said the troll.

'Yeah. Well. You too.'

The troll grinned with my face.

It turned its back on me and began to walk back the way I had come, toward the village, back to the empty house I had left that morning; and it whistled as it walked.

I've been here ever since. Hiding. Waiting. Part of the bridge.

I watch from the shadows as the people pass: walking their dogs, or talking, or doing the things that people do. Sometimes people pause beneath my bridge, to stand, or piss, or make love. And I watch them, but say nothing; and they never see me.

Fol rol de ol rol.

I'm just going to stay here, in the darkness under the arch. I can hear you all out there, trip-trapping, trip-trapping over my bridge.

Oh yes, I can hear you.

But I'm not coming out.

Don't Ask Jack

*N*obody knew where the toy had come from, which great-grandparent or distant aunt had owned it before it was given it to the nursery.

It was a box, carved and painted in gold and red. It was undoubtedly attractive and, or so the grown-ups maintained, quite valuable – perhaps even an antique. The latch, unfortunately, was rusted shut, and.the key had been lost, so the Jack could not be released from his box. Still, it was a remarkable box, heavy and carved and gilt.

The children did not play with it. It sat at the bottom of the old wooden toy box, which was the same size and age as a pirate's treasure chest, or so the children thought. The Jack-in-the-Box was buried beneath dolls and trains, clowns and paper stars and old conjuring tricks, and crippled marionettes with their strings irrevocably tangled, with dressing-up clothes (here the tatters of a long-ago wedding dress, there a black silk hat, crusted with age and time) and costume jewellery, broken hoops and tops and hobby-horses. Under them all was Jack's box.

The children did not play with it. They whispered among themselves, alone in the attic nursery. On grey days when the wind howled about the house and rain rattled the slates and pattered down the eaves, they told each other stories about Jack, although they had never seen him. One claimed that Jack was an evil wizard, placed in the box as punishment for crimes too awful to describe; another (I am certain that it must have been one of the girls) maintained that Jack's box was Pandora's Box and he had been placed in the box as guardian to prevent the bad things inside it from coming out once more. They would not even touch the box, if they could help it, although when, as happened from time to time, an adult would comment on the absence of that sweet old Jack-in-the-Box, and retrieve it from the chest, and place it in a position of honour on the mantelpiece, then the children would pluck up their courage and, later, hide it away once more in the darkness.

The children did not play with the Jack-in-the-Box. And when they grew up and left the great house, the attic nursery was closed up and almost forgotten.

Almost, but not entirely. For each of the children, separately, remembered walking alone in the moon's blue light, on his or her own bare feet, up to the nursery. It was almost like sleepwalking, feet soundless on the wood of the stairs, on the threadbare nursery carpet. Remembered opening the treasure chest, pawing through the dolls and the clothes and pulling out the box.

And then the child would touch the catch, and the lid would open, slow as a sunset, and the music would begin to play, and Jack came out. Not with a pop and a bounce: he was no spring-heeled Jack. But deliberately, intently, he would rise from the box and motion to the child to come closer, closer, and smile.

And there in the moonlight, he told them each things they could never quite remember, things they were never able entirely to forget.

The oldest boy died in the Great War. The youngest, after their parents died, inherited the house, although it was taken from him when he was found in the cellar one night with cloths and paraffin and matches, trying to burn the great house to the ground. They took him to the madhouse, and perhaps he is there still.

The other children, who had once been girls and now were women, declined, each and every one, to return to the house in which they had grown up; and the windows of the house were boarded up, and the doors were all locked with huge iron keys, and the sisters visited it as often as they visited their eldest brother's grave, or the sad thing that had once been their younger brother, which is to say, never.

Years have passed, and the girls are old women, and owls and bats have made their homes in the old attic nursery, rats build their nests among the forgotten toys. The creatures gaze uncuriously at the faded prints on the wall, and stain the remnants of the carpet with their droppings.

And deep within the box within the box, Jack waits and smiles, holding his secrets. He is waiting for the children. He can wait for ever.

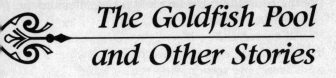

The Goldfish Pool
and Other Stories

*I*t was raining when I arrived in L.A., and I felt
myself surrounded by a hundred old movies.

There was a limo driver in a black uniform waiting
for me at the airport, holding a white sheet of cardboard
with my name misspelled neatly upon it.

'I'm taking you straight to your hotel, sir,' said the
driver. He seemed vaguely disappointed that I didn't
have any real luggage for him to carry, just a battered
overnight bag stuffed with T-shirts, underwear, and
socks.

'Is it far?'

He shook his head. 'Maybe twenty-five, thirty
minutes. You ever been to L.A. before?'

'No.'

'Well, what I always say, L.A. is a thirty-minute
town. Wherever you want to go, it's thirty minutes
away. No more.'

He hauled my bag into the boot of the car, which
he called the trunk, and opened the door for me to
climb into the back.

'So where you from?' he asked, as we headed out

of the airport into the slick wet neonspattered streets.

'England.'

'England, eh?'

'Yes. Have you ever been there?'

'Nosir. I've seen movies. You an actor?'

'I'm a writer.'

He lost interest. Occasionally he would swear at other drivers, under his breath.

He swerved suddenly, changing lanes. We passed a four-car pileup in the lane we had been in.

'You get a little rain in this city, all of a sudden everybody forgets how to drive,' he told me. I burrowed further into the cushions in the back. 'You get rain in England, I hear.' It was a statement, not a question.

'A little.'

'More than a little. Rains every day in England.' He laughed. 'And thick fog. Real thick, thick fog.'

'Not really.'

'Whaddaya mean, no?' he asked, puzzled, defensive. 'I've seen movies.'

We sat in silence then, driving through the Hollywood rain; but after a while he said: 'Ask them for the room Belushi died in.'

'Pardon?'

'Belushi. John Belushi. It was your hotel he died in. Drugs. You heard about that?'

'Oh. Yes.'

'They made a movie about his death. Some fat guy, didn't look nothing like him. But nobody tells the real truth about his death. Y'see, he wasn't alone. There were two other guys with him. Studios didn't want any shit. But you're a limo driver, you hear things.'

'Really?'

'Robin Williams and Robert De Niro. They were there with him. All of them going doo-doo on the happy dust.'

The hotel building was a white mock-gothic chateau. I said good-bye to the chauffeur and checked in; I did not ask about the room in which Belushi had died.

I walked out to my chalet through the rain, my overnight bag in my hand, clutching the set of keys that would, the desk clerk told me, get me through the various doors and gates. The air smelled of wet dust and, curiously enough, cough mixture. It was dusk, almost dark.

Water splashed everywhere. It ran in rills and rivulets across the courtyard. It ran into a small fishpond that jutted out from the side of a wall in the courtyard.

I walked up the stairs into a dank little room. It seemed a poor kind of a place for a star to die.

The bed seemed slightly damp, and the rain drummed a maddening beat on the air-conditioning system.

I watched a little television – the rerun wasteland: 'Cheers' segued imperceptibly into 'Taxi', which flickered into black and white and became 'I Love Lucy' – then stumbled into sleep.

I dreamed of drummers intermittently drumming, only thirty minutes away.

The phone woke me. 'Hey-hey-hey-hey. You made it okay then?'

'Who is this?'

'It's Jacob at the studio. Are we still on for breakfast, hey-hey?'

'Breakfast . . .?'

'No problem. I'll pick you up at your hotel in

thirty minutes. Reservations are already made. No problems. You got my messages?'

'I . . .'

'Faxed 'em through last night. See you.'

The rain had stopped. The sunshine was warm and bright: proper Hollywood light. I walked up to the main building, walking on a carpet of crushed eucalyptus leaves – the cough medicine smell from the night before.

They handed me an envelope with a fax in it – my schedule for the next few days, with messages of encouragement and faxed handwritten doodles in the margin, saying things like *This is Gonna be a Blockbuster!* and *Is this Going to be a Great Movie or What!* The fax was signed by Jacob Klein, obviously the voice on the phone. I had never before had any dealings with a Jacob Klein.

A small red sports car drew up outside the hotel. The driver got out and waved at me. I walked over. He had a trim, pepper-and-salt beard, a smile that was almost bankable, and a gold chain around his neck. He showed me a copy of *Sons of Man*.

He was Jacob. We shook hands.

'Is David around? David Gambol?'

David Gambol was the man I'd spoken to earlier on the phone when arranging the trip. He wasn't the producer. I wasn't certain quite what he was. He described himself as 'attached to the project'.

'David's not with the studio anymore. I'm kind of running the project now, and I want you to know I'm really psyched. Hey-hey.'

'That's good?'

We got in the car. 'Where's the meeting?' I asked.

He shook his head. 'It's not a meeting,' he said. 'It's

a breakfast.' I looked puzzled. He took pity on me. 'A kind of pre-meeting meeting,' he explained.

We drove from the hotel to a mall somewhere half an hour away while Jacob told me how much he enjoyed my book and how delighted he was that he'd become attached to the project. He said it was his idea to have me put up in the hotel – 'Give you the kind of Hollywood experience you'd never get at the Four Seasons or Ma Maison, right?' – and asked me if I was staying in the chalet in which John Belushi had died. I told him I didn't know, but that I rather doubted it.

'You know who he was with, when he died? They covered it up, the studios.'

'No. Who?'

'Meryl and Dustin.'

'This is Meryl Streep and Dustin Hoffman we're talking about?'

'Sure.'

'How do you know this?'

'People talk. It's Hollywood. You know?'

I nodded as if I did know, but I didn't.

People talk about books that write themselves, and it's a lie. Books don't write themselves. It takes thought and research and backache and notes and more time and more work than you'd believe.

Except for *Sons of Man*, and that one pretty much wrote itself.

The irritating question they ask us – us being writers – is: 'Where do you get your ideas?'

And the answer is: Confluence. Things come together. The right ingredients and suddenly: *Abracadabra!*

It began with a documentary on Charles Manson I

was watching more or less by accident (it was on a videotape a friend lent me after a couple of things I *did* want to watch): there was footage of Manson, back when he was first arrested, when people thought he was innocent and that it was the government picking on the hippies. And up on the screen was Manson – a charismatic, good-looking, messianic orator. Someone you'd crawl barefoot into Hell for. Someone you could kill for.

The trial started; and, a few weeks into it, the orator was gone, replaced by a shambling, apelike gibberer, with a cross carved into its forehead. Whatever the genius was was no longer there. It was gone. But it had been there.

The documentary continued: a hard-eyed ex-con who had been in prison with Manson, explaining, 'Charlie Manson? Listen, Charlie was a joke. He was a nothing. We laughed at him. You know? He was a nothing!'

And I nodded. There was a time before Manson was the charisma king, then. I thought of a benediction, something given, that was taken away.

I watched the rest of the documentary obsessively. Then, over a black-and-white still, the narrator said something. I rewound, and he said it again.

I had an idea. I had a book that wrote itself.

The thing the narrator had said was this: that the infant children Manson had fathered on the women of The Family were sent to a variety of children's homes for adoption, with court-given surnames that were certainly not Manson.

And I thought of a dozen twenty-five-year-old Mansons. Thought of the charisma-thing descending on all of them at the same time. Twelve young Mansons, in their glory, gradually being pulled toward L.A. from all over the world. And a Manson daughter trying desperately to stop them from coming together and, as the back cover blurb told us, 'realizing their terrifying destiny'.

I wrote *Sons of Man* at white heat: it was finished in a month, and I sent it to my agent, who was surprised by it ('Well, it's not like your other stuff, dear,' she said helpfully), and she sold it after an auction – my first – for more money than I had thought possible. (My other books, three collections of elegant, allusive and elusive ghost stories, had scarcely paid for the computer on which they were written.)

And then it was bought – prepublication – by Hollywood, again after an auction. There were three or four studios interested: I went with the studio who wanted me to write the script. I knew it would never happen, knew they'd never come through. But then the faxes began to spew out of my machine, late at night – most of them enthusiastically signed by one Dave Gambol; one morning I signed five copies of a contract thick as a brick; a few weeks later my agent reported the first cheque had cleared and tickets to Hollywood had arrived, for 'preliminary talks'. It seemed like a dream.

The tickets were business class. It was the moment I saw the tickets were business class that I knew the dream was real.

I went to Hollywood in the bubble bit at the top of the jumbo jet, nibbling smoked salmon and holding a hot-off-the-presses hardback of *Sons of Man*.

So. Breakfast.

They told me how much they loved the book. I

didn't quite catch anybody's name. The men had beards or baseball caps or both; the women were astoundingly attractive, in a sanitary sort of way.

Jacob ordered our breakfast, and paid for it. He explained that the meeting coming up was a formality.

'It's your book we love,' he said. 'Why would we have bought your book if we didn't want to make it? Why would we have hired *you* to write it if we didn't want the specialness you'd bring to the project. The *you-ness*.'

I nodded, very seriously, as if literary me-ness was something I had spent many hours pondering.

'An idea like this. A book like this. You're pretty unique.'

'One of the uniquest,' said a woman named Dina or Tina or possibly Deanna.

I raised an eyebrow. 'So what am I meant to do at the meeting?'

'Be receptive,' said Jacob. 'Be positive.'

The drive to the studio took about half an hour in Jacob's little red car. We drove up to the security gate, where Jacob had an argument with the guard. I gathered that he was new at the studio and had not yet been issued a permanent studio pass.

Nor, it appeared, once we got inside, did he have a permanent parking place. I still do not understand the ramifications of this: from what he said, parking places had as much to do with status at the studio as gifts from the emperor determined one's status in the court of ancient China.

We drove through the streets of an oddly flat New York and parked in front of a huge old bank.

Ten minutes' walk, and I was in a conference room,

with Jacob and all the people from breakfast, waiting for someone to come in. In the flurry I'd rather missed who the someone was and what he or she did. I took out my copy of my book and put it in front of me, a talisman of sorts.

Someone came in. He was tall, with a pointy nose and a pointy chin, and his hair was too long – he looked like he'd kidnapped someone much younger and stolen their hair. He was an Australian, which surprised me.

He sat down.

He looked at me.

'Shoot,' he said.

I looked at the people from the breakfast, but none of them were looking at me – I couldn't catch anyone's eye. So I began to talk: about the book, about the plot, about the end, the showdown in the L.A. nightclub, where the good Manson girl blows the rest of them up. Or thinks she does. About my idea for having one actor play all the Manson boys.

'Do you believe this stuff?' It was the first question from the Someone.

That one was easy. It was one I'd already answered for at least two dozen British journalists.

'Do I believe that a supernatural power possessed Charles Manson for a while and is even now possessing his many children? No. Do I believe that something strange was happening? I suppose I must do. Perhaps it was simply that, for a brief while, his madness was in step with the madness of the world outside. I don't know.'

'Mm. This Manson kid. He could be Keanu Reaves?'

God, no, I thought. Jacob caught my eye and nodded desperately. 'I don't see why not,' I said. It was all imagination anyway. None of it was real.

'We're cutting a deal with his people,' said the Someone, nodding thoughtfully.

They sent me off to do a treatment for them to approve. And by *them*, I understood they meant the Australian Someone, although I was not entirely sure.

Before I left, someone gave me $700 and made me sign for it: two weeks *per diem*.

I spent two days doing the treatment. I kept trying to forget the book, and structure the story as a film. The work went well. I sat in the little room and typed on a notebook computer the studio had sent down for me, and printed out pages on the bubble-jet printer the studio sent down with it. I ate in my room.

Each afternoon I would go for a short walk down Sunset Boulevard. I would walk as far as the 'almost all-nite' bookstore, where I would buy a newspaper. Then I would sit outside in the hotel courtyard for half an hour, reading a newspaper. And then, having had my ration of sun and air, I would go back into the dark, and turn my book back into something else.

There was a very old black man, a hotel employee, who would walk across the courtyard each day with almost painful slowness and water the plants and inspect the fish. He'd grin at me as he went past, and I'd nod at him.

On the third day I got up and walked over to him as he stood by the fish pool, picking out bits of rubbish by hand: a couple of coins and a cigarette packet.

'Hello,' I said.

'Suh,' said the old man.

I thought about asking him not to call me sir, but I couldn't think of a way to put it that might not cause offence. 'Nice fish.'

He nodded and grinned. 'Ornamental carp. Brought here all the way from China.'

We watched them swim around the little pool.

'I wonder if they get bored.'

He shook his head. 'My grandson, he's an ichthyologist, you know what that is?'

'Studies fishes.'

'Uh-huh. He says they only got a memory that's like thirty seconds long. So they swim around the pool, it's always a surprise to them, going "I never been here before." They meet another fish they known for a hundred years, they say, "Who are you, stranger?" '

'Will you ask your grandson something for me?' The old man nodded. 'I read once that carp don't have set life spans. They don't age like we do. They die if they're killed by people or predators or disease, but they don't just get old and die. Theoretically they could live for ever.'

He nodded. 'I'll ask him. It sure sounds good. These three – now, this one, I call him Ghost, he's only four, five years old. But the other two, they came here from China back when I was first here.'

'And when was that?'

'That would have been, in the Year of Our Lord Nineteen Hundred and Twenty-four. How old do I look to you?'

I couldn't tell. He might have been carved from old wood. Over fifty and younger than Methuselah. I told him so.

'I was born in 1906. God's truth.'

'Were you born here, in L.A.?'

He shook his head. 'When I was born, Los Angeles wasn't nothin' but an orange grove, a long way from New York.' He sprinkled fish food on the surface of the water. The three fish bobbed up, pale-white silvered ghost carp, staring at us, or seeming to, the O's of their mouths continually opening and closing, as if they were talking to us in some silent, secret language of their own.

I pointed to the one he had indicated. 'So he's Ghost, yes?'

'He's Ghost. That's right. That one under the lily – you can see his tail, there, see? – he's called Buster, after Buster Keaton. Keaton was staying here when we got the older two. And this one's our Princess.'

Princess was the most recognizable of the white carp. She was a pale cream colour, with a blotch of vivid crimson along her back, setting her apart from the other two.

'She's lovely.'

'She surely is. She surely is all of that.'

He took a deep breath then and began to cough, a wheezing cough that shook his thin frame. I was able then, for the first time, to see him as a man in his nineties.

'Are you all right?'

He nodded. 'Fine, fine, fine. Old bones,' he said. 'Old bones.'

We shook hands, and I returned to my treatment and the gloom.

I printed out the completed treatment, faxed it off to Jacob at the studio.

The next day he came over to the chalet. He looked upset.

'Everything okay? Is there a problem with the treatment?'

'Just shit going down. We made this movie with

 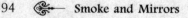

'. . .' and he named a well-known actress who had been in a few successful films a couple of years before. 'Can't lose, huh? Only she is not as young as she was, and she insists on doing her own nude scenes, and that's not a body anybody wants to see, believe me.

'So the plot is, there's this photographer who is persuading women to take their clothes off for him. Then he *shtups* them. Only no one believes he's doing it. So the chief of police – played by Ms Lemme Show the World My Naked Butt – realises that the only way she can arrest him is if she pretends to be one of the women. So she sleeps with him. Now, there's a twist . . .'

'She falls in love with him?'

'Oh. Yeah. And then she realises that women will always be imprisoned by male images of women, and to prove her love for him, when the police come to arrest the two of them she sets fire to all the photographs and dies in the fire. Her clothes burn off first. How does that sound to you?'

'Dumb.'

'That was what we thought when we saw it. So we fired the director and recut it and did an extra day's shoot. Now she's wearing a wire when they make out. And when she starts to fall in love with him, she finds out that he killed her brother. She has a dream in which her clothes burn off, then she goes out with the SWAT team to try to bring him in. But he gets shot by her little sister, who he's also been *shtupping*.'

'Is it any better?'

He shakes his head. 'It's junk. If she'd let us use a stand-in for the nude sequences, maybe we'd be in better shape.'

'What did you think of the treatment?'

'What?'

'My treatment? The one I sent you?'

'Sure. That treatment. We loved it. We all loved it. It was great. Really terrific. We're all really excited.'

'So what's next?'

'Well, as soon as everyone's had a chance to look it over, we'll get together and talk about it.'

He patted me on the back and went away, leaving me with nothing to do in Hollywood.

I decided to write a short story. There was an idea I'd had in England before I'd left. Something about a small theatre at the end of a pier. Stage magic as the rain came down. An audience who couldn't tell the difference between magic and illusion, and to whom it would make no difference if every illusion was real.

That afternoon, on my walk, I bought a couple of books on Stage Magic and Victorian Illusions in the 'almost all-nite' bookshop. A story, or the seed of it anyway, was there in my head, and I wanted to explore it. I sat on the bench in the courtyard and browsed through the books. There was, I decided, a specific atmosphere that I was after.

I was reading about the Pockets Men, who had pockets filled with every small object you could imagine and would produce whatever you asked on request. No illusion – just remarkable feats of organization and memory. A shadow fell across the page. I looked up.

'Hullo again,' I said to the old black man.

'Suh,' he said.

'Please don't call me that. It makes me feel like I ought to be wearing a suit or something.' I told him my name.

He told me his: 'Pious Dundas.'

'Pious?' I wasn't sure that I'd heard him correctly. He nodded proudly.

'Sometimes I am, and sometimes I ain't. It's what my mamma called me, and it's a good name.'

'Yes.'

'So what are you doing here, suh?'

'I'm not sure. I'm meant to be writing a film, I think. Or at least, I'm waiting for them to tell me to start writing a film.'

He scratched his nose. 'All the film people stayed here, if I started to tell you them all now, I could talk till a week next Wednesday and I wouldn't have told you the half of them.'

'Who were your favourites?'

'Harry Langdon. He was a gentleman. George Sanders. He was English, like you. He'd say, "Ah, Pious. You must pray for my soul." And I'd say, "Your soul's your own affair, Mister Sanders," but I prayed for him just the same. And June Lincoln.'

'June Lincoln?'

His eyes sparkled, and he smiled. 'She was the queen of the silver screen. She was finer than any of them: Mary Pickford or Lillian Gish or Theda Bara or Louise Brooks . . . She was the finest. She had "it". You know what "it" was?'

'Sex appeal.'

'More than that. She was everything you ever dreamed of. You'd see a June Lincoln picture, you wanted to . . .' he broke off, waved one hand in small circles, as if he were trying to catch the missing words. 'I don't know. Go down on one knee, maybe, like a knight in shinin' armour to the queen. June Lincoln, she was the best of them. I told my grandson about her, he tried to find something for the VCR, but no go.

Nothing out there anymore. She only lives in the heads of old men like me.' He tapped his forehead.

'She must have been quite something.'

He nodded.

'What happened to her?'

'She hung herself. Some folks said it was because she wouldn't have been able to cut the mustard in the talkies, but that ain't true: she had a voice you'd remember if you heard it just once. Smooth and dark, her voice was, like an Irish coffee. Some say she got her heart broken by a man, or by a woman, or that it was gambling, or gangsters, or booze. Who knows? They were wild days.'

'I take it that you must have heard her talk.'

He grinned. 'She said, "Boy, can you find what they did with my wrap?" and when I come back with it, then she said, "You're a fine one, boy." And the man who was with her, he said, "June, don't tease the help" and she smiled at me and gave me five dollars and said "He don't mind, do you, boy?" and I just shook my head. Then she made the thing with her lips, you know?'

'A *moue*?'

'Something like that. I felt it here.' He tapped his chest. 'Those lips. They could take a man apart.'

He bit his lower lip for a moment, and focused on forever. I wondered where he was, and when. Then he looked at me once more.

'You want to see her lips?'

'How do you mean?'

'You come over here. Follow me.'

'What are we . . .?' I had visions of a lip print in cement, like the handprints outside Grauman's Chinese Theatre.

He shook his head, and raised an old finger to his mouth. *Silence*.

I closed the books. We walked across the courtyard. When he reached the little fish-pool, he stopped.

'Look at the Princess,' he told me.

'The one with the red splotch, yes?'

He nodded. The fish reminded me of a Chinese dragon: wise and pale. A ghost fish, white as old bone, save for the blotch of scarlet on its back – an inch-long double-bow shape. It hung in the pool, drifting, thinking.

'That's it,' he said. 'On her back. See?'

'I don't quite follow you.'

He paused and stared at the fish.

'Would you like to sit down?' I found myself very conscious of Mr Dundas's age.

'They don't pay me to sit down,' he said, very seriously. Then he said, as if he were explaining something to a small child, 'It was like there were gods in those days. Today, it's all television: small heroes. Little people in the boxes. I see some of them here. Little people.

'The stars of the old times: They was giants, painted in silver light, big as houses . . . and when you met them, they were *still* huge. People believed in them.

'They'd have parties here. You worked here, you saw what went on. There was liquor, and weed, and goings-on you'd hardly credit. There was this one party . . . the film was called *Hearts of the Desert*. You ever heard of it?'

I shook my head.

'One of the biggest movies of 1926, up there with *What Price Glory* with Victor McLaglen and Dolores Del Rio and *Ella Cinders* starring Colleen Moore. You heard of them?'

I shook my head again.

'You ever heard of Warner Baxter? Belle Bennett?'

'Who were they?'

'Big, big stars in 1926.' He paused for a moment. '*Hearts of the Desert*. They had the party for it here, in the hotel, when it wrapped. There was wine and beer and whiskey and gin – this was Prohibition days, but the studios kind of owned the police force, so they looked the other way; and there was food, and a deal of foolishness; Ronald Colman was there and Douglas Fairbanks – the father, not the son – and all the cast and the crew; and a jazz band played over there where those chalets are now.

'And June Lincoln was the toast of Hollywood that night. She was the Arab princess in the film. Those days, Arabs meant passion and lust. These days . . . well, things change.

'I don't know what started it all. I heard it was a dare or a bet; maybe she was just drunk. I thought she was drunk. Anyhow, she got up, and the band was playing soft and slow. And she walked over here, where I'm standing right now, and she plunged her hands right into this pool. She was laughing, and laughing, and laughing . . .

'Miss Lincoln picked up the fish – reached in and took it, both hands she took it in – and she picked it up from the water, and then she held it in front of her face.

'Now, I was worried, because they'd just brought these fish in from China and they cost two hundred dollars apiece. That was before I was looking after the fish, of course. Wasn't me that'd lose it from my wages. But still, two hundred dollars was a whole lot of money in those days.

'Then she smiled at all of us, and she leaned down and she kissed it, slow like, on its back. It didn't wriggle or nothin', it just lay in her hand, and she kissed it with her lips like red coral, and the people at the party laughed and cheered.

'She put the fish back in the pool, and for a moment it was as if it didn't want to leave her – it stayed by her, nuzzling her fingers. And then the first of the fireworks went off, and it swam away.

'Her lipstick was red as red as red, and she left the shape of her lips on the fish's back. – There. Do you see?'

Princess, the white carp with the coral red mark on her back, flicked a fin and continued on her eternal series of thirty-second journeys around the pool. The red mark did look like a lip print.

He sprinkled a handful of fish food on the water, and the three fish bobbed and gulped to the surface.

I walked back in to my chalet, carrying my books on old illusions. The phone was ringing: it was someone from the studio. They wanted to talk about the treatment. A car would be there for me in thirty minutes.

'Will Jacob be there?'

But the line was already dead.

The meeting was with the Australian Someone and his assistant, a bespectacled man in a suit. His was the first suit I'd seen so far, and his spectacles were a vivid blue. He seemed nervous.

'Where are you staying?' asked the Someone.

I told him.

'Isn't that where Belushi . . .?'

'So I've been told.'

He nodded. 'He wasn't alone, when he died.'

'No?'

He rubbed one finger along the side of his pointy nose. 'There were a couple of other people at the party. They were both directors, both as big as you could get at that point. You don't need names. I found out about it when I was making the last Indiana Jones film.'

An uneasy silence. We were at a huge round table, just the three of us, and we each had a copy of the treatment I had written in front of us. Finally I said:

'What did you think of it?'

They both nodded, more or less in unison.

And then they tried, as hard as they could, to tell me they hated it while never saying anything that might conceivably upset me. It was a very odd conversation.

'We have a problem with the third act,' they'd say, implying vaguely that the fault lay neither with me nor with the treatment, nor even with the third act, but with them.

They wanted the people to be more sympathetic. They wanted sharp lights and shadows, not shades of grey. They wanted the heroine to be a hero. And I nodded and took notes.

At the end of the meeting I shook hands with the Someone, and the assistant in the blue-rimmed spectacles took me off through the corridor maze to find the outside world and my car and my driver.

As we walked, I asked if the studio had a picture anywhere of June Lincoln.

'Who?' His name, it turned out, was Greg. He pulled out a small notebook and wrote something down in it with a pencil.

'She was a silent screen star. Famous in 1926.'

'Was she with the studio?'

'I have no idea,' I admitted. 'But she was famous.

Even more famous than Marie Provost.'

'Who?'

' "A winner who became a doggie's dinner." One of the biggest stars of the silent screen. Died in poverty when the talkies came in and was eaten by her dachshund. Nick Lowe wrote a song about her.'

'Who?'

' "*I knew the bride when she used to rock and roll.*" Anyway, June Lincoln. Can someone find me a photo?'

He wrote something more down on his pad. Stared at it for a moment. Then wrote down something else. Then he nodded.

We had reached the daylight, and my car was waiting.

'By the way,' he said, 'you should know that he's full of shit.'

'I'm sorry?'

'Full of shit. It wasn't Spielberg and Lucas who were with Belushi. It was Bette Midler and Linda Ronstadt. It was a coke orgy. Everybody knows that. He's full of shit. And he was just a junior studio accountant for chrissakes on the Indiana Jones movie. Like it was his movie. Asshole.'

We shook hands. I got in the car and went back to the hotel.

The time difference caught up with me that night, and I woke, utterly and irrevocably, at 4 A.M.

I got up, peed, then I pulled on a pair of jeans (I sleep in a T-shirt) and walked outside.

I wanted to see the stars, but the lights of the city were too bright, the air too dirty. The sky was a dirty, starless yellow, and I thought of all the constellations I could see from the English countryside, and I felt, for the first time, deeply, stupidly homesick.

I missed the stars.

I wanted to work on the short story or to get on with the film script. Instead, I worked on a second draft of the treatment.

I took the number of Junior Mansons down to five from twelve and made it clearer from the start that one of them, who was now male, wasn't a bad guy and the other four most definitely were.

They sent over a copy of a film magazine. It had the smell of old pulp paper about it, and was stamped in purple with the studio name and with the word ARCHIVES underneath. The cover showed John Barrymore, on a boat.

The article inside was about June Lincoln's death. I found it hard to read and harder still to understand: it hinted at the forbidden vices that led to her death, that much I could tell, but it was as if it were hinting in a cipher to which modern readers lacked any key. Or perhaps, on reflection, the writer of her obituary knew nothing and was hinting into the void.

More interesting – at any rate, more comprehensible – were the photos. A full-page, black-edged photo of a woman with huge eyes and a gentle smile, smoking a cigarette (the smoke was airbrushed in, to my way of thinking very clumsily: had people ever been taken in by such clumsy fakes?); another photo of her in a staged clinch with Douglas Fairbanks; a small photograph of her standing on the running board of a car, holding a couple of tiny dogs.

She was, from the photographs, not a contemporary beauty. She lacked the transcendence of a Louise Brooks, the sex appeal of a Marilyn Monroe, the sluttish elegance of a Rita Hayworth. She was a twenties starlet as dull as any other twenties starlet. I saw no mystery in her huge eyes, her bobbed hair. She had perfectly made-up cupid's bow lips. I had no idea what she would have looked like if she had been alive and around today.

Still, she was real; she had lived. She had been worshipped and adored by the people in the movie palaces. She had kissed the fish, and walked in the grounds of my hotel seventy years before: no time in England, but an eternity in Hollywood.

I went in to talk about the treatment. None of the people I had spoken to before were there. Instead, I was shown in to see a very young man in a small office, who never smiled and who told me how much he loved the treatment and how pleased he was that the studio owned the property.

He said he thought the character of Charles Manson was particularly cool, and that maybe – 'once he was fully dimensionalized' – Manson could be the next Hannibal Lecter.

'But. Um. Manson. He's real. He's in prison now. His people killed Sharon Tate.'

'Sharon Tate?'

'She was an actress. A film star. She was pregnant and they killed her. She was married to Polanski.'

'*Roman* Polanski?'

'The director. Yes.'

He frowned. 'But we're putting together a deal with Polanski.'

'That's good. He's a good director.'

'Does he know about this?'

'About what? The book? Our film? Sharon Tate's death?'

He shook his head: none of the above. 'It's a three-picture deal. Julia Roberts is semi-attached to it. You say Polanski doesn't know about this treatment?'

'No, what I said was—'

He checked his watch.

'Where are you staying?' he asked. 'Are we putting you up somewhere good?'

'Yes, thank you,' I said. 'I'm a couple of chalets away from the room in which Belushi died.'

I expected another confidential couple of stars: to be told that John Belushi had kicked the bucket in company with Julie Andrews and Miss Piggy the Muppet. I was wrong.

'Belushi's dead?' he said, his young brow furrowing. 'Belushi's not dead. We're doing a picture with Belushi.'

'This was the brother,' I told him. 'The brother died, years ago.'

He shrugged. 'Sounds like a shithole,' he said. 'Next time you come out, tell them you want to stay in the Bel Air. You want us to move you out there now?'

'No, thank you,' I said. 'I'm used to it where I am.'

'What about the treatment?' I asked.

'Leave it with us.'

I found myself becoming fascinated by two old theatrical illusions I found in my books: 'The Artist's Dream' and 'The Enchanted Casement'. They were metaphors for something, of that I was certain; but the story that ought to have accompanied them was not yet there. I'd write first sentences that did not make it to first paragraphs, first paragraphs that never made it to first pages. I'd write them on the computer, then exit without saving anything.

I sat outside in the courtyard and stared at the

two white carp and the one scarlet and white carp. They looked, I decided, like Escher drawings of fish, which surprised me, as it had never occurred to me there was anything even slightly realistic in Escher's drawings.

Pious Dundas was polishing the leaves of the plants. He had a bottle of polisher and a cloth.

'Hi, Pious.'

'Suh.'

'Lovely day.'

He nodded, and coughed, and banged his chest with his fist, and nodded some more.

I left the fish, sat down on the bench.

'Why haven't they made you retire?' I asked. 'Shouldn't you have retired fifteen years ago?'

He continued polishing. 'Hell no, I'm a landmark. They can *say* that all the stars in the sky stayed here, but *I* tell folks what Cary Grant had for breakfast.'

'Do you remember?'

'Heck no. But *they* don't know that.' He coughed again. 'What you writing?'

'Well, last week I wrote a treatment for this film. And then I wrote another treatment. And now I'm waiting for . . . something.'

'So what *are* you writing?'

'A story that won't come right. It's about a Victorian magic trick called "The Artist's Dream". An artist comes on to the stage, carrying a big canvas, which he puts on an easel. It's got a painting of a woman on it. And he looks at the painting and despairs of ever being a real painter. Then he sits down and goes to sleep, and the painting comes to life, steps down from the frame and tells him not to give up. To keep fighting. He'll be a great painter one day. She climbs back into the frame.

The lights dim. Then he wakes up, and it's a painting again . . .'

'. . . and the other illusion,' I told the woman from the studio, who had made the mistake of feigning interest at the beginning of the meeting, 'was called "The Enchanted Casement". A window hangs in the air and faces appear in it, but there's no one around. I think I can get a strange sort of parallel between the enchanted casement and probably television: seems like a natural candidate, after all.'

'I like "Seinfeld",' she said. 'You watch that show? It's about nothing. I mean, they have whole episodes about nothing. And I liked Garry Shandling before he did the new show and got mean.'

'The illusions,' I continued, 'like all great illusions, make us question the nature of reality. But they also frame – pun, I suppose, intentionalish – the issue of what entertainment would turn into. Films before they had films, telly before there was ever TV.'

She frowned. 'Is this a movie?'

'I hope not. It's a short story, if I can get it to work.'

'So let's talk about the movie.' She flicked through a pile of notes. She was in her mid-twenties and looked both attractive and sterile. I wondered if she was one of the women who had been at the breakfast on my first day, a Deanna or a Tina.

She looked puzzled at something and read: '*I Knew the Bride When She Used to Rock and Roll?*'

'He wrote that down? That's not this film.'

She nodded. 'Now, I have to say that some of your treatment is kind of . . . *contentious*. The Manson thing . . . well, we're not sure it's going to fly. Could we take him out?'

'But that's the whole point of the thing. I mean, the book is called *Sons of Man*; it's about Manson's children. If you take him out, you don't have very much, do you? I mean, this is the book you bought.' I held it up for her to see: my talisman. 'Throwing out Manson is like, I don't know, it's like ordering a pizza and then complaining when it arrives because it's flat, round, and covered in tomato sauce and cheese.'

She gave no indication of having heard anything I had said. She asked, 'What do you think about *When We Were Badd* as a title? Two *d*'s in Badd.'

'I don't know. For this?'

'We don't want people to think that it's religious. *Sons of Man*. It sounds like it might be kind of anti-Christian.'

'Well, I do kind of imply that the power that possesses the Manson children is in some way a kind of demonic power.'

'You do?'

'In the book.'

She managed a pitying look, of the kind that only people who know that books are, at best, properties on which films can be loosely based, can bestow on the rest of us.

'Well, I don't think the studio would see that as appropriate,' she said.

'Do you know who June Lincoln was?' I asked her. She shook her head.

'David Gambol? Jacob Klein?'

She shook her head once more, a little impatiently. Then she gave me a typed list of things she felt needed fixing, which amounted to pretty much everything. The list was TO: me and a number of other people, whose names I didn't recognise, and it was FROM: Donna Leary.

I said Thank you, Donna, and went back to the hotel.

I was gloomy for a day. And then I thought of a way to redo the treatment that would, I thought, deal with all of Donna's list of complaints.

Another day's thinking, a few days' writing, and I faxed the third treatment off to the studio.

Pious Dundas brought his scrapbook over for me to look at, once he felt certain that I was genuinely interested in June Lincoln – named, I discovered, after the month and the President, born Ruth Baumgarten in 1903. It was a leatherbound old scrapbook, the size and weight of a family Bible.

She was twenty-four when she died.

'I wish you could've seen her,' said Pious Dundas. 'I wish some of her films had survived. She was so big. She was the greatest star of all of them.'

'Was she a good actress?'

He shook his head decisively. 'Nope.'

'Was she a great beauty? If she was, I just don't see it.'

He shook his head again. 'The camera liked her, that's for sure. But that wasn't it. Back row of the chorus had a dozen girls prettier'n her.'

'Then what was it?'

'She was a star.' He shrugged. 'That's what it means to be a star.'

I turned the pages: cuttings, reviewing films I'd never heard of – films for which the only negatives and prints had long ago been lost, mislaid, or destroyed by the fire department, nitrate negatives being a notorious fire hazard; other cuttings from film magazines: June Lincoln at play, June Lincoln at rest, June Lincoln on the set of *The Pawnbroker's Shirt*, June Lincoln wearing a huge fur coat – which somehow dated the photograph more than the strange bobbed hair or the ubiquitous cigarettes.

'Did you love her?'

He shook his head. 'Not like you would love a woman . . .' he said.

There was a pause. He reached down and turned the pages.

'And my wife would have killed me if she'd heard me say this . . .'

Another pause.

'But yeah. Skinny dead white woman. I suppose I loved her.' He closed the book.

'But she's not dead to you, is she?'

He shook his head. Then he went away. But he left me the book to look at.

The secret of the illusion of 'The Artist's Dream' was this: It was done by carrying the girl in, holding tight on to the back of the canvas. The canvas was supported by hidden wires, so, while the artist casually, easily, carried in the canvas and placed it on the easel, he was also carrying in the girl. The painting of the girl on the easel was arranged like a roller blind, and it rolled up or down.

'The Enchanted Casement', on the other hand, was, literally, done with mirrors: an angled mirror which reflected the faces of people standing out of sight in the wings.

Even today many magicians use mirrors in their acts to make you think you are seeing something you are not.

It was easy, when you knew how it was done.

'Before we start,' he said, 'I should tell you I don't read treatments. I tend to feel it inhibits my creativity. Don't worry, I had a secretary do a précis, so I'm up to speed.'

He had a beard and long hair and looked a little like Jesus, although I doubted that Jesus had such perfect teeth. He was, it appeared, the most important person I'd spoken to so far. His name was John Ray, and even I had heard of him, although I was not entirely sure what he did: his name tended to appear at the beginning of films, next to words like EXECUTIVE PRODUCER. The voice from the studio that had set up the meeting told me that they, the studio, were most excited about the fact that he had 'attached himself to the project'.

'Doesn't the précis inhibit your creativity, too?'

He grinned. 'Now, we all think you've done an amazing job. Quite stunning. There are just a few things that we have a problem with.'

'Such as?'

'Well, the Manson thing. And the idea about these kids growing up. So we've been tossing around a few scenarios in the office: try this for size. There's a guy called, say, Jack Badd – two *d*'s, that was Donna's idea—'

Donna bowed her head modestly.

'They put him away for satanic abuse, fried him in the chair, and as he dies he swears he'll come back and destroy them all.

'Now, it's today, and we see these young boys getting hooked on a video arcade game called *Be Badd*. His face on it. And as they play the game he like, starts to possess them. Maybe there could be something strange about his face, a Jason or Freddy thing.' He stopped, as if he were seeking approval.

So I said, 'So who's making these video games?'

He pointed a finger at me and said, 'You're the writer, sweet-heart. You want us to do all your work for you?'

I didn't say anything. I didn't know what to say.

Think movies, I thought. *They understand movies.* I said, 'But surely, what you're proposing is like doing *The Boys from Brazil* without Hitler.'

He looked puzzled.

'It was a film by Ira Levin,' I said. No flicker of recognition in his eyes. '*Rosemary's Baby.*' He continued to look blank. '*Sliver.*'

He nodded; somewhere a penny had dropped. 'Point taken,' he said. 'You write the Sharon Stone part, we'll move heaven and earth to get her for you. I have an in to her people.'

So I went out.

That night it was cold, and it shouldn't have been cold in L.A., and the air smelled more of cough drops than ever.

An old girlfriend lived in the L.A. area and I resolved to get hold of her. I phoned the number I had for her and began a quest that took most of the rest of the evening. People gave me numbers, and I rang them, and other people gave me numbers, and I rang them, too.

Eventually I phoned a number, and I recognised her voice.

'Do you know where I am?' she said.

'No,' I said. 'I was given this number.'

'This is a hospital room,' she said. 'My mother's. She had a brain haemorrhage.'

'I'm sorry. Is she all right?'

'No.'

'I'm sorry.'

There was an awkward silence.

'How are you?' she asked.

'Pretty bad,' I said.

I told her everything that had happened to me so far. I told her how I felt.

'Why is it like this?' I asked her.

'Because they're scared.'

'Why are they scared? What are they scared of?'

'Because you're only as good as the last hits you can attach your name to.'

'Huh?'

'If you say yes to something, the studio may make a film, and it will cost twenty or thirty million dollars, and if it's a failure, you will have your name attached to it and will lose status. If you say no, you don't risk losing status.'

'Really?'

'Kind of.'

'How do you know so much about all this? You're a musician, you're not in films.'

She laughed wearily: 'I live out here. Everybody who lives out here knows this stuff. Have you tried asking people about their screenplays?'

'No.'

'Try it sometime. Ask anyone. The guy in the gas station. Anyone. They've all got them.' Then someone said something to her, and she said something back, and she said, 'Look, I've got to go,' and she put down the phone.

I couldn't find the heater, if the room had a heater, and I was freezing in my little chalet room, like the one

Belushi died in, same uninspired framed print on the wall, I had no doubt, same chilly dampness in the air.

I ran a hot bath to warm myself up, but I was even chillier when I got out.

White goldfish sliding to and fro in the water, dodging and darting through the lily pads. One of the goldfish had a crimson mark on its back that might, conceivably, have been perfectly lip-shaped: the miraculous stigmata of an almost-forgotten goddess. The grey early-morning sky was reflected in the pool.

I stared at it gloomily.

'You okay?'

I turned. Pious Dundas was standing next to me.

'You're up early.'

'I slept badly. Too cold.'

'You should have called the front desk. They'd've sent you down a heater and extra blankets.'

'It never occurred to me.'

His breathing sounded awkward, laboured.

'You okay?'

'Heck no. I'm old. You get to my age, boy, you won't be okay either. But I'll be here when you've gone. How's work going?'

'I don't know. I've stopped working on the treatment, and I'm stuck on "The Artist's Dream" – this story I'm doing about Victorian stage magic. It's set in an English seaside resort in the rain. With the magician performing magic on the stage, which somehow changes the audience. It touches their hearts.'

He nodded, slowly. ' "The Artist's Dream" . . .' he said. 'So. You see yourself as the artist or the magician?'

'I don't know,' I said. 'I don't think I'm either of them.'

I turned to go and then something occurred to me.

'Mister Dundas,' I said. 'Have you got a screenplay? One you wrote?'

He shook his head.

'You *never* wrote a screenplay?'

'Not me,' he said.

'Promise?'

He grinned. 'I promise,' he said.

I went back to my room. I thumbed through my U.K. hardback of *Sons of Man* and wondered that anything so clumsily written had even been published, wondered why Hollywood had bought it in the first place, why they didn't want it, now that they had bought it.

I tried to write 'The Artist's Dream' some more, and failed miserably. The characters were frozen. They seemed unable to breathe, or move, or talk.

I went into the toilet, pissed a vivid yellow stream against the porcelain. A cockroach ran across the silver of the mirror.

I went back into the sitting room, opened a new document, and wrote:

I'm thinking about England in the rain,
a strange theatre on the pier: a trail
of fear and magic, memory and pain.

The fear should be of going bleak insane,
the magic should be like a fairytale.
I'm thinking about England in the rain.

The loneliness is harder to explain –
an empty place inside me where I fail,
of fear and magic, memory and pain.

I think of a magician and a skein
of truth disguised as lies. You wear a veil.
I'm thinking about England in the rain . . .

The shapes repeat like some bizarre refrain
and here's a sword, a hand, and there's a grail
of fear and magic, memory and pain.

The wizard waves his wand and we turn pale,
tells us sad truths, but all to no avail.
I'm thinking about England, in the rain
of fear and magic, memory and pain.

I didn't know if it was any good or not, but that didn't
matter. I had written something new and fresh I hadn't
written before, and it felt wonderful.

I ordered breakfast from room service and re-
quested a heater and a couple of extra blankets.

The next day I wrote a six-page treatment for a film
called *When We Were Badd*, in which Jack Badd, a serial
killer with a huge cross carved into his forehead, was
killed in the electric chair and came back in a video
game and took over four young men. The fifth young
man defeated Badd by burning the original electric
chair, which was now on display, I decided, in the wax
museum where the fifth young man's girlfriend worked
during the day. By night she was an exotic dancer.

The hotel desk faxed it off to the studio, and I went
to bed.

I went to sleep, hoping that the studio would
formally reject it and that I could go home.

In the theatre of my dreams, a man with a beard and a

baseball cap carried on a movie screen, and then he walked off-stage. The silver screen hung in the air, unsupported.

A flickery silent film began to play upon it: a woman who came out and stared down at me. It was June Lincoln who flickered on the screen, and it was June Lincoln who walked down from the screen and sat on the edge of my bed.

'Are you going to tell me not to give up?' I asked her.

On some level I knew it was a dream. I remember, dimly, understanding why this woman was a star, remember regretting that none of her films had survived.

She was indeed beautiful in my dream, despite the livid mark which went all the way around her neck.

'Why on earth would I do that?' she asked. In my dream she smelled of gin and old celluloid, although I do not remember the last dream I had where anyone smelled of anything. She smiled, a perfect black-and-white smile. 'I got out, didn't I?'

Then she stood up and walked around the room.

'I can't believe this hotel is still standing,' she said. 'I used to fuck here.' Her voice was filled with crackles and hisses. She came back to the bed and stared at me, as a cat stares at a hole.

'Do you worship me?' she asked.

I shook my head. She walked over to me and took my flesh hand in her silver one.

'Nobody remembers anything anymore,' she said. 'It's a thirty-minute town.'

There was something I had to ask her. 'Where are the stars?' I asked. 'I keep looking up in the sky, but they aren't there.'

She pointed at the floor of the chalet. 'You've been

looking in the wrong places,' she said. I had never before noticed that the floor of the chalet was a sidewalk and each paving stone contained a star and a name – names I didn't know: Clara Kimball Young, Linda Arvidson, Vivian Martin, Norma Talmadge, Olive Thomas, Mary Miles Minter, Seena Owen . . .

June Lincoln pointed at the chalet window. 'And out there.' The window was open, and through it I could see the whole of Hollywood spread out below me – the view from the hills: an infinite spread of twinkling multicoloured lights.

'Now, aren't those better than stars?' she asked.

And they were. I realised I could see constellations in the street lamps and the cars.

I nodded.

Her lips brushed mine.

'Don't forget me,' she whispered, but she whispered it sadly, as if she knew that I would.

I woke up with the telephone shrilling. I answered it, growled a mumble into the handpiece.

'This is Gerry Quoint, from the studio. We need you for a lunch meeting.'

Mumble something mumble.

'We'll send a car,' he said. 'The restaurant's about half an hour away.'

The restaurant was airy and spacious and green, and they were waiting for me there.

By this point I would have been surprised if I *had* recognised anyone. John Ray, I was told over hors d'oeuvres, had 'split over contract disagreements', and Donna had gone with him, 'obviously'.

Both of the men had beards; one had bad skin. The woman was thin and seemed pleasant.

They asked where I was staying, and, when I told them, one of the beards told us (first making us all agree that this would go no further) that a politician named Gary Hart and one of the Eagles were both doing drugs with Belushi when he died.

After that they told me that they were looking forward to the story.

I asked the question. 'Is this for *Sons of Man* or *When We Were Badd*? Because,' I told them, 'I have a problem with the latter.'

They looked puzzled.

It was, they told me, for *I Knew the Bride When She Used to Rock and Roll*. Which was, they told me, both High Concept and Feel Good. It was also, they added, Very Now, which was important in a town in which an hour ago was Ancient History.

They told me that they thought it would be a good thing if our hero could rescue the young lady from her loveless marriage, and if they could rock and roll together at the end.

I pointed out that they needed to buy the film rights from Nick Lowe, who wrote the song, and then that, no, I didn't know who his agent was.

They grinned and assured me that that wouldn't be a problem.

They suggested I turn over the project in my mind before I started on the treatment, and each of them mentioned a couple of young stars to bear in mind when I was putting together the story.

And I shook hands with all of them and told them that I certainly would.

I mentioned that I thought that I could work on it best back in England.

And they said that that would be fine.

Some days before, I'd asked Pious Dundas whether anyone was with Belushi in the chalet, on the night that he died.

If anyone would know, I figured, he would.

'He died alone,' said Pious Dundas, old as Methuselah, unblinking. 'It don't matter a rat's ass whether there was anyone with him or not. He died alone.'

It felt strange to be leaving the hotel.

I went up to the front desk.

'I'll be checking out later this afternoon.'

'Very good, sir.'

'Would it be possible for you to . . . the, uh, the groundkeeper. Mister Dundas. An elderly gentleman. I don't know. I haven't seen him around for a couple of days. I wanted to say good-bye.'

'To one of the groundsmen?'

'Yes.'

She stared at me, puzzled. She was very beautiful, and her lipstick was the colour of a blackberry bruise. I wondered whether she was waiting to be discovered.

She picked up the phone and spoke into it, quietly.

Then, 'I'm sorry, sir. Mister Dundas hasn't been in for the last few days.'

'Could you give me his phone number?'

'I'm sorry, sir. That's not our policy.' She stared at me as she said it, letting me know that she *really* was *so* sorry . . .

'How's your screenplay?' I asked her.

'How did you know?' she asked.

'Well—'

'It's on Joel Silver's desk,' she said. 'My friend Arnie, he's my writing partner, and he's a courier. He dropped it off with Joel Silver's office, like it came from a regular agent or somewhere.'

'Best of luck,' I told her.

'Thanks,' she said, and smiled with her blackberry lips.

Information had two Dundas, P's listed, which I thought was both unlikely and said something about America, or at least Los Angeles.

The first turned out to be a Ms Persephone Dundas.

At the second number, when I asked for Pious Dundas, a man's voice said, 'Who is this?'

I told him my name, that I was staying in the hotel, and that I had something belonging to Mr Dundas.

'Mister. My grandfa's dead. He died last night.'

Shock makes clichés happen for real: I felt the blood drain from my face; I caught my breath.

'I'm sorry. I liked him.'

'Yeah.'

'It must have been pretty sudden.'

'He was old. He got a cough.' Someone asked him who he was talking to, and he said nobody, then he said, 'Thanks for calling.'

I felt stunned.

'Look, I have his scrapbook. He left it with me.'

'That old film stuff?'

'Yes.'

A pause.

'Keep it. That stuff's no good to anybody. Listen, mister, I gotta run.'

A click, and the line went silent.

I went to pack the scrapbook in my bag and was startled, when a tear splashed on the faded leather cover, to discover that I was crying.

* * *

I stopped by the pool for the last time, to say good-bye to Pious Dundas, and to Hollywood.

Three ghost white carp drifted, fins flicking minutely, through the eternal present of the pool.

I remembered their names: Buster, Ghost and Princess; but there was no longer any way that anyone could have told them apart.

The car was waiting for me, by the hotel lobby. It was a thirty-minute drive to the airport, and already I was starting to forget.

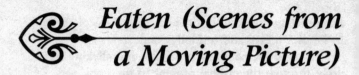

Eaten (Scenes from a Moving Picture)

INT. WEBSTER'S OFFICE. DAY.
As WEBSTER sits
reading the L.A. Times, MCBRIDE walks in
and tells in

FLASHBACK

how his SISTER came
to Hollywood eleven months ago
to make her fortune, and to meet the stars.
Of how he'd heard from friends that she'd 'gone
strange'.
Imagining the needle, or far worse,
he travels out to Hollywood himself
and finds her standing underneath a bridge.
Her skin is pale. She screams at him 'Get lost!'
and sobs and runs. A TALL MAN DRESSED IN
BLACK
grabs hold his sleeve, tells him to let it drop
'Forget your sister,' but of course he can't . . .

* * *

(IN SEPIA
we see the two as teens,
a YOUNG MCBRIDE and SISTER way back when,
giggles beneath the porch, 'I'll show you mine,'
closer perhaps than siblings ought to be . . .
PAN UP
to watch a passing butterfly.
We hear them breathe and fumble in the dark:
IN CLOSE-UP now he spurts into her hand,
she licks her palm: first makes a face, then smiles . . .
HOLD on her lips and teeth and on her tongue.)

END FLASHBACK
Webster says he'll take the case,
says something flip and hard about LA,
like how it eats young girls and spits them out,
and takes a hundred dollars on account.

CUT TO
THE PURPLE PUSSY. INT. A DIVE,
THREE NAKED WOMEN dance for dollar bills
Webster comes in, and talks to one of them,
slips her a twenty, shows a photograph,
the stripper – standing close enough that he
could touch her (but they've bouncers on patrol
wired steroid cases who will break your wrists) –
admits she thinks she knows the girl he means.
Then Webster leaves.

INT. WEBSTER'S CONDO. NIGHT.
A video awaits him at his home.
It shows A WOMAN lovelier than life
Shot from the ribcage up (her breasts exposed)
Advising him to 'let this whole thing drop,

forget it,' promising she'll see him soon . . .

DISSOLVE TO
INT. McBride'S HOTEL ROOM. NIGHT.
McBride's alone and lying on the bed,
He's watching soft-core porn on pay-per-view
Naked. He rubs his cock with Vaseline,
lazy and slow, he doesn't want to come.
A BANG upon the window. He sits up,
flaccid and scared (he's on the second floor)
and opens up the window of his room.
HIS SISTER enters, looking almost dead,
implores him to forget her. He says no.
The sister shambles over to the door.
A WOMAN DRESSED IN BLACK waits in the hall.
Brunette in leather, kinky as all hell,
who steps over the threshold with a smile.
And they have sex.

                    The sister stands alone,
She watches as the Brunette takes McBride
(her skin's necrotic blue. She's fully dressed).
The Brunette gestures curtly with her hand,
Off come the sister's clothes. She looks a mess:
her skin's all scarred and scored; one nipple's gone.
She takes her gloves off and we see her hands:
her fingers look like ribs, or chicken wings,
well-chewed, and rescued from a garbage can –
dry bones with scraps of flesh and cartilage.
She puts her fingers in the Brunette's mouth . . .
AND FADE TO BLACK.

INT. WEBSTER'S OFFICE. DAY.
THE PHONE RINGS. It's McBride. 'Just drop the case.

126 ❧— Smoke and Mirrors

I've found my sister, and I'm going home.
You've got five hundred dollars, and my thanks.'
PULL BACK on Webster, puzzled and confused.

MONTAGE of WEBSTER here. A week goes by,
we see him eating, pissing, drinking, drunk.
We watch him throw HIS GIRLFRIEND out of bed.
We see him play the video again . . .
The VIDEO GIRL stares at him and says
she'll see him soon. 'I promise, Webster, soon.'

CUT TO
THE PLACE OF EATERS, UNDERGROUND.
Pale people stand like cattle in a pen.
We see McBride. The flesh is off his chest.
White meat is good. We're looking through his ribs:
his heart is still. His lungs, however, breathe,
inflate, deflate. And tears of pus run down
his sunken cheeks. He pisses in the muck.
It doesn't steam. He wishes he were dead.

A DREAM:
As Webster tosses in his bed
He sees McBride, a corpse beneath a bridge,
all INTERCUT with lots of shots of food,
to make our theme explicit: this is art.

EXT. L.A. DAY.
WEBSTER's become obsessed.
He has to find the woman from the screen.
He beats somebody up, fucks someone else,
fixated on 'I'll see you, Webster, soon'.

He's thrown in prison. And they come for him

Eaten (Scenes from a Moving Picture) —⟫ 127

THE MAN IN BLACK attending THE BRUNETTE,
Open his cell with keys, escort him out,
and leave the prison building. Through a door.
They walk him to the car park. They go down,
below the car park, deep beneath the town,
past shadowed writhing things that suck and hiss
and glossy things that laugh, and things that scream.
Now other feeder-folk are walking past . . .
They handcuff Webster to A TINY MAN
who's covered with vaginas and with teeth,
and escorts Webster to

THE QUEEN'S SALON.

(An interjection here: my wife awoke,
scared by an evil dream. 'You hated me.
You brought these women home I didn't know,
but they knew me, and then we had a fight,
and after we had shouted you stormed out.
You said you'd find a girl to fuck and eat.'

This scares me just a little. As we write
we summon little demons. So I shrug.)

The handcuffs are removed. He's left alone.
The hangings are red velvet, then they lift,
reveal the Queen. We recognise her face,
the woman we saw on the VCR.
'The world divides so sweetly, neatly up
into the feeder-folk, into their prey.'
That's what she says. Her voice is soft and sweet.

Imagine honey-ants: the tiny head,
the chest, the tiny arms, the tiny hands,

and after that the bloat of honey-swell,
the abdomen enormous as it hangs
translucent, made of honey, sweet as lust.

The QUEEN has quite a perfect little face,
her breasts are pale, blue-veined; her nipples pink;
her hands are white. But then, below her breasts
the whole swells like a whale or like a shrine,
a human honey-ant, she's huge as rooms,
as elephants, as dinosaurs, as love.
Her flesh is opalescent, and she calls
poor WEBSTER to her. And he nods and comes.
(She must be over twenty-five feet long.)
She orders him to take off all his clothes.
His cock is hard. He shivers. He looks lost.
He moans 'I'm harder than I've ever been'.
Then, with her mouth, she licks and tongues his
    cock . . .

We linger here. The language of the eye
becomes a bland, unflinching, blowjob porn,
(her lips are glossy, and her tongue is red).
HOLD on her face. We hear him gasping 'Oh.
Oh baby. Yes. Oh. Take it in your mouth.'
And then she opens up her mouth, and grins,
and bites his cock off.
                              Spurting blood pumps out
into her mouth. She hardly spills a drop.
We never do pan up to see his face,
just her. It's what they call the money shot.

Then, when his cock's gone down, and blood's
    congealed,
we see his face. He looks all dazed and healed.

Some feeders come and take him out of there.
Down in the pens he's chained beside McBride.
Deep in the mud lie carcasses picked clean
who grin at them and dream of being soup.

Poor things.

We're almost done.

We'll leave them there.

CUT to some lonely doorway, where A TRAMP
has three cold fingers up ANOTHER TRAMP,
they're starving but they fingerfuck like hell,
and underneath the layers of old clothes
beneath the cardboard, newspaper and cloth,
their genders are impossible to tell.

PAN UP:

to watch a butterfly go past.

The White Road

'. . . I wish that you would visit me one day,
in my house.
There are such sights I would show you.'

My intended lowers her eyes, and, yes, she shivers.
Her father and his friends all hoot and cheer.

'*That's* never a story, Mister Fox,' chides a pale woman
in the corner of the room, her hair corn-fair,
her eyes the grey of cloud, meat on her bones,
she curves, and smiles crooked and amused.

'Madam, I am no storyteller,' and I bow, and ask,
'Perhaps, you have a story for us?' I raise an eyebrow.
Her smile remains.
She nods, then stands, her lips move:

'A girl from the town, a plain girl, was betrayed by her
        lover,
a scholar. So when her blood stopped flowing,
and her belly swole beyond disguising,

she went to him, and wept hot tears. He stroked her
    hair,
swore that they would marry, that they would run,
in the night,
together,
to his aunt. She believed him;
even though she had seen the glances in the hall
he gave to his master's daughter,
who was fair, and rich, she believed him.
Or she believed that she believed.

'There was something sly about his smile,
his eyes so black and sharp, his rufous hair. Something
that sent her early to their trysting place,
beneath the oak, beside the thornbush,
something that made her climb the tree and wait.
Climb a tree, and in her condition.
Her love arrived at dusk, skulking by owl-light,
carrying a bag,
from which he took a mattock, shovel, knife.
He worked with a will, beside the thornbush,
beneath the oaken tree,
he whistled gently, and he sang, as he dug her grave,
that old song . . .
Shall I sing it for you, now, good folk?'

She pauses, and as a one we clap and we holloa
—or almost as a one:
My intended, her hair so dark, her cheeks so pink,
her lips so red,
seems distracted.

The fair girl (Who is she? A guest of the inn, I hazard)
sings:

'A fox went out on a shiny night
And he begged for the moon to give him light
For he'd many miles to go that night
Before he'd reach his den-O!
Den-O! Den-O!
He'd many miles to go that night, before he'd reach his
    den-O.'

Her voice is sweet and fine, but the voice of my
intended is finer.

'And when her grave was dug –
A small hole it was, for she was a little thing,
even big with child she was a little thing –
he walked below her, back and a forth,
rehearsing her hearsing, thus:
—*Good evening, my pigsnie, my love,*
my, but you look a treat in the moon's light,
mother of my child-to-be. Come, let me hold you.
And he'd embrace the midnight air with one hand,
and with the other, holding his short but wicked knife,
he'd stab and stab the dark.

'She trembled in her oak above him. Breathed so softly,
but still she shook. And once he looked up and said,
—*Owls, I'll wager,* and another time, *Fie! Is that a cat*
up there? Here, puss . . . But she was still,
bethought herself a branch, a leaf, a twig. At dawn
he took his mattock, spade and knife and left
all grumbling and gudgeoned of his prey.

'They found her later wandering, her wits
had left her. There were oak leaves in her hair,
and she sang:

The bough did bend
The bough did break
I saw the hole
The fox did make

We swore to love
We swore to marry
I saw the blade
The fox did carry

'They say that her babe, when it was born,
had a fox's paw on her and not a hand.
Fear is the sculptress, midwives claim. The scholar fled.'

And she sits down, to general applause.
The smile twitches, hides about her lips: I know it's
    there,
it waits in her grey eyes. She stares at me, amused.

'I read that in the Orient foxes follow priests and
    scholars,
in disguise as women, houses, mountains, gods,
    processions,
always discovered by their tails—' so I begin,
but my intended's father intercedes.
'Speaking of tales – my dear, you said you had a tale?'

My intended flushes. There are no rose petals,
save for her cheeks. She nods and says:

'My story, Father? My story is the story of a dream I
    dreamed.'

Her voice is so quiet and soft, we hush ourselves to hear,

outside the inn just the night sounds: An owl hoots,
but, as the old folk say, I live too near the wood
to be frightened by an owl.

She looks at me.

'You, sir. In my dream you rode to me, and called,
—*Come to my house, my sweet, away down the white road.*
There are such sights I would show you.
I asked how I would find your house, down the white
     chalk road,
for it's a long road, and a dark one, under trees
that make the light all green and gold when the sun is
     high,
but shade the road at other times. At night
it's pitch-black; there is no moonlight on the white
     road . . .

'And you said, Mister Fox – and this is most curious,
     but dreams
are treacherous and curious and dark –
that you would cut the throat of a sow pig,
and you would walk her home behind your fine black
     stallion.
You smiled,
smiled, Mister Fox, with your red lips and your green
     eyes,
eyes that could snare a maiden's soul, and your yellow
     teeth,
which could eat her heart—'

'God forbid,' I smiled. All eyes were on me then, not
     her,
though hers was the story. Eyes, such eyes.

'So, in my dream, it became my fancy to visit your
    great house,
as you had so often entreated me to do,
to walk its glades and paths, to see the pools,
the statues you had brought from Greece, the yews,
the poplar walk, the grotto, and the bower.
And, as this was but a dream, I did not wish
to take a chaperone
– some withered, juiceless prune
who would not appreciate your house, Mister Fox; who
would not appreciate your pale skin,
nor your green eyes,
nor your engaging ways.

'So I rode the white chalk road, following the red
    blood path,
on Betsy, my filly. The trees above were green.
A dozen miles straight, and then the blood
led me off across meadows, over ditches, down a gravel
    path
(but now I needed sharp eyes to catch the blood –
a drip, a drop: The pig must have been dead as anything),
and I reined my filly in front of a house.
And such a house. A palladian delight, immense,
a landscape of its own, windows, columns,
a white stone monument to verticality, expansive.

'There was a sculpture in the garden, before the house,
A Spartan child, stolen fox half-concealed in its robe,
the fox biting the child's stomach, gnawing the vitals
    away,
the stoic child bravely saying nothing –
what could it say, cold marble that it was?
There was pain in its eyes, and it stood,

upon a plinth on which were carved eight words.
I walked around it, and I read:
Be bold,
be bold,
but not too bold.

'I tethered little Betsy in the stables,
between a dozen night black stallions
each with blood and madness in his eyes.
I saw no one.
I walked to the front of the house and up the great steps.
The huge doors were locked fast,
no servants came to greet me when I knocked.
In my dream (for do not forget, Mister Fox, that this
        was
my dream. You look so pale) the house fascinated me,
the kind of curiosity (you know this,
Mister Fox, I see it in your eyes) that kills
cats.

'I found a door, a small door, off the latch,
and pushed my way inside.
Walked corridors, lined with oak, with shelves,
with busts, with trinkets,
I walked, my feet silent on the scarlet carpet,
until I reached the great hall.
It was there again, in red stones that glittered,
set into the white marble of the floor,
it said:
Be bold,
be bold,
but not too bold.
Or else your life's blood
shall run cold.

'There were stairs, wide, carpeted in scarlet,
off the great hall,
and I walked up them, silently, silently.
Oak doors: and now
I was in the dining room, or so I am convinced,
for the remnants of a grisly supper
were abandoned, cold and fly-buzzed.
Here was a half-chewed hand, there, crisped and picked,
a face, a woman's face, who must in life, I fear,
have looked like me.'

'Heavens defend us all from such dark dreams,' her
    father cried.
'Can such things be?'

'It is not so,' I assured him. The fair woman's smile
glittered behind her grey eyes. People
need assurances.

'Beyond the supper room was a room,
a huge room, this inn would fit in that room,
piled promiscuously with rings and bracelets,
necklaces, pearl drops, ball gowns, fur wraps,
lace petticoats, silks and satins. Ladies' boots,
and muffs, and bonnets: a treasure cave and dressing
    room –
diamonds and rubies underneath my feet.

'Beyond that room I knew myself in Hell.
In my dream . . .
I saw many heads. The heads of young women. I saw a
    wall
on which dismembered limbs were nailed.
A heap of breasts. The piles of guts, of livers, lights,

the eyes, the . . .
No. I cannot say. And all around the flies were buzzing,
one low droning buzz.
—*Bëelzebubzebubzebub*, they buzzed. I could not breathe,
I ran from there and sobbed against a wall.'

'A fox's lair indeed,' says the fair woman.
('It was not so,' I mutter.)
'They are untidy creatures, so to litter
about their dens the bones and skins and feathers
of their prey. The French call him *Renard*,
the Scottish, *Tod*.'

'One cannot help one's name,' says my intended's
    father.
He is almost panting now, they all are:
in the firelight, the fire's heat, lapping their ale.
The wall of the inn was hung with sporting prints.

She continues:
'From outside I heard a crash and a commotion.
I ran back the way I had come, along the red carpet,
down the wide staircase – too late! – the main door
    was opening!
I threw myself down the stairs – rolling, tumbling –
fetched up hopelessly beneath a table,
where I waited, shivered, prayed.'

She points at me. 'Yes, you, sir. You came in,
crashed open the door, staggered in, you, sir,
dragging a young woman
by her red hair and by her throat.
Her hair was long and unconfined, she screamed and
    strove

to free herself. You laughed, deep in your throat,
were all a-sweat, and grinned from ear to ear.'

She glares at me. The colour's in her cheeks.
'You pulled a short old broadsword, Mister Fox,
    and as she screamed,
you slit her throat, again from ear to ear,
I listened to her bubbling, sighing, shriek,
and closed my eyes and prayed until she stopped.
And after much, much, much too long, she stopped.

'And I looked out. You smiled, held up your sword,
your hands agore-blood—'

'In your dream,' I tell her.

'In my dream.
She lay there on the marble, as you sliced
you hacked, you wrenched, you panted, and you stabbed.
You took her head from her shoulders,
thrust your tongue between her red wet lips.
You cut off her hands. Her pale white hands.
You sliced open her bodice, you removed each breast.
Then you began to sob and howl.
Of a sudden,
clutching her head, which you carried by the hair,
the flame red hair,
you ran up the stairs.

'As soon as you were out of sight,
I fled through the open door.
I rode my Betsy home, down the white road.'

All eyes upon me now. I put down my ale

on the old wood of the table.
'It is not so,'
I told her,
told all of them.
'It was not so, and
God forbid
it should be so. It was
an evil dream. I wish such dreams
on no one.'

'Before I fled the charnel house,
before I rode poor Betsy into a lather,
before we fled down the white road,
the blood still red
(And was it a pig whose throat you slit, Mister Fox?)
before I came to my father's inn,
before I fell before them speechless,
my father, brothers, friends—'

All honest farmers, fox-hunting men.
They are stamping their boots, their black boots.

'—before that, Mister Fox,
I seized, from the floor, from the bloody floor,
her hand, Mister Fox. The hand of the woman
you hacked apart before my eyes.'

'It is not so—'

'It was no dream. You creature. You Bluebeard.'

'It was not so—'

'You Gilles-de-Rais. You monster.'

'And God forbid it should be so!'

She smiles now, lacking mirth or warmth.
The brown hair curls around her face,
roses twining about a bower.
Two spots of red are burning on her cheeks.

'Behold, Mister Fox! Her hand! Her poor pale hand!'
She pulls it from her breasts (gently freckled,
I had dreamed of those breasts),
tosses it down upon the table.
It lays in front of me.
Her father, brothers, friends,
they stare at me hungrily,
and I pick up the small thing.

The hair was red indeed and rank. The pads and claws
were rough. One end was bloody,
but the blood had dried.

'This is no hand,' I tell them. But the first
fist knocks the wind from out of me,
an oaken cudgel hits my shoulder,
as I stagger,
the first black boot kicks me down onto the floor.
And then a rain of blows beats down on me,
I curl and mewl and pray and grip the paw
so tightly.

Perhaps I weep.

I see her then,
the pale fair girl, the smile has reached her lips,
her skirts so long as she slips, grey-eyed,

amused beyond all bearing, from the room.
She'd many a mile to go that night.
And as she leaves,
from my vantage place upon the floor,
I see the brush, the tail between her legs;
I would have called,
but I could speak no more. Tonight she'll be running
four-footed, sure-footed, down the white road.

What if the hunters come?
What if they come?

Be bold, I whisper once, before I die. *But not too bold* . . .

And then my tale is done.

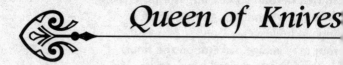

The reappearance of the lady is a matter of individual taste.
— WILL GOLDSTON, *TRICKS AND ILLUSIONS*

When I was a boy, from time to time,
I stayed with my grandparents
(old people: I knew they were old –
chocolates in their house
remained uneaten until I came to stay,
this, then, was ageing).
My grandfather always made breakfast at sunup:
a pot of tea, for her and him and me,
some toast and marmalade
(the Silver Shred and the Gold). Lunch and dinner,
those were my grandmother's to make, the kitchen
was again her domain, all the pans and spoons,
the mincer, all the whisks and knives, her loyal subjects.
She would prepare the food with them, singing her
    little songs:
Daisy, Daisy, give me your answer do,
or sometimes,

You made me love you, I didn't want to do it,
  didn't want to do it.
She had no voice, not one to speak of.

Business was very slow.
My grandfather spent his days at the top of the house,
in his tiny darkroom where I was not permitted to go,
bringing out paper faces from the darkness,
the cheerless smiles of other people's holidays.
My grandmother would take me for grey walks along
    the promenade.
Mostly I would explore
the small wet grassy space behind the house,
the blackberry brambles, and the garden shed.

It was a hard week for my grandparents
Forced to entertain a wide-eyed boy-child, so
one night they took me to the King's Theatre. The
    King's . . .

Variety!
The lights went down, red curtains rose.
A popular comedian of the day
came on, stammered out his name (his catchphrase).
pulled out a sheet of glass, and stood half-behind it,
raising the arm and leg that we could see;
reflected,
he seemed to fly – it was his trademark,
so we all laughed and cheered. He told a joke or two,
quite badly. His haplessness, his awkwardness,
these were what we had come to see.
Bemused and balding and bespectacled,
he reminded me a little of my grandfather.
And then the comedian was done.

Queen of Knives —⟫ 145

Some ladies danced all legs across the stage.
A singer sang a song I didn't know.

The audience were old people,
like my grandparents, tired and retired,
all of them laughing and applauding.

In the interval my grandfather
queued for a choc ice and a couple of tubs.
We ate our ices as the lights went down.
The SAFETY CURTAIN rose, and then the real curtain.

The ladies danced across the stage again,
and then the thunder rolled, the smoke went puff,
a conjurer appeared and bowed. We clapped.

The lady walked on, smiling from the wings:
glittered. Shimmered. Smiled.
We looked at her, and in that moment flowers grew,
and silks and pennants tumbled from his fingertips.

The flags of all nations, said my grandfather, nudging me.
They were up his sleeve.
Since he was a young man
(I could not imagine him as a child),
my grandfather had been, by his own admission,
one of the people who knew how things worked.
He had built his own television,
my grandmother told me, when they were first married;
it was enormous, though the screen was small.
This was in the days before television programmes;
they watched it, though,
unsure whether it was people or ghosts they were seeing.
He had a patent, too, for something he invented,

but it was never manufactured.
Stood for the local council, but he came in third.
He could repair a shaver or a wireless,
develop your film, or build a house for dolls.
(The doll's house was my mother's. We still had it at
    my house;
shabby and old, it sat out in the grass, all rained-on and
    forgot.)

The glitter lady wheeled on a box.
The box was tall: grown-up-person-sized and black.
She opened up the front.
They turned it round and banged upon the back.
The lady stepped inside, still smiling.
The magician closed the door on her.
When it was opened, she had gone.
He bowed.

Mirrors, explained my grandfather. *She's really still inside*.
At a gesture, the box collapsed to matchwood.
A trapdoor, assured my grandfather;
Grandma hissed him silent.

The magician smiled, his teeth were small and crowded;
he walked, slowly, out into the audience.
He pointed to my grandmother, he bowed.
a Middle European bow,
and invited her to join him on the stage.
The other people clapped and cheered.
My grandmother demurred. I was so close
to the magician that I could smell his aftershave
and whispered 'Me, oh, me . . .' But still,
he reached his long fingers for my grandmother.
Pearl, go on up, said my grandfather. *Go with the man*.

My grandmother must have been, what? Sixty, then?
She had just stopped smoking,
was trying to lose some weight. She was proudest
of her teeth, which, though tobacco-stained, were all
    her own.
My grandfather had lost his, as a youth,
riding his bicycle; he had the bright idea
to hold on to a bus to pick up speed.
The bus had turned,
and Grandpa kissed the road.
She chewed hard licorice, watching TV at night,
or sucked hard caramels, perhaps to make him wrong.

She stood up, then, a little slowly.
Put down the paper tub half-full of ice cream,
the little wooden spoon –
went down the aisle, and up the steps.
And on the stage.

The conjurer applauded her once more –
A good sport. That was what she was. A sport.
Another glittering woman came from the wings,
bringing another box –
This one was red.

That's her, nodded my grandfather, *the one
who vanished off before. You see? That's her.*
Perhaps it was. All I could see
was a woman who sparkled, standing next to my
    grandmother
(who fiddled with her pearls and looked embarrassed).
The lady smiled and faced us, then she froze,
a statue, or a window mannequin.
The magician pulled the box,

with ease,
down to the front of stage, where my grandmother waited.
A moment or so of chitchat:
where she was from, her name, that kind of thing.
They'd never met before? She shook her head.

The magician opened the door,
my grandmother stepped in.

Perhaps it's not the same one, admitted my grandfather,
on reflection,
I think she had darker hair, the other girl.
I didn't know.
I was proud of my grandmother, but also embarrassed,
hoping she'd do nothing to make me squirm,
that she wouldn't sing one of her songs.

She walked into the box. They shut the door.
he opened a compartment at the top, a little door. We saw
my grandmother's face. *Pearl? Are you all right, Pearl?*
My grandmother smiled and nodded.
The magician closed the door.

The lady gave him a long thin case,
so he opened it. Took out a sword
and rammed it through the box.

And then another, and another,
and my grandfather chuckled and explained,
*The blade slides in the hilt, and then a fake
slides out the other side.*

Then he produced a sheet of metal, which
he slid into the box half the way up.

It cut the thing in half. The two of them,
the woman and the man, lifted the top
half of the box up and off, and put it on the stage,
with half my grandma in.

The top half.

He opened up the little door again, for a moment,
My grandmother's face beamed at us, trustingly.
When he closed the door before,
she went down a trapdoor,
and now she's standing halfway up,
my grandfather confided.
She'll tell us how it's done when it's all over.
I wanted him to stop talking: I needed the magic.

Two knives now, through the half-a-box,
at neck height.
Are you there, Pearl? asked the magician. *Let us know*
—do you know any songs?

My grandmother sang *Daisy, Daisy.*
He picked up the part of the box,
with the little door in it – the head part –
and he walked about, and she sang
Daisy, Daisy, first at one side of the stage,
then at the other.

That's him, said my grandfather, *and he's throwing his*
    voice.
It sounds like Grandma, I said.
Of course it does, he said. *Of course it does.*
He's good, he said. *He's good. He's very good.*

The conjuror opened up the box again,
now hatbox-sized. My grandmother had finished *Daisy,
    Daisy,*
and was on a song which went:
*My my, here we go, the driver's drunk and the horse won't
    go,*
now we're going back, now we're going back,
back back back to London Town.

She had been born in London. Told me ominous
    tales
from time to time to time
of her childhood. Of the children who ran into her
    father's shop
shouting *Shonky shonky sheeny*, running away;
she would not let me wear a black shirt because,
she said, she remembered the marches through the
    East End.
Moseley's blackshirts. Her sister got an eye blackened.

The conjurer took a kitchen knife,
pushed it slowly through the red hatbox.
And then the singing stopped.

He put the boxes back together,
pulled out the knives and swords, one by one by one.
He opened the compartment in the top: my grand-
    mother smiled,
embarrassed, at us, displaying her own old teeth.
He closed the compartment, hiding her from view.
Pulled out the last knife.
Opened the main door again,
and she was gone.
A gesture, and the red box vanished, too.

It's up his sleeve, my grandfather explained, but seemed
    unsure.

The conjurer made two doves fly from a burning plate.
A puff of smoke, and he was gone as well.

She'll be under the stage now, or backstage,
said my grandfather,
having a cup of tea. She'll come back to us with
    flowers,
or with chocolates. I hoped for chocolates.
The dancing girls again.
The comedian, for the last time.
And all of them came on together at the end.
The grand finale, said my grandfather. *Look sharp,*
perhaps she'll be back on now.

But no. They sang
    when you're riding along
    on the crest of the wave
    and the sun is in the sky.

The curtain went down, and we shuffled out into the
    lobby.
We loitered for a while.
Then we went down to the stage door
and waited for my grandmother to come out.
The conjurer came out in street clothes;
the glitter woman looked so different in a mac.

My grandfather went to speak to him. He shrugged,
told us he spoke no English and produced
a half-a-crown from behind my ear,
and vanished off into the dark and rain.

I never saw my grandmother again.

We went back to their house, and carried on.
My grandfather now had to cook for us.
And so for breakfast, dinner, lunch, and tea,
we had golden toast and silver marmalade
and cups of tea.
'Till I went home.

He got so old after that night
as if the years took him all in a rush.
Daisy, Daisy, he'd sing, *give me your answer, do.*
If you were the only girl in the world and I were the only boy.
My old man said follow the van.
My grandfather had the voice in the family,
they said he could have been a cantor,
but there were snapshots to develop,
radios and razors to repair. . .
his brothers were a singing duo: the Nightingales,
had been on television in the early days.

He bore it well. Although, quite late one night,
I woke, remembering the licorice sticks in the pantry,
I walked downstairs.
My grandfather stood there in his bare feet.

And, in the kitchen, all alone,
I saw him stab a knife into a box.
You made me love you.
I didn't want to do it.

The Facts in the Case of the Departure of Miss Finch

*T*o begin at the end: I arranged the thin slice of pickled ginger, pink and translucent, on top of the pale yellowtail flesh, and dipped the whole arrangement – ginger, fish and vinegared rice – into the soy sauce, flesh-side down; then I devoured it in a couple of bites.

'I think we ought to go to the police,' I said.

'And tell them what, exactly?' asked Jane.

'Well, we could file a missing persons report, or something. I don't know.'

'And where did you last see the young lady?' asked Jonathan, in his most policemanlike tones. 'Ah, I see. Did you know that wasting police time is normally considered an offence, sir?'

'But the whole circus...'

'These are transient persons, sir, of legal age. They come and go. If you have their names, I suppose I can take a report...'

Gloomily, I devoured a salmon-skin roll. 'Well, then,' I said, 'why don't we go to the papers?'

'Brilliant idea,' said Jonathan, in the sort of tone of voice which indicates that the person talking doesn't think it's a brilliant idea at all.

'Jonathan's right,' said Jane. 'They won't listen to us.'

'Why wouldn't they believe us? We're reliable. Honest citizens. All that.'

'You're a fantasy writer,' she said. 'You make up stuff like this for a living. No-one's going to believe you.'

'But you two saw it all as well. You'd back me up.'

'Jonathan's got a new series on cult horror movies coming out in the autumn. They'll say he's just trying to get cheap publicity for the show. And I've got another book coming out. Same thing.'

'So you're saying that we can't tell anyone?' I sipped my green tea.

'No,' Jane said, reasonably, 'we can tell anyone we want. It's making them believe us that's problematic. Or, if you ask me, impossible.'

The pickled ginger was sharp on my tongue. 'You may be right,' I said. 'And Miss Finch is probably much happier wherever she is right now than she would be here.'

'But her name isn't Miss Finch,' said Jane, 'it's—' and she said our former companion's real name.

'I know. But it's what I thought when I first saw her,' I explained. 'Like in one of those movies. You know. When they take off their glasses and put down their hair. "Why, Miss Finch. You're beautiful." '

'She certainly was that,' said Jonathan, 'in the end, anyway.' And he shivered at the memory.

There. So now you know: that's how it all ended, and how the three of us left it, several years ago. All that remains is the beginning, and the details.

For the record, I don't expect you to believe any of this. Not really. I'm a liar by trade, after all, albeit, I like to think, an honest liar. If I belonged to a gentleman's club I'd recount it over a glass or two of port late in the evening as the fire burned low, but I am a member of no such club, and I'll write it better than ever I'd tell it. So here you will learn of Miss Finch (whose name, as you already know, was not Finch, nor anything like it, since I'm changing names here to disguise the guilty) and how it came about that she was unable to join us for sushi. Believe it or not, just as you wish. I am not even certain that I can believe it anymore. It all seems such a long way away.

I could find a dozen beginnings. Perhaps it might be best to begin in a hotel room, in London, a few years ago. It was 11 A.M. The phone began to ring, which surprised me. I hurried over to answer it.

'Hello?' It was too early in the morning for anyone in America to be phoning me, and there was no-one in England who was meant to know that I was even in the country.

'Hi,' said a familiar voice, adopting an American accent of monumentally unconvincing proportions. 'This is Hiram P. Muzzledexter of Colossal Pictures. We're working on a film that's a remake of *Raiders of the Lost Ark* but instead of Nazis it has women with enormous knockers in it. We've heard that you were astonishingly well-supplied in the trouser department and might be willing to take on the part of our male lead, Minnesota Jones . . .'

'Jonathan?' I said. 'How on earth did you find me here?'

'You knew it was me,' he said, aggrieved, his voice losing all trace of the improbable accent and returning to his native London.

'Well, it sounded like you,' I pointed out. 'Anyway,

you didn't answer my question. No-one's meant to know that I was here.'

'I have my ways,' he said, not very mysteriously. 'Listen, if Jane and I were to offer to feed you sushi – something I recall you eating in quantities that put me in mind of feeding time at London Zoo's Walrus House – and if we offered to take you the theatre before we fed you, what would you say?'

'Not sure. I'd say "Yes" I suppose. Or "What's the catch?". I might say that.'

'Not exactly a catch,' said Jonathan. 'I wouldn't exactly call it a *catch*. Not a real catch. Not really.'

'You're lying, aren't you?'

Somebody said something near the phone, and then Jonathan said, 'Hang on, Jane wants a word.' Jane is Jonathan's wife.

'How are you?' she said.

'Fine, thanks.'

'Look,' she said, 'You'd be doing us a tremendous favour – not that we wouldn't love to see you, because we would, but you see, there's someone . . .'

'She's your friend,' said Jonathan, in the background.

'She's *not* my friend. I hardly know her,' she said, away from the phone, and then, to me, 'Um, look, there's someone we're sort of lumbered with. She's not in the country for very long, and I wound up agreeing to entertain her and look after her tomorrow night. She's pretty frightful, actually. And Jonathan heard that you were in town from someone at your film company, and we thought you might be perfect to make it all less awful, so please say yes.'

So I said yes.

In retrospect, I think the whole thing might have

been the fault of the late Ian Fleming, creator of James Bond. I had read an article the previous month, in which Ian Fleming had advised any would-be writer who had a book to get done that wasn't getting written to go to a hotel to write it. I had, not a novel, but a film script that wasn't getting written; so I bought a plane ticket to London, promised the film company that they'd have a finished script in three weeks' time, and took a room in an eccentric hotel in Little Venice.

I told no-one in England that I was there. Had people known, my days and nights would have been spent seeing them, not staring at a computer screen and, sometimes, writing.

Truth to tell, I was bored half out of my mind, and ready to welcome any interruption.

Early the next evening I arrived at Jonathan and Jane's house, which was more or less in Hampstead. There was a small green sports car parked outside. Up the stairs, and I knocked at the door. Jonathan answered it; he wore an impressive suit. His light-brown hair was longer than I remembered it from the last time I had seen him, in life or on television.

'Hello,' said Jonathan. 'The show we were going to take you to has been cancelled. But we can go to something else, if that's okay with you.'

I was about to point out that I didn't know what we were originally going to see, so a change of plan would make no difference to me, but Jonathan was already leading me into the living room, establishing that I wanted fizzy water to drink, assuring me that we'd still be eating sushi and that Jane would be coming downstairs as soon as she had finished putting the children to bed.

They had just redecorated the living room, in a style Jonathan described as Moorish brothel. 'It didn't set out to be a Moorish brothel,' he explained. 'Or any kind of a brothel really. It was just where we ended up. The brothel look.'

'Has he told you all about Miss Finch?' asked Jane. Her hair had been red the last time I had seen her. Now it was dark brown; and she curved like a Raymond Chandler simile.

'Who?'

'We were talking about Ditko's inking style,' apologised Jonathan. 'And the Neal Adams issues of *Jerry Lewis*.'

'But she'll be here any moment. And he has to know about her before she gets here.'

Jane is, by profession, a journalist, but had become a bestselling author almost by accident. She had written a companion volume to accompany a television series about two paranormal investigators, which had risen to the top of the bestseller lists and stayed there.

Jonathan had originally become famous hosting an evening talk show, and had since parlayed his gonzo charm into a variety of fields. He's the same person whether the camera is on or off, which is not always true of television folk.

'It's a kind of family obligation,' Jane explained. 'Well, not exactly *family*.'

'She's Jane's friend,' said her husband, cheerfully.

'She is *not* my friend. But I couldn't exactly say no to them, could I? And she's only in the country for a couple of days.'

And who Jane could not say no to, and what the obligation was, I never was to learn, for at the moment the doorbell rang, and I found myself being introduced to Miss Finch. Which, as I have mentioned, was not her name.

She wore a black leather cap and a black leather coat, and black, black hair, pulled tightly back into a small bun, done up with a pottery tie. She wore make-up, so expertly applied to give an impression of severity that a professional dominatrix might have envied her. Her lips were tight together, and she glared at the world through a pair of definite black-rimmed spectacles – they punctuated her face much too definitely to ever be mere glasses.

'So,' she said, as if she were pronouncing a death sentence, 'we're going to the theatre, then.'

'Well, yes and no,' said Jonathan. 'I mean, yes, we are still going out, but we're not going to be able to see *The Romans in Britain*.'

'Good,' said Miss Finch. 'In poor taste anyway. Why anyone would have thought that nonsense would make a musical I do not know.'

'So we're going to a circus,' said Jane, reassuringly. 'And then we're going to eat sushi.'

Miss Finch's lips tightened. 'I do not approve of circuses,' she said.

'There aren't any animals in this circus,' said Jane.

'Good,' said Miss Finch, and she sniffed. I was beginning to understand why Jane and Jonathan had wanted me along.

The rain was pattering down as we left the house, and the street was dark. We squeezed ourselves into the sports car and headed out into London. Miss Finch and I were in the tiny back seat of the car, pressed uncomfortably close together.

Jane told Miss Finch that I was a writer, and told me that Miss Finch was a biologist.

'Biogeologist actually,' Miss Finch corrected her. 'Were you serious about eating sushi, Jonathan?'

'Er, yes. Why? Don't you like sushi?'

'Oh, I'll eat *my* food cooked,' she said, and began to list for us all the various flukes, worms and parasites that lurk in the flesh of fish and which are only killed by cooking. She told us of their life cycles while the rain pelted down, slicking night-time London into garish neon colours. Jane shot me a sympathetic glance from the passenger seat, then she and Jonathan went back to scrutinising a handwritten set of directions to wherever we were going. We crossed the Thames at London Bridge while Miss Finch lectured us about blindness, madness and liver failure; and she was just elaborating on the symptoms of elephantiasis as proudly as if she had invented them herself, when we pulled up in a small back street in the neighbourhood of Southwark Cathedral.

'So where's the circus?' I asked.

'Somewhere around here,' said Jonathan. 'They contacted us about being on the Christmas special. I tried to pay for tonight's show, but they insisted on comping us in.'

'I'm sure it will be fun,' said Jane, hopefully.

Miss Finch sniffed.

A fat, bald man, dressed as a monk, ran down the pavement toward us. 'There you are!' he said. 'I've been keeping an eye out for you. You're late. It'll be starting in a moment.' He turned around and scampered back the way he had come, and we followed him. The rain splashed on his bald head and ran down his face, turning his Fester Addams make-up into streaks of white and brown. He pushed open a door in the side of a wall.

'In here.'

We went in. There were about fifty people in there already, dripping and steaming while a tall woman in bad vampire make-up holding a small torch walked around checking tickets, tearing off stubs, selling tickets to anyone who didn't have one. A small, stocky woman immediately in front of us shook the rain from her umbrella and glowered about her fiercely. 'This'd better be gud,' she told the young man with her – her son, I suppose. She paid for tickets for both of them.

The vampire woman reached us, recognised Jonathan and said 'Is this your party? Four people? Yes? You're on the guest list.' which provoked a suspicious stare in our direction from the stocky woman.

A recording of a clock ticking began to play. A clock struck twelve (it was barely eight by my watch), and the wooden double-doors at the far end of the room creaked open. 'Enter . . . of your own free will!' boomed a voice, and it laughed maniacally. We walked through the door into darkness.

It smelled of wet bricks and of decay. I knew then where we were: there are networks of old cellars that run beneath some of the overground train tracks – vast, empty, linked rooms of various sizes and shapes. Some of them are used for storage by wine merchants and used-car sellers; some are squatted in, until the lack of light and facilities drives the squatters back into the daylight; most of them stand empty, waiting for the inevitable arrival of the wrecking ball and the open air and the time when all their secrets and mysteries will be no more.

A train rattled by above us.

We shuffled forward, led by Uncle Fester and the vampire woman, into a sort of a holding pen where we stood and waited.

'I hope we're going to be able to sit down after this,' said Miss Finch.

When we were all settled the flashlights went out, and the spotlights went on.

The people came out. Some of them rode motorbikes and dune buggies. They ran and they laughed and they swung and they cackled. Whoever had dressed them had been reading too many comics, I thought, or watched *Mad Max* too many times. There were punks and nuns and vampires and monsters and strippers and the living dead.

They danced and capered around us while the Ringmaster – identifiable by his top hat – sang Alice Cooper's song 'Welcome to My Nightmare', and sang it very badly.

'I know Alice Cooper,' I muttered to myself, misquoting something half-remembered, 'And you, sir, are no Alice Cooper.'

'It's pretty naff,' agreed Jonathan.

Jane shushed us. As the last notes faded away the Ringmaster was left alone in the spotlight. He walked around our enclosure while he talked.

'Welcome, welcome, one and all, to the Theatre of Night's Dreaming,' he said.

'Fan of yours,' whispered Jonathan.

'I think it's a *Rocky Horror Show* line,' I whispered back.

'Tonight you will all be witnesses to monsters undreamed-of, freaks and creatures of the night, to displays of ability to make you shriek with fear – and laugh with joy. We shall travel,' he told us, 'from room to room – and in each of these subterranean caverns another nightmare, another delight, another display of wonder awaits you! Please – for your own safety –

I must reiterate this! – Do not leave the spectating area marked out for you in each room – on pain of doom, bodily injury, and the loss of your immortal soul! Also, I must stress that the use of flash photography or of any recording devices is utterly forbidden.'

And with that, several young women holding pencil flashlights led us into the next room.

'No seats then,' said Miss Finch, unimpressed.

The First Room

In the first room a smiling blonde woman wearing a spangled bikini, with needle-tracks down her arms, was chained by a hunchback and Uncle Fester to a large wheel.

The wheel spun slowly around, and a fat man in a red cardinal's costume threw knives at the woman, outlining her body. Then the hunchback blindfolded the cardinal, who threw the last three knives straight and true to outline the woman's head. He removed his blindfold. The woman was untied and lifted down from the wheel. They took a bow. We clapped.

Then the cardinal took a trick knife from his belt and pretended to cut the woman's throat with it. Blood spilled down from the knife-blade. A few members of the audience gasped, and one excitable girl gave a small scream, while her friends giggled.

The cardinal and the spangled woman took their final bow. The lights went down. We followed the flashlights down a brick-lined corridor.

The Second Room

The smell of damp was worse in here. It smelled like a cellar, musty and forgotten. I could hear somewhere the drip of rain. The Ringmaster introduced the Creature – 'Stitched together in the laboratories of the night, the Creature is capable of astonishing feats of strength'. The Frankenstein's monster make-up was less than convincing, but the Creature lifted a stone block with fat Uncle Fester sitting on it, and he held back the dune buggy (driven by the vampire woman) at full throttle. For his *pièce de resistance* he blew up a hot water bottle, then popped it.

'Roll on the sushi,' I muttered to Jonathan.

Miss Finch pointed out, quietly, that in addition to the danger of parasites, it was also the case that bluefin tuna, swordfish and Chilean seabass were all being overfished and could soon be rendered extinct, since they were not reproducing fast enough to catch up.

The Third Room

went up for a long way into the darkness. The original ceiling had been removed at some time in the past, and the new ceiling was the roof of the empty warehouse far above us. The room buzzed at the corners of vision with the blue-purple of ultraviolet light. Teeth and shirts and flecks of lint began to glow in the darkness. A low, throbbing music began. We looked up to see, high above us, a skeleton, an alien, a werewolf and an angel. Their costumes fluoresced in the UV, and they glowed like old dreams high above us, on trapezes. They swung back and forth, in time with the music, and then, as one, they let go and tumbled down toward us.

We gasped, but before they reached us they

bounced on the air, and rose up again, like yo-yos, and clambered back on their trapezes. We realised that they were attached to the roof by rubber cords, invisible in the darkness, and they bounced and dove and swam through the air above us while we clapped and gasped and watched them in happy silence.

The Fourth Room

was little more than a corridor: the ceiling was low, and the Ringmaster strutted into the audience and picked two people out of the crowd – the stocky woman, and a tall black man wearing a sheepskin coat and tan gloves, pulled them up in front of us. He announced that he would be demonstrating his hypnotic powers. He made a couple of passes in the air, and rejected the stocky woman. Then he asked the man to step up onto a box.

'It's a set-up,' muttered Jane. 'He's a plant.'

A guillotine was wheeled on. The ringmaster cut a watermelon in half, to demonstrate how sharp the blade was. Then he made the man put his hand under the guillotine, and dropped the blade. The gloved hand dropped into the basket, and blood spurted from the open cuff.

Miss Finch squeaked.

Then the man picked his hand out of the basket and chased the Ringmaster around us, while the Benny Hill Show music played.

'Artificial hand,' said Jonathan.

'I saw it coming,' said Jane.

Miss Finch blew her nose into a tissue. 'I think it's all in very questionable taste,' she said. Then they led us to

The Fifth Room

and all the lights went on. There was a makeshift wooden table along one wall, with a young bald man selling beer and orange juice and bottles of water, and signs showed the way to the toilets in the room next door. Jane went to get the drinks, and Jonathan went to use the toilets, which left me to make awkward conversation with Miss Finch.

'So,' I said, 'I understand you've not been back in England long.'

'I've been in Komodo,' she told me. 'Studying the dragons. Do you know why they grew so big?'

'Er...'

'They adapted to prey upon the pygmy elephants.'

'There were pygmy elephants?' I was interested. This was much more fun than being lectured on sushi flukes.

'Oh yes. It's basic island biogeology – animals on islands will naturally tend toward either gigantism or pygmyism. There are equations, you see...' As Miss Finch talked her face became more animated, and I found myself warming to her as she explained why and how some animals grew while others shrank.

Jane brought us our drinks; Jonathan came back from the toilet, cheered and bemused by having been asked to sign an autograph while he was pissing.

'Tell me,' said Jane, 'I've been reading a lot of cryptozoological journals for the next of the Guides to the Unexplained I'm doing. As a biologist—'

'Biogeologist,' interjected Miss Finch.

'Yes. What do you think the chances are of pre-historic animals being alive today, in secret, unknown to science?'

'It's very unlikely,' said Miss Finch, as if she were

telling us off. 'There is, at any rate, no "lost world" off on some island, filled with mammoths and smilodons and aepyornis . . .'

'Sounds a bit rude,' said Jonathan. 'A what?'

'Aepyornis. A giant flightless prehistoric bird,' said Jane.

'I knew that really,' he told her.

'Although of course, they're *not* prehistoric,' said Miss Finch. 'The last Aepyornises were killed off by Portuguese sailors on Madagascar about 300 years ago. And there are fairly reliable accounts of a pygmy mammoth being presented at the Russian court in the sixteenth century, and a band of something which from the descriptions we have were almost definitely some kind of sabre-tooth – the Smilodons – were brought in from North Africa by Vespasian to die in the circus. So these things aren't all prehistoric. Often, they're historic.'

'I wonder what the point of the sabre-teeth would be,' I said. 'You'd think they'd get in the way.'

'Nonsense,' said Mss Finch. 'Smilodon was a most efficient hunter. Must have been – the sabre-teeth are repeated a number of times in the fossil record. I wish with all my heart that there were some left today. But there aren't. We know the world too well.'

'It's a big place,' said Jane, doubtfully, and then the lights were flickered on and off, and a ghastly, disembodied voice told us to walk into the next room, that the latter half of the show was not for the faint of heart, and that later tonight, for one night only, the Circus of Night's Dreaming would be proud to present The Cabinet of Wishes Fulfill'd.

We threw away our plastic glasses, and we shuffled into

 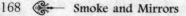

The Sixth Room

'Presenting,' announced the Ringmaster, 'The Painmaker!'

The spotlight swung up to reveal an abnormally thin young man in bathing trunks, hanging from hooks through his nipples. Two of the punk girls helped him down to the ground, and handed him his props. He hammered a six-inch nail into his nose, lifted weights with a piercing through his tongue, put several ferrets into his bathing trunks, and, for his final trick, allowed the taller of the punk girls to use his stomach as a dartboard for accurately flung hypodermic needles.

'Wasn't he on the show, years ago?' asked Jane.

'Yeah,' said Jonathan. 'Really nice guy. He lit a firework held in his teeth.'

'I thought you said there were no animals,' said Miss Finch. 'How do you think those poor ferrets feel about being stuffed into that young man's nether regions?'

'I suppose it depends mostly on whether they're boy ferrets or girl ferrets,' said Jonathan, cheerfully.

The Seventh Room

contained a rock and roll comedy act, with some clumsy slapstick. A nun's breasts were revealed, and the hunchback lost his trousers.

The Eighth Room

was dark. We waited in the darkness for something to happen. I wanted to sit down. My legs ached, I was tired and cold and I'd had enough.

Then someone started to shine a light at us. We blinked and squinted and covered our eyes.

'Tonight,' an odd voice said, cracked and dusty. Not

the Ringmaster, I was sure of that. 'Tonight, one of you shall get a wish. One of you will gain all that you desire, in the Cabinet of Wishes Fulfill'd. Who shall it be?'

'Ooh. That's a hard one. At a guess, another plant in the audience,' I whispered, remembering the one-handed man in the fourth room.

'Shush,' said Jane.

'Who will it be? You sir? You madam?' A figure came out of the darkness and shambled towards us. It was hard to see him properly, for he held a portable spotlight. I wondered if he were wearing some kind of ape costume, for his outline seemed inhuman, and he moved as gorillas move. Perhaps it was the man who had played 'The Creature'. 'Who shall it be, eh?' We squinted at him, edged out of his way.

And then he pounced. 'Aha! I think we have our volunteer,' he said, leaping over the rope-barrier that separated the audience from the show area around us. He grabbed Miss Finch by the hand.

'I really don't think so,' said Miss Finch, but she was being dragged away from us, too nervous, too polite, fundamentally too English to make a scene. He pulled her into the darkness and she was gone to us.

Jonathan swore. 'I don't think she's going to let us forget this in a hurry,' he said.

The lights went on. A man dressed as a giant fish then proceeded to ride a motorbike around the room several times. Then he stood up on the seat as it went around. Then he sat down and drove the bike up and down the walls of the room, and then he hit a brick and skidded and fell over, and the bike landed on top of him.

The hunchback and the topless nun ran on and pulled the bike off the man in the fish-suit and hauled him away.

'I just broke my sodding leg,' he was saying, in a dull, numb voice. 'It's sodding broken. My sodding leg,' as they carried him out.

'Do you think that was meant to happen,' asked a girl in the crowd near to us.

'No,' said the man beside her.

Slightly shaken, Uncle Fester and the vampire woman ushered us forward, into

The Ninth Room

where Miss Finch awaited us.

It was a huge room. I knew that, even in the thick darkness. Perhaps the dark intensifies the other senses; perhaps it's simply that we are always processing more information than we imagine. Echoes of our shuffling and coughing came back to us from walls hundreds of feet away.

And then I became convinced, with a certainty bordering upon madness, that there were great beasts in the darkness, and that they were watching us hungrily.

Slowly the lights came on, and we saw Miss Finch. I wonder to this day where they got the costume.

Her black hair was down. The spectacles were gone. The costume, what little there was of it, fitted her perfectly. She held a spear, and she stared at us without emotion. Then the great cats padded into the light next to her. One of them threw its head back and roared.

Someone began to wail. I could smell the sharp animal stench of urine.

The animals were the size of tigers, but unstriped; they were the colour of a sandy beach at evening. Their eyes were topaz, and their breath smelled of fresh meat and of blood.

I stared at their jaws: the sabre-teeth were indeed teeth, not tusks: huge, overgrown fangs, made for rending, for tearing, for ripping meat from the bone.

The great cats began to pad around us, circling, slowly. We huddled together, closing ranks, each of us remembering in our guts what it was like in the old times, long gone, when we hid in our caves as the night came and the beasts went on the prowl, remembering when we were prey.

The smilodons, if that was what they were, seemed uneasy, wary. Their tails switched whiplike from side to side, impatiently. Miss Finch said nothing. She just stared at her animals.

Then the stocky woman raised her umbrella and waved it at one of the great cats. 'Keep back, you ugly brute,' she told it.

It growled at her, and extended back, like a cat about to spring.

The stocky woman went pale, but she kept her umbrella pointed out like a sword. She made no move to run, in the torchlit darkness beneath the city.

And then it sprang, batting her to the ground with one huge velvet paw. It stood over her, triumphantly, and it roared so deeply that I could feel it in the pit of my stomach. The stocky woman seemed to have passed out, which was, I felt, a mercy: with luck, she would not know when the blade-like fangs tore at her old flesh like twin daggers.

I looked around for some way out, but the other tiger was prowling around us, keeping us herded within the rope enclosure like frightened sheep.

I could hear Jonathan muttering the same three

dirty words, over and over and over.

'We're going to die, aren't we?' I heard myself say.

'I think so,' said Jane.

Then Miss Finch pushed her way through the rope barrier, and she took the great cat by the scruff of its neck and pulled it back. It resisted, and she thwacked it on the nose with the end of her spear. Its tail went down between its legs, and it backed away from the fallen woman, cowed and obedient.

There was no blood, that I could see, and I hoped that she was only unconscious.

In the back of the cellar room light was slowly coming up. It seemed as if dawn were breaking. I could see a jungle mist wreathing about huge ferns and hostas; and I could hear, as if from a great way off, the chirp of crickets and the call of strange birds awaking to greet the new day.

And part of me – the writer part of me, the bit that has noted the particular way the light hit the broken glass in the puddle of blood even as I staggered out from a car crash, and has observed in exquisite detail the way that my heart was broken, or did not break, in moments of real, profound, personal tragedy – it was that part of me that thought, 'You could get that effect with a smoke machine, some plants and a tape track. You'd need a really good lighting guy of course.'

Miss Finch scratched her left breast, unselfconsciously, then she turned her back on us and walked toward the dawn and the jungle underneath the world, flanked by two padding sabre-toothed tigers.

A bird screeched and chattered.

Then the dawn light faded back into darkness, and the mists shifted, and the woman and the animals were gone.

The stocky woman's son helped her to her feet. She opened her eyes. She looked shocked but unhurt. And when we knew that she was not hurt, for she picked up her umbrella, and leaned on it, and glared at us all, why then we began to applaud.

No-one came to get us. I could not see Uncle Fester or the vampire woman anywhere. So unescorted we all walked on into

The Tenth Room

It was set up for what would obviously have been the grand finale. There were even plastic seats arranged, for us to sit and watch the show. We sat down on the seats and we waited, but nobody from the circus came out, and, it became apparent to us all after some time, no-one was going to come.

People began to shuffle into the next room. I heard a door open, and the noise of traffic and the rain.

I looked at Jane and Jonathan, and we got up and walked out. In the last room was an unmanned table upon which were laid out souvenirs of the circus: posters and CDs and badges, and an open cash-box. Sodium yellow light spilled in from the street outside, through an open door, and the wind gusted at the unsold posters, flapping the corners up and down impatiently.

'Should we wait for her?' one of us said, and I wish I could say that it was me. But the others shook their heads, and we walked out into the rain, which had by now subsided to a low and gusty drizzle.

After a short walk down narrow roads, in the rain and the wind, we found our way to the car. I stood on the pavement, waiting for the back door to be unlocked to let me in, and over the rain and the noise of the city I thought I heard a tiger, somewhere close by, for there was a low roar that made the whole world shake. But perhaps it was only the passage of a train.

Changes

I.

*L*ater, they would point to his sister's death, the cancer that ate her twelve-year-old life, tumours the size of duck eggs in her brain, and him a boy of seven, snot-nosed and crew-cut, watching her die in the white hospital with his wide brown eyes, and they would say, 'That was the start of it all,' and perhaps it was.

In *Reboot* (dir. Robert Zemeckis, 2018), the biopic, they jump-cut to his teens, and he's watching his science teacher die of AIDS, following their argument over dissecting a large pale-stomached frog.

'Why should we take it apart?' says the young Rajit as the music swells. 'Instead, should we not give it life?' His teacher, played by the late James Earl Jones, looks shamed and then inspired, and he lifts his hand from his hospital bed to the boy's bony shoulder. 'Well, if anyone can do it, Rajit, you can,' he says in a deep bass rumble.

The boy nods and stares at us with a dedication in his eyes that borders upon fanaticism.

This never happened.

II.

It is a grey November day, and Rajit is now a tall man in his forties with dark-rimmed spectacles, which he is not currently wearing. The lack of spectacles emphasises his nudity. He is sitting in the bath as the water gets cold, practising the conclusion to his speech. He stoops a little in everyday life, although he is not stooping now, and he considers his words before he speaks. He is not a good public speaker.

The apartment in Brooklyn, which he shares with another research scientist and a librarian, is empty today. His penis is shrunken and nutlike in the tepid water. 'What this means,' he says loudly and slowly, 'is that the war against cancer has been won.'

Then he pauses, takes a question from an imaginary reporter on the other side of the bathroom.

'Side effects?' he replies to himself in an echoing bathroom voice. 'Yes, there are some side effects. But as far as we have been able to ascertain, nothing that will create any permanent changes.'

He climbs out of the battered porcelain bathtub and walks, naked, to the toilet bowl, into which he throws up, violently, the stage fright pushing through him like a gutting knife. When there is nothing more to throw up and the dry heaves have subsided, Rajit rinses his mouth with Listerine, gets dressed, and takes the subway into central Manhattan.

III.

It is, as *Time* magazine will point out, a discovery that would 'change the nature of medicine every bit as fundamentally and as importantly as the discovery of penicillin.'

'What if,' says Jeff Goldblum, playing the adult Rajit in the biopic, 'just – what if – you could reset the body's genetic code? So many ills come because the body has forgotten what it should be doing. The code has become scrambled. The program has become corrupted. What if . . . what if you could fix it?'

'You're crazy,' retorts his lovely blonde girlfriend, in the movie. In real life he has no girlfriend; in real life Rajit's sex life is a fitful series of commercial transactions between Rajit and the young men of the AAA-Ajax Escort Agency.

'Hey,' says Jeff Goldblum, putting it better than Rajit ever did, 'it's like a computer. Instead of trying to fix the glitches caused by a corrupted program one by one, symptom by symptom, you can just reinstall the program. All the information's there all along. We just have to tell our bodies to go and recheck the RNA and the DNA – reread the program if you will. And then reboot.'

The blonde actress smiles, and stops his words with a kiss, amused and impressed and passionate.

IV.

The woman has cancer of the spleen and of the lymph nodes and abdomen: non-Hodgkin's lymphoma. She also has pneumonia. She has agreed to Rajit's request to use an experimental treatment on her. She also knows that claiming to cure cancer is illegal in America. She was a fat woman until recently. The weight has fallen from her, and she reminds Rajit of a snowman in the sun: each day she melts, each day she is, he feels, less defined.

'It is not a drug as you understand it,' he tells her.

'It is a set of chemical instructions.' She looks blank. He injects two ampules of a clear liquid into her veins.

Soon she sleeps.

When she awakes, she is free of cancer. The pneumonia kills her soon after that.

Rajit has spent the two days before her death wondering how he will explain the fact that, as the autopsy demonstrates beyond a doubt, the patient now has a penis and is, in every respect, functionally and chromosomally male.

V.

It is twenty years later in a tiny apartment in New Orleans (although it might as well be in Moscow, or Manchester, or Paris, or Berlin). Tonight is going to be a big night, and Jo/e is going to stun.

The choice is between a Polonaise crinoline-style eighteenth-century French court dress (fibreglass bustle, underwired decolletage setting off lace-embroidered crimson bodice) and a reproduction of Sir Philip Sidney's court dress in black velvet and silver thread, complete with ruff and codpiece. Eventually, and after weighing all the options, Jo/e plumps for cleavage over cock. Twelve hours to go: Jo/e opens the bottle with the red pills, each little red pill marked with an X, and pops two of them. It's 10 A.M., and Jo/e goes to bed, begins to masturbate, penis semihard, but falls asleep before coming.

The room is very small. Clothes hang from every surface. An empty pizza box sits on the floor. Jo/e snores loudly, normally, but when freebooting Jo/e makes no sound at all, and might as well be in some kind of coma.

Jo/e wakes at 10 P.M., feeling tender and new. Back when Jo/e first started on the party scene, each change would prompt a severe self-examination, peering at moles and nipples, foreskin or clit, finding out which scars had vanished and which ones had remained. But Jo/e's now an old hand at this and puts on the bustle, the petticoat, the bodice and the gown, new breasts (high and conical) pushed together, petticoat trailing the floor, which means Jo/e can wear the forty-year-old pair of Doctor Martens boots underneath (you never know when you'll need to run, or to walk or to kick, and silk slippers do no one any favours).

High, powder-look wig completes the look. And a spray of cologne. Then Jo/e's hand fumbles at the petticoat, a finger pushes between the legs (Jo/e wears no knickers, claiming a desire for authenticity to which the Doc Martens give the lie) and then dabs it behind the ears, for luck, perhaps, or to help pull. The taxi rings the door at 11:05, and Jo/e goes downstairs. Jo/e goes to the ball.

Tomorrow night Jo/e will take another dose; Jo/e's job identity during the week is strictly male.

VI.

Rajit never viewed the gender-rewriting action of Reboot as anything more than a side effect. The Nobel prize was for anti-cancer work (rebooting worked for most cancers, it was discovered, but not all of them).

For a clever man, Rajit was remarkably shortsighted. There were a few things he failed to foresee. For example:

That there would be people who, dying of cancer, would rather die than experience a change in gender.

That the Catholic Church would come out against Rajit's chemical trigger, marketed by this point under the brand name Reboot, chiefly because the gender change caused a female body to reabsorb into itself the flesh of a fetus as it rebooted itself: males cannot be pregnant. A number of other religious sects would come out against Reboot, most of them citing Genesis I: 27, 'Male and female created He them,' as their reason.

Sects that came out against Reboot included: Islam; Christian Science; the Russian Orthodox Church; the Roman Catholic Church (with a number of dissenting voices); the Unification Church; Orthodox Trek Fandom; Orthodox Judaism; the Fundamentalist Alliance of the U.S.A.

Sects that came out in favour of Reboot use where deemed the appropriate treatment by a qualified medical doctor included: most Buddhists; the Church of Jesus Christ of Latter-Day Saints; the Greek Orthodox Church; the Church of Scientology; the Anglican Church (with a number of dissenting voices); New Trek Fandom; Liberal and Reform Judaism; the New Age Coalition of America.

Sects that initially came out in favour of using Reboot recreationally: None.

While Rajit realised that Reboot would make gender-reassignment surgery obsolete, it never occurred to him that anyone might wish to take it for reasons of desire or curiosity or escape. Thus, he never foresaw the black market in Reboot and similar chemical triggers; nor that, within fifteen years of Reboot's commercial release and FDA approval, illegal sales of the designer Reboot knock-offs (*bootlegs*, as they were soon known) would outsell heroine and cocaine, gram for gram, more than ten times over.

VII.

In several of the New Communist States of Eastern Europe possession of bootlegs carried a mandatory death sentence.

In Thailand and Mongolia it was reported that boys were being forcibly rebooted into girls to increase their worth as prostitutes.

In China newborn girls were rebooted to boys: families would save all they had for a single dose. The old people died of cancer as before. The subsequent birthrate crisis was not perceived as a problem until it was too late, the proposed drastic solutions proved difficult to implement and led, in their own way, to the final revolution.

Amnesty International reported that in several of the Pan-Arabic countries men who could not easily demonstrate that they had been born male and were not, in fact, women escaping the veil were being imprisoned and, in many cases, raped and killed. Most Arab leaders denied that either phenomenon was occurring or had ever occurred.

VIII.

Rajit is in his sixties when he reads in *The New Yorker* that the word *change* is gathering to itself connotations of deep indecency and taboo.

Schoolchildren giggle embarrassedly when they encounter phrases like 'I needed a change' or 'Time for change' or 'The Winds of Change' in their studies of pre-twenty-first-century literature. In an English class in Norwich horrified smutty sniggers greet a fourteen-year-old's discovery of 'A change is as good as a rest.'

A representative of the King's English Society

writes a letter to *The Times*, deploring the loss of another perfectly good word to the English language.

Several years later a youth in Streatham is successfully prosecuted for publicly wearing a T-shirt with the slogan I'M A CHANGED MAN! printed clearly upon it.

IX.

Jackie works in *Blossoms*, a nightclub in West Hollywood. There are dozens, if not hundreds of Jackies in Los Angeles, thousands of them across the country, hundreds of thousands across the world.

Some of them work for the government, some for religious organizations, or for businesses. In New York, London and Los Angeles, people like Jackie are on the door at the places that the in-crowds go.

This is what Jackie does. Jackie watches the crowd coming in and thinks, *Born M now F, born F now M, born M now M, born M now F, born F now F* . . .

On 'Natural Nights' (crudely, *unchanged*) Jackie says, 'I'm sorry, you can't come in tonight' a lot. People like Jackie have a 97 per cent accuracy rate. An article in *Scientific American* suggests that birth gender recognition skills might be genetically inherited: an ability that always existed but had no strict survival values until now.

Jackie is ambushed in the small hours of the morning, after work, in the back of the *Blossoms* parking lot. And as each new boot crashes or thuds into Jackie's face and chest and head and groin, Jackie thinks, *Born M now F, born F now F, born F now M, born M now M* . . .

When Jackie gets out of the hospital, vision in one eye only, face and chest a single huge purple-green bruise, there is a message, sent with an enormous bunch of exotic flowers, to say that Jackie's job is still open.

However, Jackie takes the bullet train to Chicago, and from there takes a slow train to Kansas City, and stays there, working as a housepainter and electrician, professions for which Jackie had trained a long time before, and does not go back.

X.

Rajit is now in his seventies. He lives in Rio de Janeiro. He is rich enough to satisfy any whim; he will, however, no longer have sex with anyone. He eyes them all distrustfully from his apartment's window, staring down at the bronzed bodies on the Copacabana, wondering.

The people on the beach think no more of him than a teenager with chlamydia gives thanks to Alexander Fleming. Most of them imagine that Rajit must be dead by now. None of them care either way.

It is suggested that certain cancers have evolved or mutated to survive rebooting. Many bacterial and viral diseases can survive rebooting. A handful even thrive upon rebooting, and one – a strain of gonorrhoea – is hypothesised to use the process in its vectoring, initially remaining dormant in the host body and becoming infectious only when the genitalia have reorganised into that of the opposite gender.

Still, the average Western human life span is increasing.

Why some freebooters – recreational Reboot users – appear to age normally, while others give no indication of ageing at all, is something that puzzles scientists. Some claim that the latter group is actually ageing on a cellular level. Others maintain that it is too soon to tell and that no one knows anything for certain.

Rebooting does not reverse the ageing process; however, there is evidence that, for some, it may arrest it. Many of the older generation, who have until now been resistant to rebooting for pleasure, begin to take it regularly – freebooting – whether they have a medical condition that warrants it or no.

XI.

Loose coins become known as *coinage* or, occasionally, *specie*.

The process of making different or altering is now usually known as *shifting*.

XII.

Rajit is dying of prostate cancer in his Rio apartment. He is in his early nineties. He has never taken Reboot; the idea now terrifies him. The cancer has spread to the bones of his pelvis and to his testes.

He rings the bell. There is a short wait for the nurse's daily soap opera to be turned off, the cup of coffee put down. Eventually his nurse comes in.

'Take me out into the air,' he says to the nurse, his voice hoarse. At first the nurse affects not to understand him. He repeats it, in his rough Portuguese. A shake of the head from his nurse.

He pulls himself out of the bed – a shrunken figure, stooped so badly as to be almost hunchbacked, and so frail that it seems that a storm would blow him over – and begins to walk toward the door of the apartment.

His nurse tries, and fails, to dissuade him. And then the nurse walks with him to the apartment hall and holds his arm as they wait for the elevator. He has not left the apartment in two years; even before the cancer, Rajit did not leave the apartment. He is almost blind.

The nurse walks him out into the blazing sun, across the road, and down onto the sand of the Copacabana.

The people on the beach stare at the old man, bald and rotten, in his antique pyjamas, gazing about him with colourless once-brown eyes through bottle-thick dark-rimmed spectacles.

He stares back at them.

They are golden and beautiful. Some of them are asleep on the sand. Most of them are naked, or they wear the kind of bathing attire that emphasises and punctuates their nakedness.

Rajit knows them, then.

Later, much later, they made another biopic. In the final sequence the old man falls to his knees on the beach, as he did in real life, and blood trickles from the open flap of his pyjama bottoms, soaking the faded cotton and puddling darkly onto the soft sand. He stares at them all, looking from one to another with awe upon his face, like a man who has finally learned how to stare at the sun.

He said one word only as he died, surrounded by the golden people, who were not men, who were not women.

He said, 'Angels.'

And the people watching the biopic, as golden, as beautiful, as *changed* as the people on the beach, knew that that was the end of it all.

And in any way that Rajit would have understood, it was.

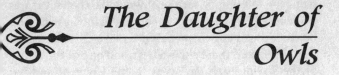

The Daughter of Owls

From *The Remaines of Gentilisme & Judaisme*
by John Aubrey, R.S.S. (1686–87), (pp 262–263)

I had this story from my friend Edmund Wyld Esq.
who had it from Mr Farringdon, who said it was
old in his time. In the Town of Dymton a newly-born
girl was left one night on the steps of the Church,
where the Sexton found her there the next morning,
and she had hold of a curious thing, *viz*.:—yᵉ pellet of
an Owle, which when crumbled showed the usual
composition of an Hoot-owle's pellet, thus: skin and
teeth and small bones.

The old wyves of the Town sayed as follows: that
the girl was the daughter of Owls, and that she should
be burnt to death, for she was not borne of woeman.
Notwithstanding, wiser Heads and Greybeards
prevayled, and the babe was taken to the Convent (for
this was shortly after the Papish times, and the Convent

had been left empty, for the Townefolke thought it was a place of Dyvills and such, and Hoot-owles and Screach-owles and many bats did make theyr homes in the tower) and there she was left, and one of the wyves of the Towne each day went to the Convent and fed the babe &c.

It was prognostickated that ye babe would dye, wch she did not doe: instead she grew year onn and about until she was a mayd of xiiii summers. She was the prittiest thing you ever did see, a fine young lass, who spent her dais and nights behind high stone walls with no-one never to see, but a Towne wyfe who came every morn. One market daie the good-wife talked too loudly of the girl's prittyness, & also that she could not speak, for she had never learned the manner of it.

The men of Dymton, the grey-beards and the young men, spoke to-gether, saying: if wee were to visit her, who would know? (Meaning by *visit*, that they did intend to ravish her.)

It was putt about thus: that ye menfolk would go a-hunting all in a company, when the Moon would be fulle: wch it beeing, they crep't one by one from theyr houses and mett outside the Convent, & the Reeve of Dymton unlocked the gate & one by one they went in. They found her hiding in the cellar, being startled by ye noyse.

The Maid was more pritty even than they had heard: her hair was red wch was uncommon, & she wore but a white shift, & when she saw them she was much afrayd for she had never seen no Men before, save only the woemen who brought her vittles: & she stared at them with huge eyes & she uttered small cries, as if she were imploring them nott to hurte her.

The Townefolk merely laughed for they meant

mischiefe & were wicked cruel men: & they came at her in the moon's light.

Then the girl began a-screaching & a-wayling, but that did not stay them from theyr purpos. & the grate window went dark & the light of the moon was blockt: & there was the sound of mighty wings; but the men did not see it as they were intent on theyr ravishment.

The folk of Dymton in theyr beds that night dreamed of hoots & screaches and howells: & of grate birds: & they dreamed that they were become littel mice & ratts.

On the morrow, when the sun was high, the goodwives of the Town went through Dymton a-hunting High & Low for theyr Husbands & theyr Sonnes; w^{ch}, coming to the Convent, they fownd, on the Cellar stones, ye pellets of owles: & in the pellets they discovered hair & buckles & coins, & small bones: & also a quantity of straw upon the floor.

And the men of Dymton was none of them seen agane. However, for some years therafter, some said they saw ye Maid in high Places, like the highest Oke trees & steeples &c; this being always in the dusk, and at night, & no-one could rightly sware, if it were her or no.

(She was a white figure:—but Mr E. Wyld could not remember him rightly whether folk said that she wore cloathes or was naked.)

The truth of it I know not, but it is a merrye tale & one wch I write down here.

Shoggoth's Old Peculiar

*B*enjamin Lassiter was coming to the unavoidable conclusion that the woman who had written *A Walking Tour of the British Coastline*, the book he was carrying in his backpack, had never been on a walking tour of any kind, and would probably not recognise the British coastline if it were to dance through her bedroom at the head of a marching band, singing 'I'm the British Coastline' in a loud and cheerful voice while accompanying itself on the kazoo.

He had been following her advice for five days now and had little to show for it, except blisters and a backache. *All British seaside resorts contain a number of bed-and-breakfast establishments, who will be only too delighted to put you up in the 'off-season'* was one such piece of advice. Ben had crossed it out and written in the margin beside it: *All British seaside resorts contain a handful of bed-and-breakfast establishments, the owners of which take off to Spain or Provence or somewhere on the last day of September, locking the doors behind them as they go.*

He had added a number of other marginal notes,

too. Such as *Do not repeat not under any circumstances order fried eggs again in any roadside cafe* and *What is it with the fish-and-chips thing?* and *No they are not.* That last was written beside a paragraph which claimed that, if there was one thing that the inhabitants of scenic villages on the British coastline were pleased to see, it was a young American tourist on a walking tour.

For five hellish days, Ben had walked from village to village, had drunk sweet tea and instant coffee in cafeterias and cafes and stared out at grey rocky vistas and at the slate-coloured sea, shivered under his two thick sweaters, got wet, and failed to see any of the sights that were promised.

Sitting in the bus shelter in which he had unrolled his sleeping bag one night, he had begun to translate key descriptive words: *charming* he decided, meant *nondescript; scenic* meant *ugly but with a nice view if the rain ever lets up; delightful* probably meant *We've never been here and don't know anyone who has.* He had also come to the conclusion that the more exotic the name of the village, the duller the village.

Thus it was that Ben Lassiter came, on the fifth day, somewhere north of Bootle, to the village of Innsmouth, which was rated neither *charming, scenic* nor *delightful* in his guidebook. There were no descriptions of the rusting pier, nor the mounds of rotting lobster pots upon the pebbly beach.

On the seafront were three bed-and-breakfasts next to each other: Sea View, Mon Repose and Shub Niggurath, each with a neon VACANCIES sign turned off in the window of the front parlour, each with a CLOSED FOR THE SEASON notice thumbtacked to the front door.

There were no cafes open on the seafront. The lone fish-and-chip shop had a CLOSED sign up. Ben waited outside for it to open as the grey afternoon light faded into dusk. Finally a small, slightly frog-faced woman came down the road, and she unlocked the door of the shop. Ben asked her when they would be open for business, and she looked at him, puzzled, and said, 'It's Monday, dear. We're never open on Monday.' Then she went into the fish-and-chip shop and locked the door behind her, leaving Ben cold and hungry on her doorstep.

Ben had been raised in a dry town in northern Texas: the only water was in backyard swimming pools, and the only way to travel was in an air-conditioned pickup truck. So the idea of walking, by the sea, in a country where they spoke English of a sort, had appealed to him. Ben's hometown was double dry: it prided itself on having banned alcohol thirty years before the rest of America leapt onto the Prohibition bandwagon, and on never having got off again; thus all Ben knew of pubs was that they were sinful places, like bars, only with cuter names. The author of *A Walking Tour of the British Coastline* had, however, suggested that pubs were good places to go to find local colour and local information, that one should always 'stand one's round', and that some of them sold food.

The Innsmouth pub was called *The Book of Dead Names* and the sign over the door informed Ben that the proprietor was one *A. Al-Hazred*, licensed to sell wines and spirits. Ben wondered if this meant that they would serve Indian food, which he had eaten on his arrival in Bootle and rather enjoyed. He paused at the signs directing him to the *Public Bar* or the *Saloon Bar*, wondering if British Public Bars were private like their Public Schools, and eventually, because it sounded more like something you would find in a Western, going into the Saloon Bar.

The Saloon Bar was almost empty. It smelled like last week's spilled beer and the day-before-yesterday's cigarette smoke. Behind the bar was a plump woman with bottle-blonde hair. Sitting in one corner were a couple of gentlemen wearing long grey raincoats and scarves. They were playing dominoes and sipping dark brown foam-topped beerish drinks from dimpled glass tankards.

Ben walked over to the bar. 'Do you sell food here?'

The barmaid scratched the side of her nose for a moment, then admitted, grudgingly, that she could probably do him a ploughman's.

Ben had no idea what this meant and found himself, for the hundredth time, wishing that *A Walking Tour of the British Coastline* had an American-English phrase book in the back. 'Is that food?' he asked.

She nodded.

'Okay. I'll have one of those.'

'And to drink?'

'Coke, please.'

'We haven't got any Coke.'

'Pepsi, then.'

'No Pepsi.'

'Well, what do you have? Sprite? 7UP? Gatorade?'

She looked blanker than previously. Then she said, 'I think there's a bottle or two of cherryade in the back.'

'That'll be fine.'

'It'll be five pounds and twenty pence, and I'll bring you over your ploughman's when it's ready.'

Ben decided as he sat at a small and slightly sticky wooden table, drinking something *fizzy* that both looked and tasted a bright chemical red, that a ploughman's was probably a steak of some kind. He reached this conclusion, coloured, he knew, by wishful thinking, from imagining rustic, possibly even bucolic, ploughmen leading their plump oxen through fresh-ploughed fields at sunset and because he could, by then, with equanimity and only a little help from others, have eaten an entire ox.

'Here you go. Ploughman's,' said the barmaid, putting a plate down in front of him.

That a ploughman's turned out to be a rectangular slab of sharp-tasting cheese, a lettuce leaf, an undersized tomato with a thumb-print in it, a mound of something wet and brown that tasted like sour jam, and a small, hard, stale roll, came as a sad disappointment to Ben, who had already decided that the British treated food as some kind of punishment. He chewed the cheese and the lettuce leaf, and cursed every ploughman in England for choosing to dine upon such swill.

The gentlemen in grey raincoats, who had been sitting in the corner, finished their game of dominoes, picked up their drinks, and came and sat beside Ben. 'What you drinking'?' one of them asked, curiously.

'It's called cherryade,' he told them. 'It tastes like something from a chemical factory.'

'Interesting you should say that,' said the shorter of the two. 'Interesting you should say that. Because I had a friend worked in a chemical factory and he *never drank cherryade*.' He paused dramatically and then took a sip of his brown drink. Ben waited for him to go on, but that appeared to be that; the conversation had stopped.

In an effort to appear polite, Ben asked, in his turn, 'So, what are *you* guys drinking?'

The taller of the two strangers, who had been looking lugubrious, brightened up. 'Why, that's exceedingly kind of you. Pint of Shoggoth's Old Peculiar for me, please.'

'And for me, too,' said his friend. 'I could murder a Shoggoth's. 'Ere, I bet that would make a good advertising slogan. "I could murder a Shoggoth's." I should write to them and suggest it. I bet they'd be very glad of me suggestin' it.'

Ben went over to the barmaid, planning to ask her for two pints of Shoggoth's Old Peculiar and a glass of water for himself, only to find she had already poured three pints of the dark beer. *Well*, he thought, *might as well be hung for a sheep as a lamb*, and he was certain it couldn't be worse than the cherryade. He took a sip. The beer had the kind of flavour which, he suspected, advertisers would describe as *full-bodied*, although if pressed they would have to admit that the body in question had been that of a goat.

He paid the barmaid and manoeuvered his way back to his new friends.

'So. What you doin' in Innsmouth?' asked the taller of the two. 'I suppose you're one of our American cousins, come to see the most famous of English villages.'

'They named the one in America after this one, you know,' said the smaller one.

'Is there an Innsmouth in the States?' asked Ben.

'I should say so,' said the smaller man. 'He wrote about it all the time. Him whose name we don't mention.'

'I'm sorry?' said Ben.

The little man looked over his shoulder, then he hissed, very loudly, 'H. P. Lovecraft!'

'I told you not to mention that name,' said his friend, and he took a sip of the dark brown beer. 'H. P. Lovecraft. H. P. bloody Lovecraft. H. bloody P. bloody Love bloody 'craft.' He stopped to take a breath. 'What did *he* know. Eh? I mean, what did he bloody know?'

Ben sipped his beer. The name was vaguely familiar; he remembered it from rummaging through the pile of old-style vinyl LPs in the back of his father's garage. 'Weren't they a rock group?'

'Wasn't talkin' about any rock group. I mean the writer.'

Ben shrugged. 'I've never heard of him,' he admitted. 'I really mostly only read Westerns. And technical manuals.'

The little man nudged his neighbour. 'Here. Wilf. You hear that? He's never heard of him.'

'Well. There's no harm in that. *I* used to read that Zane Grey,' said the taller.

'Yes. Well. That's nothing to be proud of. This bloke – what did you say your name was?'

'Ben. Ben Lassiter. And you are . . .?'

The little man smiled; he looked awfully like a frog, thought Ben. 'I'm Seth,' he said. 'And my friend here is called Wilf.'

'Charmed,' said Wilf.

'Hi,' said Ben.

'Frankly,' said the little man, 'I agree with you.'

'You do?' said Ben, perplexed.

The little man nodded. 'Yer. H. P. Lovecraft. I don't know what the fuss is about. He couldn't bloody write.' He slurped his stout, then licked the foam from his lips with a long and flexible tongue. 'I mean, for starters, you look at them words he used. *Eldritch*. You know what *eldritch* means?'

Ben shook his head. He seemed to be discussing literature with two strangers in an English pub while drinking beer. He wondered for a moment if he had become someone else, while he wasn't looking. The beer tasted less bad, the farther down the glass he went, and was beginning to erase the lingering aftertaste of the cherryade.

'*Eldritch*. Means weird. Peculiar. Bloody odd. That's what it means. I looked it up. In a dictionary. And *gibbous*?'

Ben shook his head again.

'*Gibbous* means the moon was nearly full. And what about that one he was always calling us, eh? Thing. Wossname. Starts with a *b*. Tip of me tongue . . .'

'Bastards?' suggested Wilf.

'Nah. Thing. You know. *Batrachian*. That's it. Means looked like frogs.'

'Hang on,' said Wilf. 'I thought they was, like, a kind of camel.'

Seth shook his head vigorously. 'S'definitely frogs. Not camels. Frogs.'

Wilf slurped his Shoggoth's. Ben sipped his, carefully, without pleasure.

'So?' said Ben.

'They've got two humps,' interjected Wilf, the tall one.

'Frogs?' asked Ben.

'Nah. Batrachians. Whereas your average dromedary camel, he's only got one. It's for the long journey through the desert. That's what they eat.'

'Frogs?' asked Ben.

'Camel humps.' Wilf fixed Ben with one bulging yellow eye. 'You listen to me, matey-me-lad. After you've been out in some trackless desert for three or four weeks, a plate of roasted camel hump starts looking particularly tasty.'

Seth looked scornful. 'You've never eaten a camel hump.'

'I might have done,' said Wilf.

'Yes, but you haven't. You've never even been in a desert.'

'Well, let's say, just supposing I'd been on a pilgrimage to the Tomb of Nyarlathotep . . .'

'The black king of the ancients who shall come in the night from the east and you shall not know him, you mean?'

'Of course that's who I mean.'

'Just checking.'

'Stupid question, if you ask me.'

'You could of meant someone else with the same name.'

'Well, it's not exactly a common name, is it? Nyarlathotep. There's not exactly going to be two of them, are there? "Hello, my name's Nyarlathotep, what a coincidence meeting you here, funny them bein' two of us," I don't exactly think so. Anyway, so I'm trudging through them trackless wastes, thinking to myself, I could murder a camel hump . . .'

'But you haven't, have you? You've never been out of Innsmouth harbour.'

'Well . . . No.'

'There.' Seth looked at Ben triumphantly. Then he leaned over and whispered into Ben's ear, 'He gets like this when he gets a few drinks into him, I'm afraid.'

'I heard that,' said Wilf.

'Good,' said Seth. 'Anyway. H. P. Lovecraft. He'd write one of his bloody sentences. Ahem. "The gibbous moon hung low over the eldritch and batrachian inhabitants of squamous Dulwich." What does he mean, eh? *What does he mean?* I'll tell you what he bloody means. What he bloody means is that the moon was nearly full, and everybody what lived in Dulwich was bloody peculiar frogs. That's what he means.'

'What about the other thing you said?' asked Wilf.

'What?'

'*Squamous*. Wossat mean, then?'

Seth shrugged. 'Haven't a clue,' he admitted. 'But he used it an awful lot.'

There was another pause.

'I'm a student,' said Ben. 'Gonna be a metallurgist.' Somehow he had managed to finish the whole of his first pint of Shoggoth's Old Peculiar, which was, he realised, pleasantly shocked, his first alcoholic beverage. 'What do you guys do?'

'We,' said Wilf, 'are acolytes.'

'Of Great Cthulhu,' said Seth proudly.

'Yeah?' said Ben. 'And what exactly does that involve?'

'My shout,' said Wilf. 'Hang on.' Wilf went over to the barmaid and came back with three more pints. 'Well,' he said, 'what it involves is, technically speaking, not a lot right now. The acolytin' is not really what you might call laborious employment in the middle of its busy season. That is, of course, because of his bein' asleep. Well, not exactly *asleep*. More like, if you want to put a finer point on it, *dead*.'

' "In his house at Sunken R'lyeh dead Cthulhu lies dreaming," ' interjected Seth. 'Or, as the poet has it, "That is not dead what can eternal lie—" '

' "But in Strange Aeons—" ' chanted Wilf.

'—and by *Strange* he means *bloody peculiar*—'

'Exactly. We are not talking your normal Aeons here at all.'

' "But in Strange Aeons even Death can die." '

Ben was mildly surprised to find that he seemed to be drinking another full-bodied pint of Shoggoth's Old Peculiar. Somehow the taste of rank goat was less offensive on the second pint. He was also delighted to notice that he was no longer hungry, that his blistered feet had stopped hurting, and that his companions were charming, intelligent men whose names he was having difficulty in keeping apart. He did not have enough experience with alcohol to know that this was one of the symptoms of being on your second pint of Shoggoth's Old Peculiar.

'So right now,' said Seth, or possibly Wilf, 'the business is a bit light. Mostly consisting of waiting.'

'And praying,' said Wilf, if he wasn't Seth.

'And praying. But pretty soon now, that's all going to change.'

'Yeah?' asked Ben. 'How's that?'

'Well,' confided the taller one. 'Any day now, Great Cthulhu (currently impermanently deceased), who is our boss, will wake up in his undersea living-sort-of quarters.'

'And then,' said the shorter one, 'he will stretch and yawn and get dressed—'

'Probably go to the toilet, I wouldn't be at all surprised.'

'Maybe read the papers.'

'—And having done all that, he will come out of the ocean depths and consume the world utterly.'

Ben found this unspeakably funny. 'Like a ploughman's,' he said.

'Exactly. Exactly. Well put, the young American gentleman. Great Cthulhu will gobble the world up like a ploughman's lunch, leaving but only the lump of Branston pickle on the side of the plate.'

'That's the brown stuff?' asked Ben. They assured him that it was, and he went up to the bar and brought them back another three pints of Shoggoth's Old Peculiar.

He could not remember much of the conversation that followed. He remembered finishing his pint, and his new friends inviting him on a walking tour of the village, pointing out the various sights to him 'that's where we rent our videos, and that big building next door is the Nameless Temple of Unspeakable Gods and on Saturday mornings there's jumble sale in the crypt . . .'

He explained to them his theory of the walking tour book and told them, emotionally, that Innsmouth was both *scenic* and *charming*. He told them that they were the best friends he had ever had and that Innsmouth was *delightful*.

The moon was nearly full, and in the pale moonlight both of his new friends did look remarkably like huge frogs. Or possibly camels.

The three of them walked to the end of the rusted pier, and Seth and/or Wilf pointed out to Ben the ruins of Sunken R'lyeh in the bay, visible in the moonlight, beneath the sea, and Ben was overcome by what he kept explaining was a sudden and unforeseen attack of seasickness and was violently and unendingly sick over the metal railings into the black sea below . . .

After that it all got a bit odd.

Ben Lassiter awoke on the cold hillside with his head pounding and a bad taste in his mouth. His head was resting on his backpack. There was rocky moorland on each side of him, and no sign of a road, and no sign of any village, scenic, charming, delightful, or even picturesque.

He stumbled and limped almost a mile to the nearest road and walked along it until he reached a petrol station.

They told him that there was no village anywhere locally named Innsmouth. No village with a pub called *The Book of Dead Names*. He told them about two men, named Wilf and Seth, and a friend of theirs, called Strange Ian, who was fast asleep somewhere, if he wasn't dead, under the sea. They told him that they didn't think much of American hippies who wandered about the countryside taking drugs, and that he'd probably feel better after a nice cup of tea and a tuna and cucumber sandwich, but that if he was dead set on wandering the country taking drugs, young Ernie who worked the afternoon shift would be all too happy to sell him a nice little bag of homegrown cannabis, if he could come back after lunch.

Ben pulled out his *A Walking Tour of the British Coastline* book and tried to find Innsmouth in it to prove to them that he had not dreamed it, but he was unable to locate the page it had been on – if ever it had been there at all. Most of one page, however, had been ripped out, roughly, about halfway through the book.

And then Ben telephoned a taxi, which took him to Bootle railway station, where he caught a train, which took him to Manchester, where he got on an aeroplane, which took him to Chicago, where he changed planes and flew to Dallas, where he got another plane going north, and he rented a car and went home.

He found the knowledge that he was over 600 miles away from the ocean very comforting; although, later in life, he moved to Nebraska to increase the distance from the sea: there were things he had seen, or thought he had seen, beneath the old pier that night that he would never be able to get out of his head. There were things that lurked beneath grey raincoats that man was not meant to know. *Squamous*. He did not need to look it up. He knew. They were *squamous*.

A couple of weeks after his return home Ben posted his annotated copy of *A Walking Tour of the British Coastline* to the author, care of her publisher, with an extensive letter containing a number of helpful suggestions for future editions. He also asked the author if she would send him a copy of the page that had been ripped from his guidebook, to set his mind at rest; but he was secretly relieved, as the days turned into months, and the months turned into years and then into decades, that she never replied.

There was a computer game, I was given it,
one of my friends gave it to me, he was playing it,
he said, it's brilliant, you should play it,
and I did, and it was.

I copied it off the disk he gave me
for anyone, I wanted everyone to play it.
Everyone should have this much fun.
I sent it upline to bulletin boards
but mainly I got it out to all of my friends.

(Personal contact. That's the way it was given to me.)

My friends were like me: some were scared of viruses,
someone gave you a game on disk, next week or Friday
    the 13th
it reformatted your hard disk or corrupted your memory.
But this one never did that. This was dead safe.

Even my friends who didn't like computers started to
    play:

as you get better the game gets harder;
maybe you never win but you can get pretty good.
I'm pretty good.

Of course I have to spend a lot of time playing it.
So do my friends. And their friends.
And just the people you meet, you can see them,
walking down the old motorways
or standing in queues, away from their computers,
away from the arcades that sprang up overnight,
but they play it in their heads in the meantime,
combining shapes,
puzzling over contours, putting colours next to colours,
twisting signals to new screen sections,
listening to the music.

Sure, people think about it, but mainly they play it.
My record's eighteen hours at a stretch.
40,012 points, 3 fanfares.

You play through the tears, the aching wrist, the hunger,
    after a while
it all goes away.
All of it except the game, I should say.

There's no room in my mind anymore; no room for
    other things.
We copied the game, gave it to our friends.
It transcends language, occupies our time,
sometimes I think I'm forgetting things these days.

I wonder what happened to the TV. There used to be TV.
I wonder what will happen when I run out of canned
    food.

I wonder where all the people went. And then I realise
   how,
if I'm fast enough, I can put a black square next to a
   red line,
mirror it and rotate them so they both disappear,
clearing the left block
for a white bubble to rise . . .

(So they both disappear.)

And when the power goes off for good then I
Will play it in my head until I die.

 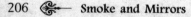

Looking for the Girl

I was nineteen in 1965, in my drainpipe trousers with my hair quietly creeping down toward my collar. Every time you turned on the radio the Beatles were singing *Help!* and I wanted to be John Lennon with all the girls screaming after me, always ready with a cynical quip. That was the year I bought my first copy of *Penthouse* from a small tobacconist's in the King's Road. I paid my few furtive shillings and went home with it stuffed up my jumper, occasionally glancing down to see if it had burnt a hole in the fabric.

The copy has long since been thrown away, but I'll always remember it: sedate letters about censorship; a short story by H. E. Bates and an interview with an American novelist I had never heard of; a fashion spread of mohair suits and paisley ties, all to be bought on Carnaby Street. And best of all, there were girls, of course; and best of all the girls, there was Charlotte.

Charlotte was nineteen, too.

All the girls in that long-gone magazine seemed identical with their perfect plastic flesh; not a hair out of place (you could almost smell the lacquer); smiling wholesomely at the camera while their eyes squinted at you through forest-thick eyelashes: white lipstick; white teeth, white breasts, bikini-bleached. I never gave a thought to the strange positions they had coyly arranged themselves into to avoid showing the slightest curl or shadow of pubic hair – I wouldn't have known what I was looking at anyway. I had eyes only for their pale bottoms and breasts, their chaste but inviting come-on glances.

Then I turned the page, and I saw Charlotte. She was different from the others. Charlotte *was* sex; she wore sexuality like a translucent veil, like a heady perfume.

There were words beside the pictures, and I read them in a daze. 'The entrancing Charlotte Reave is nineteen . . . a resurgent individualist and beat poet, contributor to *FAB* magazine . . .' Phrases stuck to my mind as I pored over the flat pictures: she posed and pouted in a Chelsea flat – the photographer's, I guessed – and I knew that I needed her.

She was my age. It was fate.

Charlotte.

Charlotte was nineteen.

I bought *Penthouse* regularly after that, hoping she'd appear again. But she didn't. Not then.

Six months later my mum found a shoebox under my bed and looked inside it. First she threw a scene, then she threw out all the magazines, finally she threw me out. The next day I got a job and a bedsit in Earl's Court, without, all things considered, too much trouble.

My job, my first, was at an electrical shop off the Edgware Road. All I could do was change a plug, but in those days people could afford to get an electrician in to do just that. My boss told me I could learn on the job.

I lasted three weeks. My first job was a proper

thrill – changing the plug on the bedside light of an English film star, who had achieved fame through his portrayal of laconic Cockney Casanovas. When I got there he was in bed with two honest-to-goodness dolly birds. I changed the plug and left – it was all very proper. I didn't even catch a glimpse of nipple, let alone get invited to join them.

Three weeks later I got fired and lost my virginity on the same day. It was a posh place in Hampstead, empty apart from the maid, a little dark-haired woman a few years older than me. I got down on my knees to change the plug, and she climbed on a chair next to me to dust off the top of a door. I looked up: under her skirt she was wearing stockings, and suspenders, and, so help me, nothing else. I discovered what happened in the bits the pictures didn't show you.

So I lost my cherry under a dining room table in Hampstead. You don't see maidservants anymore. They have gone the way of the bubble car and the dinosaur.

It was afterward that I lost my job. Not even my boss, convinced as he was of my utter incompetence, believed I could have taken three hours to change a plug – and I wasn't about to tell him that I'd spent two of the hours I'd been gone hiding underneath the dining room table when the master and mistress of the house came home unexpectedly, was I?

I got a succession of short-lived jobs after that: first as a printer, then as a typesetter, before I wound up in a little ad agency above a sandwich shop in Old Compton Street.

I carried on buying *Penthouse*. Everybody looked like an extra in 'The Avengers', but they looked like that in real life. Articles on Woody Allen and Sappho's island, Batman and Vietnam, strippers in action wielding whips, fashion and fiction and sex.

The suits gained velvet collars, and the girls messed up their hair. Fetish was fashion. London was swinging, the magazine covers were psychedelic, and if there wasn't acid in the drinking water, we acted as if there ought to have been.

I saw Charlotte again in 1969, long after I'd given up on her. I thought that I had forgotten what she looked like. Then one day the head of the agency dropped a *Penthouse* on my desk – there was a cigarette ad we'd placed in it that he was particularly pleased with. I was twenty-three, a rising star, running the art department as if I knew what I was doing, and sometimes I did.

I don't remember much about the issue itself; all I remember is Charlotte. Hair wild and tawny, eyes provocative, smiling like she knew all the secrets of life, and she was keeping them close to her naked chest. Her name wasn't Charlotte then, it was Melanie, or something like that. The text said that she was nineteen.

I was living with a dancer called Rachel at the time, in a flat in Camden Town. She was the best-looking, most delightful woman I've ever known, was Rachel. And I went home early with those pictures of Charlotte in my briefcase, and locked myself in the bathroom, and I wanked myself into a daze.

We broke up shortly after that, me and Rachel.

The ad agency boomed – everything in the sixties boomed – and in 1971 I was given the task of finding 'The Face' for a clothing label. They wanted a girl who would epitomize everything sexual; who would wear their clothes as if she were about to reach up and rip them off – if some man didn't get there first. And I knew the perfect girl: Charlotte.

I phoned *Penthouse*, who didn't know what I was

talking about, but, reluctantly, put me in touch with both of the photographers who had shot her in the past. The man at *Penthouse* didn't seem convinced when I told them it was the same girl each time.

I got hold of the photographers, trying to find her agency.

They said she didn't exist.

At least not in any way you could pin down, she didn't. Sure, both of them knew the girl I meant. But as one of them told me, 'Like, *weird*,' she'd come to them. They'd paid her a modelling fee and sold the pictures. No, they didn't have any addresses for her.

I was twenty-six and a fool. I saw immediately what must be happening: I was being given the runaround. Some other ad agency had obviously signed her, was planning a big campaign around her, had paid the photographers to keep quiet. I cursed and I shouted at them over the phone. I made outrageous financial offers.

They told me to fuck off.

And the next month she was in *Penthouse*. No longer a psychedelic tease mag, it had become classier – the girls had grown pubic hair, had man-eating glints in their eyes. Men and women romped in soft focus through cornfields, pink against the gold.

Her name, said the text, was Belinda. She was an antique dealer. It was Charlotte, all right, although her hair was dark and piled in rich ringlets over her head. The text also gave her age: nineteen.

I phoned my contact at *Penthouse* and got the name of the photographer, John Felbridge. I rang him. Like the others, he claimed to know nothing about her, but by now I'd learned a lesson. Instead of shouting at him down the telephone line, I gave him a job, on a fairly sizeable account, shooting a small boy eating ice cream.

Felbridge was long-haired, in his late thirties, with a ratty fur coat and plimsolls that were flapping open, but a good photographer. After the shoot, I took him out for a drink, and we talked about the lousy weather, and photography, and decimal currency, and his previous work, and Charlotte.

'So you were saying you'd seen the pictures in *Penthouse*?' Felbridge said.

I nodded. We were both slightly drunk.

'I'll tell you about that girl. You know something? She's why I want to give up glamour work and go legit. Said her name was Belinda.'

'How did you meet her?'

'I'm getting to that, aren't I? I thought she was from an agency, didn't I? She knocks on the door, I think strewth! and invite her in. She said she wasn't from an agency, she says she's selling . . .' He wrinkled his brow, confused. 'Isn't that odd? I've forgotten what she was selling. Maybe she wasn't selling anything. I don't know. I'll forget me own name next.

'I knew she was something special. Asked her if she'd pose, told her it was kosher, I wasn't just trying to get into her pants, and she agrees. Click, flash! Five rolls, just like that. As soon as we're finished, she's got her clothes back on, heads out the door pretty-as-you-please. "What about your money?" I says to her. "Send it to me," she says, and she's down the steps and onto the road.'

'So you *have* got her address?' I asked, trying to keep the interest out of my voice.

'No. Bugger all. I wound up setting her fee aside in case she comes back.'

I remember, in with the disappointment, wondering whether his Cockney accent was real or merely fashionable.

'But what I was leading up to is this. When the pictures came back, I knew I'd . . . well, as far as tits and fanny went, no – as far as the whole photographing women thing went – I'd done it all. She *was* women, see? I'd *done* it. No, no, let me get you one. My shout. Bloody Mary, wasn't it? I gotter say, I'm looking forward to our future work together. . .'

There wasn't to be any future work.

The agency was taken over by an older, bigger firm, who wanted our accounts. They incorporated the initials of the firm into their own and kept on a few top copywriters, but they let the rest of us go.

I went back to my flat and waited for the offers of work to pour in, which they didn't, but a friend of a girlfriend of a friend starting chatting to me late one night in a club (music by a guy I'd never heard of, name of David Bowie. He was dressed as a spaceman, the rest of his band were in silver cowboy outfits. I didn't even listen to the songs), and the next thing you know I was managing a rock band of my own, the Diamonds of Flame. Unless you were hanging around the London club scene in the early seventies you'll never have heard of them, although they were a very good band. Tight, lyrical. Five guys. Two of them are currently in world-league supergroups. One of them's a plumber in Walsall; he still sends me Christmas cards. The other two have been dead for fifteen years: anonymous ODs. They went within a week of each other, and it broke up the band.

It broke me up, too. I dropped out after that – I wanted to get as far away from the city and that lifestyle as I could. I bought a small farm in Wales. I was happy there, too, with the sheep and the goats and the cabbages. I'd probably be there today if it hadn't been for her and *Penthouse*.

I don't know where it came from; one morning I went outside to find the magazine lying in the yard, in the mud, face down. It was almost a year old. She wore no makeup and was posed in what looked like a very high-class flat. For the first time I could see her pubic hair, or I could have if the photo hadn't been artistically fuzzed and just a fraction out of focus. She looked as if she were coming out of the mist.

Her name, it said, was Lesley. She was nineteen.

And after that I just couldn't stay away anymore. I sold the farm for a pittance and came back to London in the last days of 1976.

I went on the dole, lived in a council flat in Victoria, got up at lunchtime, hit the pubs until they closed in the afternoons, read newspapers in the library until opening time, then pub-crawled until closing time. I lived off my dole money and drank from my savings account.

I was thirty and I felt much older. I started living with an anonymous blonde punkette from Canada I met in a drinking club in Greek Street. She was the barmaid, and one night, after closing, she told me she'd just lost her digs, so I offered her the sofa at my place. She was only sixteen, it turned out, and she never got to sleep on the sofa. She had small, pomegranate breasts, a skull tattooed on her back, and a junior Bride of Frankenstein hairdo. She said she'd done everything and believed in nothing. She would talk for hours about the way the world was moving toward a condition of anarchy, claimed that there was no hope and no future; but she fucked like she'd just invented fucking. And I figured that was good.

She'd come to bed wearing nothing but a spiky black leather dog collar and masses of messy black eye makeup. She spat sometimes, just gobbed on the pavement, when we were walking, which I hated, and she made me take her to the punk clubs, to watch her gob and swear and pogo. Then I really felt old. I liked some of the music, though: *Peaches*, stuff like that. And I saw the Sex Pistols play live. They were rotten.

Then the punkette walked out on me, claiming that I was a boring old fart, and she took up with an extremely plump Arab princeling.

'I thought you didn't believe in anything,' I called after her as she climbed into the Roller he sent to collect her.

'I believe in hundred quid blowjobs and mink sheets,' she called back, one hand playing with a strand of her Bride of Frankenstein hairdo. 'And a gold vibrator. I believe in that.'

So she went away to an oil fortune and a new wardrobe, and I checked my savings and found I was dead broke – practically penniless. I was still sporadically buying *Penthouse*. My sixties soul was both deeply shocked and profoundly thrilled by the amount of flesh now on view. Nothing was left to the imagination, which, at the same time, attracted and repelled me.

Then, near the end of 1977, *she* was there again.

Her hair was multicoloured, my Charlotte, and her mouth was as crimson as if she'd been eating raspberries. She lay on satin sheets with a jeweled mask on her face and a hand between her legs, ecstatic, orgasmic, all I ever wanted: Charlotte.

She was appearing under the name of Titania and was draped with peacock feathers. She worked, I was informed by the insectile black words that crept around her photographs, in an estate agent's in the South. She liked sensitive, honest men. She was nineteen.

And goddamn it, she *looked* nineteen. And I was

broke, on the dole with just over a million others, and going nowhere.

I sold my record collection, and my books, all but four copies of *Penthouse*, and most of the furniture, and I bought myself a fairly good camera. Then I phoned all the photographers I'd known when I was in advertising almost a decade before.

Most of them didn't remember me, or they said they didn't. And those that did, didn't want an eager young assistant who wasn't young anymore and had no experience. But I kept trying and eventually got hold of Harry Bleak, a silver-haired old boy with his own studios in Crouch End and a posse of expensive little boyfriends.

I told him what I wanted. He didn't even stop to think about it. 'Be here in two hours.'

'No catches?'

'Two hours. No more.'

I was there.

For the first year I cleaned the studio, painted backdrops, and went out to the local shops and streets to beg, buy or borrow appropriate props. The next year he let me help with the lights, set up shots, waft smoke pellets and dry ice around, and make the tea. I'm exaggerating – I only made the tea once; I make terrible tea. But I learned a hell of a lot about photography.

And suddenly it was 1981, and the world was newly romantic, and I was thirty-five and feeling every minute of it. Bleak told me to look after the studio for a few weeks while he went off to Morocco for a month of well-earned debauchery.

She was in *Penthouse* that month. More coy and prim than before, waiting for me neatly between advertisements for stereos and Scotch. She was called

Dawn, but she was still my Charlotte, with nipples like beads of blood on her tanned breasts, dark fuzzy thatch between forever legs, shot on location on a beach somewhere. She was only nineteen, said the text. Charlotte. Dawn.

Harry Bleak was killed travelling back from Morocco: a bus fell on him.

It's not funny, really – he was on a car ferry coming back from Calais, and he snuck down into the car hold to get his cigars, which he'd left in the glove compartment of the Merc.

The weather was rough, and a tourist bus (belonging, I read in the papers, and was told at length by a tearful boyfriend, to a shopping co-op in Wigan) hadn't been chained down properly. Harry was crushed against the side of his silver Mercdes.

He had always kept that car spotless.

When the will was read I discovered that the old bastard had left me his studio. I cried myself to sleep that night, got stinking drunk for a week, and then opened for business.

Things happened between then and now. I got married. It lasted three weeks, then we called it a day. I guess I'm not the marrying type. I got beaten up by a drunken Glaswegian on a train late one night, and the other passengers pretended it wasn't happening. I bought a couple of terrapins and a tank, put them in the flat over the studio, and called them Rodney and Kevin. I became a fairly good photographer. I did calendars, advertising, fashion and glamour work, little kids and big stars: the works.

And one spring day in 1985, I met Charlotte.

I was alone in the studio on a Thursday morning, unshaven and barefoot. It was a free day, and I was going to spend it cleaning the place and reading the papers. I had left the studio doors open, letting the fresh air in to replace the stink of cigarettes and spilled wine of the shoot the night before, when a woman's voice said, 'Bleak Photographic?'

'That's right,' I said, not turning around, 'but Bleak's dead. I run the place now.'

'I want to model for you,' she said.

I turned around. She was about five foot six, with honey-coloured hair, olive green eyes, a smile like cold water in the desert.

'Charlotte?'

She tilted her head to one side. 'If you like. Do you want to take my picture?'

I nodded dumbly. Plugged in the umbrellas, stood her up against a bare brick wall, and shot off a couple of test Polaroids. No special makeup, no set, just a few lights, a Hasselblad, and the most beautiful girl in my world.

After a while, she began to take off her clothes. I did not ask her to. I don't remember saying *anything* to her. She undressed and I carried on taking photographs.

She knew it all. How to pose, to preen, to stare. Silently she flirted with the camera, and with me standing behind it, moving around her, clicking away. I don't remember stopping for anything, but I must have changed films, because I wound up with a dozen rolls at the end of the day.

I suppose you think that after the pictures were taken, I made love with her. Now, I'd be a liar if I said I've never screwed models in my time, and, for that matter, some of them have screwed me. But I didn't touch her. She was my dream; and if you touch a dream it vanishes, like a soap bubble.

And anyway, I simply couldn't touch her.

'How old are you?' I asked her just before she left, when she was pulling on her coat and picking up her bag.

'Nineteen,' she told me without looking around, and then she was out the door.

She didn't say good-bye.

I sent the photos to *Penthouse*. I couldn't think of anywhere else to send them. Two days later I got a call from the art editor. 'Loved the girl! Real face-of-the-eighties stuff. What are her vital statistics?'

'Her name is Charlotte,' I told him. 'She's nineteen.'

And now I'm thirty-nine, and one day I'll be fifty, and she'll still be nineteen. But someone else will be taking the photographs.

Rachel, my dancer, married an architect.

The blonde punkette from Canada runs a multi-national fashion chain. I do some photographic work for her from time to time. Her hair's cut short, and there's a smudge of gray in it, and she's a lesbian these days. She told me she's still got the mink sheets, but she made up the bit about the gold vibrator.

My ex-wife married a nice bloke who owns two video rental shops, and they moved to Slough. They have twin boys.

I don't know what happened to the maid.

And Charlotte?

In Greece the philosophers are debating, Socrates is drinking hemlock, and she's posing for a sculpture of Erato, muse of light poetry and lovers, and she's nineteen.

In Crete she's oiling her breasts, and she's jumping bulls in the ring while King Minos applauds, and someone's painting her likeness on a wine jar, and she's nineteen.

In 2065 she's stretched out on the revolving floor of a holographic photographer, who records her as an erotic dream in Living Sensolove, imprisons the sight and sound and the very smell of her in a tiny diamond matrix. She's only nineteen.

And a caveman outlines Charlotte with a burnt stick on the wall of the temple cave, filling in the shape and the texture of her with earths and berry dyes. Nineteen.

Charlotte is there, in all places, all times, sliding through our fantasies, a girl forever.

I want her so much it makes me hurt sometimes. That's when I take down the photographs of her and just look at them for a while, wondering why I didn't try to touch her, why I wouldn't really even speak to her when she was there, and never coming up with an answer that I could understand.

That's why I've written this all down, I suppose.

This morning I noticed yet another gray hair at my temple. Charlotte is nineteen. Somewhere.

 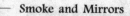

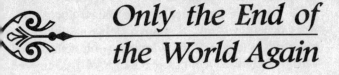

Only the End of
the World Again

*I*t was a bad day: I woke up naked in the bed with a cramp in my stomach, feeling more or less like hell. Something about the quality of the light, stretched and metallic, like the colour of a migraine, told me it was afternoon.

The room was freezing – literally: there was a thin crust of ice on the inside of the windows. The sheets on the bed around me were ripped and clawed, and there was animal hair in the bed. It itched.

I was thinking about staying in bed for the next week – I'm always tired after a change – but a wave of nausea forced me to disentangle myself from the bedding and to stumble, hurriedly, into the apartment's tiny bathroom.

The cramps hit me again as I got to the bathroom door. I held on to the door frame and I started to sweat. Maybe it was a fever; I hoped I wasn't coming down with something.

The cramping was sharp in my guts. My head felt swimmy. I crumpled to the floor, and, before I could manage to raise my head enough to find the toilet bowl, I began to spew.

I vomited a foul-smelling thin yellow liquid; in it was a dog's paw – my guess was a Doberman's, but I'm not really a dog person; a tomato peel; some diced carrots and sweet corn; some lumps of half-chewed meat, raw; and some fingers. They were fairly small pale fingers, obviously a child's.

'Shit.'

The cramps eased up, and the nausea subsided. I lay on the floor with stinking drool coming out of my mouth and nose, with the tears you cry when you're being sick drying on my cheeks.

When I felt a little better, I picked up the paw and the fingers from the pool of spew and threw them into the toilet bowl, flushed them away.

I turned on the tap, rinsed out my mouth with the briny Innsmouth water, and spat it into the sink. I mopped up the rest of the sick as best I could with washcloth and toilet paper. Then I turned on the shower and stood in the bathtub like a zombie as the hot water sluiced over me.

I soaped myself down, body and hair. The meagre lather turned grey; I must have been filthy. My hair was matted with something that felt like dried blood, and I worked at it with the bar of soap until it was gone. Then I stood under the shower until the water turned icy.

There was a note under the door from my landlady. It said that I owed her for two weeks' rent. It said that all the answers were in the Book of Revelations. It said that I made a lot of noise coming home in the early hours of this morning, and she'd thank me to be quieter in future. It said that when the Elder Gods rose up from the ocean, all the scum of the Earth, all the nonbelievers, all the human garbage and the wastrels and deadbeats would be swept away, and the world would be cleansed by ice and deep water. It said that she felt she ought to remind me that she had assigned me a shelf in the refrigerator when I arrived and she'd thank me if in the future I'd keep to it.

I crumpled the note, dropped it on the floor, where it lay alongside the Big Mac cartons and the empty pizza cartons and the long-dead dried slices of pizza.

It was time to go to work.

I'd been in Innsmouth for two weeks, and I disliked it. It smelled fishy. It was a claustrophobic little town: marshland to the east, cliffs to the west, and, in the centre, a harbour that held a few rotting fishing boats and was not even scenic at sunset. The yuppies had come to Innsmouth in the eighties anyway, bought their picturesque fisherman's cottages overlooking the harbour. The yuppies had been gone for some years now, and the cottages by the bay were crumbling, abandoned.

The inhabitants of Innsmouth lived here and there in and around the town and in the trailer parks that ringed it, filled with dank mobile homes that were never going anywhere.

I got dressed, pulled on my boots, put on my coat, and left my room. My landlady was nowhere to be seen. She was a short pop-eyed woman who spoke little, although she left extensive notes for me pinned to doors and placed where I might see them; she kept the house filled with the smell of boiling seafood: huge pots were always simmering on the kitchen stove, filled with things with too many legs and other things with no legs at all.

There were other rooms in the house, but no one else rented them. No one in their right mind would come to Innsmouth in winter.

Outside the house it didn't smell much better. It was colder, though, and my breath steamed in the sea air. The snow on the streets was crusty and filthy; the clouds promised more snow.

A cold salty wind came up off the bay. The gulls were screaming miserably. I felt shitty. My office would be freezing, too. On the corner of Marsh Street and Leng Avenue was a bar, *The Opener*, a squat building with small dark windows that I'd passed two dozen times in the last couple of weeks. I hadn't been in before, but I really needed a drink, and besides, it might be warmer in there. I pushed open the door.

The bar was indeed warm. I stamped the snow off my boots and went inside. It was almost empty and smelled of old ashtrays and stale beer. A couple of elderly men were playing chess by the bar. The barman was reading a battered old gilt-and-green-leather edition of the poetical works of Alfred, Lord Tennyson.

'Hey. How about a Jack Daniel's, straight up?'

'Sure thing. You're new in town,' he told me, putting his book face down on the bar, pouring the drink into a glass.

'Does it show?'

He smiled, passed me the Jack Daniel's. The glass was filthy, with a greasy thumbprint on the side, and I shrugged and knocked back the drink anyway. I could barely taste it.

'Hair of the dog?' he said.

'In a manner of speaking.'

'There is a belief,' said the barman, whose fox-red hair was tightly greased back, 'that the *lykanthropoi* can be returned to their natural forms by thanking them, while they're in wolf form, or by calling them by their given names.'

'Yeah? Well, thanks.'

He poured another shot for me, unasked. He looked a little like Peter Lorre, but then, most of the folk in Innsmouth look a little like Peter Lorre, including my landlady.

I sank the Jack Daniel's, this time felt it burning down into my stomach, the way it should.

'It's what they say. I never said I believed it.'

'What *do* you believe?'

'Burn the girdle.'

'Pardon?'

'The *lykanthropoi* have girdles of human skin, given to them at their first transformation by their masters in Hell. Burn the girdle.'

One of the old chess players turned to me then, his eyes huge and blind and protruding. 'If you drink rainwater out of warg-wolf's pawprint, that'll make a wolf of you, when the moon is full,' he said. 'The only cure is to hunt down the wolf that made the print in the first place and cut off its head with a knife forged of virgin silver.'

'Virgin, huh?' I smiled.

His chess partner, bald and wrinkled, shook his head and croaked a single sad sound. Then he moved his queen and croaked again.

There are people like him all over Innsmouth.

I paid for the drinks and left a dollar tip on the bar. The barman was reading his book once more and ignored it.

Outside the bar big wet kissy flakes of snow had begun to fall, settling in my hair and eyelashes. I hate snow. I hate New England. I hate Innsmouth: it's no place to be alone, but if there's a good place to be alone, I've not found it yet. Still, business has kept me on the move for more moons than I like to think about. Business, and other things.

I walked a couple of blocks down Marsh Street – like most of Innsmouth, an unattractive mixture of eighteenth-century American Gothic houses, late-nineteenth-century stunted brownstones, and late-twentieth prefab grey-brick boxes – until I got to a boarded-up fried chicken joint, and I went up the stone steps next to the store and unlocked the rusting metal security door.

There was a liquor store across the street; a palmist was operating on the second floor.

Someone had scrawled graffiti in black marker on the metal: JUST DIE, it said. Like it was easy.

The stairs were bare wood; the plaster was stained and peeling. My one-room office was at the top of the stairs.

I don't stay anywhere long enough to bother with my name in gilt on glass. It was handwritten in block letters on a piece of ripped cardboard that I'd thumbtacked to the door.

LAWRENCE TALBOT

ADJUSTER

I unlocked the door to my office and went in.

I inspected my office, while adjectives like *seedy* and *rancid* and *squalid* wandered through my head, then gave up, outclassed. It was fairly unprepossessing – a desk, an office chair, an empty filing cabinet; a window, which gave you a terrific view of the liquor store and the empty palmist's. The smell of old cooking grease permeated from the store below. I wondered how long the fried chicken joint had been boarded up; I imagined a multitude of black cockroaches swarming over every surface in the darkness beneath me.

'That's the shape of the world that you're thinking of there,' said a deep dark voice, deep enough that I felt it in the pit of my stomach.

There was an old armchair in one corner of the office. The remains of a pattern showed through the patina of age and grease the years had given it. It was the colour of dust.

The fat man sitting in the armchair, his eyes still tightly closed, continued: 'We look about in puzzlement at our world, with a sense of unease and disquiet. We think of ourselves as scholars in arcane liturgies, single men trapped in worlds beyond our devising. The truth is far simpler: there are things in the darkness beneath us that wish us harm.'

His head was lolled back on the armchair, and the tip of his tongue poked out of the corner of his mouth.

'You read my mind?'

The man in the armchair took a slow deep breath that rattled in the back of his throat. He really was immensely fat, with stubby fingers like discoloured sausages. He wore a thick old coat, once black, now an indeterminate grey. The snow on his boots had not entirely melted.

'Perhaps. The end of the world is a strange concept. The world is always ending, and the end is always being averted, by love or foolishness or just plain old dumb luck.

'Ah well. It's too late now: The Elder Gods have chosen their vessels. When the moon rises . . .'

A thin trickle of drool came from one corner of his

mouth, oozed down in a thread of silver to his collar. Something scuttled from his collar into the shadows of his coat.

'Yeah? What happens when the moon rises?'

The man in the armchair stirred, opened two little eyes, red and swollen, and blinked them in waking.

'I dreamed I had many mouths,' he said, his new voice oddly small and breathy for such a huge man. 'I dreamed every mouth was opening and closing independently. Some mouths were talking, some whispering, some eating, some waiting in silence.'

He looked around, wiped the spittle from the corner of his mouth, sat back in the chair, blinking puzzledly. 'Who are you?'

'I'm the guy who rents this office,' I told him.

He belched suddenly, loudly. 'I'm sorry,' he said in his breathy voice, and lifted himself heavily from the armchair. He was shorter than I was, when he was standing. He looked me up and down blearily. 'Silver bullets,' he pronounced after a short pause. 'Old-fashioned remedy.'

'Yeah,' I told him. 'That's so obvious – must be why I didn't think of it. Gee, I could just kick myself. I really could.'

'You're making fun of an old man,' he told me.

'Not really. I'm sorry. Now, out of here. Some of us have work to do.'

He shambled out. I sat down in the swivel chair at the desk by the window and discovered, after some minutes, through trial and error, that if I swivelled the chair to the left, it fell off its base.

So I sat still and waited for the dusty black telephone on my desk to ring while the light slowly leaked away from the winter sky.

Ring.

A man's voice: *Had I thought about aluminum siding?* I put down the phone.

There was no heating in the office. I wondered how long the fat man had been asleep in the armchair.

Twenty minutes later the phone rang again. A crying woman implored me to help her find her five-year-old daughter, missing since last night, stolen from her bed. The family dog had vanished, too.

I don't do missing children, I told her. *I'm sorry: too many bad memories.* I put down the telephone, feeling sick again.

It was getting dark now, and, for the first time since I had been in Innsmouth, the neon sign across the street flicked on. It told me that MADAME EZEKIEL performed TAROT READINGS AND PALMISTRY.

Red neon stained the falling snow the colour of new blood.

Armageddon is averted by small actions. That's the way it was. That's the way it always has to be.

The phone rang a third time. I recognised the voice; it was the aluminum siding man again. 'You know,' he said chattily, 'transformation from man to animal and back being, by definition, impossible, we need to look for other solutions. Depersonalization, obviously, and likewise some form of projection. Brain damage? Perhaps. Pseudoneurotic schizophrenia? Laughably so. Some cases have been treated with intravenous thioridazine hydrochloride.'

'Successfully?'

He chuckled. 'That's what I like. A man with a sense of humour. I'm sure we can do business.'

'I told you already. I don't need aluminum siding.'

'Our business is more remarkable than that and of

far greater importance. You're new in town, Mr Talbot. It would be a pity if we found ourselves at, shall we say, loggerheads?'

'You can say whatever you like, pal. In my book you're just another adjustment, waiting to be made.'

'We're ending the world, Mr Talbot. The Deep Ones will rise out of their ocean graves and eat the moon like a ripe plum.'

'Then I won't ever have to worry about full moons anymore, will I?'

'Don't try to cross us,' he began, but I growled at him, and he fell silent.

Outside my window the snow was still falling.

Across Marsh Street, in the window directly opposite mine, the most beautiful woman I had ever seen stood in the ruby glare of her neon sign, and she stared at me.

She beckoned with one finger.

I put down the phone on the aluminum siding man for the second time that afternoon, and went downstairs, and crossed the street at something close to a run; but I looked both ways before I crossed.

She was dressed in silks. The room was lit only by candles and stank of incense and patchouli oil.

She smiled at me as I walked in, beckoned me over to her seat by the window. She was playing a card game with a tarot deck, some version of solitaire. As I reached her, one elegant hand swept up the cards, wrapped them in a silk scarf, placed them gently in a wooden box.

The scents of the room made my head pound. I hadn't eaten anything today, I realised; perhaps that was what was making me lightheaded. I sat down across the table from her, in the candlelight.

She extended her hand and took my hand in hers.

She stared at my palm, touched it, softly, with her forefinger.

'Hair?' She was puzzled.

'Yeah, well. I'm on my own a lot.' I grinned. I had hoped it was a friendly grin, but she raised an eyebrow at me anyway.

'When I look at you,' said Madame Ezekiel, 'this is what I see. I see the eye of a man. Also I see the eye of a wolf. In the eye of a man I see honesty, decency, innocence. I see an upright man who walks on the square. And in the eye of wolf I see a groaning and a growling, night howls and cries, I see a monster running with blood-flecked spittle in the darkness of the borders of the town.'

'How can you see a growl or a cry?'

She smiled. 'It is not hard,' she said. Her accent was not American. It was Russian, or Maltese, or Egyptian perhaps. 'In the eye of the mind we see many things.'

Madame Ezekiel closed her green eyes. She had remarkably long eyelashes; her skin was pale, and her black hair was never still – it drifted gently around her head, in the silks, as if it were floating on distant tides.

'There is a traditional way,' she told me. 'A way to wash off a bad shape. You stand in running water, in clear spring water, while eating white rose petals.'

'And then?'

'The shape of darkness will be washed from you.'

'It will return,' I told her, 'with the next full of the moon.'

'So,' said Madame Ezekiel, 'once the shape is washed from you, you open your veins in the running water. It will sting mightily, of course. But the river will carry the blood away.'

She was dressed in silks, in scarves and cloths of a hundred different colours, each bright and vivid, even in the muted light of the candles.

Her eyes opened.

'Now,' she said, 'the tarot.' She unwrapped her deck from the black silk scarf that held it, passed me the cards to shuffle. I fanned them, riffed and bridged them.

'Slower, slower,' she said. 'Let them get to know you. Let them love you, like . . . like a woman would love you.'

I held them tightly, then passed them back to her.

She turned over the first card. It was called *The Warwolf.* It showed darkness and amber eyes, a smile in white and red.

Her green eyes showed confusion. They were the green of emeralds. 'This is not a card from my deck,' she said and turned over the next card. 'What did you do to my cards?'

'Nothing, ma'am. I just held them. That's all.'

The card she had turned over was *The Deep One.* It showed something green and faintly octopoid. The thing's mouths – if they were indeed mouths and not tentacles – began to writhe on the card as I watched.

She covered it with another card, and then another, and another. The rest of the cards were blank pasteboard.

'Did you do that?' She sounded on the verge of tears.

'No.'

'Go now,' she said.

'But—'

'*Go.*' She looked down, as if trying to convince herself I no longer existed.

I stood up, in the room that smelled of incense and candlewax, and looked out of her window, across the street. A light flashed briefly in my office window. Two men with flashlights were walking around. They opened the empty filing cabinet, peered around, then took up their positions, one in the armchair, the other behind the door, waiting for me to return. I smiled to myself. It was cold and inhospitable in my office, and with any luck they would wait there for hours until they finally decided I wasn't coming back.

So I left Madame Ezekiel turning over her cards, one by one, staring at them as if that would make the pictures return; and I went downstairs and walked back down Marsh Street until I reached the bar.

The place was empty now; the barman was smoking a cigarette, which he stubbed out as I came in.

'Where are the chess fiends?'

'It's a big night for them tonight. They'll be down at the bay. Let's see. You're a Jack Daniel's? Right?'

'Sounds good.'

He poured it for me. I recognised the thumbprint from the last time I had the glass. I picked up the volume of Tennyson poems from the bar top.

'Good book?'

The fox-haired barman took his book from me, opened it, and read:

'Below the thunders of the upper deep;

Far, far beneath in the abysmal sea,

His ancient dreamless, uninvaded sleep

The Kraken sleepeth . . .'

I'd finished my drink. 'So? What's your point?'

He walked around the bar, took me over to the window. 'See? Out there?'

He pointed toward the west of the town, toward

the cliffs. As I stared a bonfire was kindled on the cliff tops; it flared and began to burn with a copper-green flame.

'They're going to wake the Deep Ones,' said the barman. 'The stars and the planets and the moon are all in the right places. It's time. The dry lands will sink, and the seas shall rise...'

' "For the world shall be cleansed with ice and floods, and I'll thank you to keep to your own shelf in the refrigerator," ' I said.

'Sorry?'

'Nothing. What's the quickest way to get up to those cliffs?'

'Back up Marsh Street. Hang a left at the Church of Dagon till you reach Manuxet Way, then just keep on going.' He pulled a coat off the back of the door and put it on. 'C'mon. I'll walk you up there. I'd hate to miss any of the fun.'

'You sure?'

'No one in town's going to be drinking tonight.' We stepped out, and he locked the door to the bar behind us.

It was chilly in the street, and fallen snow blew about the ground like white mists. From street level, I could no longer tell if Madame Ezekiel was in her den above her neon sign or if my guests were still waiting for me in my office.

We put our heads down against the wind, and we walked.

Over the noise of the wind I heard the barman talking to himself:

'Winnow with giant arms the slumbering green,' he was saying.

'There hath he lain for ages and will lie

Battening upon huge seaworms in his sleep,
Until the latter fire shall heat the deep;
Then once by men and angels to be seen,
In roaring he shall rise . . .'

He stopped there, and we walked on together in silence with blown snow stinging our faces.

And on the surface die, I thought, but said nothing out loud.

Twenty minutes' walking and we were out of Innsmouth. Manuxet Way stopped when we left the town, and it became a narrow dirt path, partly covered with snow and ice, and we slipped and slid our way up it in the darkness.

The moon was not yet up, but the stars had already begun to come out. There were so many of them. They were sprinkled like diamond dust and crushed sapphires across the night sky. You can see so many stars from the seashore, more than you could ever see back in the city.

At the top of the cliff, behind the bonfire, two people were waiting – one huge and fat, one much smaller. The barman left my side and walked over to stand beside them, facing me.

'Behold,' he said, 'the sacrificial wolf.' There was now an oddly familiar quality to his voice.

I didn't say anything. The fire was burning with green flames, and it lit the three of them from below: classic spook lighting.

'Do you know why I brought you up here?' asked the barman, and I knew then why his voice was familiar: it was the voice of the man who had attempted to sell me aluminum siding.

'To stop the world ending?'

He laughed at me then.

The second figure was the fat man I had found asleep in my office chair. 'Well, if you're going to get eschatalogical about it . . .' he murmured in a voice deep enough to rattle walls. His eyes were closed. He was fast asleep.

The third figure was shrouded in dark silks and smelled of patchouli oil. It held a knife. It said nothing.

'This night,' said the barman, 'the moon is the moon of the Deep Ones. This night are the stars configured in the shapes and patterns of the dark old times. This night, if we call them, they will come. If our sacrifice is worthy. If our cries are heard.'

The moon rose, huge and amber and heavy, on the other side of the bay, and a chorus of low croaking rose with it from the ocean far beneath us.

Moonlight on snow and ice is not daylight, but it will do. And my eyes were getting sharper with the moon: in the cold waters men like frogs were surfacing and submerging in a slow water dance. Men like frogs, and women, too: it seemed to me that I could see my landlady down there, writhing and croaking in the bay with the rest of them.

It was too soon for another change; I was still exhausted from the night before; but I felt strange under that amber moon.

'Poor wolf-man,' came a whisper from the silks. 'All his dreams have come to this: a lonely death upon a distant cliff.'

I will dream if I want to, I said, *and my death is my own affair*. But I was unsure if I had said it out loud.

Senses heighten in the moon's light; I heard the roar of the ocean still, but now, overlaid on top of it, I could hear each wave rise and crash; I heard the splash of the frog people; I heard the drowned whispers of the dead in the bay; I heard the creak of green wrecks far beneath the ocean.

Smell improves, too. The aluminum siding man was human, while the fat man had other blood in him.

And the figure in the silks . . .

I had smelled her perfume when I wore man-shape. Now I could smell something else, less heady, beneath it. A smell of decay, of putrefying meat and rotten flesh.

The silks fluttered. She was moving toward me. She held the knife.

'Madame Ezekiel?' My voice was roughening and coarsening. Soon I would lose it all. I didn't understand what was happening, but the moon was rising higher and higher, losing its amber colour and filling my mind with its pale light.

'Madame Ezekiel?'

'You deserve to die,' she said, her voice cold and low. 'If only for what you did to my cards. They were old.'

'I don't die,' I told her. ' "Even a man who is pure in heart, and says his prayers by night." Remember?'

'It's bullshit,' she said. 'You know what the oldest way to end the curse of the werewolf is?'

'No.'

The bonfire burned brighter now; burned with the green of the world beneath the sea, the green of algae and of slowly drifting weed; burned with the colour of emeralds.

'You simply wait till they're in human shape, a whole month away from another change; then you take the sacrificial knife and you kill them. That's all.'

I turned to run, but the barman was behind me, pulling my arms, twisting my wrists up into the small of my back. The knife glinted pale silver in the moon-light. Madame Ezekiel smiled.

She sliced across my throat.

Blood began to gush and then to flow. And then it slowed and stopped . . .

—The pounding in the front of my head, the pressure in the back. All a roiling change a how-wow-row-now change a red wall coming toward me from the night

—I tasted stars dissolved in brine, fizzy and distant and salt

—my fingers prickled with pins and my skin was lashed with tongues of flame my eyes were topaz I could taste the night

My breath steamed and billowed in the icy air.

I growled involuntarily, low in my throat. My forepaws were touching the snow.

I pulled back, tensed, and sprang at her.

There was a sense of corruption that hung in the air, like a mist, surrounding me. High in my leap, I seemed to pause, and something burst like a soap bubble . . .

I was deep, deep in the darkness under the sea, standing on all fours on a slimy rock floor at the entrance of some kind of citadel built of enormous rough-hewn stones. The stones gave off a pale glow-in-the-dark light; a ghostly luminescence, like the hands of a watch.

A cloud of black blood trickled from my neck.

She was standing in the doorway in front of me. She was now six, maybe seven feet high. There was flesh on her skeletal bones, pitted and gnawed, but the silks were weeds, drifting in the cold water, down there in the dreamless deeps. They hid her face like a slow green veil.

There were limpets growing on the upper surfaces of her arms and on the flesh that hung from her ribcage.

I felt like I was being crushed. I couldn't think anymore.

She moved toward me. The weed that surrounded her head shifted. She had a face like the stuff you don't want to eat in a sushi counter, all suckers and spines and drifting anemone fronds; and somewhere in all that I knew she was smiling.

I pushed with my hind legs. We met there, in the deep, and we struggled. It was so cold, so dark. I closed my jaws on her face and felt something rend and tear.

It was almost a kiss, down there in the abysmal deep . . .

I landed softly on the snow, a silk scarf locked between my jaws. The other scarves were fluttering to the ground. Madame Ezekiel was nowhere to be seen.

The silver knife lay on the ground in the snow. I waited on all fours in the moonlight, soaking wet. I shook myself, spraying the brine about. I heard it hiss and spit when it hit the fire.

I was dizzy and weak. I pulled the air deep into my lungs.

Down, far below, in the bay, I could see the frog people hanging on the surface of the sea like dead things; for a handful of seconds, they drifted back and forth on the tide, then they twisted and leapt, and each by each they *plop-plopped* down into the bay and vanished beneath the sea.

There was a scream. It was the fox-haired bartender, the popeyed aluminum siding salesman, and he was staring at the night sky, at the clouds that were drifting in, covering the stars, and he was screaming. There was rage and there was frustration in that cry, and it scared me.

He picked up the knife from the ground, wiped the snow from the handle with his fingers, wiped the blood from the blade with his coat. Then he looked across at me. He was crying. 'You bastard,' he said. 'What did you do to her?'

I would have told him I didn't do anything to her, that she was still on guard far beneath the ocean, but I couldn't talk any more, only growl and whine and howl.

He was crying. He stank of insanity and of disappointment. He raised the knife and ran at me, and I moved to one side.

Some people just can't adjust even to tiny changes. The barman stumbled past me, off the cliff, into nothing.

In the moonlight blood is black, not red, and the marks he left on the cliff side as he fell and bounced and fell were smudges of black and dark grey. Then, finally, he lay still on the icy rocks at the base of the cliff until an arm reached out from the sea and dragged him, with a slowness that was almost painful to watch, under the dark water.

A hand scratched the back of my head. It felt good.

'What was she? Just an avatar of the Deep Ones, sir. An eidolon, a manifestation, if you will, sent up to us from the uttermost deeps to bring about the end of the world.'

I bristled.

'No, it's over – for now. You disrupted her, sir. And the ritual is most specific. Three of us must stand together and call the sacred names while innocent blood pools and pulses at our feet.'

I looked up at the fat man and whined a query. He

patted me on the back of the neck sleepily.

'Of course she doesn't love you, boy. She hardly even exists on this plane in any material sense.'

The snow began to fall once more. The bonfire was going out.

'Your change tonight, incidentally, I would opine, is a direct result of the self-same celestial configurations and lunar forces that made tonight such a perfect night to bring back my old friends from Underneath . . .'

He continued talking in his deep voice, and perhaps he was telling me important things. I'll never know, for the appetite was growing inside me, and his words had lost all but the shadow of any meaning; I had no further interest in the sea or the cliff-top or the fat man.

There were deer running in the woods beyond the meadow: I could smell them on the winter's night's air.

And I was, above all things, hungry.

I was naked when I came to myself again, early the next morning, a half-eaten deer next to me in the snow. A fly crawled across its eye, and its tongue lolled out of its dead mouth, making it look comical and pathetic, like an animal in a newspaper cartoon.

The snow was stained a fluorescent crimson where the deer's belly had been torn out.

My face and chest were sticky and red with the stuff. My throat was scabbed and scarred, and it stung; by the next full moon, it would be whole once more.

The sun was a long way away, small and yellow, but the sky was blue and cloudless, and there was no breeze. I could hear the roar of the sea some distance away.

I was cold and naked and bloody and alone. *Ah well*, I thought, *it happens to all of us in the beginning. I just get it once a month.*

I was painfully exhausted, but I would hold out until I found a deserted barn or a cave; and then I was going to sleep for a couple of weeks.

A hawk flew low over the snow toward me with something dangling from its talons. It hovered above me for a heartbeat, then dropped a small grey squid in the snow at my feet and flew upward. The flaccid thing lay there, still and silent and tentacled in the bloody snow.

I took it as an omen, but whether good or bad I couldn't say and I didn't really care any more; I turned my back to the sea, and on the shadowy town of Innsmouth, and began to make my way toward the city.

Listen, Talbot. Somebody's killing my people,
said Roth, growling down the phone like the sea in a
     shell.
Find out who and why and stop them.

Stop them how? I asked.

Whatever it takes, he said. *But I don't want them walking
     away*
after you stopped them, if you get me.
And I got him. And I was hired.

Now you listen: this was back in the twenty-twenties
in L.A., down on Venice Beach.
Gar Roth owned the business in that part of the world,
dealt in stims and pumps and steroids,
recreationals, built up quite a following.
All the buff kids, boys in thongs popping pumpers,
girls popping curves and fearmoans and whoremoans,
all of them loved Roth. He had the shit.
The force took his payoffs to look the other way;

 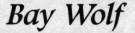

he owned the beach world, from Laguna Beach north
    to Malibu,
built a beach hall where the buff and the curvy
hung and sucked and flaunted.

Oh, but that city worshipped the flesh; and theirs was
    the flesh.
They were partying. Everyone was partying,
dusted, shot up, cranked out,
the music was so loud you could hear it with your
    bones,
and that was when something took them, quietly,
whatever it was. It cracked their heads. It tore them
    into offal.
No one heard the screams over the boom of the oldies
    and the surf.
That was the year of the death metal revival.
It took maybe a dozen of them away, dragged them
    into the sea,
death in the early morning.
Roth said he thought it was a rival drug cartel,
posted more guards, had choppers circling, floaters
    watching
for when it came back. As it did, again, again.
But the cameras and the vids showed nothing at all.

They had no idea what it was, but still,
it ripped them limb from limb and head from neck,
tore saline bags out from ballooning breasts,
left steroid-shrunken testes on the beach
like tiny world-shaped creatures in the sand.
Roth had been hurt: The beach was not the same,
and that was when he called me on the phone.

I stepped over several sleeping cuties of all sexes,
tapped Roth on the shoulder. Before
I could blink, a dozen big guns
were pointing at my chest and head,
so I said, *Hey, I'm not a monster.*
Well, I'm not your monster, anyway.
Not yet.

I gave him my card. *Talbot*, he said.
You're the adjuster I spoke to?
That's right, I told him, tough-talking in the afternoon,
and you got stuff that needs adjusting.
This is the deal, I said.
I take your problem out. You pay and pay and pay.

Roth said, *Sure, like we said. Whatever. Deal.*
Me? I'm thinking it's the Eurisraeli Mafia
or the Chinks. You scared of them?

No, I told him. *Not scared.*

I kind of wished I'd been there in the glory days:
Now Roth's pretty people were getting kind of thin on
    the ground,
none of them, close up,
as plump and curvy as they'd seemed from farther
    away.

At dusk the party starts.
I tell Roth that I hated death metal the first time
    around.
He says I must be older than I look.
They play real loud. The speakers make the seashore
    pump and thump.

I strip down then for action and I wait
on four legs in the hollow of a dune.
And days and nights I wait. And wait. And wait.

Where the fuck are you and your people?
asked Roth on the third day. *What the fuck am I paying
    you for?*
Nothing on the beach last night but some big dog.
But I just smiled. *No sign of the problem so far, whatever
    it is,*
I said.
And I've been here all the time.
I tell you it's the Israeli Mafia, he said.
I never trusted those Europeans.

Third night comes.
The moon is huge and a chemical red.
Two of them are playing in the surf.
boy and girl play,
the hormones still a little ahead of the drugs. She's
    giggling,
and the surf crashes slowly.
It would be suicide if the enemy came every night.
But the enemy does not come every night,
so they run through the surf,
splashing, screaming with pleasure. I got sharp ears
(all the better to hear them with) and good eyes
(all the better to see them with)
and they're so fucking young and happy fucking I could
    spit.

The hardest thing, for such a one as me:
the gift of death should go to such as those.
She screamed first. The red moon was high

and just a day past full.
I watched her tumble into the surf, as if
the water were twenty feet deep, not two,
as if she were being sucked under. The boy just ran,
a stream of clear piss splashing from the jut in his speedos,
stumbling and wailing and away.

It came out of the water slowly, like a man in bad
    monster movie makeup.
It carried the bronzed girl in its arms. I yawned,
like big dogs yawn, and licked my flanks.

The creature bit the girl's face off, dropped what was
    left on the sand,
and I thought: *meat and chemicals, how quickly they
become meat and chemicals, just one bite and they're
meat and chemicals . . .*
Roth's men came down then with fear in their eyes,
automatic weapons in their hands. It picked them up
and ripped them open, dropped them on the moonlit
    sand.

The thing walked stiffly up the beach, white sand
    adhering
to its green-gray feet, webbed and clawed.
Top of the world, Ma, it howled.
What kind of mother, I thought, *gives birth to something
    like that?*
And from high on the beach I could hear Roth
    screaming, *Talbot,*
Talbot you asshole. Where are you?

I got up and stretched and loped naked down the beach.
Well, hi, I said.

Hey, pooch, he said.
I'm gonna rip your hairy leg off and push it down your
*   throat.*
That's no way to say hi, I told him.
I'm Grand Al, he said.
And who are you? Jojo the yapping dog-faced boy?
I'm going to whip and rip and tear you into shit.

Avaunt, foul beast, I said.
He stared at me with eyes that glittered like two crack
    pipes.
Avaunt? Shit, boy. Who's going to make me?
Me, I quipped. *I am.*
I'm one of the avaunt guard.
He just looked blank, and hurt, a bit confused, and
for a moment I almost felt sorry for him.

And then the moon came out from behind a cloud,
and I began to howl.

His skin was fishskin pale,
his teeth were sharp as sharks',
his fingers were webbed and clawed,
and, growling, he lunged for my throat.

And he said, *What are you?*
He said, *Ow, no, ow.*
He said, *Hey, shit, this isn't fair.*
Then he said nothing at all, not words now,
no more words,
because I had ripped off his arm
and left it,
fingers spastically clutching nothing,
on the beach.

Grand Al ran for the waves, and I loped after him.
The waves were salt: his blood stank.
I could taste it, black in my mouth.

He swam, and I followed, down and down,
and when I felt my lungs bursting,
the world crushing my throat and head and mind and
    chest,
monsters turning to suffocate me,
we came into the tumbled wreckage of an offshore oil
    rig,
and that was where Grand Al had gone to die.

This must have been the place that he was spawned,
this rusting rig abandoned in the sea.
He was three-quarters dead when I arrived.
I left him to die: weird fishy food he would have been,
a dish of stray prions. Dangerous meat. But still,
I kicked him in the jaw, stole one sharklike tooth
that I'd knocked loose, to bring me luck.
She came upon me then, all fang and claw.

Why should it be so strange that the beast had a
    mother?
So many of us have mothers.
Go back fifty years and everyone had a mother.

She wailed for her son, she wailed and keened.
She asked me how I could be so unkind.
She squatted, stroked his face, and then she groaned.
After, we spoke, hunting for common ground.

What we did is no business of yours.
It was no more than you or I have done before,

And whether I loved her or I killed her, her son was
    dead as the gulf.

Rolling, pelt to scales,
her neck between my teeth,
my claws raking her back . . .
Lalalalalala. This is the oldest song.

Later I walked out of the surf.
Roth was waiting in the dawn.
I dropped Grand Al's head down upon the beach,
fine white sand clung in clumps to the wet eyes.

This was your problem, I told him.
Yeah, he's dead, I said.
And now? he asked.
Danegeld, I told him.

You think he was working for the Chinks? he asked.
Or the Eurisraeli Mafia? Or who?
He was a neighbour, I said. *Wanted you to keep the noise
    down.*
You think? he said.
I know, I told him, looking at the head.
Where did he come from? asked Roth.
I pulled my clothes on, tired from the change.
Meat and chemicals, I whispered.

He knew I lied, but wolves are born to lie.
I sat down on the beach to watch the bay,
stared at the sky as dawn turned into day,
and daydreamed of a day when I might die.

Fifteen Painted Cards from a Vampire Tarot

0. The Fool

'What do you want?'

The young man had come to the graveyard every night for a month now. He had watched the moon paint the cold granite and the fresh marble and the old moss-covered stones and statues in its cold light. He had started at shadows and at owls. He had watched courting couples, and drunks, and teenagers taking nervous shortcuts: all the people who come through the graveyard at night.

He slept in the day. Nobody cared. He stood alone in the night and shivered, in the cold. It came to him then that he was standing on the edge of a precipice.

The voice came from the night all around him, in his head and out of it.

'What do you want?' it repeated.

He wondered if he dared to turn and look, realised he did not.

'Well? You come here every night, in a place where the living are not welcome. I have seen you. Why?'

'I wanted to meet you,' he said, without looking around. 'I want to live for ever.' His voice cracked as he said it.

He had stepped over the precipice. There was no going back. In his imagination, he could already feel the prick of needle-sharp fangs in his neck, a sharp prelude to eternal life.

The sound began. It was low and sad, like the rushing of an underground river. It took him several long seconds to recognise it as laughter.

'This is not life,' said the voice.

It said nothing more, and after a while the young man knew he was alone in the graveyard.

1. The Magician

They asked St Germain's manservant if his master was truly a thousand years old, as it was rumoured he had claimed.

'How would I know?' the man replied. 'I have only been in the master's employ for three hundred years.'

2. The Priestess

Her skin was pale, and her eyes were dark and her hair was dyed a raven black. She went on a daytime talk show and proclaimed herself a vampire queen. She showed the cameras her dentally crafted fangs, and brought on ex-lovers who, in various stages of embarrassment, admitted that she had drawn their blood, and that she drank it.

'You can be seen in a mirror, though?' asked the talk show hostess. She was the richest woman in America, and had got that way by bringing the freaks and the hurt and the lost out in front of her cameras, and showing their pain to the world.

The studio audience laughed.

The woman seemed slightly affronted. 'Yes. Contrary to what people may think, vampires can be seen in mirrors and on television cameras.'

'Well, that's one thing you finally got right, honey,' said the hostess of the daytime talk show. But she put her hand over her microphone as she said it, and it was never broadcast.

5. The Pope

This is my body, he said, two thousand years ago. *This is my blood.*

It was the only religion that delivered exactly what it promised: life eternal, for its adherents.

There are some of us alive today who remember him. And some of us claim that he was a messiah, and some think that he was just a man with very special powers. But that misses the point. Whatever he was, he changed the world.

6. The Lovers

After she was dead, she began to come to him, in the night. He grew pale, and there were deep circles under his eyes. At first, they thought he was mourning her. And then, one night, he was gone from the village.

It was hard for them to get permission to disinter her, but get it they did. They hauled up the coffin and they unscrewed it. Then they prized what they found out of the box. There was six inches of water in the bottom of the box: the iron had coloured it a deep, orangish red. There were two bodies in the coffin: hers, of course, and his. He was more decayed than she was. Later, someone wondered aloud how both of them had fitted in a coffin built for one. Especially given her condition, he said; for she was very obviously very pregnant.

This caused some confusion, for she had not been noticeably pregnant when she was buried.

Still later they dug her up for one last time, at the request of the church authorities, who had heard rumours of what had been found in the grave. Her stomach was flat. The local doctor told them all that it had just been gas and bloating as the stomach swelled. The townsfolk nodded sagely, almost as if they believed him.

7. The Chariot

It was genetic engineering at its finest: they created a breed of human to sail the stars: they needed to be possessed of impossibly long life-spans, for the distances between the stars were vast; space was limited, and their food supplies needed to be compact; they needed to be able to process local sustenance, and to colonise the worlds they found with their own kind.

The homeworld wished the colonists well, and sent them on their way. They removed all traces of their location from the ships' computers first, however, to be on the safe side.

10. The Wheel of Fortune

What did you do with the doctor? she asked, and laughed. I thought the doctor came in here ten minutes ago.

I'm sorry, I said. I was hungry. And we both laughed.

I'll go find her for you, she said.

I sat in the doctor's office, picking my teeth. After a while the assistant came back.

I'm sorry, she said. The doctor must have stepped out for a while. Can I make an appointment for you for next week?

I shook my head. I'll call, I said. But, for the first time that day, I was lying.

11. Justice

'It is not human,' said the magistrate, 'and it does not deserve the trial of a human thing.'

'Ah,' said the advocate. 'But we cannot execute without a trial: there are the precedents. A pig, that had eaten a child who had fallen into its sty. It was found guilty and hanged. A swarm of bees, found guilty of stinging an old man to death, was burned by the public hangman. We owe the hellish creature no less.'

The evidence against the baby was incontestable. It amounted to this: a woman had brought the baby from the country. She said it was hers, and that her husband was dead. She lodged at the house of a coach maker and his wife. The old coach maker complained of melancholia and lassitude, and was, with his wife and their lodger, found dead by their servant. The baby was alive in its cradle, pale and wide-eyed, and there was blood on its face and lips.

The jury found the little thing guilty, beyond all doubt, and condemned it to death.

The executioner was the town butcher. In the sight of all the town he cut the babe in two, and flung the pieces onto the fire.

His own baby had died earlier that same week. Infant mortality in those days was a hard thing but common. The butcher's wife had been brokenhearted.

She had already left the town, to see her sister in the city, and, within the week, the butcher joined her. The three of them – butcher, wife and babe – made the prettiest family you ever did see.

14. Temperance

She said she was a vampire. One thing I knew already, the woman was a liar. You could see it in her eyes. Black as coals they were, but she never quite looked at you, staring at invisibles over your shoulder, behind you, above you, two inches in front of your face.

'What does it taste like?' I asked her. This was in the parking lot, behind the bar. She worked the graveyard shift in the bar, mixed the finest drinks but never drank anything herself.

'V8 juice,' she said. 'Not the low-sodium kind, but the original. Or a salty gazpacho.'

'What's gazpacho?'

'A sort of cold vegetable soup.'

'You're shitting me.'

'No.'

'So you drink blood? Just like I drink V8?'

'Not exactly,' she said. 'If *you* get sick of drinking V8 you can drink something else.'

'Yeah,' I said. 'Actually, I don't like V8 much.'

'See?' she said. 'In China it's not blood we drink, it's spinal fluid.'

'What's that taste like?'

'Nothing much. Clear broth.'

'You've tried it?'

'I know people.'

I tried to figure out if I could see her reflection in the wing mirror of the truck we were leaning against, but it was dark, and I couldn't tell.

15. The Devil

This is his portrait. Look at his flat, yellow teeth, his ruddy face. He has horns, and he carries a foot-long wooden stake in one hand, and his wooden mallet in the other.

Of course, there is no such thing as the devil.

16. The Tower

The tower's built of stone and spite,
Without a sound, without a sight,
– The biter bit, the bitter bite
(It's better to be out at night).

17. The Star

The older, richer, ones follow the winter, taking the long nights where they find them. Still, they prefer the northern hemisphere to the south.

'You see that star?' they say, pointing to one of the stars in the constellation of Draco, the Dragon. 'We came from there. One day we shall return.'

The younger ones sneer and jeer and laugh at this. Still, as the years become centuries, they find themselves becoming homesick for a place they have never been; and they find the northern climes reassuring, as long as Draco twines about the greater and lesser Bears, up near chill Polaris.

19. The Sun

'Imagine', she said, 'that there was something in the sky that was going to hurt you, perhaps even kill you. A huge eagle or something. Imagine that if you went out in daylight the eagle would get you.'

'Well,' she said. 'That's how it is for us. Only it's not a bird. It's bright, beautiful, dangerous daylight, and I haven't seen it now in a hundred years.'

20. Judgement

It's a way of talking about lust without talking about lust, he told them.

It is a way of talking about sex, and fear of sex, and death, and fear of death, and what else is there to talk about?

22. The World

'You know the saddest thing,' she said. 'The saddest thing is that we're you.'

I said nothing.

'In your fantasies,' she said, 'my people are just like you. Only better. We don't die, or age, or suffer from pain or cold or thirst. We're snappier dressers. We possess the wisdom of the ages. And if we crave blood, well, it is no more than the way you people crave food, or affection, or sunlight – and besides, it gets us out of the house. Crypt. Coffin. Whatever. That's the fantasy.'

'And the reality is?' I asked her.

'We're you,' she said. 'We're you, with all your fuckups and all the things that make you human – all your fears and lonelinesses and confusions . . . none of that gets better.

'But we're colder than you are. Deader. I miss daylight and food and knowing how it feels to touch someone and care. I remember life, and meeting people as people and not just as things to feed on or control, and I remember what it was to *feel* something, anything, happy or sad or *anything* . . .' And then she stopped.

'Are you crying?' I asked.

'We don't cry,' she told me.

Like I said, the woman was a liar.

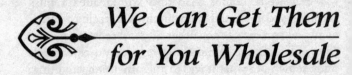

We Can Get Them for You Wholesale

*P*eter Pinter had never heard of Aristippus of the Cyrenaics, a lesser-known follower of Socrates who maintained that the avoidance of trouble was the highest attainable good; however, he had lived his uneventful life according to this precept. In all respects except one (an inability to pass up a bargain, and which of us is entirely free from that?), he was a very moderate man. He did not go to extremes. His speech was proper and reserved; he rarely overate; he drank enough to be sociable and no more; he was far from rich and in no wise poor. He liked people and people liked him. Bearing all that in mind, would you expect to find him in a lowlife pub on the seamier side of London's East End, taking out what is colloquially known as a 'contract' on someone he hardly knew? You would not. You would not even expect to find him in the pub.

And until a certain Friday afternoon, you would have been right. But the love of a woman can do strange things to a man, even one so colourless as Peter Pinter, and the discovery that Miss Gwendolyn Thorpe, twenty-three years of age, of 9, Oaktree Terrace, Purley, was messing about (as the vulgar would put it) with a smooth young gentleman from the accounting department – *after*, mark you, she had consented to wear an engagement ring, composed of real ruby chips, nine-carat gold, and something that might well have been a diamond (£37.50) that it had taken Peter almost an entire lunch hour to choose – can do very strange things to a man indeed.

After he made this shocking discovery, Peter spent a sleepless Friday night, tossing and turning with visions of Gwendolyn and Archie Gibbons (the Don Juan of the Clamages accounting department) dancing and swimming before his eyes – performing acts that even Peter, if he were pressed, would have to admit were most improbable. But the bile of jealousy had risen up within him, and by the morning Peter had resolved that his rival should be done away with.

Saturday morning was spent wondering how one contacted an assassin, for, to the best of Peter's knowledge, none were employed by Clamages (the department store that employed all three of the members of our eternal triangle and, incidentally, furnished the ring), and he was wary of asking anyone outright for fear of attracting attention to himself.

Thus it was that Saturday afternoon found him hunting through the Yellow Pages.

ASSASSINS, he found, was not between ASPHALT CONTRACTORS and ASSESSORS (QUANTITY); KILLERS was not between KENNELS and KINDERGARTENS; MURDERERS was not between MOWERS and MUSEUMS. PEST CONTROL looked promising; however closer investigation of the pest control advertisements showed them to be almost solely concerned with 'rats, mice, fleas, cockroaches, rabbits, moles and rats' (to quote from one that Peter felt was rather hard on rats) and not really what he had in mind. Even so, being of a careful nature, he dutifully inspected the entries in that category, and at the bottom of the second page, in small print, he found a firm that looked promising.

'*Complete discreet disposal of irksome and unwanted mammals, etc.*' went the entry, '*Ketch, Hare, Burke and Ketch. The Old Firm.*' It went on to give no address, but only a telephone number.

Peter dialled the number, surprising himself by so doing. His heart pounded in his chest, and he tried to look nonchalant. The telephone rang once, twice, three times. Peter was just starting to hope that it would not be answered and he could forget the whole thing when there was a click and a brisk young female voice said, 'Ketch Hare Burke Ketch. Can I help you?'

Carefully not giving his name, Peter said, 'Er, how big – I mean, what size mammals do you go up to? To, uh, dispose of?'

'Well, that would all depend on what size sir requires.'

He plucked up all his courage. 'A person?'

Her voice remained brisk and unruffled. 'Of course, sir. Do you have a pen and paper handy? Good. Be at the Dirty Donkey pub, off Little Courtney Street, E3, tonight at eight o'clock. Carry a rolled-up copy of the *Financial Times* – that's the pink one, sir – and our operative will approach you there.' Then she put down the phone.

Peter was elated. It had been far easier than he had imagined. He went down to the newsagent's and bought a copy of the *Financial Times*, found Little Courtney Street in his *A–Z of London*, and spent the rest of the afternoon watching football on the television and imagining the smooth young gentleman from accounting's funeral.

It took Peter a while to find the pub. Eventually he spotted the pub sign, which showed a donkey and was indeed remarkably dirty.

The Dirty Donkey was a small and more or less filthy pub, poorly lit, in which knots of unshaven people wearing dusty donkey jackets stood around eyeing each other suspiciously, eating crisps and drinking pints of Guinness, a drink that Peter had never cared for. Peter held his *Financial Times* under one arm as conspicuously as he could, but no one approached him, so he bought a half of shandy and retreated to a corner table. Unable to think of anything else to do while waiting, he tried to read the paper, but, lost and confused by a maze of grain futures and a rubber company that was selling something or other short (quite what the short somethings were he could not tell), he gave it up and stared at the door.

He had waited almost ten minutes when a small busy man hustled in, looked quickly around him, then came straight over to Peter's table and sat down.

He stuck out his hand. 'Kemble. Burton Kemble of Ketch Hare Burke Ketch. I hear you have a job for us.'

He didn't look like a killer. Peter said so.

'Oh, lor' bless us, no. I'm not actually part of our workforce, sir. I'm in sales.'

Peter nodded. That certainly made sense. 'Can we – er – talk freely here?'

'Sure. Nobody's interested. Now then, how many people would you like disposed of?'

'Only one. His name's Archibald Gibbons and he

works in Clamages accounting department. His address is . . .'

Kemble interrupted. 'We can go into all that later, sir, if you don't mind. Let's just quickly go over the financial side. First of all, the contract will cost you five hundred pounds . . .'

Peter nodded. He could afford that and in fact had expected to have to pay a little more.

'. . . although there's always the special offer,' Kemble concluded smoothly.

Peter's eyes shone. As I mentioned earlier, he loved a bargain and often bought things he had no imaginable use for in sales or on special offers. Apart from this one failing (one that so many of us share), he was a most moderate young man. 'Special offer?'

'Two for the price of one, sir.'

Mmm. Peter thought about it. That worked out at only £250 each, which couldn't be bad no matter how you looked at it. There was only one snag. 'I'm afraid I don't *have* anyone else I want killed.'

Kemble looked disappointed. 'That's a pity, sir. For two we could probably have even knocked the price down to, well, say four hundred and fifty pounds for the both of them.'

'Really?'

'Well, it gives our operatives something to do, sir. If you must know' – and here he dropped his voice – 'there really isn't enough work in this particular line to keep them occupied. Not like the old days. Isn't there just *one* other person you'd like to see dead?'

Peter pondered. He hated to pass up a bargain, but couldn't for the life of him think of anyone else. He liked people. Still, a bargain was a bargain . . .

'Look,' said Peter. 'Could I think about it and see you here tomorrow night?'

The salesman looked pleased. 'Of course, sir,' he said. 'I'm sure you'll be able to think of someone.'

The answer – the obvious answer – came to Peter as he was drifting off to sleep that night. He sat straight up in bed, fumbled the bedside light on, and wrote a name down on the back of an envelope, in case he forgot it. To tell the truth, he didn't think that he could forget it, for it was painfully obvious, but you can never tell with these late-night thoughts.

The name that he had written down on the back of the envelope was this: *Gwendolyn Thorpe*.

He turned the light off, rolled over, and was soon asleep, dreaming peaceful and remarkably unmurderous dreams.

Kemble was waiting for him when he arrived in the Dirty Donkey on Sunday night. Peter bought a drink and sat down beside him.

'I'm taking you up on the special offer,' he said by way of greeting.

Kemble nodded vigorously. 'A very wise decision, if you don't mind me saying so, sir.'

Peter Pinter smiled modestly, in the manner of one who read the *Financial Times* and made wise business decisions. 'That will be four hundred and fifty pounds, I believe?'

'Did I say four hundred and fifty pounds, sir? Good gracious me, I do apologize. I beg your pardon, I was thinking of our bulk rate. It would be four hundred and seventy-five pounds for two people.'

Disappointment mingled with cupidity on Peter's bland and youthful face. That was an extra £25.

However, something that Kemble had said caught his attention.

'Bulk rate?'

'Of course, but I doubt that sir would be interested in that.'

'No, no, I am. Tell me about it.'

'Very well, sir. Bulk rate, four hundred and fifty pounds, would be for a large job. Ten people.'

Peter wondered if he had heard correctly. 'Ten people? But that's only forty-five pounds each.'

'Yes, sir. It's the large order that makes it profitable.'

'I see,' said Peter, and 'Hmm,' said Peter, and 'Could you be here the same time tomorrow night?'

'Of course, sir.'

Upon arriving home, Peter got out a scrap of paper and a pen. He wrote the numbers one to ten down one side and then filled it in as follows:

1. . . . *Archie G.*

2. . . . *Gwennie.*

3. . . .

and so forth.

Having filled in the first two, he sat sucking his pen, hunting for wrongs done to him and people the world would be better off without.

He smoked a cigarette. He strolled around the room.

Aha! There was a physics teacher at a school he had attended who had delighted in making his life a misery. What was the man's name again? And for that matter, was he still alive? Peter wasn't sure, but he wrote *The Physics Teacher, Abbot Street Secondary School* next to the number three. The next came more easily – his department head had refused to raise his salary a couple of months back; that the raise had eventually come was immaterial. *Mr Hunterson* was number four.

When he was five, a boy named Simon Ellis had poured paint on his head while another boy named James somebody-or-other had held him down and a girl named Sharon Hartsharpe had laughed. They were numbers five through seven, respectively.

Who else?

There was the man on television with the annoying snicker who read the news. He went on the list. And what about the woman in the flat next door with the little yappy dog that shat in the hall? He put her and the dog down on nine. Ten was the hardest. He scratched his head and went into the kitchen for a cup of coffee, then dashed back and wrote *My Great-Uncle Mervyn* down in the tenth place. The old man was rumored to be quite affluent, and there was a possibility (albeit rather slim) that he could leave Peter some money.

With the satisfaction of an evening's work well done, he went off to bed.

Monday at Clamages was routine; Peter was a senior sales assistant in the books department, a job that actually entailed very little. He clutched his list tightly in his hand, deep in his pocket, rejoicing in the feeling of power that it gave him. He spent a most enjoyable lunch hour in the canteen with young Gwendolyn (who did not know that he had seen her and Archie enter the stockroom together) and even smiled at the smooth young man from the accounting department when he passed him in the corridor.

He proudly displayed his list to Kemble that evening.

The little salesman's face fell.

'I'm afraid this isn't ten people, Mr Pinter,' he

We Can Get Them for You Wholesale ⟶ 267

explained. 'You've counted the woman in the next-door flat *and* her dog as one person. That brings it to eleven, which would be an extra' – his pocket calculator was rapidly deployed – 'an extra seventy pounds. How about if we forget the dog?'

Peter shook his head. 'The dog's as bad as the woman. Or worse.'

'Then I'm afraid we have a slight problem. Unless . . .'

'What?'

'Unless you'd like to take advantage of our whole-sale rate. But of course sir wouldn't be . . .'

There are words that do things to people; words that make people's faces flush with joy, excitement, or passion. *Environmental* can be one; *occult* is another. *Wholesale* was Peter's. He leaned back in his chair. 'Tell me about it,' he said with the practised assurance of an experienced shopper.

'Well, sir,' said Kemble, allowing himself a little chuckle, 'we can, uh, *get* them for you wholesale, seventeen pounds fifty each, for every quarry after the first fifty, or a tenner each for every one over two hundred.'

'I suppose you'd go down to a fiver if I wanted a thousand people knocked off?'

'Oh no, sir,' Kemble looked shocked. 'If you're talking those sorts of figures, we can do them for a quid each.'

'One *pound*?'

'That's right, sir. There's not a big profit margin on it, but the high turnover and productivity more than justifies it.'

Kemble got up. 'Same time tomorrow, sir?'

Peter nodded.

One thousand pounds. One thousand people. Peter Pinter didn't even *know* a thousand people. Even so . . . there were the Houses of Parliament. He didn't like politicians; they squabbled and argued and carried on so.

And for that matter . . .

An idea, shocking in its audacity. Bold. Daring. Still, the idea was there and it wouldn't go away. A distant cousin of his had married the younger brother of an earl or a baron or something . . .

On the way home from work that afternoon, he stopped off at a little shop that he had passed a thousand times without entering. It had a large sign in the window – guaranteeing to trace your lineage for you and even draw up a coat of arms if you happened to have mislaid your own – and an impressive heraldic map.

They were very helpful and phoned him up just after seven to give him their news.

If approximately fourteen million, seventy-two thousand, eight hundred and eleven people died, he, Peter Pinter, would be *King of England*.

He didn't have fourteen million, seventy-two thousand, eight hundred and eleven pounds: but he suspected that when you were talking in those figures, Mr Kemble would have one of his special discounts.

Mr Kemble did.

He didn't even raise an eyebrow.

'Actually,' he explained, 'it works out quite cheaply; you see, we wouldn't have to do them all individually. Small-scale nuclear weapons, some judicious bombing, gassing, plague, dropping radios in swimming pools, and then mopping up the stragglers. Say four thousand pounds.'

'Four thou—? That's incredible!'

The salesman looked pleased with himself. 'Our operatives will be glad of the work, sir.' He grinned. 'We pride ourselves on servicing our wholesale customers.'

The wind blew cold as Peter left the pub, setting the old sign swinging. It didn't look much like a dirty donkey, thought Peter. More like a pale horse.

Peter was drifting off to sleep that night, mentally rehearsing his coronation speech, when a thought drifted into his head and hung around. It would not go away. Could he – could he *possibly* be passing up an even larger saving than he already had? Could he be missing out on a bargain?

Peter climbed out of bed and walked over to the phone. It was almost 3 A.M., but even so . . .

His Yellow Pages lay open where he had left it the previous Saturday, and he dialled the number.

The phone seemed to ring forever. There was a click and a bored voice said, 'Burke Hare Ketch. Can I help you?'

'I hope I'm not phoning too late . . .' he began.

'Of course not, sir.'

'I was wondering if I could speak to Mr Kemble.'

'Can you hold? I'll see if he's available.'

Peter waited for a couple of minutes, listening to the ghostly crackles and whispers that always echo down empty phone lines.

'Are you there, caller?'

'Yes, I'm here.'

'Putting you through.' There was a buzz, then 'Kemble speaking.'

'Ah, Mr Kemble. Hello. Sorry if I got you out of bed or anything. This is, um, Peter Pinter.'

 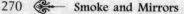

'Yes, Mr Pinter?'

'Well, I'm sorry it's so late, only I was wondering . . . How much would it cost to kill everybody? Everybody in the world?'

'Everybody? All the people?'

'Yes. How much? I mean, for an order like that, you'd have to have some kind of a big discount. How much would it be? For everyone?'

'Nothing at all, Mr Pinter.'

'You mean you wouldn't do it?'

'I mean we'd do it for nothing, Mr Pinter. We only have to be asked, you see. We always have to be asked.'

Peter was puzzled. 'But – when would you start?'

'Start? Right away. Now. We've been ready for a long time. But we had to be asked, Mr Pinter. Good night. It *has* been a *pleasure* doing business with you.'

The line went dead.

Peter felt strange. Everything seemed very distant. He wanted to sit down. What on earth had the man meant? 'We always have to be asked.' It was definitely strange. Nobody does anything for nothing in this world; he had a good mind to phone Kemble back and call the whole thing off. Perhaps he had overreacted, perhaps there was a perfectly innocent reason why Archie and Gwendolyn had entered the stockroom together. He would talk to her; that's what he'd do. He'd talk to Gwennie first thing tomorrow morning . . .

That was when the noises started.

Odd cries from across the street. A catfight? Foxes probably. He hoped someone would throw a shoe at them. Then, from the corridor outside his flat, he heard a muffled clumping, as if someone were dragging something very heavy along the floor. It stopped. Someone knocked on his door, twice, very softly.

Outside his window the cries were getting louder. Peter sat in his chair, knowing that somehow, somewhere, he had missed something. Something important. The knocking redoubled. He was thankful that he always locked and chained his door at night.

They'd been ready for a long time, but they had to be asked . . .

When the thing came through the door, Peter started screaming, but he really didn't scream for very long.

One Life,
Furnished in Early
Moorcock

*T*he Pale albino prince lofted on high his great black
sword. 'This is Stormbringer,' he said, 'and it will
suck your soul right out.'

The Princess sighed. 'Very well!' she said. 'If that is
what you need to get the energy you need to fight the
Dragon Warriors, then you must kill me and let your
broad sword feed on my soul.'

'I do not want to do this,' he said to her.

'That's okay,' said the princess and with that she
ripped her flimsy gown and bared her chest to him. 'That
is my heart,' she said, pointing with her finger, 'and that
is where you must plunge.'

He had never got any farther than that. That had
been the day he had been told he was being moved up
a year, and there hadn't been much point after that.
He'd learned not to try and continue stories from one
year to another. Now, he was twelve.

It was a pity, though.

The essay title had been 'Meeting My Favourite
Literary Character', and he'd picked Elric. He'd toyed
with Corum, or Jerry Cornelius, or even Conan the

Barbarian, but Elric of Melnibone won, hands down, just like he always did.

Richard had first read *Stormbringer* three years ago, at the age of nine. He'd saved up for a copy of *The Singing Citadel* (something of a cheat, he decided, on finishing: only one Elric story) and then borrowed the money from his father to buy *The Sleeping Sorceress*, found in a spin rack while they were on holiday in Scotland last summer. In *The Sleeping Sorceress* Elric met Erikose and Corum, two other aspects of the Eternal Champion, and they all got together.

Which meant, he realised when he finished the book, that the Corum books and the Erikose books and even the Dorian Hawkmoon books were really Elric books, too, so he began buying them, and he enjoyed them.

They weren't as good as Elric, though. Elric was the best.

Sometimes he'd sit and draw Elric, trying to get him right. None of the paintings of Elric on the covers of the books looked like the Elric that lived in his head. He drew the Elrics with a fountain pen in empty school exercise books he had obtained by deceit. On the front cover he'd write his name: RICHARD GREY. DO NOT STEAL.

Sometimes he thought he ought to go back and finish writing his Elric story. Maybe he could even sell it to a magazine. But then, what if Moorcock found out? What if he got into trouble?

The classroom was large, filled with wooden desks. Each desk was carved and scored and ink-stained by its occupant, an important process. There was a blackboard on the wall with a chalk drawing on it: a fairly accurate representation of a male penis, heading towards a Y shape, intended to represent the female genitalia.

The door downstairs banged, and someone ran up the stairs. 'Grey, you spazmo, what're you doing up here? We're meant to be down on the Lower Acre. You're playing football today.'

'We are? I am?'

'It was announced at assembly this morning. And the list is up on the games notice board.' J.B.C. MacBride was sandy-haired, bespectacled, only marginally more organised than Richard Grey. There were two J. MacBrides, which was how he ranked a full set of initials.

'Oh.'

Grey picked up a book (*Tarzan at the Earth's Core*) and headed off after him. The clouds were dark grey, promising rain or snow.

People were forever announcing things he didn't notice. He would arrive in empty classes, miss organised games, arrive at school on days when everyone else had gone home. Sometimes he felt as if he lived in a different world to everyone else.

He went off to play football, *Tarzan at the Earth's Core* shoved down the back of his scratchy blue football shorts.

He hated the showers and the baths. He couldn't understand why they had to use both, but that was just the way it was.

He was freezing, and no good at games. It was beginning to become a matter of perverse pride with him that in his years at the school so far, he hadn't scored a goal, or hit a run, or bowled anyone out, or done anything much except be the last person to be picked when choosing sides.

Elric, proud pale prince of the Melniboneans, would

never have had to stand around on a football pitch in the middle of winter, wishing the game would be over.

Steam from the shower room, and his inner thighs were chapped and red. The boys stood naked and shivering in a line, waiting to get under the showers and then to get into the baths.

Mr Murchison, eyes wild and face leathery and wrinkled, old and almost bald, stood in the changing rooms directing naked boys into the shower, then out of the shower and into the baths. 'You boy. Silly little boy. Jamieson. Into the shower, Jamieson. Atkinson, you baby, get under it properly. Smiggins, into the bath. Goring, take his place in the shower . . .'

The showers were too hot. The baths were freezing cold and muddy.

When Mr Murchison wasn't around, boys would flick each other with towels, joke about each others' penises, about who had pubic hair, who didn't.

'Don't be an idiot,' hissed someone near Richard. 'What if the Murch comes back. He'll kill you.' There was some nervous giggling.

Richard turned and looked. An older boy had an erection, was rubbing his hand up and down it slowly under the shower, displaying it proudly to the room.

Richard turned away.

Forgery was too easy.

Richard could do a passable imitation of the Murch's signature, for example, and an excellent version of his housemaster's handwriting and signature. His housemaster was a tall, bald, dry man named Trellis. They had disliked each other for years.

Richard used the signatures to get blank exercise books from the stationery office, which dispensed paper, pencils, pens and rulers on the production of a note signed by a teacher.

Richard wrote stories and poems and drew pictures in the exercise books.

After the bath, Richard towelled himself off and dressed hurriedly; he had a book to get back to, a lost world to return to.

He walked out of the building slowly, tie askew, shirttail flapping, reading about Lord Greystoke, wondering whether there really was a world inside the world where dinosaurs flew and it was never night.

The daylight was beginning to go, but there were still a number of boys outside the school, playing with tennis balls: a couple played conkers by the bench. Richard leaned against the redbrick wall and read, the outside world closed off, the indignities of changing rooms forgotten.

'You're a disgrace, Grey.'

Me?

'Look at you. Your tie's all crooked. You're a disgrace to the school. That's what you are.'

The boy's name was Lindfield, two school years above him, but already as big as an adult. 'Look at your tie. I mean, *look* at it.' Lindfield pulled at Richard's green tie, pulled it tight into a hard little knot. 'Pathetic.'

Lindfield and his friends wandered off.

Elric of Melnibone was standing by the redbrick walls of the school building, staring at him. Richard pulled at the knot in his tie, trying to loosen it. It was cutting into his throat.

His hands fumbled around his neck.

He couldn't breathe; but he was not concerned about breathing. He was worried about standing.

Richard had suddenly forgotten how to stand. It was a relief to discover how soft the brick path he was standing on had become as it slowly came up to embrace him.

They were standing together under a night sky hung with a thousand huge stars, by the ruins of what might once have been an ancient temple.

Elric's ruby eyes stared down at him. They looked, Richard thought, like the eyes of a particularly vicious white rabbit that Richard had once had, before it gnawed through the wire of the cage and fled into the Sussex countryside to terrify innocent foxes. His skin was perfectly white; his armour, ornate and elegant, traced with intricate patterns, perfectly black. His fine white hair blew about his shoulders as if in a breeze, but the air was still.

—*So you want to be a companion to heroes?* he asked. His voice was gentler than Richard had imagined it would be.

Richard nodded.

Elric put one long finger beneath Richard's chin, lifted his face up. *Blood eyes*, thought Richard. *Blood eyes*.

—*You're no companion, boy*, he said in the High Speech of Melnibone.

Richard had always known he would understand the High Speech when he heard it, even if his Latin and French had always been weak.

—*Well, what* am *I, then?* he asked. *Please tell me. Please?*

Elric made no response. He walked away from Richard, into the ruined temple.

Richard ran after him.

Inside the temple Richard found a life waiting for him, all ready to be worn and lived, and inside that life, another. Each life he tried on, he slipped into and it pulled him farther in, farther away from the world he came from; one by one, existence following existence, rivers of dreams and fields of stars, a hawk with a sparrow clutched in its talons flies low above the grass, and here are tiny intricate people waiting for him to fill their heads with life, and thousands of years pass and he is engaged in strange work of great importance and sharp beauty, and he is loved, and he is honoured, and then a pull, a sharp tug, and it's . . .

. . . it was like coming up from the bottom of the deep end of a swimming pool. Stars appeared above him and dropped away and dissolved into blues and greens, and it was with a deep sense of disappointment that he became Richard Grey and came to himself once more, filled with an unfamiliar emotion. The emotion was a specific one, so specific that he was surprised, later, to realise that it did not have its own name: a feeling of disgust and regret at having to return to something he had thought long since done with and abandoned and forgotten and dead.

Richard was lying on the ground, and Lindfield was pulling at the tiny knot of his tie. There were other boys around, faces staring down at him, worried, concerned, scared.

Lindfield pulled the tie loose. Richard struggled to pull air, he gulped it, clawed it into his lungs.

'We thought you were faking. You just went over.' Someone said that.

'Shut up,' said Lindfield. 'Are you all right? I'm sorry. I'm really sorry. Christ. I'm sorry.'

For one moment, Richard thought he was apologizing for having called him back from the world beyond the temple.

Lindfield was terrified, solicitous, desperately worried. He had obviously never almost killed anyone before. As he walked Richard up the stone steps to the matron's office, Lindfield explained that he had returned from the school tuck-shop, found Richard unconscious on the path, surrounded by curious boys, and had realised what was wrong. Richard rested for a little in the matron's office, where he was given a bitter soluble aspirin, from a huge jar, in a plastic tumbler of water, then was shown in to the headmaster's study.

'God, but you look scruffy, Grey!' said the headmaster, puffing irritably on his pipe. 'I don't blame young Lindfield at all. Anyway, he saved your life. I don't want to hear another word about it.'

'I'm sorry,' said Grey.

'That will be all,' said the headmaster in his cloud of scented smoke.

'Have you picked a religion yet?' asked the school chaplain, Mr Aliquid.

Richard shook his head. 'I've got quite a few to choose from,' he admitted.

The school chaplain was also Richard's biology teacher. He had recently taken Richard's biology class, fifteen thirteen-year-old boys and Richard, just twelve, across the road to his little house opposite the school. In the garden Mr Aliquid had killed, skinned, and dismembered a rabbit with a small sharp knife. Then he'd taken a foot pump and blown up the rabbit's bladder like a balloon until it had popped, spattering the boys with blood. Richard threw up, but he was the only one who did.

'Hm,' said the chaplain.

The chaplain's study was lined with books. It was

one of the few masters' studies that was in any way comfortable.

'What about masturbation? Are you masturbating excessively?' Mr Aliquid's eyes gleamed.

'What's excessively?'

'Oh. More than three or four times a day, I suppose.'

'No,' said Richard. 'Not excessively.'

He was a year younger than anyone else in his class; people forgot about that sometimes.

Every weekend he travelled to North London to stay with his cousins for bar mitzvah lessons taught by a thin ascetic cantor, *frummer* than *frum*, a cabalist and keeper of hidden mysteries onto which he could be diverted with a well-placed question. Richard was an expert at well-placed questions.

Frum was orthodox, hard-line Jewish. No milk with meat, and two washing machines for the two sets of plates and cutlery.

Thou shalt not seethe a kid in its mother's milk.

Richard's cousins in North London were *frum*, although the boys would secretly buy cheeseburgers after school and brag about it to each other.

Richard suspected his body was hopelessly polluted already. He drew the line at eating rabbit, though. He had eaten rabbit, and disliked it, for years before he figured out what it was. Every Thursday there was what he believed to be a rather unpleasant chicken stew for school lunch. One Thursday he found a rabbit's paw floating in his stew, and the penny dropped. After that on Thursdays, he filled up on bread and butter.

On the underground train to North London, he'd scan the faces of the other passengers, wondering if any of them were Michael Moorcock.

If he met Moorcock, he'd ask him how to get back to the ruined temple.

If he met Moorcock, he'd be too embarrassed to speak.

Some nights when his parents were out, he'd try to phone Michael Moorcock.

He'd phone directory enquiries and ask for Moorcock's number.

'Can't give it to you, love. It's ex-directory.'

He'd wheedle and cajole, and always fail, to his relief. He didn't know what he would say to Moorcock if he succeeded.

He put ticks in the front of his Moorcock novels, on the By the Same Author page, for the books he read.

That year there seemed to be a new Moorcock book every week. He'd pick them up at Victoria station on the way to bar mitzvah lessons.

There were a few he simply couldn't find – *Stealer of Souls, Breakfast in the Ruins* – and eventually, nervously, he ordered them from the address in the back of the books. He got his father to write him a cheque.

When the books arrived, they contained a bill for 25 pence: the prices of the books were higher than originally listed. But still, he now had a copy of *Stealer of Souls* and a copy of *Breakfast in the Ruins*.

At the back of *Breakfast in the Ruins* was a biography of Moorcock that said he'd died of lung cancer the year before.

Richard was upset for weeks. That meant there wouldn't be any more books, ever.

That fucking biography. Shortly after it came out, I was at a Hawkwind gig, stoned out of my brain, and these people kept coming up to me, and I thought I was dead. They kept saying, 'You're dead, you're dead.' Later I realised that they were saying, 'But we thought you were dead.'

– Michael Moorcock, in conversation, Notting Hill, 1976

There was the Eternal Champion, and then there was the Companion to Champions. Moonglum was Elric's companion, always cheerful, the perfect foil to the pale prince, who was prey to moods and depressions.

There was a multiverse out there, glittering and magic. There were the agents of balance, the Gods of Chaos, and the Lords of Order. There were the older races, tall, pale and elfin, and the young kingdoms, filled with people like him. Stupid, boring, normal people.

Sometimes he hoped that Elric could find peace away from the black sword. But it didn't work that way. There had to be the both of them – the white prince and the black sword.

Once the sword was unsheathed, it lusted for blood, needed to be plunged into quivering flesh. Then it would drain the soul from the victim, feed his or her energy into Elric's feeble frame.

Richard was becoming obsessed with sex; he had even had a dream in which he was having sex with a girl. Just before waking, he dreamed what it must be like to have an orgasm – it was an intense and magical feeling of love, centred on your heart; that was what it was, in his dream.

A feeling of deep, transcendent, spiritual bliss.

Nothing he experienced ever matched up to that dream.

Nothing even came close.

The Karl Glogauer in *Behold the Man* was not the Karl Glogauer of *Breakfast in the Ruins*, Richard decided; still, it gave him an odd, blasphemous pride to read *Breakfast in the Ruins* in the school chapel in the choir stalls. As long as he was discreet no one seemed to care.

He was the boy with the book. Always and forever.

His head swam with religions: the weekend was now given to the intricate patterns and language of Judaism; each weekday morning to the wood-scented, stained-glass solemnities of the Church of England; and the nights belonged to his own religion, the one he made up for himself, a strange, multicoloured pantheon in which the Lords of Chaos (Arioch, Xiombarg, and the rest) rubbed shoulders with the Phantom Stranger from the DC Comics and Sam the trickster-Buddha from Zelazny's *Lord of Light*, and vampires and talking cats and ogres, and all the things from the Lang coloured Fairy books: in which all mythologies existed simultaneously in a magnificent anarchy of belief.

Richard had, however, finally given up (with, it must be admitted, a little regret) his belief in Narnia. From the age of six – for half his life – he had believed devoutly in all things Narnian; until, last year, rereading *The Voyage of the Dawn Treader* for perhaps the hundredth time, it had occurred to him that the transformation of the unpleasant Eustace Scrub into a dragon and his subsequent conversion to belief in Aslan the lion was terribly similar to the conversion of St Paul on the road to Damascus; if his blindness were a dragon . . .

This having occurred to him, Richard found correspondences everywhere, too many to be simple coincidence.

Richard put away the Narnia books, convinced, sadly, that they were allegory; that an author (whom he had trusted) had been attempting to slip something past him. He had had the same disgust with the Professor Challenger stories, when the bull-necked old professor became a convert to Spiritualism; it was not that Richard had any problems with believing in ghosts – Richard believed, with no problems or contradictions, in *everything* – but Conan Doyle was preaching, and it showed through the words. Richard was young, and innocent in his fashion, and believed that authors should be trusted, and that there should be nothing hidden beneath the surface of a story.

At least the Elric stories were honest. There was nothing going on beneath the surface there: Elric was the etiolated prince of a dead race, burning with self-pity, clutching Stormbringer, his dark-bladed broadsword – a blade which sang for lives, which ate human souls, and which gave their strength to the doomed and weakened albino.

Richard read and reread the Elric stories, and he felt pleasure each time Stormbringer plunged into an enemy's chest, somehow felt a sympathetic satisfaction as Elric drew his strength from the soul-sword, like a heroin addict in a paperback thriller with a fresh supply of smack.

Richard was convinced that one day the people from Mayflower Books would come after him for their 25 pence. He never dared buy any more books through the mail.

* * *

J.B.C. MacBride had a secret.

'You mustn't tell anyone.'

'Okay.'

Richard had no problem with the idea of keeping secrets. In later years he realised that he was a walking repository of old secrets, secrets that his original confidants had probably long forgotten.

They were walking, with their arms over each other's shoulders, up to the woods at the back of the school.

Richard had, unasked, been gifted with another secret in these woods: it is here that three of Richard's school friends have meetings with girls from the village and where, he has been told, they display to each other their genitalia.

'I can't tell you who told me any of this.'

'Okay,' said Richard.

'I mean, it's true. And it's a deadly secret.'

'Fine.'

MacBride had been spending a lot of time recently with Mr Aliquid, the school chaplain.

'Well, everybody has two angels. God gives them one and Satan gives them one. So when you get hypnotized, Satan's angel takes control. And that's how Ouija boards work. It's Satan's angel. And you can implore your God's angel to talk through you. But real enlightenment only occurs when you can talk to your angel. He tells you secrets.'

This was the first time that it had occurred to Grey that the Church of England might have its own esoterica, its own hidden cabala.

The other boy blinked owlishly. 'You mustn't tell anyone that. I'd get into trouble if they knew I'd told you.'

'Fine.'

There was a pause.

'Have you ever wanked off a grown-up?' asked MacBride.

'No.' Richard's own secret was that he had not yet begun to masturbate. All of his friends masturbated, continually, alone and in pairs or groups. He was a year younger than them and couldn't understand what the fuss was about; the whole idea made him uncomfortable.

'Spunk everywhere. It's thick and oozy. They try to get you to put their cocks in your mouth when they shoot off.'

'Eugh.'

'It's not that bad.' There was a pause. 'You know, Mr Aliquid thinks you're very clever. If you wanted to join his private religious discussion group, he might say yes.'

The private discussion group met at Mr Aliquid's small bachelor house across the road from the school in the evenings, twice a week after prep.

'I'm not Christian.'

'So? You still come top of the class in Divinity, Jewboy.'

'No thanks. Hey, I got a new Moorcock. One you haven't read. It's an Elric book.'

'You haven't. There isn't a new one.'

'Is. It's called *The Jade Man's Eyes*. It's printed in green ink. I found it in a bookshop in Brighton.'

'Can I borrow it after you?'

'Course.'

It was getting chilly, and they walked back, arm in arm. Like Elric and Moonglum, thought Richard to himself, and it made as much sense as MacBride's angels.

* * *

Richard had daydreams in which he would kidnap Michael Moorcock and make him tell Richard the secret.

If pushed, Richard would be unable to tell you what kind of thing the secret was. It was something to do with writing; something to do with gods.

Richard wondered where Moorcock got his ideas from.

Probably from the ruined temple, he decided, in the end, although he could no longer remember what the temple looked like. He remembered a shadow, and stars, and the feeling of pain at returning to something he thought long finished.

He wondered if that was where all authors got their ideas from or just Michael Moorcock.

If you had told him that they just made it all up, out of their heads, he would never have believed you. There had to be a place the magic came from.

Didn't there?

This bloke phoned me up from America the other night, he said, 'Listen, man, I have to talk to you about your religion.' I said, 'I don't know what you're talking about. I haven't got any fucking religion.'

– Michael Moorcock, in conversation, Notting Hill, 1976

It was six months later. Richard had been bar mitzvahed and would be changing schools soon. He and J.B.C. MacBride were sitting on the grass outside the school in the early evening, reading books. Richard's parents were late picking him up from school.

Richard was reading *The English Assassin*. MacBride was engrossed in *The Devil Rides Out*.

Richard found himself squinting at the page. It wasn't properly dark yet, but he couldn't read any more. Everything was turning into greys.

'Mac? What do you want to be when you grow up?'

The evening was warm, and the grass was dry and comfortable.

'I don't know. A writer, maybe. Like Michael Moorcock. Or T.H. White. How about you?'

Richard sat and thought. The sky was a violet-grey, and a ghost moon hung high in it, like a sliver of a dream. He pulled up a blade of grass and slowly shredded it between his fingers, bit by bit. He couldn't say 'A writer' as well now. It would seem like he was copying. And he didn't want to be a writer. Not really. There were other things to be.

'When I grow up,' he said, pensively, eventually, 'I want to be a wolf.'

'It'll never happen,' said MacBride.

'Maybe not,' said Richard. 'We'll see.'

The lights went on in the school windows, one by one, making the violet sky seem darker than it was before, and the summer evening was gentle and quiet. At that time of year, the day lasts forever, and the night never really comes.

'I'd like to be a wolf. Not all the time. Just sometimes. In the dark. I would run through the forests as a wolf at night,' said Richard, mostly to himself. 'I'd never hurt anyone. Not that kind of wolf. I'd just run and run forever in the moonlight, through the trees, and never get tired or out of breath, and never have to stop. That's what I want to be when I grow up...'

One Life, Furnished in Early Moorcock   289

He pulled up another long stalk of grass, expertly stripped the blades from it, and slowly began to chew the stem.

And the two children sat alone in the grey twilight, side by side, and waited for the future to start.

Cold Colours

I.

Woken at nine o'clock by the postman,
who turns out not to be the postman but an itinerant
    seller of pigeons,
crying,
'Fat pigeons, pure pigeons, dove white, slate grey,
living, breathing pigeons,
none of your reanimated muck here, sir.'

I have pigeons and to spare and I tell him so.
He tells me he's new in this business,
used to be part of a moderately successful
financial securities analysis company
but was laid off, replaced by a computer RS232'd to a
quartz sphere.

'Still, mustn't grumble, one door opens, another one
slams,
got to keep up with the times, sir, got to keep up with
the times.'
He thrusts me a free pigeon

(To attract new custom, sir,
once you've tried one of our pigeons, you'll never look
    at another)
and struts down the stairs, singing,
'Pigeons alive-oh, alive alive-oh.'

Ten o'clock after I've bathed and shaved
(unguents of eternal youth and of certain sexual
    attraction applied from plastic vessels)
I take the pigeon into my study;
I refresh the chalk circle around my old Dell 310,
hang wards at each corner of the monitor,

and do what is needful with the pigeon.

Then I turn the computer to on: It chugs and
    hums,
inside it fans blow like storm winds on old oceans
ready to drown poor merchantmen.
Autoexec complete it bleeps:
I'll do, I'll do, I'll do . . .

II.

Two o'clock and walking through familiar London
– or what was familiar London before the cursor
    deleted certain certainties –
I watch a suit and tie man giving suck
to the Psion Organizer lodged in his breast pocket,
its serial interface like a cool mouth hunting his chest
    for sustenance,
familiar feeling, and I'm watching my breath steam in
the air.

Cold as a witch's tit these days is London,
you'd never think it was November,
and from underground the sounds of trains rumble.
Mysterious: tube trains are almost legendary in these
    times,
stopping only for virgins and the pure of heart,
first stop Avalon, Lyonesse, or the Isles of the Blessed.
    Maybe
you get a postcard and maybe you don't.
Anyway, looking down any chasm demonstrates
conclusively
there is no room under London for subways;
I warm my hands at a pit.
Flames lick upward.

Far below a smiling demon spots me, waves, mouths
    carefully,
as one does to the deaf, or distant, or to foreigners.
Its sales performance is spotless: It mimes a Dwarrow
    Clone,
mimes software beyond my wildest,
Albertus Magnus ARChived on three floppies,
Claviculae Solomon for VGA, CGA, four-colour or
    monochrome,
mimes
and mimes
and mimes.

The tourists lean over the riftways to Hell,
staring at the damned
(perhaps the worst part of damnation;
eternal torture is bearable in noble silence, alone,
but an audience, eating crisps and chips and chestnuts,
an audience who aren't even really that interested . . .

They must feel like something at the zoo,
the damned).

Pigeons flutter around Hell, dancing on the updrafts,
race memory perhaps telling them
that somewhere around here there should be four lions,
unfrozen water, one stone man above;
the tourists cluster around.
One does a deal with the demon: a ten-pack of blank
    floppies for his soul.
One has recognised a relative in the flames and is
waving:
    Coooee! Coooeee! Uncle Joseph! Look, Nerissa, it's
    your Great-Uncle Joe
    that died before you was born,
    that's him down there, in the Slough, up to his
    eyes in boiling scum
    with the worms crawling in and out of his face.
    Such a lovely man.
    We all cried at his funeral.
    Wave to your uncle, Nerissa, wave to your uncle.

The pigeon man lays limed twigs on the cracked paving
stones,
then sprinkles breadcrumbs and waits.
He raises his cap to me.
'This morning's pigeon, sir, I trust it was satisfactory?'
I allow that it was and toss him a golden shilling
(which he touches surreptitiously to the iron of his
    gauntlet,
checking for fairy gold, then palms).

Tuesday, I tell him. Come on Tuesdays.

III.

Bird-legged cottages and huts crowd the London streets,
stepping spindly over the taxis, shitting embers over
    cyclists,
queuing in the streets behind the buses,
chuckchuckchuckchuckchuurck, they murmur.
Old women with iron teeth gaze out of the windows,
then return to their magic mirrors,
or to their housework,
Hoovering through fog and filthy air.

IV.

Four o'clock in Old Soho,
rapidly becoming a backwater of lost technology.
The ratcheting grate of charms being wound up
with clockwork silver keys
grinds out from every backstreet Watchmaker's,
Abortionist's, Philtre & Tobacconist's.

It's raining.

Bulletin board kids drive pimpmobiles in floppy hats,
modem panders
anoracked kid-kings of signal to noise;
and all their neon-lit stippled stable flirting and turning
    under the lights,
succubi and incubi with sell-by dates and Smart Card
    eyes,
all yours, if you've got your number,
know your expiry date, all that.
One of them winks at me
(flashes on, on-off, off-off-on),
noise swallows signal in fumbled fellatio.

(I cross two fingers,
a binary precaution against hex,
effective as superconductor or simple superstition.)
Two poltergeists share a take-away. Old Soho always
    makes me nervous.
Brewer Street. A hiss from an alley: Mephistopheles
    opens his brown coat,
flashes me the lining (databased old invocations,
Magians lay ghosts – with diagrams), curses, and begins:
    Blight an enemy?
    Wither a harvest?
    Barren a consort?
    Debase an innocent?
    Ruin a party . . .?
    For you, sir? No, sir? Reconsider, I beg you.
    Just a little of your blood smudged on this printout
    and you can be the proud possessor of a new voice
    synthesizer, listen—
He stands a Zenith portable on a table he makes from
    a modest suitcase,
attracting a small audience in the process, plugs in the
    voicebox, types at the
c> prompt: GO
and it recites in voice exact and fine:
*Orientis princeps Beëlzebub, inferni irredentista menarche
    et demigorgon, propitiamus vows . . .*

I hurry onward, hurry down the street
while paper ghosts, old printouts, dog my heels,
and hear him patter like a market man:
    Not twenty
    not eighteen
    not fifteen
    Cost me twelve lady so help me Satan but to you?

 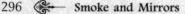

Because I like your pretty face
because I want to raise your spirits.

Five.
That's right.

Five.

Sold to the lady with the lovely eyes . . .

V.

The archbishop hunches glaucous blind in the darkness
    on the edge of St Paul's,
small, birdlike, luminous, humming *I/O, I/O, I/O.*
It's almost six and the rush-hour traffic in stolen dreams
and expanded memory hustles the pavement below
    us.

I hand the man my jug.
He takes it, carefully, and shuffles back into the waiting
    cathedral shadows.
When he returns the jug is full once more.
I josh, 'Guaranteed holy?'
He traces one word in the frozen dirt: WYSIWYG
and does not smile back.

(Wheezy wig. Whisky whig.)
He coughs grey, milk phlegm,
spits onto the steps.

What I see in the jug: it looks holy enough, but you
    can't know for sure,
not unless you are yourself a siren or a fetch,

coagulating out of a telecom mouthpiece, riding the bleep,
an invocation, some really Wrong Number; then you
    can tell from holy.
I've dumped telephones in buckets of the stuff before
    now,
watched things begin to form
then bubble and hiss as the water gets to them:
lustrated and asperged, the Final Sanction.
One afternoon
there was a queue of them, trapped on the tape of my
    ansaphone:
I copied it to floppy and filed it away.
You want it?
Listen, everything's for sale.

The priest needs shaving, and he's got the shakes.
His wine-stained vestments do little to keep him warm.
I give him money.
(Not much. After all,
it's just water, some creatures are so stupid
They'll do you a Savini gunk-dissolve
if you sprinkle them with Perrier
for chrissakes, whining the whole time,
All my evil, my beautiful evil.)

The old priest pockets the coin, gives me
a bag of crumbs as a bonus,
sits on his steps, hugging himself.

I feel the need to say something before I leave.
Look, I tell him, it's not your fault.
It's just a multi-user system.
You weren't to know.
If prayers could be networked,

if saintware were up and running,
if you could make your side as reliable as they've made
theirs . . .
'What You See,' he mutters desolately,
'What You See Is What You Get.' He crumbles a
communion wafer
throws it down for the pigeons,
makes no attempt to catch even the slowest bird.

Cold wars produce bad losers.
I go home.

VI.

News at Ten. And here is Abel Drugger, reading it:

VII.

The corners of my eyes catch hasty, bloodless motion—
a mouse?
Well, certainly a peripheral of some kind.

VIII.

It's bedtime. I feed the pigeons,
then undress.
Contemplate downloading a succubus from a board,
maybe just call up a sidekick
(there's public-domain stuff, bawds and bauds,
shareware, no need to pay a fortune,
even copy-protected stuff can be copied, passed about,
everything has a price, any of us).
Dryware, wetware, hardware, software,
blackware, darkware,

nightware, nightmare...
The modem sits inviting beside the phone,
red eyes.
I let it rest –
you can't trust anybody these days.
You download, hell, you don't know where what came
    from anymore,
who had it last.
Well, aren't you? Aren't you scared of viruses?
Even the better protected files corrupt,
and the best protected corrupt absolutely.

In the kitchen I hear the pigeons billing and queuing,
dreaming of left-handed knives,
of athanors and mirrors.

Pigeon blood stains the floor of my study.

Alone, I sleep. And all alone I dream

IX.

Perhaps I wake in the night, suddenly comprehending
something, reach out,
scribble on the back of an old bill
my revelation, my newfound understanding,
knowing that morning will render it prosaic,
knowing that magic is a night-time thing,
then remembering when it still was...
Revelation retreats to cliché, listen:
    Things seemed simpler before we kept computers.

X.

Waking or dreaming from outside I hear
wild sabbats, screaming winds, tape hum, metal
    machine music;
witches astride ghetto blasters crowd the moon,
then land on the heath their naked flanks aglisten.
No one pays anything to attend the meet, each has it
    taken care of in advance,
baby bones with fat still clinging to them;
these things are direct debit, standing order,
and I see
    or think I see
a face I recognise and all of them queue up to kiss his
    ass,
let's rim the Devil, boys, cold seed,
and in the dark he turns and looks at me:
    One door opens, another one slams,
    I trust that everything is satisfactory?
    We do what we can, everybody's got the right to
    turn an honest penny;
    we're all bankrupt, sir,
    we're all redundant,
    but we make the best of it, whistle through the
    Blitz,
    that's the business. Fair trade is no robbery.
    Tuesday morning, then, sir, with the pigeons?

I nod and draw the curtains. Junk mail is everywhere.
They'll get to you,
one way or another they'll get to you; someday
I'll find my tube train underground, I'll pay no fare,
just 'This is Hell, and I want out of it,'
and then things will be simple once again.

It will come for me like a dragon down a dark tunnel.

 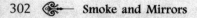

The Sweeper of Dreams

*A*fter all the dreaming is over, after you wake, and leave the world of madness and glory for the mundane day-lit daily grind, through the wreckage of your abandoned fancies walks the sweeper of dreams.

Who knows what he was when he was alive? Or if, for that matter, he ever was alive. He certainly will not answer your questions. The sweeper talks little, in his gruff grey voice, and when he does speak it is mostly about the weather and the prospects, victories and defeats of certain sports teams. He despises everyone who is not him.

Just as you wake he comes to you, and he sweeps up kingdoms and castles, and angels and owls, mountains and oceans. He sweeps up the lust and the love and the lovers, the sages who are not butterflies, the flowers of meat, the running of the deer and the sinking of the *Lusitania*. He sweeps up everything you left behind in your dreams, the life you wore, the eyes through which you gazed, the examination paper you were never able to find. One by one he sweeps them away: the sharp-toothed woman who sank her teeth into your face; the nuns in the woods; the dead arm that broke through the tepid water of the bath; the scarlet worms that crawled in your chest when you opened your shirt.

He will sweep it up – everything you left behind when you woke. And then he will burn it, to leave the stage fresh for your dreams tomorrow.

Treat him well, if you see him. Be polite with him. Ask him no questions. Applaud his teams' victories, commiserate with him over their losses, agree with him about the weather. Give him the respect he feels is his due.

For there are people he no longer visits, the sweeper of dreams, with his hand-rolled cigarettes and his dragon tattoo.

You've seen them. They have mouths that twitch, and eyes that stare, and they babble and they mewl and they whimper. Some of them walk the cities in ragged clothes, their belongings under their arms. Others of their number are locked in the dark, in places where they can no longer harm themselves or others. They are not mad, or rather, the loss of their sanity is the lesser of their problems. It is worse than madness. They will tell you, if you let them: they are the ones who live, each day, in the wreckage of their dreams.

And if the sweeper of dreams leaves you, he will never come back.

Foreign Parts

The VENEREAL DISEASE is disease contracted as a consequence of impure connexion. The fearful constitutional consequences which may result from this affection, – consequences, the fear of which may haunt the mind for years, which may taint the whole springs of health, and be transmitted to circulate in the young blood of innocent offspring, – are indeed terrible considerations, too terrible not to render the disease one of those which must unhesitatingly be placed under medical care.

— SPENCER THOMAS, M.D., L.R.C.S. (EDIN.),
A DICTIONARY OF DOMESTIC MEDICINE AND HOUSEHOLD SURGERY, 1882

*S*imon Powers didn't like sex. Not really.
He disliked having someone else in the same bed as himself; he suspected that he came too soon; he always felt uncomfortably that his performance was in some way being graded, like a driving test or a practical examination.

He had got laid in college a few times and once, three years ago, after the office New Year's party. But that had been that, and as far as Simon was concerned, he was well out of it.

It occurred to him once, during a slack time at the office, that he would have liked to have lived in the days of Queen Victoria, where well-brought-up women were no more than resentful sex dolls in the bedroom: they'd unlace their stays, loosen their petticoats (revealing pinkish-white flesh) then lie back and suffer the indignities of the carnal act – an indignity it would never even occur to them that they were meant to enjoy.

He filed it away for later, another masturbatory fantasy.

Simon masturbated a great deal. Every night – sometimes more than that if he was unable to sleep. He could take as long, or as short, a time to climax as he wished. And in his mind he had had them all. Film and television stars; women from the office; schoolgirls; the naked models who pouted from the crumpled pages of *Fiesta*; faceless slaves in chains; tanned boys with bodies like Greek gods . . .

Night after night they paraded in front of him.

It was safer that way.

In his mind.

And afterward he'd fall asleep, comfortable and safe in a world he controlled, and he'd sleep without dreaming. Or at least, he never remembered his dreams in the morning.

The morning it started he was woken by the radio ('Two hundred killed and many others believed to be injured; and now over to Jack for the weather and traffic news . . .'), dragged himself out of bed, and stumbled, bladder aching, into the bathroom.

He pulled up the toilet seat and urinated. It felt like he was pissing needles.

He needed to urinate again after breakfast – less painfully, since the flow was not as heavy – and three more times before lunch.

Each time it hurt.

He told himself that it couldn't be a venereal disease. That was something that other people got, and something (he thought of his last sexual encounter, three years in the past) that you got from other people. You couldn't really catch it from toilet seats, could you? Wasn't that just a joke?

Simon Powers was twenty-six, and he worked in a large London bank, in the securities division. He had few friends at work. His only real friend, Nick Lawrence, a lonely Canadian, had recently transferred to another branch, and Simon sat by himself in the staff canteen, staring out at the Docklands Lego landscape, picking at a limp green salad.

Someone tapped him on the shoulder.

'Simon, I heard a good one today. Wanna hear?' Jim Jones was the office clown, a dark-haired, intense young man who claimed he had a special pocket on his boxer shorts, for condoms.

'Um. Sure.'

'Here you go. What's the collective noun for people who work in banks?'

'The what?'

'Collective noun. You know, like a flock of sheep, a pride of lions. Give up?'

Simon nodded.

'A wunch of bankers.'

Simon must have looked puzzled, because Jim

sighed and said, 'Wunch of bankers. *Bunch of wankers.* God, you're slow . . .' Then, spotting a group of young women at a far table, Jim straightened his tie and carried his tray over to them.

He could hear Jim telling his joke to the women, this time with added hand movements.

They all got it immediately.

Simon left his salad on the table and went back to work.

That night he sat in his chair in his bedsitter flat with the television turned off, and he tried to remember what he knew about venereal diseases.

There was syphilis, which pocked your face and drove the Kings of England mad; gonorrhoea – the clap – a green oozing and more madness; crabs, little pubic lice, which nested and itched (he inspected his pubic hairs through a magnifying glass, but nothing moved); AIDS, the eighties plague, a plea for clean needles and safer sexual habits (but what could be safer than a clean wank for one into a fresh handful of white tissues?); herpes, which had something to do with cold sores (he checked his lips in the mirror, they looked fine). That was all he knew.

And he went to bed and fretted himself to sleep, without daring to masturbate.

That night he dreamed of tiny women with blank faces, walking in endless rows between gargantuan office blocks, like an army of soldier ants.

Simon did nothing about the pain for another two days. He hoped it would go away, or get better on its own. It didn't. It got worse. The pain continued for up to an hour after urination; his penis felt raw and bruised inside.

And on the third day, he phoned his doctor's

surgery to make an appointment. He had dreaded having to tell the woman who answered the phone what the problem was, and so he was relieved, and perhaps just a little disappointed, when she didn't ask but simply made an appointment for the following day.

He told his senior at the bank that he had a sore throat and would need to see the doctor about it. He could feel his cheeks burn as he told her, but she did not remark on this, merely told him that that would be fine.

When he left her office, he found that he was shaking.

It was a grey wet day when he arrived at the doctor's surgery. There was no queue, and he went straight in to the doctor. Not his regular doctor, Simon was comforted to see. This was a young Pakistani, of about Simon's age, who interrupted Simon's stammered recitation of symptoms to ask:

'Urinating more than usual, are we?'

Simon nodded.

'Any discharge?'

Simon shook his head.

'Right ho. I'd like you to take down your trousers, if you don't mind.'

Simon took them down. The doctor peered at his penis. 'You do have a discharge, you know,' he said.

Simon did himself up again.

'Now, Mr Powers, tell me, do you think it possible that you might have picked up from someone, a, uh, venereal disease?'

Simon shook his head vigorously. 'I haven't had sex with anyone—' he had almost said 'anyone else' '—in almost three years.'

'No?' The doctor obviously didn't believe him. He smelled of exotic spices and had the whitest teeth Simon had ever seen. 'Well, you have either contracted gonorrhoea or NSU. Probably NSU: nonspecific urethritis. Which is less famous and less painful than gonorrhoea, but it can be a bit of an old bastard to treat. You can get rid of gonorrhoea with one big dose of antibiotics. Kills the bugger off . . .' He clapped his hands twice. Loudly. 'Just like that.'

'You don't know, then?'

'Which one it is? Good Lord, no. I'm not even going to try to find out. I'm sending you to a special clinic, which takes care of all of that kind of thing. I'll give you a note to take with you.' He pulled a pad of headed notepaper from a drawer. 'What is your profession, Mr Powers?'

'I work in a bank.'

'A teller?'

'No.' He shook his head. 'I'm in securities. I clerk for two assistant managers.' A thought occurred to him. 'They don't have to know about this, do they?'

The doctor looked shocked. 'Good gracious, no.'

He wrote a note, in a careful, round handwriting, stating that Simon Powers, age twenty-six, had something that was probably NSU. He had a discharge. Said he had had no sex for three years. In discomfort. Please could they let him know the results of the tests. He signed it with a squiggle. Then he handed Simon a card with the address and phone number of the special clinic on it. 'Here you are. This is where you go. Not to worry – happens to lots of people. See all the cards I have here? Not to worry – you'll soon be right as rain. Phone them when you get home and make an appointment.'

Simon took the card and stood up to go.

'Don't worry,' said the doctor. 'It won't prove difficult to treat.'

Simon nodded and tried to smile.

He opened the door to go out.

'And, at any rate, it's nothing really nasty, like syphilis,' said the doctor.

The two elderly women sitting outside in the hallway waiting area looked up delightedly at this fortuitous overheard, and stared hungrily at Simon as he walked away.

He wished he were dead.

On the pavement outside, waiting for the bus home, Simon thought: *I've* got a venereal disease. I've *got* a venereal disease. I've got a *venereal disease*. Over and over, like a mantra.

He should toll a bell as he walked.

On the bus he tried not to get too close to his fellow passengers. He was certain they knew (couldn't they read the plague marks on his face?); and at the same time he was ashamed he was forced to keep it a secret from them.

He got back to the flat and went straight into the bathroom, expecting to see a decayed horror-movie face, a rotting skull fuzzy with blue mould, staring back at him from the mirror. Instead, he saw a pink-cheeked bank clerk in his mid-twenties, fair-haired, perfect-skinned.

He fumbled out his penis and scrutinised it with care. It was neither a gangrenous green nor a leprous white, but looked perfectly normal, except for the slightly swollen tip and the clear discharge that lubricated the hole. He realised that his white underpants had been stained across the crotch by the leak.

Simon felt angry with himself and angrier with God for having given him a (say it) (*dose of the clap*) obviously meant for someone else.

He masturbated that night for the first time in four days.

He fantasised a schoolgirl in blue cotton panties who changed into a policewoman, then two police-women, then three.

It didn't hurt at all until he climaxed; then he felt as if someone were pushing a switchblade through the inside of his cock. As if he were ejaculating a pin-cushion.

He began to cry then in the darkness, but whether from the pain, or from some other reason, less easy to identify, even Simon was unsure.

That was the last time he masturbated.

The clinic was located in a dour Victorian hospital in central London. A young man in a white coat looked at Simon's card, and took his doctor's note, and told him to take a seat.

Simon sat down on an orange plastic chair covered with brown cigarette burns.

He stared at the floor for a few minutes. Then, having exhausted that form of entertainment, he stared at the walls, and finally, having no other option, at the other people.

They were all male, thank God – women were on the next floor up – and there were more than a dozen of them.

The most comfortable were the macho building-site types, here for their seventeenth or seventieth time, looking rather pleased with themselves, as if whatever they had caught were proof of their virility.

There were a few city gents in ties and suits. One of them looked relaxed; he carried a mobile telephone. Another, hiding behind a *Daily Telegraph*, was blushing, embarrassed to be there; there were little men with wispy moustaches and tatty raincoats – newspaper sellers, perhaps, or retired teachers; a rotund Malaysian gentleman who chain-smoked filterless cigarettes, lighting each cigarette from the butt of the one before, so the flame never went out, but was transmitted from one dying cigarette to the next. In one corner sat a scared gay couple. Neither of them looked more than eighteen. This was obviously their first appointment as well, the way they kept glancing around. They were holding hands, white-knuckled and discreetly. They were terrified.

Simon felt comforted. He felt less alone.

'Mister Powers, please,' said the man at the desk. Simon stood up, conscious that all eyes were upon him, that he'd been identified and named in front of all these people. A cheerful, red-haired doctor in a white coat was waiting.

'Follow me,' he said.

They walked down some corridors, through a door (on which DR. J. BENHAM was written in felt pen on a white sheet of paper scotch-taped to the frosted glass), into a doctor's office.

'I'm Doctor Benham,' said the doctor. He didn't offer to shake hands. 'You have a note from your doctor?'

'I gave it to the man at the desk.'

'Oh.' Dr Benham opened a file on the desk in front of him. There was a computer printout label on the side. It said:

REG'D 2 JLY 90. MALE. 90/00666.L
POWERS, SIMON, MR.
BORN 12 OCT 63. SINGLE.

Benham read the note, looked at Simon's penis, and handed him a sheet of blue paper from the file. It had the same label, stuck to the top.

'Take a seat in the corridor,' he told him. 'A nurse will collect you.'

Simon waited in the corridor.

'They're very fragile,' said the sunburnt man sitting next to him, by accent a South African or perhaps Zimbabwean. Colonial accent, at any rate.

'I'm sorry?'

'Very fragile. Venereal diseases. Think about it. You can catch a cold or flu simply by being in the same room as someone who's got it. Venereal diseases need warmth and moisture, and intimate contact.'

Not mine, thought Simon, but he didn't say anything.

'You know what I'm dreading?' said the South African.

Simon shook his head.

'Telling my wife,' said the man, and he fell silent.

A nurse came and took Simon away. She was young and pretty, and he followed her into a cubicle. She took the blue slip of paper from him.

'Take off your jacket and roll up your right sleeve.'

'My jacket?'

She sighed. 'For the blood test.'

'Oh.'

The blood test was almost pleasant, compared to what came next.

'Take down your trousers,' she told him. She had a

marked Australian accent. His penis had shrunk, tightly pulled in on itself; it looked grey and wrinkled. He found himself wanting to tell her that it was normally much larger, but then she picked up a metal instrument with a wire loop at the end, and he wished it were even smaller. 'Squeeze your penis at the base and push forward a few times.' He did so. She stuck the loop into the head of his penis and twisted it around the inside. He winced at the pain. She smeared the discharge onto a glass slide. Then she pointed to a glass jar on a shelf. 'Can you urinate into that for me, please?'

'What, from here?'

She pursed her lips. Simon suspected that she must have heard that joke thirty times a day since she had been working there.

She went out of the cubicle and left him alone to pee.

Simon found it difficult to pee at the best of times, often having to wait around in toilets until all the people had gone. He envied men who could casually walk into toilets, unzip, and carry on cheerful conversations with their neighbours in the adjoining urinal, all the while showering the white porcelain with yellow urine. Often he couldn't do it at all.

He couldn't do it now.

The nurse came in again. 'No luck? Not to worry. Take a seat back in the waiting room, and the doctor will call you in a minute.'

'Well,' said Dr Benham. 'You have NSU. Nonspecific urethritis.'

Simon nodded, and then he said, 'What does that mean?'

'It means you don't have gonorrhoea, Mister Powers.'

'But I haven't had sex with, with anyone, for...'

'Oh, that's nothing to worry about. It can be a quite spontaneous disease – you need not, um, indulge, to pick it up.' Benham reached into a desk drawer and pulled out a bottle of pills. 'Take one of these four times a day before meals. Stay off alcohol, no sex, and don't drink milk for a couple of hours after taking one. Got it?'

Simon grinned nervously.

'I'll see you next week. Make an appointment downstairs.'

Downstairs they gave him a red card with his name on and the time of his appointment. It also had a number on: 90/00666.L.

Walking home in the rain, Simon paused outside a travel agents'. The poster in the window showed a beach in the sun and three bronzed women in bikinis, sipping long drinks.

Simon had never been abroad.

Foreign places made him nervous.

As the week went on, the pain went away; and four days later Simon found himself able to urinate without flinching.

Something else was happening, however.

It began as a tiny seed, which took root in his mind, and grew. He told Dr Benham about it at his next appointment.

Benham was puzzled.

'You're saying that you don't feel your penis is your own anymore, then, Mister Powers?'

'That's right, Doctor.'

'I'm afraid I don't quite follow you. Is there some kind of loss of sensation?'

Simon could feel his penis inside his trousers, felt

the sensation of cloth against flesh. In the darkness it began to stir.

'Not at all. I can feel everything like I always could. It's just it feels ... well, different, I suppose. Like it isn't really part of me anymore. Like it ...' He paused. 'Like it belongs to someone else.'

Dr Benham shook his head. 'To answer your question, Mr Powers, that isn't a symptom of NSU – although it's a perfectly valid psychological reaction for someone who has contracted it. A, uh, feeling of disgust with yourself, perhaps, which you've externalized as a rejection of your genitalia.'

That sounds about right, thought Dr Benham. He hoped he had got the jargon correct. He had never paid much attention to his psychology lectures or textbooks, which might explain, or so his wife maintained, why he was currently serving out a stint in a London VD clinic.

Powers looked a little soothed.

'I was just a bit worried, Doctor, that's all.' He chewed his lower lip. 'Um, what exactly *is* NSU?'

Benham smiled, reassuringly. 'Could be any one of a number of things. NSU is just our way of saying we don't know exactly what it is. It's not gonorrhoea. It's not chlamydia. 'Nonspecific,' you see. It's an infection, and it responds to antibiotics. Which reminds me ...' He opened a desk drawer and took out a new week's supply.

'Make an appointment downstairs for next week. No sex. No alcohol.'

No sex? thought Simon. *Not bloody likely*.

But when he walked past the pretty Australian nurse in the corridor, he felt his penis begin to stir again, begin to get warm and to harden.

Benham saw Simon the following week. Tests showed he still had the disease.

Benham shrugged.

'It's not unusual for it to hang on for this long. You say you feel no discomfort?'

'No. None at all. And I haven't seen any discharge, either.'

Benham was tired, and a dull pain throbbed behind his left eye. He glanced down at the tests in the folder. 'You've still got it, I'm afraid.'

Simon Powers shifted his seat. He had large watery blue eyes and a pale unhappy face. 'What about the other thing, Doctor?'

The doctor shook his head. 'What other thing?'

'I *told* you,' said Simon. 'Last week. I *told* you. The feeling that my, um, my penis wasn't, isn't *my* penis anymore.'

Of course, thought Benham. *It's that patient*. There was never any way he could remember the procession of names and faces and penises, with their awkwardness, and their braggadocio, and their sweaty nervous smells, and their sad little diseases.

'Mm. What about it?'

'It's spreading, Doctor. The whole lower half of my body feels like it's someone else's. My legs and everything. I can feel them, all right, and they go where I want them to go, but sometimes I get the feeling that if they wanted to go somewhere else – if they wanted to go walking off into the world – they could, and they'd take me with them.

'I wouldn't be able to do anything to stop it.'

Benham shook his head. He hadn't really been listening. 'We'll change your antibiotics. If the others haven't knocked this disease out by now, I'm sure these will. They'll probably get rid of this other feeling as well – it's probably just a side effect of the antibiotics.'

The young man just stared at him.

Benham felt he should say something else. 'Perhaps you should try to get out more,' he said.

The young man stood up.

'Same time next week. No sex, no booze, no milk after the pills.' The doctor recited his litany.

The young man walked away. Benham watched him carefully, but could see nothing strange about the way he walked.

On Saturday night Dr Jeremy Benham and his wife, Celia, attended a dinner party held by a professional colleague. Benham sat next to a foreign psychiatrist.

They began to talk, over the hors d'oeuvres.

'The trouble with telling folks you're a psychiatrist,' said the psychiatrist, who was American, and huge, and bullet-headed, and looked like a merchant marine, 'is you get to watch them trying to act normal for the rest of the evening.' He chuckled, low and dirty.

Benham chuckled, too, and since he was sitting next to a psychiatrist, he spent the rest of the evening trying to act normally.

He drank too much wine with his dinner.

After the coffee, when he couldn't think of anything else to say, he told the psychiatrist (whose name was Marshall, although he told Benham to call him Mike) what he could recall of Simon Powers's delusions.

Mike laughed. 'Sounds fun. Maybe a tiny bit spooky. But nothing to worry about. Probably just a hallucination caused by a reaction to the antibiotics. Sounds a little like Capgras's Syndrome. You heard about that over here?'

Benham nodded, then thought, then said, 'No.' He poured himself another glass of wine, ignoring his wife's pursed lips and almost imperceptibly shaken head.

'Well, Capgras's Syndrome,' said Mike, 'is this funky delusion. Whole piece on it in *The Journal of American Psychiatry* about five years back. Basically, it's where a person believes that the important people in his or her life – family members, workmates, parents, loved ones, whatever – have been replaced by – get this! – exact doubles.

'Doesn't apply to everyone they know. Just selected people. Often just one person in their life. No accompanying delusions, either. Just that one thing. Acutely emotionally disturbed people with paranoid tendencies.'

The psychiatrist picked his nose with his thumbnail. 'I ran into a case myself, couple, two, three years back.'

'Did you cure him?'

The psychiatrist gave Benham a sideways look and grinned, showing all his teeth. 'In psychiatry, Doctor – unlike, perhaps, the world of sexually transmitted disease clinics – there is no such thing as a cure. There is only adjustment.'

Benham sipped the red wine. Later it occurred to him that he would never have said what he said next if it wasn't for the wine. Not aloud, anyway. 'I don't suppose . . .' He paused, remembering a film he had seen as a teenager. (Something about *bodysnatchers*?) 'I don't suppose that anyone ever checked to see if those people had been removed and replaced by exact doubles . . .?'

Mike – Marshall – whatever – gave Benham a very

funny look indeed and turned around in his chair to talk to his neighbour on the other side.

Benham, for his part, carried on trying to act normally (whatever that was) and failed miserably. He got very drunk indeed, started muttering about 'fucking colonials', and had a blazing row with his wife after the party was over, none of which were particularly normal occurrences.

Benham's wife locked him out of their bedroom after the argument.

He lay on the sofa downstairs, covered by a crumpled blanket, and masturbated into his underpants, his hot seed spurting across his stomach.

In the small hours he was woken by a cold sensation around his loins.

He wiped himself off with his dress shirt and returned to sleep.

Simon was unable to masturbate.

He wanted to, but his hand wouldn't move. It lay beside him, healthy, fine; but it was as if he had forgotten how to make it respond. Which was silly, wasn't it?

Wasn't it?

He began to sweat. It dripped from his face and forehead onto the white cotton sheets, but the rest of his body was dry.

Cell by cell, something was reaching up inside him. It brushed his face tenderly, like the kiss of a lover; it was licking his throat, breathing on his cheek. Touching him.

He had to get out of the bed. He couldn't get out of the bed.

He tried to scream, but his mouth wouldn't open. His larynx refused to vibrate.

Simon could still see the ceiling, lit by the lights of passing cars. The ceiling blurred: His eyes were still his own, and tears were oozing out of them, down his face, soaking the pillow.

They don't know what I've got, he thought. *They said I had what everyone else gets. But I didn't catch that. I've caught something different.*

Or maybe, he thought, as his vision clouded over and the darkness swallowed the last of Simon Powers, *it caught me*.

Soon after that, Simon got up, and washed, and inspected himself carefully in front of the bathroom mirror. Then he smiled, as if he liked what he saw.

Benham smiled. 'I'm pleased to tell you,' he said, 'that I can give you a clean bill of health.'

Simon Powers stretched in his seat, lazily, and nodded. 'I feel terrific,' he said.

He did look well, Benham thought. Glowing with health. He seemed taller as well. A very attractive young man, decided the doctor. 'So, uh, no more of those feelings?'

'Feelings?'

'Those feelings you were telling me about. That your body didn't belong to you anymore.'

Simon waved a hand, gently, fanning his face. The cold weather had broken, and London was stewing in a sudden heatwave; it didn't feel like England anymore. Simon seemed amused.

'All of this body belongs to me, Doctor. I'm certain of that.'

Simon Powers (90/00666.L SINGLE. MALE.) grinned

like the world belonged to him as well.

The doctor watched him as he walked out of the surgery. He looked stronger now, less fragile.

The next patient on Jeremy Benham's appointment card was a twenty-two-year-old boy. Benham was going to have to tell him he was HIV positive. *I hate this job*, he thought. *I need a holiday*.

He walked down the corridor to call the boy in and pushed past Simon Powers, talking animatedly to a pretty young Australian nurse. 'It must be a lovely place,' he was telling her. 'I want to see it. I want to go everywhere. I want to meet *everyone*.' He was resting a hand on her arm, and she was making no move to free herself from it.

Dr Benham stopped beside them. He touched Simon on the shoulder. 'Young man,' he said. 'Don't let me see you back here.'

Simon Powers grinned. 'You won't see me here again, Doctor,' he said. 'Not as such, anyway. I've packed in my job. I'm going around the world.'

They shook hands. Powers's hand was warm and comfortable and dry.

Benham walked away, but could not avoid hearing Simon Powers, still talking to the nurse.

'It's going to be so great,' he was saying to her. Benham wondered if he was talking about sex or world travel, or possibly, in some way, both.

'I'm going to have such *fun*,' said Simon. 'I'm loving it already.'

Vampire Sestina

I wait here at the boundaries of dream,
all shadow-wrapped. The dark air tastes of night,
so cold and crisp, and I wait for my love.
The moon has bleached the colour from her stone.
She'll come, and then we'll stalk this pretty world
alive to darkness and the tang of blood.

It is a lonely game, the quest for blood,
but still, a body's got the right to dream
and I'd not give it up for all the world.
The moon has leeched the darkness from the night.
I stand in shadows, staring at her stone:
Undead, my lover . . . O, undead my love?

I dreamt you while I slept today and love
meant more to me than life – meant more than blood.
The sunlight sought me, deep beneath my stone,
more dead than any corpse but still a-dream
until I woke as vapor into night
and sunset forced me out into the world.

For many centuries I've walked the world
dispensing something that resembled love –
a stolen kiss, then back into the night
contented by the life and by the blood.
And come the morning I was just a dream,
cold body chilling underneath a stone.

I said I would not hurt you. Am I stone
to leave you prey to time and to the world?
I offered you a truth beyond your dreams
while all *you* had to offer was your love.
I told you not to worry and that blood
tastes sweeter on the wing and late at night.

Sometimes my lovers rise to walk the night . . .
Sometimes they lie, cold corpse beneath a stone,
and never know the joys of bed and blood,
of walking through the shadows of the world;
instead they rot to maggots. O my love
they whispered you had risen, in my dream.

I've waited by your stone for half the night
but you won't leave your dream to hunt for blood.
Good night, my love. I offered you the world.

Mouse

*T*hey had a number of devices that would kill the mouse fast, others that would kill it more slowly. There were a dozen variants on the traditional mousetrap, the one Regan tended to think of as a Tom and Jerry trap: a metal spring trap that would slam down at a touch, breaking the mouse's back; there were other gadgets on the shelves – ones that suffocated the mouse, others that electrocuted it, or even drowned it, each safe in its multicoloured cardboard package.

'These weren't quite what I was looking for,' said Regan.

'Well, that's all we got in the way of traps,' said the woman, who wore a large plastic name tag that said her name was BECKY and that she LOVES WORKING FOR YOU AT MACREA'S ANIMAL FEED AND SPECIALTY STORE. 'Now, over here—'

She pointed to a stand-alone display of HUN-GREE-CAT MOUSE POISON sachets. A little rubber mouse lay on the top of the display, his legs in the air.

Regan experienced a sudden memory flash, unbidden: Gwen, extending an elegant pink hand, her fingers curled upward. 'What's that?' she said. It was the week before he had left for America.

'I don't know,' said Regan. They were in the bar of a small hotel in the West Country, burgundy-coloured carpets, fawn-coloured wallpaper. He was nursing a gin and tonic; she was sipping her second glass of Chablis. Gwen had once told Regan that blondes should only drink white wine; it looked better. He laughed until he realised she meant it.

'It's a dead one of *these*,' she said, turning her hand over so the fingers hung like the legs of a slow pink animal. He smiled. Later he paid the bill, and they went upstairs to Regan's room . . .

'No. Not poison. You see, I don't want to kill it,' he told the saleswoman, Becky.

She looked at him curiously, as if he had just begun to speak in a foreign tongue. 'But you said you wanted mousetraps . . .?'

'Look, what I want is a humane trap. It's like a corridor. The mouse goes in, the door shuts behind it, it can't get out.'

'So how do you kill it?'

'You don't kill it. You drive a few miles away and let it go. And it doesn't come back to bother you.'

Becky was smiling now, examining him as if he were just the most darling thing, just the sweetest, dumbest, cutest little thing. 'You stay here,' she said. 'I'll check out back.'

She walked through a door marked EMPLOYEES ONLY. She had a nice bottom, thought Regan, and was sort of attractive, in a dull Midwestern sort of way.

He glanced out the window. Janice was sitting in the car, reading her magazine: a red-haired woman in a dowdy housecoat. He waved at her, but she wasn't looking at him.

Becky put her head back through the doorway. 'Jackpot!' she said. 'How many you want?'

'Two?'

'No problem.' She was gone again and returned with two small green plastic containers. She rang them up on the cash register, and as he fumbled through his notes and coins, still unfamiliar, trying to put together the correct change, she examined the traps, smiling, turning the packets over in her hands.

'My lord,' she said. 'Whatever will they think of next?'

The heat slammed Regan as he stepped out of the store.

He hurried over to the car. The metal door handle was hot in his hand; the engine was idling.

He climbed in. 'I got two,' he said. The air-conditioning in the car was cool and pleasant.

'Seatbelt on,' said Janice. 'You've really got to learn to drive over here.' She put down her magazine.

'I will,' he said. 'Eventually.'

Regan was scared of driving in America: it was like driving on the other side of a mirror.

They said nothing else, and Regan read the instructions on the back of the mousetrap boxes. According to the text, the main attraction of this type of trap was that you never needed to see, touch, or handle the mouse. The door would close behind it, and that would be that. The instructions said nothing about not killing the mouse.

When they got home, he took the traps out of the boxes, put a little peanut butter in one, down at the far end, a lump of cooking chocolate in the other, and placed them on the floor of the pantry, one against the wall, the other near the hole that the mice seemed to be using to gain access to the pantry.

The traps were only corridors. A door at one end, a wall at the other.

In bed that night Regan reached out and touched Janice's breasts as she slept; touched them gently, not wanting to wake her. They were perceptibly fuller. He wished he found large breasts erotic. He found himself wondering what it must be like to suck a woman's breasts while she was lactating. He could imagine sweetness, but no specific taste.

Janice was sound asleep, but still she moved toward him.

He edged away; lay there in the dark, trying to remember how to sleep, hunting through alternatives in his mind. It was so hot, so stuffy. When they'd lived in Ealing he'd fallen asleep instantly, he was certain.

There was a sharp scream from the garden. Janice stirred and rolled away from him. It had sounded almost human. Foxes can sound like small children in pain – Regan had heard this long ago. Or perhaps it was a cat. Or a night bird of some kind.

Something had died, anyway, in the night. Of that there was no doubt at all.

The next morning one of the traps had been sprung, although when Regan opened it carefully, it proved to be empty. The chocolate bait had been nibbled. He opened the door to the trap once more and replaced it by the wall.

Janice was crying to herself in the lounge. Regan stood beside her; she reached out her hand, and he held it tightly. Her fingers were cold. She was still wearing her nightgown, and she had put on no makeup.

Later she made a phone call.

A package arrived for Regan shortly before noon by Federal Express, containing a dozen floppy disks, each filled with numbers for him to inspect and sort and classify.

He worked at the computer until six, sitting in front of a small metal fan that whirred and rattled and moved the hot air around.

He turned on the radio that evening while he cooked.

'. . . what my book *tells* everyone. What the liberals don't *want* us to know.' The voice was high, nervous, arrogant.

'Yeah. Some of it was, well kinda hard to believe.' The host was encouraging: a deep radio voice, reassuring and easy on the ears.

'Of *course* it's hard to believe. It runs against everything they *want* you to believe. The liberals and the how-mo-sexuals in the media, they don't *let* you know the truth.'

'Well, we all know that, friend. We'll be right back after this song.'

It was a country and western song. Regan kept the radio tuned to the local National Public Radio station; sometimes they broadcast the BBC World Service News. Someone must have retuned it, he supposed, although he couldn't imagine who.

He took a sharp knife and cut through the chicken breast with care, parting the pink flesh, slicing it into strips all ready to stir-fry, listening to the song.

Somebody's heart was broken; somebody no longer cared. The song ended. There was a commercial for beer. Then the men began to talk again.

'Thing is, nobody believes it at first. But I got the *do*cuments. I got the *pho*tographs. You read my book. *You'll* see. It's the unholy alliance, and I *do* mean unholy, between the so-called pro-choice lobby, the medical community, and how-mo-sexuals. The how-mos *need* these murders because that's where they get the little children they use to e*xper*iment with to find a cure for AIDS.

'I mean, those liberals talk about *Nazi* atrocities, but nothing those Nazis did comes in even *close* to what *they're* doing, even as we speak. They take these human foetuses and they graft them onto little mice to create these human-mouse hybrid creatures for their experiments. *Then* they inject them with AIDS. . .'

Regan found himself thinking of Mengele's wall of strung eyeballs. Blue eyes and brown eyes and hazel . . .

'Shit!' He'd sliced into his thumb. He pushed it into his mouth, bit down on it to stop the bleeding, ran into the bathroom, and began to hunt for a Band-Aid.

'Remember, I'll need to be out of the house by ten tomorrow.' Janice was standing behind him. He looked at her blue eyes in the bathroom mirror. She looked calm.

'Fine.' He pulled the Band-Aid onto his thumb, hiding and binding the wound, and turned to face her.

'I saw a cat in the garden today,' she said. 'A big grey one. Maybe it's a stray.'

'Maybe.'

'Did you think any more about getting a pet?'

'Not really. It'd just be something else to worry about. I thought we agreed: no pets.'

She shrugged.

They went back into the kitchen. He poured oil

into the frying pan and lit the gas. He dropped the strips of pink flesh into the pan and watched them shrink and discolour and change.

Janice drove herself to the bus station early the next morning. It was a long drive into the city, and she'd be in no condition to drive when she was ready to return. She took five hundred dollars with her, in cash.

Regan checked the traps. Neither of them had been touched. Then he prowled the corridors of the house.

Eventually, he phoned Gwen. The first time he misdialled, his fingers slipping on the buttons of the phone, the long string of digits confusing him. He tried again.

A ringing, then her voice on the line. 'Allied Accountancy Associates. Good afternoon.'

'Gwennie? It's me.'

'Regan? It's you, isn't it? I was hoping you'd call eventually. I missed you.' Her voice was distant; transatlantic crackle and hum taking her farther away from him.

'It's expensive.'

'Any more thoughts about coming back?'

'I don't know.'

'So how's wifeykins?'

'Janice is . . .' He paused. Sighed. 'Janice is just fine.'

'I've started fucking our new sales director,' said Gwen. 'After your time. You don't know him. You've been gone for six months now. I mean, what's a girl to do?'

It occurred then to Regan that that was what he hated most about women: their practicality. Gwen had always made him use a condom, although he disliked condoms, while she had also used a diaphragm and a spermicide. Regan felt that somewhere in all there a level of spontaneity, of romance, of passion, was lost. He liked sex to be something that just happened, half in his head, half out of it. Something sudden and dirty and powerful.

His forehead began to throb.

'So what's the weather like out there?' Gwen asked brightly.

'It's hot,' said Regan.

'Wish it was here. It's been raining for weeks.'

He said something about it being lovely to hear her voice again. Then he put down the phone.

Regan checked the traps. Still empty.

He wandered into his office and flipped on the TV.

'. . . this is a little one. That's what *foetus* means. And one day she'll grow up to be a big one. She's got little fingers, little toes – she's even got little toenails.'

A picture on the screen: red and pulsing and indistinct. It cut to a woman with a huge smile, cuddling a baby.

'Some little ones like her will grow up to be nurses, or teachers, or musicians. One day one of them may even be President.'

Back to the pink thing, filling the screen.

'But *this* little one will never grow up to be a big one. She's going to be killed tomorrow. And her mother says it isn't murder.'

He flipped channels until he found 'I Love Lucy', the perfect background nothing, then he turned on the computer and got down to work.

After two hours spent chasing an error of under a hundred dollars through seemingly endless columns of figures, his head began to ache. He got up and walked into the garden.

He missed having a garden; missed proper English lawns with proper English grass. The grass out here was withered, brown and sparse, the trees bearded with Spanish moss like something from a science fiction movie. He followed a track out into the woods behind the house. Something grey and sleek slipped from behind one tree to another.

'Here, kitty kitty,' called Regan. 'Here, puss puss puss.'

He walked over to the tree and looked behind it. The cat – or whatever it had been – was gone.

Something stung his cheek. He slapped at it without thought, lowered his hand to find it stained with blood, a mosquito, half-squashed, still twitching in his palm.

He went back into the kitchen and poured himself a cup of coffee. He missed tea, but it just didn't taste the same out here.

Janice got home about six.

'How was it?'

She shrugged. 'Fine.'

'Yeah?'

'Yeah.'

'I have to go back next week,' she said. 'For a checkup.'

'To make sure they didn't leave any instruments inside you?'

'Whatever,' she said.

'I've made a spaghetti Bolognese,' said Regan.

'I'm not hungry,' said Janice. 'I'm going to bed.'

She went upstairs.

Regan worked until the numbers no longer added up. He went upstairs and walked quietly into the darkened bedroom. He slipped off his clothes in the moonlight, dropped them onto the carpet, and slid between the sheets.

He could feel Janice next to him. Her body was shaking, and the pillow was wet.

'Jan?'

She had her back to him.

'It was horrible,' she whispered into her pillow. 'It hurt so much. And they wouldn't give me a proper anaesthetic or anything. They said I could have a shot of Valium if I wanted one, but they didn't have an anaesthetist there anymore. The lady said he couldn't stand the pressure and anyway it would have cost another two hundred dollars and nobody wanted to pay . . .

'It hurt so much.' She was sobbing now, gasping the words as if they were being tugged out of her. 'So much.'

Regan got out of bed.

'Where are you going?'

'I don't have to listen to this,' said Regan. 'I really don't have to listen to this.'

It was too hot in the house. Regan walked downstairs in only his underpants. He walked into the kitchen, bare feet making sticking noises on the vinyl.

One of the mousetrap doors was closed.

He picked up the trap. It felt a trifle heavier than before. He opened the door carefully, a little way. Two beady eyes stared up at him. Light brown fur. He pushed the door shut again and heard a scrabbling from inside the trap.

Now what?

He couldn't kill it. He couldn't kill anything.

The green mousetrap smelled acrid, and the bottom of it was sticky with mouse piss. Regan carried it gingerly out into the garden.

A gentle breeze had sprung up. The moon was almost full. He knelt on the ground, placed the trap carefully on the dry grass.

He opened the door of the small green corridor.

'Run away,' he whispered, feeling embarrassed at the sound of his voice in the open air. 'Run away, little mouse.'

The mouse didn't move. He could see its nose at the door of the trap.

'Come on,' said Regan. Bright moonlight; he could see everything, sharply lit and shadowed, if lacking in colour.

He nudged the trap with his foot.

The mouse made a dash for it then. It ran out from the trap, then stopped, turned, and began to hop into the woods.

Then it stopped again. The mouse looked up in Regan's direction. Regan was convinced that it was staring at him. It had tiny pink hands. Regan felt almost paternal then. He smiled, wistfully.

A streak of grey in the night, and the mouse hung, struggling uselessly, from the mouth of a large grey cat, its eyes burning green in the night. Then the cat bounded into the undergrowth.

He thought briefly of pursuing the cat, of freeing the mouse from its jaws . . .

There was a sharp scream from the woods; just a night sound, but for a moment Regan thought it sounded almost human, like a woman in pain.

He threw the little plastic mousetrap as far from him as he could. He was hoping for a satisfying crash as it hit something, but it fell soundlessly in the bushes.

Then Regan walked back inside, and he closed the door of the house behind him.

The Sea Change

Now is a good time to write this down,
now, with the rattle of the pebbles raked by the waves,
and the slanting rain cold, cold, pattering and spattering
the tin roof until I can barely hear myself think,
and over it all the wind's low howl. Believe me,
I could crawl down to the black waves now,
but that would be foolish, under the dark cloud.

'Now hear us as we cry to Thee
For those in peril on the sea.'

The old hymn hovers on my lips, unbidden,
perhaps I am singing aloud. I cannot tell.
I am not old, but when I wake I am wracked with pain,
an old sea wreck. Look at my hands.
Broken by the waves and the sea: and twisted,
they look like something I'd find on the beach, after a
      storm.
I hold my pen like an old man.

My father called a sea like this 'a widow-maker'.

My mother said the sea was always a widow-maker,
even when it was grey and smooth as sky. And she was
    right.
My father drowned in fine weather.
Sometimes I wonder if his bones have ever washed
    ashore,
or if I'd know them if they had,
twisted and sea-smoothed as they would be.

I was a lad of seventeen, cocky as any a young man
who thinks he can make the sea his mistress,
and I had promised my mother I'd not go to sea.
She'd prenticed me to a stationer, and my days were
    spent
with reams and quires; but when she died I took her
    savings
bought myself a small boat. I took my father's dusty
    nets and lobster pots,
raised a three-man crew, all older than I was,
and left the inkpots and the nibs for ever.

There were good months and bad.
Cold, cold, the sea was bitter and brine, the nets cut
my hands,
the lines were tricksy, dangerous things; still,
I'd not have given it up for the world. Not then.
The salt scent of my world made me sure I'd live
    forever.
Scudding over the waves in a fine breeze,
the sun behind me, faster than a dozen horses across
    the white wave tops,
that was living indeed.

The sea had moods. You learned that fast.

The day I write of now, she was shifty, evil-humoured,
the wind coming now and now from all four corners of
    the compass,
the waves all choppy. I could not get the measure of her.
We were all out of sight of land when I saw a hand,
saw something, reaching from the grey sea.
Remembering my father, I ran to the prow and called
    aloud.

No answer but the lonely wail of gulls.
And the air was filled with a whirr of white wings, and
    then
the swing of the wooden boom, which struck me at
    the base of the skull:
I remember the slow way the cold sea came toward
    me,
enveloped me, swallowed me, took me for its own.

I tasted salt. We are made of seawater and bone:
That's what the stationer told me when I was a boy.
It had occurred to me since that waters break to herald
    every birth,
and I am certain that those waters must taste salt –
remembering, perhaps, my own birth.
The world beneath the sea was blur. Cold, cold, cold . . .

I do not believe I truly saw her. I can not believe.
A dream, or madness, the lack of air,
the blow upon the head: That's all she was.
But when in dreams I see her, as I do, I never doubt her.
Old as the sea she was, and young as a new-formed
    breaker or a swell.
Her goblin eyes had spied me. And I knew she wanted
    me.

They say the sea folk have no souls: Perhaps
the sea is one huge soul they breathe and drink and
　　live.
She wanted me. And she would have had me; there
　　could be no doubt.
And yet . . .

They pulled me from the sea and pumped my chest
until I vomited rich seawater onto the wave-wet
　　shingle.
Cold, cold, cold I was, trembling and shivering and
　　sick.
My hands were broken and my legs were twisted,
as if I had just come up from deep water,
scrimshaw and driftwood are my bones,
carved messages hidden beneath my flesh.

The boat never came back. The crew was never more
　　seen.
I live on the charity of the village:
There, but for the mercy of the sea, they say, go we.
Some years have passed: almost a score.
And whole women view me with pity, or with scorn.

Outside my cottage the wind's howl has become a
　　screaming,
rattling the rain against the tin walls,
crunching the flinty shingle, stone against stone.

'Now hear us as we cry to Thee
For those in peril on the sea.'

Believe me, I could go down to the sea tonight,
drag myself down there on my hands and knees.

Give myself to the water and the dark.
And to the girl.
Let her suck the meat from off these tangled bones,
transmute me to something incorruptible and ivory:
to something rich and strange. But that would be
foolish.

The voice of the storm is whispering to me.
The voice of the beach is whispering to me.
The voice of the waves is whispering to me.

 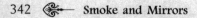

How Do You Think It Feels?

I am in bed, now. I can feel the linen sheets beneath me, warmed to body temperature, slightly rumpled. There is no-one in the bed with me.

My chest no longer hurts. I feel nothing at all. I feel just fine.

My dreams are vanishing as I wake, overexposed by the glare of the morning sun through my bedroom window, and are being replaced, slowly, by memories; and now, with only a purple flower and the scent of her still on the pillow, my memories are all of Becky, and fifteen years drifts away like confetti or falling blossom, through my hands.

She was just twenty. I was by far the older man, almost twenty-seven, with a wife, and a career, and twin little girls. And I was ready to give them all up for her.

We met at a conference, in Hamburg, in Germany. I had seen her performing in a presentation on 'The Future of Interactive Entertainment', and had found her attractive and amusing. Her hair was long and dark, her eyes were a greenish blue. At first, I was certain that she reminded me of someone I knew, and then I realised that I had never actually met the person she reminded me of: it was Emma Peel, Diana Rigg's character in the *Avengers* television series. I had loved her and longed for her, in black and white, before I ever reached my tenth birthday.

That evening, passing her in a corridor on my way to some software vendor's party, I congratulated her upon her performance. She told me that she was a professional actress, hired for the presentation ('after all, we can't all be in the West End can we?') and that her name was Rebecca.

Later, I kissed her in a doorway, and she sighed as she pressed against me.

Becky slept in my hotel room for the rest of the conference. I was head-over-heels in love, and so, I liked to think, was she. Our affair continued when we returned to England: fizzy, funny, utterly delightful, a little dangerous. It was love, I knew, and it tasted like champagne in my mind.

I spent all my free time with her, told Caroline, my wife, I was working late, needed in London, busy. Instead I was in Becky's Battersea flat with Becky.

I took joy in her body, the golden litheness of her skin, her blue-green eyes. She found it hard to relax during sex – she seemed to like the idea of it, but to be less impressed by the physical practicalities. She found oral sex faintly disgusting, giving or receiving it, and liked the sexual act best when it was over fastest. I hardly cared: the way she looked was enough for me, and the speed of her wit. I liked the way she made little doll-faces out of modelling clay, and the way the plasticine crept in dark crescents under her fingernails. She had a beautiful voice, and sometimes, spontaneously, would begin to sing – popular songs, folk songs, snatches of opera, television jingles, whatever came into her mind. Caroline did not sing, not even nursery rhymes.

Colours seemed brighter because Becky was there. I began to notice parts of life I had never seen before: I saw the elegant intricacy of flowers, because Becky loved flowers, and knew all their names; I became a fan of silent movies, because Becky loved silent movies, and I watched *The Thief of Baghdad* and *Sherlock Junior* over and over on video; I began to accumulate CDs and tapes, because Becky loved music, and I loved her, and I loved whatever she loved. I had never heard music before; never understood the black and white grace of a silent clown before; never touched, or smelled, or properly looked at, a flower, before I met her.

She told me that she needed to stop acting and to do something that would make her more money, and would bring that money in regularly. I put her in touch with a friend in the music business, and she became his personal assistant. I wondered, sometimes, if they were sleeping together, but I said nothing about it – I did not dare, although I brooded on it. I did not want to endanger what we had together, and I knew that I had no grounds from which to reproach her.

'How do you think I feel?' she asked. We were walking back to her flat from the Thai restaurant around the corner. We ate there most of the time. 'Knowing that you are going back to your wife, every night? How do you think it feels for me?'

I knew she was right. I did not want to hurt anyone yet I felt as if I were tearing myself apart. My work, at the small software company I owned, suffered. I began to nerve myself to tell Caroline that I was leaving her.

I envisioned Becky's joy at learning that I was to be only hers. It would be hard and hurtful to Caroline, and harder on the twins, but it would have to be done.

Each time I played with the twins, my two almost-identical girls (clue: look for the tiny mole above Amanda's lip, the rounder line of Jessica's jaw), their hair a lighter shade of Caroline's dark honey colour, every time I took them to the park or bathed them or tucked them in at night, it hurt me inside. But I knew what I had to do; that the pain I was feeling would soon be replaced with the perfect joy that living with Becky, loving Becky, spending every waking moment with Becky, would bring me.

It was less than a week before Christmas, and the days were as short as they were ever going to get. I took Becky out to the Thai place for dinner, and, as she licked the peanut sauce from a stick of chicken satay, I told her that, immediately after Christmas, I would soon be leaving my wife and children for her. I expected to see a smile on her face, but she said nothing, and she did not smile.

In her flat, that night, she refused to sleep with me. Instead, she told me it was all over between us. I drank too much, cried for the last time as an adult, begged her and pleaded with her to reconsider.

'You aren't any fun any more,' she said, simply and flatly, as I sat, sadly, on the floor of her living room, my back resting against the side of her battered sofa. 'You used to be fun, and funny. Now you just mope around all the time.'

'I'm sorry,' I said, pathetically. 'Really, I'm sorry. I can change.'

'See?' she said. 'No fun at all.'

Then she opened the door to her bedroom, and

went inside, closing it and locking it, finally, behind her; and I sat on the floor, and finished a bottle of whisky, all on my own, and then, maudlin drunk, I wandered about her flat, touching her things and snivelling. I read her diary. I went into the bathroom, and pulled her soiled panties from the laundry basket, and buried my face in them, breathing her scents. At one point I banged on her bedroom door, calling her name, but she did not respond, and she would not open the door.

I made the gargoyle for myself in the small hours of the morning, out of grey modelling clay.

I remember doing it. I was naked. I had found a large lump of plasticine on the mantelpiece, and I thumbed and kneaded it until it was soft and pliable, then, lost in a place of drunken, horny, angry madness, I masturbated into it, and kneaded my milky seed into the grey shapeless mess.

I have never been a sculptor, but something took shape beneath my fingers that night: blocky hands and grinning head, stumpy wings and twisted legs: I made it of my lust and self-pity and hatred, then I baptised it with the last drops of Johnny Walker Black Label and placed it over my heart, my own little gargoyle, to protect me from beautiful women with blue-green eyes and from ever feeling anything again.

I lay on the floor, with the gargoyle upon my chest; and, in moments, I slept.

When I woke up, a few hours later, her door was still locked, and it was still dark. I crawled to the bathroom, and threw up all over the toilet bowl and the floor and the scattered mess I had left of her underwear. And then I put on my clothes and went home.

I do not remember what I told my wife, when I got home. Perhaps there were things she did not wish to know. Don't ask, don't tell, all that. Perhaps Caroline teased me about Christmas drinking. I can barely remember.

I did not ever return to the flat in Battersea.

I saw Becky every couple of years, in passing, on the Tube, or in the City, never comfortably. She seemed brittle and awkward. We would say hello, and she would congratulate me on whatever my latest achievements were, for I had taken my energies and channelled them into my work, building something that was, if it was not (as it was often called) an entertainment empire, then it was at least a small principality of music and drama and interactive adventure.

Sometimes I would meet girls, smart, beautiful, wonderful girls and, as time went on, women, for whom I could have fallen; people I could have loved. But I did not love them. I did not love anybody.

Heads and hearts: and in my head I tried not to think about Becky, assured myself I did not love her, did not need her, did not think about her. But when I did think of her, when, unbidden, memories of her smile or of her eyes came to me, then I felt pain: a sharp hurt inside my rib-cage, a perceptible, actual pain inside me, as if something were squeezing sharp fingers into my heart.

And it was at these times that I imagined that I could feel the little grey gargoyle in my chest. It would wrap itself, stone-cold, about my heart, protecting me until I felt nothing at all, and I would return to my work.

Years passed: the twins grew up and they left home to go to college, and I left home too, leaving it with Caroline, and I moved into a large flat in Chelsea and lived on my own, and was, if not happy, then, at least content.

And then it was yesterday afternoon. Becky saw me first, in Hyde Park, where I was sitting on a bench, reading a company report in the springtime sun, and she ran over to me and touched my hand.

'Don't you remember your old friends?' she asked.

I looked up. 'Hello, Becky.'

'You haven't changed.'

'Neither have you,' I told her. I had silver-grey in my thick beard, and had lost most of my hair on the top, and she was a trim woman in her mid-thirties. I was not lying, though, and neither was she.

'You are doing very well,' she said. 'I read about you in the papers all the time.'

'Just means that my publicity people are earning their keep. What are you doing these days?'

She was running the press office of an independent television network. She wished, she said, that she had stuck with acting, certain that she would, by now, have been on the West End stage. She ran her hand through her long, dark hair, and smiled like Emma Peel, and I would have followed her anywhere. I closed my book and put it into the pocket of my jacket.

We walked through the park, hand in hand. The spring flowers nodded their heads at us, yellow and orange and white, as we passed.

'Makes me feel like Wordsworth,' I told her. 'All those daffodils.'

'Those are *narcissi*,' she said. 'Daffodils are a kind of *narcissus*.'

It was spring in Hyde Park, and we were almost able to forget the city surrounding us. We stopped at an ice-cream stand and bought two violently coloured frozen ice-cream confections.

'Was there someone else, back then?' I asked her, eventually, as casually as I could, licking my ice-cream. 'Someone you left me for?'

She shook her head. 'You were getting too serious,' she said. 'That was all. And I wasn't a homewrecker.'

Later that night, much later, she repeated it. 'I wasn't a homewrecker,' she said, and she stretched, languorously, and added, '– *then*. Now, I don't care.'

I had not told her that I was divorced. We had eaten sushi and sashimi in a restaurant in Greek Street, drunk enough sake to warm us and to cast a rice-wine glow over the evening. We took a golden-painted taxi back to my flat in Chelsea.

The sake was warm in my chest. In my bedroom we kissed, and hugged, and laughed. Becky examined my CD collection carefully, and then she put on the Cowboy Junkies' *The Trinity Session*, singing along in a quiet voice. This was only a few hours ago, but I cannot remember the point at which she removed her clothes. I remember her breasts, however, still beautiful, although they had lost the firmness and shape they had when she was little more than a girl: her nipples were deep red, and pronounced.

I had put on some weight. She had not.

'Will you go down on me?' she whispered, when we reached my bed, and I did. Her labia were engorged, purple, full and long, and they opened like a flower to my mouth when I began to lick her. Her clitoris swelled beneath my tongue and the salty taste of her filled my world, and I licked and teased and sucked and nibbled at her sex for what felt like hours.

She came, once, spasmodically, under my tongue, and then she pulled my head up to hers, and we kissed some more, and then, finally, she guided me inside her.

'Was your cock that big fifteen years ago?' she asked.

'I think so,' I told her.

'Mmm.'

After a while she said, 'I want you to come in my mouth.' And, soon after, I did.

We lay in silence, side by side, and she said, 'Do you hate me?'

'No,' I said, sleepily. 'I used to. I hated you for years. And I loved you, too.'

'And now?'

'No, I don't hate you any more. It's gone away. Floated off into the night, like a balloon.' I realised as I said it that I was speaking the truth.

She snuggled closer to me, pressed her warm skin against my skin. 'I can't believe I ever let you go. I won't make that mistake twice. I do love you.'

'Thank you.'

'Not, "*thank you*", idiot. Try "*I love you too*".'

'I love you too,' I echoed, and, sleepily, I kissed her still-sticky lips. And then I slept.

In my dream I felt something uncurling inside me, something moving and changing. The cold of stone, a lifetime of darkness. A rending, and a ripping, as if my heart were breaking; a moment of utter pain. Blackness and strangeness and blood.

I must have dreamed the grey dawn as well. I opened my eyes, moving away from one dream but not entirely coming awake. My chest was wide open, literally: there was a dark split that ran from my navel to my neck, and a huge, misshapen hand, plasticine-grey, was pulling back into the crack. There was long dark hair caught between the stone fingers. The hand retreated into my chest as I watched, as an insect will vanish into a crack when the lights are turned on. And, as I squinted sleepily down at it, my acceptance of the strangeness of it all my only clue that this was truly another dream, the split in my chest healed, knit and mended, and the cold hand vanished for good. I felt my eyes closing once more. I was tired, and I swam back into the comforting, sake-flavoured dark.

I slept once more, but those dreams are now lost to me.

I awoke, completely, a few moments ago, the morning sun full on my face. There was nothing beside me in the bed but a purple flower on the pillow. I am holding it now. It reminds me of an orchid, although I know little enough of flowers, and its scent is strange, salty and female.

Becky must have placed it here for me to find, when she left, while I slept.

Pretty soon now I shall have to get up. I shall get out of this bed and resume my life.

I wonder if I shall ever see her again, and I realise that I scarcely care. I can feel the sheets beneath me, and the cold air on my chest. I feel fine. I feel absolutely fine.

I feel nothing at all.

When We Went to See the End of the World by Dawnie Morningside, age 11¼

What I did on the founders day holiday was, my dad said we were going to have a picnic, and, my mum said where and I said I wanted to go to Ponydale and ride the ponies, but my dad said we were going to the end of the world and my mum said oh god and my dad said now, Tanya, its time the child got to see what was what and my mum said no, no, she just meant that shed thought that Johnsons Peculiar Garden of Lights was nice this time of year.

My mum loves Johnsons Peculiar Garden of Lights, which is in Lux, between 12th street and the river, and I like it too, especially when they give you potato sticks and you feed them to the little white chipmunks who come all the way up to the picnic table.

This is the word for the white chipmunks. Albino.

Dolorita Hunsickle says that the chipmunks tell your fortune if you catch them but I never did. She says a chipmunk told her she would grow up to be a famous ballerina and that she would die of consumption unloved in a boardinghouse in Prague.

So my dad made potato salad.

Here is the recipe.

My dads potato salad is made with tiny new potatoes, which he boils, then while their warm he pours his secret mix over them which is mayonnaise and sour cream and little onion things called chives which he sotays in bacon fat, and crunchy bacon bits. When it gets cool its the best potato salad in the world, and better than the potato salad we get at school which tastes like white sick.

We stopped at the shop and got fruit and Coca-cola and potato sticks, and they went into the box and it went into the back of the car and we went into the car and mum and dad and my baby sister, We Are On Our Way!

Where our house is, it is morning, when we leave, and we got onto the motorway and we went over the bridge over twilight, and soon it got dark. I love driving through the dark.

I sit in the back of the car and I got all scrunched singing songs that go lah lah lah in the back of my head so my dad has to go, Dawnie darling stop making that noise, but still I go lah lah lah.

Lah lah lah.

The motorway was closed for repairs so we followed signs and this is what they said: DIVERSION.

Mummy made dad lock his door, while we were driving, and she made me to lock my door too.

It got more darker as we went.

This is what I saw while we drived through the centre of the city, out of the window. I saw a beardy man who ran out when we stopped at the lights and ran a smeary cloth all over our windows.

He winked at me through the window, in the back of the car, with his old eyes.

Then he wasnt there any more, and mummy and daddy had an arguement about who he was, and whether he was good luck or bad luck. But not a bad arguement.

Their were more signs that said DIVERSION, and they were yellow.

I saw a street where the prettiest men Id ever seen blew us kisses and sung songs, and a street where I saw a woman holding the side of her face under a blue light but her face was bleeding and wet, and a street where there were only cats who stared at us.

My sister went loo loo, which means look and she said kitty.

The baby is called Melicent, but I call her Daisydaisy. Its my secret name for her. Its from a song called Daisydaisy, which goes, Daisydaisy give me your answer do Im half crazy over the love of you it wont be a stylish marriage I cant afford a carriage but youll look sweet upon the seat of a bicicle made for two.

Then we were out of the city, into the hills.

Then there were houses that were like palaces on each side of the road, set far back.

My dad was born in one of those houses, and he and mummy had the arguement about money where he says what he threw away to be with her and she says oh, so your bringing that up again are you?

I looked at the houses. I asked my Daddy which one Grandmother lived in. He said he didnt know, which he was lying. I dont know why grownups fib so much, like when they say Ill tell you later or well see when they mean no or I wont tell you at all even when your older.

In one house there were people dancing in the garden. Then the road began to wind around, and daddy was driving us through the countryside through the dark.

Look! said my mother. A white deer ran across the road with people chasing it. My dad said they were a nuisance and they were a pest and like rats with antlers, and the worst bit of hitting a deer is when it comes through the glass into the car and he said he had a friend who was kicked to death by a deer who came through the glass with sharp hooves.

And mummy said oh god like we really needed to know that, and daddy said well it happened Tanya, and mummy said honestly your incorigible.

I wanted to ask who the people chasing the deer was, but I started to sing instead going lah lah lah lah lah lah.

My dad said stop that. My mum said for gods sake let the girl express herself, and Dad said I bet you like chewing tinfoil too and my mummy said so whats that supposed to mean and Daddy said nothing and I said arent we there yet?

On the side of the road there were bonfires, and sometimes piles of bones.

We stopped on one side of a hill. The end of the world was on the other side of the hill, said my dad.

I wondered what it looked like. We parked the car in the car park. We got out. Mummy carried Daisy. Daddy carried the picnic basket. We walked over the hill, in the light of the candles they set by the path. A unicorn came up to me on the way. It was white as snow, and it nuzzled me with its mouth.

I asked daddy if I could give it an apple and he said it probably has fleas, and Mummy said it didnt. and all the time its tail went swish swish swish.

I offered it my apple it looked at me with big silver

eyes and then it snorted like this, hrrrmph, and ran away over the hill.

Baby Daisy said loo loo.

This is what it looks like at the end of the world, which is the best place in the world.

There is a hole in the ground, which looks like a very wide big hole and pretty people holding sticks and simatars that burn come up out of it. They have long golden hair. They look like princesses, only fierce. Some of them have wings and some of them dusnt.

And theres a big hole in the sky too and things are coming down from it, like the cat-heady man, and the snakes made out of stuff that looks like glitter-jel like I putted on my hair at Hallowmorn, and I saw something that looked like a big old buzzie fly, coming down from the sky. There were very many of them. As many as stars.

They dont move. They just hang there, not doing anything. I asked Daddy why they weren't moving and he said they were moving just very very slowly but I dont think so.

We set up at a picnic table.

Daddy said the best thing about the end of the world was no wasps and no moskitos. And mummy said there werent a lot of wasps in Johnsons Peculiar Garden of Lights either. I said there werent alot of wasps or moskitos at Ponydale and there were ponies too we could ride on and my Dad said hed brought us here to enjoy ourselves.

I said I wanted to go over to see if I could see the unicorn again and mummy and daddy said dont go too far.

At the next table to us were people with masks on. I went off with Daisydaisy to see them.

They sang Happy Birthday to you to a big fat lady with no clothes on, and a big funny hat. She had lots of bosoms all the way down to her tummy. I waited to see her blow out the candles on her cake, but there wasnt a cake.

Arent you going to make a wish? I said.

She said she couldnt make any more wishes. She was too old. I told her that at my last birthday when I blew out my candles all in one go I had thought about my wish for a long time, and I was going to wish that mummy and Daddy wouldn't argue any more in the night. But in the end I wished for a shetland pony but it never come.

The lady gave me a cuddle and said I was so cute that she could just eat me all up, bones and hair and everything. She smelled like sweet dried milk.

Then Daisydaisy started to cry with all her might and mane, and the lady putted me down.

I shouted and called for the unicorn, but I didnt see him. Sometimes I thought I could hear a trumpet, and sometimes I thought it was just the noise in my ears.

Then we came back to the table. Whats after the end of the world I said to my dad. Nothing he said. Nothing at all. Thats why its called the end.

Then Daisy was sick over Daddys shoes, and we cleaned it up.

I sat by the table. We ate potato salad, which I gave you the recipe for all ready, you should make it its really good, and we drank orange juice and potato sticks and squishy egg and cress sandwiches. We drank our Coca-cola.

Then Mummy said something to Daddy I didnt hear and he just hit her in the face with a big hit with his hand, and mummy started to cry.

Daddy told me to take Daisy and walk about while they talked.

I took Daisy and I said come on Daisydaisy, come on old daisybell because she was crying too, but Im too old to cry.

I couldnt hear what they were saying. I looked up at the cat face man and I tried to see if he was moving very very slowly, and I heard the trumpet at the end of the world in my head going dah dah dah.

We sat by a rock and I sang songs to Daisy lah lah lah lah lah to the sound of the trumpet in my head dah dah dah.

Lah lah lah lah lah lah lah lah.

Lah lah lah.

Then mummy and daddy came over to me and they said we were going home. But that everything was really all right. Mummys eye was all purple. She looked funny, like a lady on the television.

Daisy said owie. I told her yes, it was an owie. We got back in the car.

On the way home, nobody said anything. The baby sleeped.

There was a dead animal by the side of the road somebody had hit with a car. Daddy said it was a white deer. I thought it was the unicorn, but mummy told me that you cant kill unicorns but I think she was lying like grownups do again.

When we got to Twilight I said, if you told someone your wish, did that mean it wouldnt come true?

What wish, said Daddy?

Your birthday wish. When you blow out the candles.

He said, Wishes dont come true whether you tell them or not. Wishes, he said. He said you cant trust wishes.

I asked Mummy, and she said, whatever your father says, she said in her cold voice, which is the one she uses when she tells me off with my whole name.

Then I slept too.

And then we were home, and it was morning, and I dont want to see the end of the world again. And before I got out of the car, while mummy was carrying in Daisydaisy to the house, I closed my eyes so I couldn't see anything at all, and I wished and I wished and I wished and I wished. I wished wed gone to Ponydale. I wished wed never gone anywhere at all. I wished I was somebody else.

And I wished.

 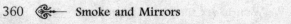

Desert Wind

There was an old man with skin baked black by the
    desert sun
who told me that, when he was young, a storm had
    separated him from his caravan
and its spices, and he walked over rock and over sand
    for days and nights,
seeing nothing but small lizards and sand-coloured rats.

But that, on the third day, he came upon a city of silken
    tents
of all bright colours. A woman led him into the largest
    tent,
crimson the silk was, and set a tray in front of him,
    gave him iced sherbet
to drink, and cushions to lie upon, and then, with scarlet
    lips, she kissed his brow.

Veiled dancers undulated in front of him, bellies like
    sand dunes,
Eyes like pools of dark water in oases, purple were all
    their silks,

and their rings were gold. He watched the dancers
while servants brought him food,
all kinds of food, and wine as white as silk and wine as
red as sin.

And then, the wine making good madness in his belly
and his head, he jumped up,
into the midst of the dancers, and danced with them,
feet stamping on the sand,
jumping and pounding, and he took the fairest of all
the dancers
in his arms and kissed her. But his lips pressed to a dry
and desert-pitted skull.

And each dancer in purple had become bones, but still
they curved and stamped
in their dance. And he felt the city of tents then like
dry sand, hissing and escaping
through his fingers, and he shivered, and buried his
head in his *burnous*,
And sobbed, so he could no longer hear the drums.

He was alone, he said, when he awoke. The tents were
gone and the *ifreets*.
The sky was blue, the sun was pitiless. That was a
lifetime ago.
He lived to tell the tale. He laughed with toothless
gums, and told us this:
He has seen the city of silken tents on the horizon
since, dancing in the haze.

I asked him if it were a mirage, and he said yes. I said it
was a dream,
and he agreed, but said it was the desert's dream, not

his. And he told me that
in a year or so, when he had aged enough for any man,
   then he would walk
into the wind, until he saw the tents. This time, he said,
   he would go on with them.

*H*e had a tattoo on his upper arm, of a small heart, done in blue and red. Beneath it was a patch of pink skin, where a name had been erased.

He was licking her left nipple, slowly. His right hand was caressing the back of her neck.

'What's wrong?' she asked.

He looked up. 'What do you mean?'

'You seem like you're. I don't know. Somewhere else,' she said. 'Oh . . . that's nice. That's really nice.'

They were in a hotel suite. It was her suite. He knew who she was, had recognised her on sight, but had been warned not to use her name.

He moved his head up to look into her eyes, moved his hand down to her breast. They were both naked from the waist up. She had a silk skirt on; he wore blue jeans.

'Well?' she said.

He put his mouth against hers. Their lips touched. Her tongue flickered against his. She sighed, pulled back. 'So what's wrong? Don't you like me?'

He grinned, reassuringly. 'Like you? I think you're

wonderful,' he said. He hugged her, tightly. Then his hand cupped her left breast, and, slowly, squeezed it. She closed her eyes.

'Well, then,' she whispered, 'what's wrong?'

'Nothing,' he said. 'It's wonderful. You're wonderful. You're very beautiful.'

'My ex-husband used to say that I used my beauty,' she told him. She ran the back of her hand across the front of his jeans, up and down. He pushed against her, arching his back. 'I suppose he was right.' She knew the name he had given her, but, certain that it was false, a name of convenience, would not call him by it.

He touched her cheek. Then he moved his mouth back to her nipple. This time, as he licked, he moved a hand down between her legs. The silk of her skirt was soft against his hand, and he cupped his fingers against her pubis and slowly increased the pressure.

'Anyway, something's wrong,' she said. 'There's something going on in that pretty head of yours. Are you sure you don't want to talk about it?'

'It's silly,' he said. 'And I'm not here for me. I'm here for you.'

She undid the buttons of his jeans. He rolled over and slid them off, dropping them onto the floor by the bed. He wore thin scarlet underpants, and his erect penis pushed against the material.

While he took off his jeans, she removed her earrings; they were made of elaborately looped silver wires. She placed them carefully beside the bed.

He laughed, suddenly.

'What was that about?' she asked.

'Just a memory. Strip poker,' he said. 'When I was a kid, I don't know, thirteen or fourteen, we used to play with the girls next door. They'd always load up with *tchotchkes* – necklaces, earrings, scarves, things like that. So when they'd lose, they'd take off one earring or whatever. Ten minutes in, we'd be nude and embarrassed, and they'd still be fully dressed.'

'So why'd you play with them?'

'Hope,' he said. He reached beneath her skirt, began to massage her labia through her white cotton panties. 'Hope that maybe we'd get a glimpse of something. Anything.'

'And did you?'

He pulled his hand away, rolled on top of her. They kissed. They pushed as they kissed, gently, crotch to crotch. Her hands squeezed the cheeks of his ass. He shook his head. 'No. But you can always dream.'

'So. What's silly? And why wouldn't I understand?'

'Because it's dumb. Because . . . I don't know what you're thinking.'

She pulled down his Jockey shorts. Ran her forefinger along the side of his penis. 'It's really big. Natalie said it would be.'

'Yeah?'

'I'm not the first person to tell you that it's big.'

'No.'

She lowered her head, kissed his penis at the base, where the spring of golden hair brushed it, then she dribbled a little saliva onto it and ran her tongue slowly up its length. She pulled back after that, stared into his blue eyes with her brown ones.

'You don't know what I'm thinking? What does that mean? Do you normally know what other people are thinking?'

He shook his head. 'Well,' he said. 'Not exactly.'

'Hold that thought,' she said. 'I'll be right back.'

She got up, walked into the bathroom, closed the

door behind her but did not lock it. There was the sound of urine splashing into a toilet bowl. It seemed to go on for a long time. The toilet was flushed; the sound of movement in the bathroom, a cupboard opening, closing; more movements.

She opened the door and came out. She was quite naked now. She looked, for the first time, slightly self-conscious. He was sitting on the bed, also naked. His hair was blond and cut very short. As she came close to him, he reached out his hands, held her waist, pulled her close to him. His face was level with her navel. He licked it, then lowered his head to her crotch, pushed his tongue between her long labia, lapped and licked.

She began to breathe faster.

While he tongued her clitoris, he pushed a finger into her vagina. It was already wet, and the finger slid in easily.

He slid his other hand down her back to the curve of her ass and let it remain there.

'So. Do you always know what people are thinking?'

He pulled his head back, her juices on his mouth. 'It's a bit stupid. I mean, I don't really want to talk about it. You'll think I'm weird.'

She reached down, tipped his chin up, kissed him. She bit his lip, not too hard, pulled at it with her teeth.

'You are weird. But I like it when you talk. And I want to know what's wrong, Mister Mind Reader.'

She sat next to him on the bed. 'You have terrific breasts,' he told her. 'Really lovely.'

She made a *moue*. 'They're not as good as they used to be. And don't change the subject.'

'I'm not changing the subject.' He lay back on the bed. 'I can't really read minds. But I sort of can. When

I'm in bed with someone. I know what makes them tick.'

She climbed on top of him, sat on his stomach. 'You're kidding.'

'No.'

He fingered her clitoris gently. She squirmed. 'Nice.' She moved back six inches. Now she was sitting on his penis, pushed flat between them. She moved on it.

'I know . . . I usually . . . do you know how hard it is to concentrate with you doing that?'

'Talk,' she said. 'Talk to me.'

'Put it in you.'

She reached down one hand, held his penis. She lifted herself up slightly, squatted down on his penis, feeding the head inside her. He arched his back, pushed up into her. She closed her eyes, then opened them and stared at him. 'Well?'

'It's just that when I'm fucking, or even in the time before fucking, well . . . I *know* things. Things I honestly don't know – or can't know. Things I don't want to know even. Abuse. Abortions. Madness. Incest. Whether they're secret sadists or stealing from their bosses.'

'For example?'

He was all the way in her now, thrusting slowly in and out. Her hands were resting on his shoulders. She leaned down, kissed him on the lips.

'Well, like it works with sex, too. Usually I know how I'm doing. In bed. With women. I know what to do. I don't have to ask. I know. If she needs a top or a bottom, a master or a slave. If she needs me to whisper "I love you" over and over while I fuck her and we lie side by side, or just needs me to piss into her mouth. I become what she wants. That's why . . . Jesus. I can't believe I'm telling you this. I mean, that's why I started doing this for a living.'

'Yeah. Natalie swears by you. She gave me your number.'

'She's so cool. Natalie. And in such great shape for her age.'

'And what does Natalie like to do, then?'

He smiled up at her. 'Trade secret,' he said. 'Sworn to secrecy. Scout's honour.'

'Hold on,' she said. She climbed off him, rolled over. 'From behind. I like it from behind.'

'I should have known that,' he said, sounding almost irritated. He got up, positioned himself behind her, ran a finger down the soft skin that covered her spine. He put his hand between her legs, then grasped his penis and pushed it into her vagina.

'Really slow,' she said.

He thrust his hips, sliding his penis into her. She gasped.

'Is that nice?' he asked.

'No,' she said. 'It hurt a little when it was all the way in. Not so deep next time. So you know stuff about women when you screw them. What do you know about me?'

'Nothing special. I'm a big fan of yours.'

'Spare me.'

One of his arms was across her breasts. His other hand touched her lips. She sucked at his forefinger, licking it. 'Well, not that big a fan. But I saw you on Letterman, and I thought you were wonderful. Really funny.'

'Thanks.'

'I can't believe we're doing this.'

'Fucking?'

'No. Talking while we're fucking.'

'I like to talk while I fuck. That's enough like this. My knees are getting tired.'

He pulled out and sat back on the bed.

'So you knew what women were thinking, and what they wanted? Hmm. Does it work for men?'

'I don't know. I've never made love to a man.'

She stared at him. Placed a finger on his forehead, ran it slowly down to his chin, tracing the line of his cheekbone on the way. 'But you're so pretty.'

'Thank you.'

'And you're a whore.'

'Escort,' he said.

'Vain, too.'

'Perhaps. And you're not?'

She grinned. 'Touché. So. You don't know what I want now?'

'No.'

She lay on her side. 'Put on a condom and fuck me in the ass.'

'You got any lubricant?'

'Bedside table.'

He took the condom and the gel from the drawer, unrolled the condom down his penis.

'I hate condoms,' he told her as he put it on. 'They make me itch. And I've got a clean bill of health. I showed you the certificate.'

'I don't care.'

'I just thought I'd mention it. That's all.'

He rubbed the lubricant into and around her anus, then he slid the head of his penis inside her.

She groaned. He paused. 'Is – is that okay?'

'Yes.'

He rocked back and forth, pushing deeper. She

grunted, rhythmically, as he did so. After a couple of minutes she said 'Enough.'

He pulled out. She rolled onto her back and pulled the soiled condom off his penis, dropped it onto the carpet.

'You can come now,' she told him.

'I'm not ready. And we could go for hours yet.'

'I don't care. Come on my stomach.' She smiled at him. 'Make yourself come. Now.'

He shook his head, but his hand was already fumbling at his penis, jerking it forward and back until he spurted in a glistening trail all over her stomach and breasts.

She reached a hand down and rubbed the milky semen lazily across her skin.

'I think you should go now,' she said.

'But you didn't come. Don't you want me to make you come?'

'I got what I wanted.'

He shook his head, confusedly. His penis was flaccid and shrunken. 'I should have known,' he said, puzzled. 'I don't. I don't know. I don't know anything.'

'Get dressed,' she told him. 'Go away.'

He pulled on his clothes, efficiently, beginning with his socks. Then he leaned over, to kiss her.

She moved her head away from his lips. 'No,' she said.

'Can I see you again?'

She shook her head. 'I don't think so.'

He was shaking. 'What about the money?' he asked.

'I paid you already,' she said. 'I paid you when you came in. Don't you remember?'

He nodded, nervously, as if he could not remember but dared not admit it. Then he patted his pockets until he found the envelope with the cash in it, and he nodded once more. 'I feel so empty,' he said, plaintively.

She scarcely noticed when he left.

She lay on the bed with a hand on her stomach, his spermatic fluid drying cold on her skin, and she tasted him in her mind.

She tasted each woman he had slept with. She tasted what he did with her friend, smiling inside at Natalie's tiny perversities. She tasted the day he lost his first job. She tasted the morning he had awakened, still drunk, in his car, in the middle of a cornfield, and, terrified, had sworn off the bottle for ever. She knew his real name. She remembered the name that had once been tattooed on his arm and knew why it could be there no longer. She tasted the colour of his eyes from the inside, and shivered at the nightmare he had in which he was forced to carry spiny fish in his mouth, and from which he woke, choking, night after night. She savoured his hungers in food and fiction, and discovered a dark sky when he was a small boy and he had stared up at the stars and wondered at their vastness and immensity, that even he had forgotten.

Even in the pettiest, most unpromising material, she had discovered, you could find real treasures. And he had a little of the talent himself, although he had never understood it, or used it for anything more than sex. She wondered, as she swam in his memories and dreams, if he would miss them, if he would ever notice that they were gone. And then, shuddering, ecstatic, she came, in bright flashes, which warmed her and took her out of herself and into the nowhere-at-all perfection of the little death.

There was a crash from the alley below. Someone had stumbled into a garbage can.

She sat up and wiped the stickiness from her skin. And then, without showering, she began to dress herself once more, deliberately, beginning with her white cotton panties and ending with her elaborate silver earrings.

In the End

*I*n the end, the Lord gave Mankind the world. All the world was Man's, save for one garden. *This is my garden*, saith the Lord, *and here you shall not enter*.

There was a man and a woman who came to the garden, and their names were Earth and Breath.

They had with them a small fruit which the Man carried, and when they arrived at the gate to the garden, the Man gave the fruit to the Woman, and the Woman gave the fruit to the Serpent with the flaming sword who guarded the Eastern Gate.

And the Serpent took the fruit and placed it upon a tree in the centre of the garden.

Then Earth and Breath knew their clothedness, and removed their garments, one by one, until they were naked; and when the Lord walked through the garden he saw the man and the woman, who no longer knew good from evil, but were satisfied, and He saw it was good.

Then the Lord opened the gates and gave Mankind the garden, and the Serpent he raised up, and it walked away proudly on four strong legs; and where it went then none but the Lord can say.

And after that there was nothing but silence in the Garden, save for the occasional sound of the man taking away a name from another animal.

A few years back all the animals went away.
We woke up one morning, and they just weren't there anymore. They didn't even leave us a note, or say good-bye. We never figured out quite where they'd gone.

We missed them.

Some of us thought that the world had ended, but it hadn't. There just weren't any more animals. No cats or rabbits, no dogs or whales, no fish in the seas, no birds in the skies.

We were all alone.

We didn't know what to do.

We wandered around lost, for a time, and then someone pointed out that just because we didn't have animals anymore, that was no reason to change our lives. No reason to change our diets or to cease testing products that might cause us harm.

After all, there were still babies.

Babies can't talk. They can hardly move. A baby is not a rational, thinking creature.

We made babies.

And we used them.

Some of them we ate. Baby flesh is tender and succulent.

We flayed their skin and decorated ourselves in it. Baby leather is soft and comfortable.

Some of them we tested.

We taped open their eyes, dripped detergents and shampoos in, a drop at a time.

We scarred them and scalded them. We burnt them. We clamped them and planted electrodes into their brains. We grafted, and we froze, and we irradiated.

The babies breathed our smoke, and the babies' veins flowed with our medicines and drugs, until they stopped breathing or until their blood ceased to flow.

It was hard, of course, but it was necessary.

No one could deny that.

With the animals gone, what else could we do?

Some people complained, of course. But then, they always do.

And everything went back to normal.

Only . . .

Yesterday, all the babies were gone.

We don't know where they went. We didn't even see them go.

We don't know what we're going to do without them.

But we'll think of something. Humans are smart. It's what makes us superior to the animals and the babies.

We'll figure something out.

Murder Mysteries

The Fourth Angel says:
> Of this order I am made one,
> From Mankind to guard this place
> That through their Guilt they have foregone
> For they have forfeited His Grace;
> Therefore all this must they shun
> Or else my Sword they shall embrace
> And myself will be their Foe
> To flame them in the Face.

— CHESTER MYSTERY CYCLE,
THE CREATION AND ADAM AND EVE, 1461

*T*his is true.

Ten years ago, give or take a year, I found myself on an enforced stopover in Los Angeles, a long way from home. It was December, and the California weather was warm and pleasant. England, however, was in the grip of fogs and snowstorms, and no planes were landing there. Each day I'd phone the airport, and each day I'd be told to wait another day.

This had gone on for almost a week.

I was barely out of my teens. Looking around today at the parts of my life left over from those days, I feel uncomfortable, as if I've received a gift, unasked, from another person: a house, a wife, children, a vocation. Nothing to do with me, I could say, innocently. If it's true that every seven years each cell in your body dies and is replaced, then I have truly inherited my life from a dead man; and the misdeeds of those times have been forgiven, and are buried with his bones.

I was in Los Angeles. Yes.

On the sixth day I received a message from an old sort-of-girlfriend from Seattle: she was in L.A., too, and she had heard I was around on the friends-of-friends network. Would I come over?

I left a message on her machine. Sure.

That evening: a small, blonde woman approached me as I came out of the place I was staying. It was already dark.

She stared at me, as if she were trying to match me to a description, and then, hesitantly, she said my name.

'That's me. Are you Tink's friend?'

'Yeah. Car's out back. C'mon. She's really looking forward to seeing you.'

The woman's car was one of the huge old boatlike jobs you only ever seem to see in California. It smelled of cracked and flaking leather upholstery. We drove out from wherever we were to wherever we were going.

Los Angeles was at that time a complete mystery to me; and I cannot say I understand it much better now. I understand London, and New York, and Paris: you can walk around them, get a sense of what's where in just a morning of wandering, maybe catch the subway. But Los Angeles is about cars. Back then I didn't drive at all; even today I will not drive in America. Memories of L.A. for me are linked by rides in other people's cars, with no sense there of the shape of the city, of the relationships between the people and the place. The regularity of the roads, the repetition of structure and form, mean that when I try to remember it as an entity, all I have is the boundless profusion of tiny lights I saw from the hill of Griffith Park one night, on my first trip to the city. It was one of the most beautiful things I had ever seen, from that distance.

'See that building?' said my blonde driver, Tink's friend. It was a redbrick Art Deco house, charming and quite ugly.

'Yes.'

'Built in the 1930s,' she said, with respect and pride.

I said something polite, trying to comprehend a city inside which fifty years could be considered a long time.

'Tink's real excited. When she heard you were in town. She was so excited.'

'I'm looking forward to seeing her again.'

Tink's real name was Tinkerbell Richmond. No lie.

She was staying with friends in a small apartment clump, somewhere an hour's drive from downtown L.A.

What you need to know about Tink: she was ten years older than me, in her early thirties; she had glossy black hair and red, puzzled lips, and very white skin, like Snow White in the fairy stories; the first time I met her I thought she was the most beautiful woman in the world.

Tink had been married for a while at some point in

her life and had a five-year-old daughter called Susan. I had never met Susan – when Tink had been in England, Susan had been staying on in Seattle, with her father.

People named Tinkerbell name their daughters Susan.

Memory is the great deceiver. Perhaps there are some individuals whose memories act like tape recordings, daily records of their lives complete in every detail, but I am not one of them. My memory is a patchwork of occurrences, of discontinuous events roughly sewn together: The parts I remember, I remember precisely, whilst other sections seem to have vanished completely.

I do not remember arriving at Tink's house, nor where her flatmate went.

What I remember next is sitting in Tink's lounge with the lights low, the two of us next to each other, on her sofa.

We made small talk. It had been perhaps a year since we had seen one another. But a twenty-one-year-old boy has little to say to a thirty-two-year-old woman, and soon, having nothing in common, I pulled her to me.

She snuggled close with a kind of sigh, and presented her lips to be kissed. In the half-light her lips were black. We kissed for a little on the couch, and I stroked her breasts through her blouse and then she said:

'We can't fuck. I'm on my period.'

'Fine.'

'I can give you a blowjob, if you'd like.'

I nodded assent, and she unzipped my jeans, and lowered her head to my lap.

After I had come, she got up and ran into the kitchen. I heard her spitting into the sink, and the sound of running water: I remember wondering why she did it, if she hated the taste that much.

Then she returned and we sat next to each other on the couch.

'Susan's upstairs, asleep,' said Tink. 'She's all I live for. Would you like to see her?'

'I don't mind.'

We went upstairs. Tink led me into a darkened bedroom. There were child-scrawl pictures all over the walls – wax-crayoned drawings of winged fairies and little palaces – and a small fair-haired girl was asleep in the bed.

'She's very beautiful,' said Tink, and kissed me. Her lips were still slightly sticky. 'She takes after her father.'

We went downstairs. We had nothing else to say, nothing else to do. Tink turned on the main light. For the first time, I noticed tiny crow's feet at the corners of her eyes, incongruous on her perfect Barbie doll face.

'I love you,' she said.

'Thank you.'

'Would you like a ride back?'

'If you don't mind leaving Susan alone . . .?'

She shrugged, and I pulled her to me for the last time.

At night Los Angeles is all lights. And shadows.

A blank, here, in my mind. I simply don't remember what happened next. She must have driven me back to the place where I was staying – how else would I have gotten there? I do not even remember kissing her good-bye. Perhaps I simply waited on the sidewalk and watched her drive away.

Perhaps.

I do know, however, that once I reached the place

I was staying, I just stood there, unable to go inside, to wash, and then to sleep, unwilling to do anything else.

I was not hungry. I did not want alcohol. I did not want to read or talk. I was scared of walking too far, in case I became lost, bedeviled by the repeating motifs of Los Angeles, spun around and sucked in so I could never find my way home again. Central Los Angeles sometimes seems to me to be nothing more than a pattern, like a set of repeating blocks: a gas station, a few homes, a mini-mall (doughnuts, photo developers, Laundromats, fast foods), and repeat until hypnotized; and the tiny changes in the mini-malls and the houses only serve to reinforce the structure.

I thought of Tink's lips. Then I fumbled in a pocket of my jacket and pulled out a packet of cigarettes.

I lit one, inhaled, blew blue smoke into the warm night air.

There was a stunted palm tree growing outside the place I was staying, and I resolved to walk for a way, keeping the tree in sight, to smoke my cigarette, perhaps even to think; but I felt too drained to think. I felt very sexless, and very alone.

A block or so down the road there was a bench, and when I reached it I sat down. I threw the stub of the cigarette onto the pavement, hard, and watched it shower orange sparks.

Someone said, 'I'll buy a cigarette off you, pal. Here.'

A hand in front of my face, holding a quarter. I looked up.

He did not look old, although I would not have been prepared to say how old he was. Late thirties, perhaps. Mid-forties. He wore a long, shabby coat, colourless under the yellow streetlamps, and his eyes were dark.

'Here. A quarter. That's a good price.'

I shook my head, pulled out the packet of Marlboros, offered him one. 'Keep your money. It's free. Have it.'

He took the cigarette. I passed him a book of matches (it advertised a telephone sex line; I remember that), and he lit the cigarette. He offered me the matches back, and I shook my head. 'Keep them. I always wind up accumulating books of matches in America.'

'Uh-huh.' He sat next to me and smoked his cigarette. When he had smoked it halfway down, he tapped the lighted end off on the concrete, stubbed out the glow, and placed the butt of the cigarette behind his ear.

'I don't smoke much,' he said. 'Seems a pity to waste it, though.'

A car careened down the road, veering from one side to the other. There were four young men in the car; the two in the front were both pulling at the wheel and laughing. The windows were wound down, and I could hear their laughter, and the two in the backseat ('*Gaary, you asshole! What the fuck are you onnn, mannnn?*'), and the pulsing beat of a rock song. Not a song I recognised. The car looped around a corner, out of sight.

Soon the sounds were gone, too.

'I owe you,' said the man on the bench.

'Sorry?'

'I owe you something. For the cigarette. And the matches. You wouldn't take the money. I owe you.'

I shrugged, embarrassed. 'Really, it's just a cigarette.

I figure, if I give people cigarettes, then if ever I'm out, maybe people will give me cigarettes.' I laughed, to show I didn't really mean it, although I did. 'Don't worry about it.'

'Mm. You want to hear a story? True story? Stories always used to be good payment. These days . . .' – he shrugged – '. . . not so much.'

I sat back on the bench, and the night was warm, and I looked at my watch: it was almost one in the morning. In England a freezing new day would already have begun: a workday would be starting for those who could beat the snow and get into work; another handful of old people, and those without homes, would have died, in the night, from the cold.

'Sure,' I said to the man. 'Sure. Tell me a story.'

He coughed, grinned white teeth – a flash in the darkness – and he began.

'First thing I remember was the Word. And the Word was God. Sometimes, when I get *really* down, I remember the sound of the Word in my head, shaping me, forming me, giving me life.

'The Word gave me a body, gave me eyes. And I opened my eyes, and I saw the light of the Silver City.

'I was in a room – a silver room – and there wasn't anything in it except me. In front of me was a window that went from floor to ceiling, open to the sky, and through the window I could see the spires of the City, and at the edge of the City, the Dark.

'I don't know how long I waited there. I wasn't impatient or anything, though. I remember that. It was like I was waiting until I was called; and I knew that some time I would be called. And if I had to wait until the end of everything and never be called, why, that was fine, too. But I'd be called, I was certain of that.

And then I'd know my name and my function.

'Through the window I could see silver spires, and in many of the other spires were windows; and in the windows I could see others like me. That was how I knew what I looked like.

'You wouldn't think it of me, seeing me now, but I was beautiful. I've come down in the world a way since then.

'I was taller then, and I had wings.

'They were huge and powerful wings, with feathers the colour of mother-of-pearl. They came out from just between my shoulder blades. They were so good. My wings.

'Sometimes I'd see others like me, the ones who'd left their rooms, who were already fulfilling their duties. I'd watch them soar through the sky from spire to spire, performing errands I could barely imagine.

'The sky above the City was a wonderful thing. It was always light, although lit by no sun – lit, perhaps, by the City itself; but the quality of light was forever changing. Now pewter-coloured light, then brass, then a gentle gold, or a soft and quiet amethyst . . .'

The man stopped talking. He looked at me, his head on one side. There was a glitter in his eyes that scared me. 'You know what amethyst is? A kind of purple stone?'

I nodded.

My crotch felt uncomfortable.

It occurred to me then that the man might not be mad; I found this far more disquieting than the alternative.

The man began talking once more. 'I don't know how long it was that I waited in my room. But time didn't mean anything. Not back then. We had all the time in the world.

'The next thing that happened to me, was when the Angel Lucifer came to my cell. He was taller than me, and his wings were imposing, his plumage perfect. He had skin the colour of sea mist, and curly silver hair, and these wonderful grey eyes...

'I say *he*, but you should understand that none of us had any sex, to speak of.' He gestured toward his lap. 'Smooth and empty. Nothing there. You know.'

'Lucifer shone. I mean it – he glowed from inside. All angels do. They're lit up from within, and in my cell the Angel Lucifer burned like a lightning storm.

'He looked at me. And he named me.

' "You are Raguel," he said. "The Vengeance of the Lord."

'I bowed my head, because I knew it was true. That was my name. That was my function.

' "There has been a ... a wrong thing," he said. "The first of its kind. You are needed."

'He turned and pushed himself into space, and I followed him, flew behind him across the Silver City to the outskirts, where the City stops and the Darkness begins; and it was there, under a vast silver spire, that we descended to the street, and I saw the dead angel.

'The body lay, crumpled and broken, on the silver sidewalk. Its wings were crushed underneath it and a few loose feathers had already blown into the silver gutter.

'The body was almost dark. Now and again a light would flash inside it, an occasional flicker of cold fire in the chest, or in the eyes, or in the sexless groin, as the last of the glow of life left it forever.

'Blood pooled in rubies on its chest and stained its

white wing feathers crimson. It was very beautiful, even in death.

'It would have broken your heart.

'Lucifer spoke to me then. "You must find who was responsible for this, and how; and take the Vengeance of the Name on whosoever caused this thing to happen."

'He really didn't have to say anything. I knew that already. The hunt, and the retribution: it was what I was created for, in the Beginning; it was what I *was*.

' "I have work to attend to," said the Angel Lucifer.

'He flapped his wings once, hard, and rose upward; the gust of wind sent the dead angel's loose feathers blowing across the street.

'I leaned down to examine the body. All luminescence had by now left it. It was a dark thing, a parody of an angel. It had a perfect, sexless face, framed by silver hair. One of the eyelids was open, revealing a placid grey eye; the other was closed. There were no nipples on the chest and only smoothness between the legs.

'I lifted the body up.

'The back of the angel was a mess. The wings were broken and twisted, the back of the head staved in; there was a floppiness to the corpse that made me think its spine had been broken as well. The back of the angel was all blood.

'The only blood on its front was in the chest area. I probed it with my forefinger, and it entered the body without difficulty.

'*He fell*, I thought. *And he was dead before he fell*.

'And I looked up at the windows that ranked the street. I stared across the Silver City. *You did this*, I thought. *I will find you, whoever you are. And I will take the Lord's vengeance upon you*.'

The man took the cigarette stub from behind his

ear, lit it with a match. Briefly I smelled the ashtray smell of a dead cigarette, acrid and harsh; then he pulled down to the unburnt tobacco, exhaled blue smoke into the night air.

'The angel who had first discovered the body was called Phanuel.

'I spoke to him in the Hall of Being. That was the spire beside which the dead angel lay. In the Hall hung the . . . the blueprints, maybe, for what was going to be . . . all this.' He gestured with the hand that held the stubby cigarette, pointing to the night sky and the parked cars and the world. 'You know. The universe.'

'Phanuel was the senior designer; working under him were a multitude of angels labouring on the details of the Creation. I watched him from the floor of the Hall. He hung in the air below the Plan, and angels flew down to him, waiting politely in turn as they asked him questions, checked things with him, invited comment on their work. Eventually he left them and descended to the floor.

' "You are Raguel," he said. His voice was high and fussy. "What need have you of me?"

' "You found the body?"

' "Poor Carasel? Indeed I did. I was leaving the Hall – there are a number of concepts we are currently constructing, and I wished to ponder one of them, *Regret* by name. I was planning to get a little distance from the City – to fly above it, I mean, not to go into the Dark outside, I wouldn't do that, although there has been some loose talk amongst . . . but, yes. I was going to rise and contemplate.

' "I left the Hall, and . . ." he broke off. He was small, for an angel. His light was muted, but his eyes were vivid and bright. I mean really bright. "Poor

Carasel. How could he *do* that to himself? How?"

' "You think his destruction was self-inflicted?"

'He seemed puzzled – surprised that there could be any other explanation. "But of course. Carasel was working under me, developing a number of concepts that shall be intrinsic to the universe when its Name shall be Spoken. His group did a remarkable job on some of the real basics – *Dimension* was one, and *Sleep* another. There were others.

' "Wonderful work. Some of his suggestions regarding the use of individual viewpoints to define dimensions were truly ingenious.

' "Anyway. He had begun work on a new project. It's one of the really major ones – the ones that I would usually handle, or possibly even Zephkiel." He glanced upward. "But Carasel had done such sterling work. And his last project was *so* remarkable. Something apparently quite trivial that he and Saraquael elevated into . . ." he shrugged. "But that is unimportant. It was *this* project that forced him into nonbeing. But none of us could ever have foreseen . . ."

' "What was his current project?"

'Phanuel stared at me. "I'm not sure I ought to tell you. All the new concepts are considered sensitive until we get them into the final form in which they will be Spoken."

'I felt myself transforming. I am not sure how I can explain it to you, but suddenly I wasn't me – I was something larger. I was transfigured: I was my function.

'Phanuel was unable to meet my gaze.

' "I am Raguel, who is the Vengeance of the Lord," I told him. "I serve the Name directly. It is my mission to discover the nature of this deed, and to take the

Name's vengeance on those responsible. My questions are to be answered."

'The little angel trembled, and he spoke fast.

' "Carasel and his partner were researching *Death*. Cessation of life. An end to physical, animated existence. They were putting it all together. But Carasel always went too far into his work – we had a terrible time with him when he was designing *Agitation*. That was when he was working on *Emotions* . . ."

' "You think Carasel died to – to research the phenomenon?"

' "Or because it intrigued him. Or because he followed his research just too far. Yes." Phanuel flexed his fingers, stared at me with those brightly shining eyes. "I trust that you will repeat none of this to any unauthorized persons, Raguel."

' "What did you do when you found the body?"

' "I came out of the Hall, as I said, and there was Carasel on the sidewalk, staring up. I asked him what he was doing, and he did not reply. Then I noticed the inner fluid, and that Carasel seemed unable, rather than unwilling, to talk to me.

' "I was scared. I did not know what to do.

' "The Angel Lucifer came up behind me. He asked me if there was some kind of problem. I told him. I showed him the body. And then . . . then his Aspect came upon him, and he communed with the Name. He burned so bright.

' "Then he said he had to fetch the one whose function embraced events like this, and he left – to seek you, I imagine.

' "As Carasel's death was now being dealt with, and his fate was no real concern of mine, I returned to work, having gained a new – and, I suspect, quite valuable – perspective on the mechanics of *Regret*.

' "I am considering taking *Death* away from the Carasel and Saraquael partnership. I may reassign it to Zephkiel, my senior partner, if he is willing to take it on. He excels on contemplative projects."

'By now there was a line of angels waiting to talk to Phanuel. I felt I had almost all I was going to get from him.

' "Who did Carasel work with? Who would have been the last to see him alive?"

' "You could talk to Saraquael, I suppose – he was his partner, after all. Now, if you'll excuse me . . ."

'He returned to his swarm of aides: advising, correcting, suggesting, forbidding.'

The man paused.

The street was quiet now; I remember the low whisper of his voice, the buzz of a cricket somewhere. A small animal – a cat perhaps, or something more exotic, a raccoon, or even a jackal – darted from shadow to shadow among the parked cars on the opposite side of the street.

'Saraquael was in the highest of the mezzanine galleries that ringed the Hall of Being. As I said, the universe was in the middle of the Hall, and it glinted and sparkled and shone. Went up quite a way, too . . .'

'The universe you mention, it was, what, a diagram?' I asked, interrupting for the first time.

'Not really. Kind of. Sorta. It was a blueprint; but it was full-sized, and it hung in the Hall, and all these angels went around and fiddled with it all the time. Doing stuff with *Gravity* and *Music* and *Klar* and whatever. It wasn't really the universe, not yet. It would be, when it was finished, and it was time for it to be properly Named.'

'But . . .' I grasped for words to express my confusion. The man interrupted me.

'Don't worry about it. Think of it as a model if that makes it easier for you. Or a map. Or a – what's the word? Prototype. Yeah. A Model-T Ford universe.' He grinned. 'You got to understand, a lot of the stuff I'm telling you, I'm translating already; putting it in a form you can understand. Otherwise I couldn't tell the story at all. You want to hear it?'

'Yes.' I didn't care if it was true or not; it was a story I needed to hear all the way through to the end.

'Good. So shut up and listen.

'So I met Saraquael in the topmost gallery. There was no one else about – just him, and some papers, and some small, glowing models.

' "I've come about Carasel," I told him.

'He looked at me. "Carasel isn't here at this time," he said. "I expect him to return shortly."

'I shook my head.

' "Carasel won't be coming back. He's stopped existing as a spiritual entity," I said.

'His light paled, and his eyes opened very wide. "He's dead?"

' "That's what I said. Do you have any ideas about how it happened?"

' "I . . . this is so sudden. I mean, he'd been talking about . . . but I had no idea that he would . . ."

' "Take it slowly."

'Saraquael nodded.

'He stood up and walked to the window. There was no view of the Silver City from his window – just a reflected glow from the City and the sky behind us, hanging in the air, and beyond that, the Dark. The wind from the Dark gently caressed Saraquael's hair as he spoke. I stared at his back.

' "Carasel is . . . no, was. That's right, isn't it? *Was*. He was always so involved. And so creative. But it was never enough for him. He always wanted to understand everything – to experience what he was working on. He was never content to just create it – to understand it intellectually. He wanted *all* of it.

' "That wasn't a problem before, when we were working on properties of matter. But when we began to design some of the Named emotions . . . he got too involved with his work.

' "And our latest project was *Death*. It's one of the hard ones – one of the big ones, too, I suspect. Possibly it may even become the attribute that's going to define the Creation for the Created: If not for *Death*, they'd be content to simply exist, but with *Death*, well, their lives will have meaning – a boundary beyond which the living cannot cross . . ."

' "So you think he killed himself?"

' "I know he did," said Saraquael. I walked to the window and looked out. Far below, a *long* way, I could see a tiny white dot. That was Carasel's body. I'd have to arrange for someone to take care of it. I wondered what we would do with it; but there would be someone who would know, whose function was the removal of unwanted things. It was not my function. I knew that.

' "How?"

'He shrugged. "I know. Recently he'd begun asking questions – questions about *Death*. How we could know whether or not it was right to make this thing, to set the rules, if we were not going to experience it ourselves. He kept talking about it."

' "Didn't you wonder about this?"

'Saraquael turned, for the first time, to look at me.

"No. That *is* our function – to discuss, to improvise, to aid the Creation and the Created. We sort it out now, so that when it all Begins, it'll run like clockwork. Right now we're working on *Death*. So obviously that's what we look at. The physical aspect; the emotional aspect; the philosophical aspect . . .

' "And the *patterns*. Carasel had the notion that what we do here in the Hall of Being creates patterns. That there are structures and shapes appropriate to beings and events that, once begun, must continue until they reach their end. For us, perhaps, as well as for them. Conceivably he felt this was one of his patterns."

' "Did you know Carasel well?"

' "As well as any of us know each other. We saw each other here; we worked side by side. At certain times I would retire to my cell across the City. Sometimes he would do the same."

'Tell me about Phanuel.'

'His mouth crooked into a smile. "He's officious. Doesn't do much – farms everything out and takes all the credit." He lowered his voice, although there was no other soul in the gallery. "To hear him talk, you'd think that *Love* was all his own work. But to his credit, he does make sure the work gets done. Zephkiel's the real thinker of the two senior designers, but he doesn't come here. He stays back in his cell in the City and contemplates; resolves problems from a distance. If you need to speak to Zephkiel, you go to Phanuel, and Phanuel relays your questions to Zephkiel . . ."

'I cut him short. "How about Lucifer? Tell me about him."

' "Lucifer? The Captain of the Host? He doesn't work here . . . He has visited the Hall a couple of times, though – inspecting the Creation. They say he reports directly to the Name. I have never spoken to him."

' "Did he know Carasel?"

' "I doubt it. As I said, he has only been here twice. I have seen him on other occasions, though. Through here." He flicked a wingtip, indicating the world outside the window. "In flight."

' "Where to?"

'Saraquael seemed to be about to say something, then he changed his mind. "I don't know."

'I looked out of the window at the Darkness outside the Silver City.

' "I may want to talk with you some more, later," I told Saraquael.

' "Very good." I turned to go. "Sir? Do you know if they will be assigning me another partner? For *Death*?"

' "No," I told him. "I'm afraid I don't."

'In the centre of the Silver City was a park – a place of recreation and rest. I found the Angel Lucifer there, beside a river. He was just standing, watching the water flow.

' "Lucifer?"

'He inclined his head. "Raguel. Are you making progress?"

' "I don't know. Maybe. I need to ask you a few questions. Do you mind?"

' "Not at all."

' "How did you come upon the body?"

' "I didn't. Not exactly. I saw Phanuel standing in the street. He looked distressed. I inquired whether there was something wrong, and he showed me the dead angel. And I fetched you."

' "I see."

'He leaned down, let one hand enter the cold water

of the river. The water splashed and rolled around it. "Is that all?"

' "Not quite. What were you doing in that part of the city?"

' "I don't see what business that is of yours."

' "It is my business, Lucifer. What were you doing there?"

' "I was . . . walking. I do that sometimes. Just walk and think. And try to understand." He shrugged.

' "You walk on the edge of the City?"

'A beat, then "Yes."

' "That's all I want to know. For now."

' "Who else have you talked to?"

' "Carasel's boss and his partner. They both feel that he killed himself – ended his own life."

' "Who else are you going to talk to?"

'I looked up. The spires of the City of the Angels towered above us. "Maybe everyone."

' "All of them?"

' "If I need to. It's my function. I cannot rest until I understand what happened, and until the Vengeance of the Name has been taken on whosoever was responsible. But I'll tell you something I *do* know."

' "What would that be?" Drops of water fell like diamonds from the Angel Lucifer's perfect fingers.

' "Carasel did not kill himself."

' "How do you know that?"

' "I am Vengeance. If Carasel had died by his own hand," I explained to the Captain of the Heavenly Host, "there would have been no call for me. Would there?"

'He did not reply.

'I flew upward into the light of the eternal morning.

'You got another cigarette on you?'

I fumbled out the red and white packet, handed him a cigarette.

'Obliged.

'Zephkiel's cell was larger than mine.

'It wasn't a place for waiting. It was a place to live, and work, and *be*. It was lined with books, and scrolls, and papers, and there were images and representations on the walls: pictures. I'd never seen a picture before.

'In the centre of the room was a large chair, and Zephkiel sat there, his eyes closed, his head back.

'As I approached him, he opened his eyes.

'They burned no brighter than the eyes of any of the other angels I had seen, but somehow they seemed to have seen more. It was something about the way he looked. I'm not sure I can explain it. And he had no wings.

' "Welcome, Raguel," he said. He sounded tired.

' "You are Zephkiel?" I don't know why I asked him that. I mean, I knew who people were. It's part of my function, I guess. Recognition. I know who *you* are.

' "Indeed. You are staring, Raguel. I have no wings, it is true, but then my function does not call for me to leave this cell. I remain here, and I ponder. Phanuel reports back to me, brings me the new things, for my opinion. He brings me the problems, and I think about them, and occasionally I make myself useful by making some small suggestions. That is my function. As yours is vengeance."

' "Yes."

' "You are here about the death of the Angel Carasel?"

' "Yes."

' "I did not kill him."

'When he said it, I knew it was true.

' "Do you know who did?"

' "That is *your* function, is it not? To discover who killed the poor thing and to take the Vengeance of the Name upon him."

' "Yes."

'He nodded.

' "What do you want to know?"

'I paused, reflecting on what I had heard that day. "Do you know what Lucifer was doing in that part of the City before the body was found?"

'The old angel stared at me. "I can hazard a guess."

' "Yes?"

' "He was walking in the Dark."

'I nodded. I had a shape in my mind now. Something I could almost grasp. I asked the last question:

' "What can you tell me about *Love*?"

'And he told me. And I thought I had it all.

'I returned to the place where Carasel's body had been. The remains had been removed, the blood had been cleaned away, the stray feathers collected and disposed of. There was nothing on the silver sidewalk to indicate it had ever been there. But I knew where it had been.

'I ascended on my wings, flew upward until I neared the top of the spire of the Hall of Being. There was a window there, and I entered.

'Saraquael was working there, putting a wingless mannikin into a small box. On one side of the box was a representation of a small brown creature with eight legs. On the other was a representation of a white blossom.

' "Saraquael?"

' "Hm? Oh, it's you. Hello. Look at this. If you were to die and to be, let us say, put into the earth in a box, which would you want laid on top of you – a spider, here, or a lily, here?"

' "The lily, I suppose."

' "Yes, that's what I think, too. But *why*? I wish . . ." He raised a hand to his chin, stared down at the two models, put first one on top of the box, then the other, experimentally. "There's so much to do, Raguel. So much to get right. And we only get one chance at it, you know. There'll just be one universe – we can't keep trying until we get it right. I wish I understood why all this was so important to Him . . ."

' "Do you know where Zephkiel's cell is?" I asked him.

' "Yes. I mean, I've never been there. But I know where it is."

' "Good. Go there. He'll be expecting you. I will meet you there."

'He shook his head. "I have work to do. I can't just . . ."

'I felt my function come upon me. I looked down at him, and I said, "You will be there. Go now."

'He said nothing. He backed away from me toward the window, staring at me; then he turned and flapped his wings, and I was alone.

'I walked to the central well of the Hall and let myself fall, tumbling down through the model of the universe: it glittered around me, unfamiliar colours and shapes seething and writhing without meaning.

'As I approached the bottom, I beat my wings, slowing my descent, and stepped lightly onto the silver floor. Phanuel stood between two angels who were both trying to claim his attention.

' "I don't care how aesthetically pleasing it would be," he was explaining to one of them. "We simply cannot put it in the centre. Background radiation would prevent any possible life-forms from even getting a foothold; and anyway, it's too unstable."

'He turned to the other. "Okay, let's see it. Hmm. So that's *Green*, is it? It's not exactly how I'd imagined it, but. Mm. Leave it with me. I'll get back to you." He took a paper from the angel, folded it over decisively.

'He turned to me. His manner was brusque, and dismissive. "Yes?"

' "I need to talk to you."

' "Mm? Well, make it quick. I have much to do. If this is about Carasel's death, I have told you all I know."

' "It is about Carasel's death. But I will not speak to you now. Not here. Go to Zephkiel's cell: he is expecting you. I will meet you there."

'He seemed about to say something, but he only nodded, walked toward the door.

'I turned to go when something occurred to me. I stopped the angel who had the *Green*. "Tell me something."

' "If I can, sir."

' "That thing." I pointed to the universe. "What's it going to be *for*?"

' "For? Why, it is the universe."

' "I know what it's called. But what purpose will it serve?"

'He frowned. "It is part of the plan. The Name wishes it; He requires *such and such*, to *these* dimensions and having *such and such* properties and ingredients. It is our function to bring it into existence, according to His wishes. I am sure *He* knows its function, but He has not revealed it to me." His tone was one of gentle rebuke.

'I nodded, and left that place.

'High above the City a phalanx of angels wheeled

and circled and dove. Each held a flaming sword that trailed a streak of burning brightness behind it, dazzling the eye. They moved in unison through the salmon pink sky. They were very beautiful. It was – you know on summer evenings when you get whole flocks of birds performing their dances in the sky? Weaving and circling and clustering and breaking apart again, so just as you think you understand the pattern, you realise you don't, and you never will? It was like that, only better.

'Above me was the sky. Below me, the shining City. My home. And outside the City, the Dark.

'Lucifer hovered a little below the Host, watching their manoeuvers.

' "Lucifer?"

' "Yes, Raguel? Have you discovered your malefactor?"

' "I think so. Will you accompany me to Zephkiel's cell? There are others waiting for us there, and I will explain everything."

'He paused. Then, "Certainly."

'He raised his perfect face to the angels, now performing a slow revolution in the sky, each moving through the air keeping perfect pace with the next, none of them ever touching. "Azazel!"

'An angel broke from the circle; the others adjusted almost imperceptibly to his disappearance, filling the space, so you could no longer see where he had been.

' "I have to leave. You are in command, Azazel. Keep them drilling. They still have much to perfect."

' "Yes, sir."

'Azazel hovered where Lucifer had been, staring up at the flock of angels, and Lucifer and I descended toward the City.

' "He's my second-in-command," said Lucifer.

"Bright. Enthusiastic. Azazel would follow you any-where."

' "What are you training them for?"

' "War."

' "With whom?"

' "How do you mean?"

' "Who are they going to fight? Who else *is* there?"

'He looked at me; his eyes were clear, and honest. "I do not know. But He has Named us to be His army. So we will be perfect. For Him. The Name is infallible and all-just and all-wise, Raguel. It cannot be otherwise, no matter what—" He broke off and looked away.

' "You were going to say?"

' "It is of no importance."

' "Ah."

'We did not talk for the rest of the descent to Zephkiel's cell.'

I looked at my watch; it was almost three. A chill breeze had begun to blow down the L.A. street, and I shivered. The man noticed, and he paused in his story. 'You okay?' he asked.

'I'm fine. Please carry on. I'm fascinated.'

He nodded.

'They were waiting for us in Zephkiel's cell: Phanuel, Saraquael and Zephkiel. Zephkiel was sitting in his chair. Lucifer took up a position beside the window.

'I walked to the centre of the room, and I began.

' "I thank you all for coming here. You know who I am; you know my function. I am the Vengeance of the Name, the arm of the Lord. I am Raguel.

'The Angel Carasel is dead. It was given to me to find out why he died, who killed him. This I have done. Now, the Angel Carasel was a designer in the Hall of

Being. He was very good, or so I am told . . .

' "Lucifer. Tell me what you were doing before you came upon Phanuel, and the body."

' "I have told you already. I was walking."

' "Where were you walking?"

' "I do not see what business that is of yours."

' "*Tell me.*"

'He paused. He was taller than any of us, tall, and proud. "Very well. I was walking in the Dark. I have been walking in the Darkness for some time now. It helps me to gain a perspective on the City – being outside it. I see how fair it is, how perfect. There is nothing more enchanting than our home. Nothing more complete. Nowhere else that anyone would want to be."

' "And what do you do in the Dark, Lucifer?"

'He stared at me. "I walk. And . . . There are voices in the Dark. I listen to the voices. They promise me things, ask me questions, whisper and plead. And I ignore them. I steel myself and I gaze at the City. It is the only way I have of testing myself – putting myself to any kind of trial. I am the Captain of the Host; I am the first among the Angels, and I must prove myself."

'I nodded. "Why did you not tell me this before?"

'He looked down. "Because I am the only angel who walks in the Dark. Because I do not want others to walk in the Dark: I am strong enough to challenge the voices, to test myself. Others are not so strong. Others might stumble, or fall."

' "Thank you, Lucifer. That is all, for now." I turned to the next angel. "Phanuel. How long have you been taking credit for Carasel's work?"

'His mouth opened, but no sound came out.

' "*Well?*"

' "I . . . I would not take credit for another's work."

' "But you did take credit for *Love*?"

'He blinked. "Yes. I did."

' "Would you care to explain to us all what *Love* is?" I asked.

'He glanced around uncomfortably. "It's a feeling of deep affection and attraction for another being, often combined with passion or desire – a need to be with another." He spoke dryly, didactically, as if he were reciting a mathematical formula. "The feeling that we have for the Name, for our Creator – that is *Love* . . . amongst other things. *Love* will be an impulse that will inspire and ruin in equal measure. We are . . ." He paused, then began once more. "We are very proud of it."

'He was mouthing the words. He no longer seemed to hold any hope that we would believe them.

' "Who did the majority of the work on *Love*? No, don't answer. Let me ask the others first. Zephkiel? When Phanuel passed the details on *Love* to you for approval, who did he tell you was responsible for it?"

'The wingless angel smiled gently. "He told me it was his project."

' "Thank you, sir. Now, Saraquael: whose was *Love*?"

' "Mine. Mine and Carasel's. Perhaps more his than mine, but we worked on it together."

' "You knew that Phanuel was claiming the credit for it?"

' " . . . Yes."

' "And you permitted this?"

' "He . . . he promised us that he would give us a good project of our own to follow. He promised that if we said nothing we would be given more big projects – and he was true to his word. He gave us *Death*."

'I turned back to Phanuel. "Well?"

' "It is true that I claimed that *Love* was mine."

' "But it was Carasel's. And Saraquael's."

' "Yes."

' "Their last project – before *Death*?"

' "Yes."

' "That is all."

'I walked over to the window, looked at the silver spires, looked at the Dark. And I began to speak.

' "Carasel was a remarkable designer. If he had one failing, it was that he threw himself too deeply into his work." I turned back to them. The Angel Saraquael was shivering, and lights were flickering beneath his skin. "Saraquael? Who did Carasel love? Who was his lover?"

'He stared at the floor. Then he stared up, proudly, aggressively. And he smiled.

' "I was."

' "Do you want to tell me about it?"

' "No." A shrug. "But I suppose I must. Very well, then.

' "We worked together. And when we began to work on *Love* . . . we became lovers. It was his idea. We would go back to his cell whenever we could snatch the time. There we touched each other, held each other, whispered endearments and protestations of eternal devotion. His welfare mattered more to me than my own. I existed for him. When I was alone, I would repeat his name to myself and think of nothing but him.

' "When I was with him . . ." he paused. He looked down. "Nothing else mattered."

'I walked to where Saraquael stood, lifted his chin with my hand, stared into his grey eyes. "Then why did you kill him?"

' "Because he would no longer love me. When we

started to work on *Death*, he . . . he lost interest. He was no longer mine. He belonged to *Death*. And if I could not have him, then his new lover was welcome to him. I could not bear his presence – I could not endure to have him near me and to know that he felt nothing for me. That was what hurt the most. I thought . . . I hoped . . . that if he was gone, then I would no longer care for him – that the pain would stop.

' "So I killed him. I stabbed him, and I threw his body from our window in the Hall of Being. But the pain has *not* stopped." It was almost a wail.

'Saraquael reached up, removed my hand from his chin. "Now what?"

'I felt my aspect begin to come upon me; felt my function possess me. I was no longer an individual – I was the Vengeance of the Lord.

'I moved close to Saraquael and embraced him. I pressed my lips to his, forced my tongue into his mouth. We kissed. He closed his eyes.

'I felt it well up within me then: a burning, a brightness. From the corner of my eyes, I could see Lucifer and Phanuel averting their faces from my light; I could feel Zephkiel's stare. And my light became brighter and brighter until it erupted – from my eyes, from my chest, from my fingers, from my lips: a white searing fire.

'The white flames consumed Saraquael slowly, and he clung to me as he burned.

'Soon there was nothing left of him. Nothing at all.

'I felt the flame leave me. I returned to myself once more.

'Phanuel was sobbing. Lucifer was pale. Zephkiel sat in his chair, quietly watching me.

'I turned to Phanuel and Lucifer. "You have seen

the Vengeance of the Lord," I told them. "Let it act as a warning to you both."

'Phanuel nodded. "It has. Oh, it has. I . . . I will be on my way, sir. I will return to my appointed post. If that is all right with you?"

' "Go."

'He stumbled to the window and plunged into the light, his wings beating furiously.

'Lucifer walked over to the place on the silver floor where Saraquael had once stood. He knelt, stared desperately at the floor as if he were trying to find some remnant of the angel I had destroyed, a fragment of ash, or bone, or charred feather, but there was nothing to find. Then he looked up at me.

' "That was not right," he said. "That was not just." He was crying; wet tears ran down his face. Perhaps Saraquael was the first to love, but Lucifer was the first to shed tears. I will never forget that.

'I stared at him impassively. "It was justice. He killed another. He was killed in his turn. You called me to my function, and I performed it."

' "But . . . he *loved*. He should have been forgiven. He should have been helped. He should not have been destroyed like that. That was *wrong*."

' "It was His will."

'Lucifer stood. "Then perhaps His will is unjust. Perhaps the voices in the Darkness speak truly, after all. How *can* this be right?"

' "It is right. It is His will. I merely performed my function."

'He wiped away the tears with the back of his hand. "No," he said, flatly. He shook his head, slowly, from side to side. Then he said, "I must think on this. I will go now."

'He walked to the window, stepped into the sky, and he was gone.

'Zephkiel and I were alone in his cell. I went over to his chair. He nodded at me. "You have performed your function well, Raguel. Shouldn't you return to your cell to wait until you are next needed?" '

The man on the bench turned toward me: his eyes sought mine. Until now it had seemed – for most of his narrative – that he was scarcely aware of me; he had stared ahead of himself, whispered his tale in little better than a monotone. Now it felt as if he had discovered me and that he spoke to me alone, rather than to the air, or the City of Los Angeles. And he said:

'I knew that he was right. But I *couldn't* have left then – not even if I had wanted to. My aspect had not entirely left me; my function was not completely fulfilled. And then it fell into place; I saw the whole picture. And like Lucifer, I knelt. I touched my forehead to the silver floor. "No, Lord," I said. "Not yet."

'Zephkiel rose from his chair. "Get up. It is not fitting for one angel to act in this way to another. It is not right. Get up!"

'I shook my head. "Father, You are no angel," I whispered.

'Zephkiel said nothing. For a moment, my heart misgave within me. I was afraid. "Father, I was charged to discover who was responsible for Carasel's death. And I do know."

' "You have taken your Vengeance, Raguel."

' "*Your* Vengeance, Lord."

'And then He sighed and sat down once more. "Ah, little Raguel. The problem with creating things is that they perform so much better than one had ever planned. Shall I ask how you recognised me?"

' "I . . . I am not certain, Lord. You have no wings. You wait at the centre of the City, supervising the Creation directly. When I destroyed Saraquael, You did not look away. You know too many things. You . . ." I paused and thought. "No, I do not know how I know. As You say, You have created me well. But I only understood who You were, and the meaning of the drama we had enacted here for You, when I saw Lucifer leave."

' "What did you understand, child?"

' "Who killed Carasel. Or, at least, who was pulling the strings. For example, who arranged for Carasel and Saraquael to work together on *Love*, knowing Carasel's tendency to involve himself too deeply in his work?"

'He was speaking to me gently, almost teasingly, as an adult would pretend to make conversation with a tiny child. "Why should anyone have 'pulled the strings', Raguel?"

' "Because nothing occurs without reason; and all the reasons are Yours. You set Saraquael up: yes, he killed Carasel. But he killed Carasel so that *I* could destroy *him*."

' "And were you wrong to destroy him?"

'I looked into His old, old eyes. "It was my function. But I do not think it was just. I think perhaps it was needed that I destroy Saraquael, in order to demonstrate to Lucifer the Injustice of the Lord."

'He smiled, then. "And whatever reason would I have for doing that?"

' "I . . . I do not know. I do not understand – no more than I understand why You created the Dark or the voices in the Darkness. But You did. You caused all this to occur."

'He nodded. "Yes. I did. Lucifer must brood on the unfairness of Saraquael's destruction. And that –

amongst other things – will precipitate him into certain actions. Poor sweet Lucifer. His way will be the hardest of all my children; for there is a part he must play in the drama that is to come, and it is a grand role."

'I remained kneeling in front of the Creator of All Things.

' "What will you do now, Raguel?" He asked me.

' "I must return to my cell. My function is now fulfilled. I have taken Vengeance, and I have revealed the perpetrator. That is enough. But – Lord?"

' "Yes, child."

' "I feel dirty. I feel tarnished. I feel befouled. Perhaps it is true that all that happens is in accordance with Your will, and thus it is good. But sometimes You leave blood on Your instruments."

'He nodded, as if He agreed with me. "If you wish, Raguel, you may forget all this. All that has happened this day." And then He said, "However, you will not be able to speak of this to any other angel, whether you choose to remember it or not."

' "I will remember it."

' "It is your choice. But sometimes you will find it is easier by far not to remember. Forgetfulness can sometimes bring freedom, of a sort. Now, if you do not mind," He reached down, took a file from a stack on the floor, opened it, "there is work I should be getting on with."

'I stood up and walked to the window. I hoped He would call me back, explain every detail of His plan to me, somehow make it all better. But He said nothing, and I left His Presence without ever looking back.'

The man was silent, then. And he remained silent – I couldn't even hear him breathing – for so long that I began to get nervous, thinking that perhaps he had fallen asleep or died.

Then he stood up.

'There you go, pal. That's your story. Do you think it was worth a couple of cigarettes and a book of matches?' He asked the question as if it was important to him, without irony.

'Yes,' I told him. 'Yes. It was. But what happened next? How did you . . . I mean, if . . .' I trailed off.

It was dark on the street now, at the edge of daybreak. One by one the streetlamps had begun to flicker out, and he was silhouetted against the glow of the dawn sky. He thrust his hands into his pockets. 'What happened? I left home, and I lost my way, and these days home's a long way back. Sometimes you do things you regret, but there's nothing you can do about them. Times change. Doors close behind you. You move on. You know?

'Eventually I wound up here. They used to say no one's ever originally from L.A. True as Hell in my case.'

And then, before I could understand what he was doing, he leaned down and kissed me, gently, on the cheek. His stubble was rough and prickly, but his breath was surprisingly sweet. He whispered into my ear: 'I never fell. I don't care what they say. I'm still doing my job, as I see it.'

My cheek burned where his lips had touched it.

He straightened up. 'But I still want to go home.'

The man walked away down the darkened street, and I sat on the bench and watched him go. I felt like he had taken something from me, although I could no longer remember what. And I felt like something had been left in its place – absolution, perhaps, or innocence, although of what, or from what, I could no longer say.

An image from somewhere: a scribbled drawing of two angels in flight above a perfect city; and over the image a child's perfect hand print, which stains the white paper blood-red. It came into my head unbidden, and I no longer know what it meant.

I stood up.

It was too dark to see the face of my watch, but I knew I would get no sleep that day. I walked back to the place I was staying, to the house by the stunted palm tree, to wash myself and to wait. I thought about angels and about Tink; and I wondered whether love and death went hand in hand.

The next day the planes to England were flying again.

I felt strange – lack of sleep had forced me into that miserable state in which everything seems flat and of equal importance; when nothing matters, and in which reality seems scraped thin and threadbare. The taxi journey to the airport was a nightmare. I was hot, and tired, and testy. I wore a T-shirt in the L.A. heat; my coat was packed at the bottom of my luggage, where it had been for the entire stay.

The airplane was crowded, but I didn't care.

The stewardess walked down the aisle with a rack of newspapers: the *Herald Tribune*, *USA Today*, and the *L.A. Times*. I took a copy of the *Times*, but the words left my head as my eyes scanned over them. Nothing that I read remained with me. No, I lie. Somewhere in the back of the paper was a report of a triple murder: two women and a small child. No names were given, and I do not know why the report should have registered as it did.

Soon I fell asleep. I dreamed about fucking Tink, while blood ran sluggishly from her closed eyes and lips. The blood was cold and viscous and clammy, and I awoke chilled by the plane's airconditioning, with an unpleasant taste in my mouth. My tongue and lips were dry. I looked out of the scratched oval window, stared down at the clouds, and it occurred to me then (not for the first time) that the clouds were in actuality another land, where everyone knew just what they were looking for and how to get back where they started from.

Staring down at the clouds is one of the things I have always liked best about flying. That, and the proximity one feels to one's death.

I wrapped myself in the thin aircraft blanket and slept some more, but if further dreams came then they made no impression upon me.

A blizzard blew up shortly after the plane landed in England, knocking out the airport's power supply. I was alone in an airport elevator at the time, and it went dark and jammed between floors. A dim emergency light flickered on. I pressed the crimson alarm button until the batteries ran down and it ceased to sound; then I shivered in my L.A. T-shirt in the corner of my little silver room. I watched my breath steam in the air, and I hugged myself for warmth.

There wasn't anything in there except me; but even so, I felt safe and secure. Soon someone would come and force open the doors. Eventually somebody would let me out; and I knew that I would soon be home.

Snow, Glass, Apples

I do not know what manner of thing she is. None of us do. She killed her mother in the birthing, but that's never enough to account for it.

They call me wise, but I am far from wise, for all that I foresaw fragments of it, frozen moments caught in pools of water or in the cold glass of my mirror. If I were wise I would not have tried to change what I saw. If I were wise I would have killed myself before ever I encountered her, before ever I caught him.

Wise, and a witch, or so they said, and I'd seen his face in my dreams and in reflections for all my life: sixteen years of dreaming of him before he reined his horse by the bridge that morning and asked my name. He helped me onto his high horse and we rode together to my little cottage, my face buried in the gold of his hair. He asked for the best of what I had; a king's right, it was.

His beard was red-bronze in the morning light, and I knew him, not as a king, for I knew nothing of kings then, but as my love. He took all he wanted from me, the right of kings, but he returned to me on the following day and on the night after that: his beard so red, his hair so gold, his eyes the blue of a summer sky, his skin tanned the gentle brown of ripe wheat.

His daughter was only a child: no more than five years of age when I came to the palace. A portrait of her dead mother hung in the princess's tower room: a tall woman, hair the colour of dark wood, eyes nut-brown. She was of a different blood to her pale daughter.

The girl would not eat with us.

I do not know where in the palace she ate.

I had my own chambers. My husband the king, he had his own rooms also. When he wanted me he would send for me, and I would go to him, and pleasure him, and take my pleasure with him.

One night, several months after I was brought to the palace, she came to my rooms. She was six. I was embroidering by lamplight, squinting my eyes against the lamp's smoke and fitful illumination. When I looked up, she was there.

'Princess?'

She said nothing. Her eyes were black as coal, black as her hair; her lips were redder than blood. She looked up at me and smiled. Her teeth seemed sharp, even then, in the lamplight.

'What are you doing away from your room?'

'I'm hungry,' she said, like any child.

It was winter, when fresh food is a dream of warmth and sunlight; but I had strings of whole apples, cored and dried, hanging from the beams of my chamber, and I pulled an apple down for her.

'Here.'

Autumn is the time of drying, of preserving, a time of picking apples, of rendering the goose fat. Winter is the time of hunger, of snow, and of death; and it is the time of the midwinter feast, when we rub the goose fat into the skin of a whole pig, stuffed with that autumn's apples; then we roast it or spit it, and we prepare to feast upon the crackling.

She took the dried apple from me and began to chew it with her sharp yellow teeth.

'Is it good?'

She nodded. I had always been scared of the little princess, but at that moment I warmed to her and, with my fingers, gently, I stroked her cheek. She looked at me and smiled – she smiled but rarely – then she sank her teeth into the base of my thumb, the Mound of Venus, and she drew blood.

I began to shriek, from pain and from surprise, but she looked at me and I fell silent.

The little princess fastened her mouth to my hand and licked and sucked and drank. When she was finished, she left my chamber. Beneath my gaze the cut that she had made began to close, to scab, and to heal. The next day it was an old scar: I might have cut my hand with a pocketknife in my childhood.

I had been frozen by her, owned and dominated. That scared me, more than the blood she had fed on. After that night I locked my chamber door at dusk, barring it with an oaken pole, and I had the smith forge iron bars, which he placed across my windows.

My husband, my love, my king, sent for me less and less, and when I came to him he was dizzy, listless, confused. He could no longer make love as a man makes love, and he would not permit me to pleasure him with my mouth: the one time I tried, he started violently, and began to weep. I pulled my mouth away and held him tightly until the sobbing had stopped, and he slept, like a child.

I ran my fingers across his skin as he slept. It was covered in a multitude of ancient scars. But I could recall no scars from the days of our courtship, save one, on his side, where a boar had gored him when he was a youth.

Soon he was a shadow of the man I had met and loved by the bridge. His bones showed, blue and white, beneath his skin. I was with him at the last: his hands were cold as stone, his eyes milky blue, his hair and beard faded and lustreless and limp. He died unshriven, his skin nipped and pocked from head to toe with tiny, old scars.

He weighed near to nothing. The ground was frozen hard, and we could dig no grave for him, so we made a cairn of rocks and stones above his body, as a memorial only, for there was little enough of him left to protect from the hunger of the beasts and the birds.

So I was queen.

And I was foolish, and young – eighteen summers had come and gone since first I saw daylight – and I did not do what I would do, now.

If it were today, I would have her heart cut out, true. But then I would have her head and arms and legs cut off. I would have them disembowel her. And then I would watch in the town square as the hangman heated the fire to white-heat with bellows, watch unblinking as he consigned each part of her to the fire. I would have archers around the square, who would shoot any bird or animal that came close to the flames, any raven or dog or hawk or rat. And I would not close my eyes until the princess was ash, and a gentle wind could scatter her like snow.

I did not do this thing, and we pay for our mistakes.

They say I was fooled; that it was not her heart. That it was the heart of an animal – a stag, perhaps, or a boar. They say that, and they are wrong.

And some say (but it is *her* lie, not mine) that I was given the heart, and that I ate it. Lies and half-truths fall like snow, covering the things that I remember, the things I saw. A landscape, unrecognizable after a snowfall; that is what she has made of my life.

There were scars on my love, her father's thighs, and on his ballock-pouch, and on his male member, when he died.

I did not go with them. They took her in the day, while she slept, and was at her weakest. They took her to the heart of the forest, and there they opened her blouse, and they cut out her heart, and they left her dead, in a gully, for the forest to swallow.

The forest is a dark place, the border to many kingdoms; no one would be foolish enough to claim jurisdiction over it. Outlaws live in the forest. Robbers live in the forest, and so do wolves. You can ride through the forest for a dozen days and never see a soul; but there are eyes upon you the entire time.

They brought me her heart. I know it was hers – no sow's heart or doe's would have continued to beat and pulse after it had been cut out, as that one did.

I took it to my chamber.

I did not eat it: I hung it from the beams above my bed, placed it on a length of twine that I strung with rowan berries, orange-red as a robin's breast, and with bulbs of garlic.

Outside the snow fell, covering the footprints of my huntsmen, covering her tiny body in the forest where it lay.

I had the smith remove the iron bars from my windows, and I would spend some time in my room each afternoon through the short winter days, gazing out over the forest, until darkness fell.

There were, as I have already stated, people in the forest. They would come out, some of them, for the Spring Fair: a greedy, feral, dangerous people; some were stunted – dwarfs and midgets and hunchbacks; others had the huge teeth and vacant gazes of idiots; some had fingers like flippers or crab claws. They would creep out of the forest each year for the Spring Fair, held when the snows had melted.

As a young lass I had worked at the fair, and they had scared me then, the forest folk. I told fortunes for the fairgoers, scrying in a pool of still water; and later, when I was older, in a disk of polished glass, its back all silvered – a gift from a merchant whose straying horse I had seen in a pool of ink.

The stallholders at the fair were afraid of the forest folk; they would nail their wares to the bare boards of their stalls – slabs of gingerbread or leather belts were nailed with great iron nails to the wood. If their wares were not nailed, they said, the forest folk would take them and run away, chewing on the stolen gingerbread, flailing about them with the belts.

The forest folk had money, though: a coin here, another there, sometimes stained green by time or the earth, the face on the coin unknown to even the oldest of us. Also they had things to trade, and thus the fair continued, serving the outcasts and the dwarfs, serving the robbers (if they were circumspect) who preyed on the rare travellers from lands beyond the forest, or on gypsies, or on the deer. (This was robbery in the eyes of the law. The deer were the queen's.)

The years passed by slowly, and my people claimed that I ruled them with wisdom. The heart still hung above my bed, pulsing gently in the night. If there were any who mourned the child, I saw no evidence: she was a thing of terror, back then, and they believed themselves well rid of her.

Spring Fair followed Spring Fair: five of them, each sadder, poorer, shoddier than the one before. Fewer of the forest folk came out of the forest to buy. Those who did seemed subdued and listless. The stallholders stopped nailing their wares to the boards of their stalls. And by the fifth year but a handful of folk came from the forest – a fearful huddle of little hairy men, and no one else.

The Lord of the Fair, and his page, came to me when the fair was done. I had known him slightly, before I was queen.

'I do not come to you as my queen,' he said.

I said nothing. I listened.

'I come to you because you are wise,' he continued. 'When you were a child you found a strayed foal by staring into a pool of ink; when you were a maiden you found a lost infant who had wandered far from her mother, by staring into that mirror of yours. You know secrets and you can seek out things hidden. My queen,' he asked, 'what is taking the forest folk? Next year there will be no Spring Fair. The travellers from other kingdoms have grown scarce and few, the folk of the forest are almost gone. Another year like the last, and we shall all starve.'

I commanded my maidservant to bring me my looking glass. It was a simple thing, a silver-backed glass disk, which I kept wrapped in a doeskin, in a chest, in my chamber.

They brought it to me then, and I gazed into it:

She was twelve and she was no longer a little child. Her skin was still pale, her eyes and hair coal-black, her lips blood-red. She wore the clothes she had worn when she left the castle for the last time – the blouse, the skirt – although they were much let-out, much mended. Over them she wore a leather cloak, and instead of boots she had leather bags, tied with thongs, over her tiny feet.

She was standing in the forest, beside a tree.

As I watched, in the eye of my mind, I saw her edge and step and flitter and pad from tree to tree, like an animal: a bat or a wolf. She was following someone.

He was a monk. He wore sackcloth, and his feet were bare and scabbed and hard. His beard and tonsure were of a length, overgrown, unshaven.

She watched him from behind the trees. Eventually he paused for the night and began to make a fire, laying twigs down, breaking up a robin's nest as kindling. He had a tinderbox in his robe, and he knocked the flint against the steel until the sparks caught the tinder and the fire flamed. There had been two eggs in the nest he had found, and these he ate raw. They cannot have been much of a meal for so big a man.

He sat there in the firelight, and she came out from her hiding place. She crouched down on the other side of the fire, and stared at him. He grinned, as if it were a long time since he had seen another human, and beckoned her over to him.

She stood up and walked around the fire, and waited, an arm's length away. He pulled in his robe until he found a coin – a tiny copper penny – and tossed it to her. She caught it, and nodded, and went to him. He pulled at the rope around his waist, and his robe swung open. His body was as hairy as a bear's. She pushed him back onto the moss. One hand crept, spiderlike, through the tangle of hair, until it closed on his manhood; the other hand traced a circle on his left nipple. He closed his eyes and fumbled one huge hand under her skirt. She lowered her mouth to the nipple she had been teasing, her smooth skin white on the furry brown body of him.

She sank her teeth deep into his breast. His eyes opened, then they closed again, and she drank.

She straddled him, and she fed. As she did so, a thin blackish liquid began to dribble from between her legs . . .

'Do you know what is keeping the travellers from our town? What is happening to the forest people?' asked the Lord of the Fair.

I covered the mirror in doeskin, and told him that I would personally take it upon myself to make the forest safe once more.

I had to, although she terrified me. I was the queen.

A foolish woman would have gone then into the forest and tried to capture the creature; but I had been foolish once and had no wish to be so a second time.

I spent time with old books. I spent time with the gypsy women (who passed through our country across the mountains to the south, rather than cross the forest to the north and the west).

I prepared myself and obtained those things I would need, and when the first snows began to fall, I was ready.

Naked, I was, and alone in the highest tower of the palace, a place open to the sky. The winds chilled my body; goose pimples crept across my arms and thighs and breasts. I carried a silver basin, and a basket in which I had placed a silver knife, a silver pin, some tongs, a grey robe, and three green apples.

I put them on and stood there, unclothed, on the tower, humble before the night sky and the wind. Had any man seen me standing there, I would have had his eyes; but there was no one to spy. Clouds scudded across the sky, hiding and uncovering the waning moon.

I took the silver knife and slashed my left arm – once, twice, three times. The blood dripped into the basin, scarlet seeming black in the moonlight.

I added the powder from the vial that hung around my neck. It was a brown dust, made of dried herbs and the skin of a particular toad, and from certain other things. It thickened the blood, while preventing it from clotting.

I took the three apples, one by one, and pricked their skins gently with my silver pin. Then I placed the apples in the silver bowl and let them sit there while the first tiny flakes of snow of the year fell slowly onto my skin, and onto the apples, and onto the blood.

When dawn began to brighten the sky I covered myself with the grey cloak, and took the red apples from the silver bowl, one by one, lifting each into my basket with silver tongs, taking care not to touch it. There was nothing left of my blood or of the brown powder in the silver bowl, nothing save a black residue, like a verdigris, on the inside.

I buried the bowl in the earth. Then I cast a glamour on the apples (as once, years before, by a bridge, I had cast a glamour on myself), that they were, beyond any doubt, the most wonderful apples in the world, and the crimson blush of their skins was the warm colour of fresh blood.

I pulled the hood of my cloak low over my face, and I took ribbons and pretty hair ornaments with me, placed them above the apples in the reed basket, and I walked alone into the forest until I came to her dwelling: a high sandstone cliff, laced with deep caves going back a way into the rock wall.

There were trees and boulders around the cliff face, and I walked quietly and gently from tree to tree without disturbing a twig or a fallen leaf. Eventually I found my place to hide, and I waited, and I watched.

After some hours, a clutch of dwarfs crawled out of the hole in the cave front – ugly, misshapen, hairy little men, the old inhabitants of this country. You saw them seldom now.

They vanished into the wood, and none of them espied me, though one of them stopped to piss against the rock I hid behind.

I waited. No more came out.

I went to the cave entrance and hallooed into it, in a cracked old voice.

The scar on my Mound of Venus throbbed and pulsed as she came toward me, out of the darkness, naked and alone.

She was thirteen years of age, my stepdaughter, and nothing marred the perfect whiteness of her skin, save for the livid scar on her left breast, where her heart had been cut from her long since.

The insides of her thighs were stained with wet black filth.

She peered at me, hidden, as I was, in my cloak. She looked at me hungrily. 'Ribbons, goodwife,' I croaked. 'Pretty ribbons for your hair . . .'

She smiled and beckoned to me. A tug; the scar on my hand was pulling me toward her. I did what I had planned to do, but I did it more readily than I had planned: I dropped my basket and screeched like the bloodless old peddler woman I was pretending to be, and I ran.

My grey cloak was the colour of the forest, and I

was fast; she did not catch me.

I made my way back to the palace.

I did not see it. Let us imagine, though, the girl returning, frustrated and hungry, to her cave, and finding my fallen basket on the ground.

What did she do?

I like to think she played first with the ribbons, twined them into her raven hair, looped them around her pale neck or her tiny waist.

And then, curious, she moved the cloth to see what else was in the basket, and she saw the red, red apples.

They smelled like fresh apples, of course; and they also smelled of blood. And she was hungry. I imagine her picking up an apple, pressing it against her cheek, feeling the cold smoothness of it against her skin.

And she opened her mouth and bit deep into it . . .

By the time I reached my chambers, the heart that hung from the roof beam, with the apples and hams and the dried sausages, had ceased to beat. It hung there, quietly, without motion or life, and I felt safe once more.

That winter the snows were high and deep, and were late melting. We were all hungry come the spring.

The Spring Fair was slightly improved that year. The forest folk were few, but they were there, and there were travellers from the lands beyond the forest.

I saw the little hairy men of the forest cave buying and bargaining for pieces of glass, and lumps of crystal and of quartz rock. They paid for the glass with silver coins – the spoils of my stepdaughter's depredations, I had no doubt. When it got about what they were buying, townsfolk rushed back to their homes and came back with their lucky crystals, and, in a few cases, with whole sheets of glass.

I thought briefly about having the little men killed, but I did not. As long as the heart hung, silent and immobile and cold, from the beam of my chamber, I was safe, and so were the folk of the forest, and, thus, eventually, the folk of the town.

My twenty-fifth year came, and my stepdaughter had eaten the poisoned fruit two winters back, when the prince came to my palace. He was tall, very tall, with cold green eyes and the swarthy skin of those from beyond the mountains.

He rode with a small retinue: large enough to defend him, small enough that another monarch – myself, for instance – would not view him as a potential threat.

I was practical: I thought of the alliance of our lands, thought of the kingdom running from the forests all the way south to the sea; I thought of my golden-haired bearded love, dead these eight years; and, in the night, I went to the prince's room.

I am no innocent, although my late husband, who was once my king, was truly my first lover, no matter what they say.

At first the prince seemed excited. He bade me remove my shift, and made me stand in front of the opened window, far from the fire, until my skin was chilled stone-cold. Then he asked me to lie upon my back, with my hands folded across my breasts, my eyes wide open – but staring only at the beams above. He told me not to move, and to breathe as little as possible. He implored me to say nothing. He spread my legs apart.

It was then that he entered me.

As he began to thrust inside me, I felt my hips raise, felt myself begin to match him, grind for grind, push for push. I moaned. I could not help myself.

Snow, Glass, Apples ➤ 427

His manhood slid out of me. I reached out and touched it, a tiny, slippery thing.

'Please,' he said softly. 'You must neither move nor speak. Just lie there on the stones, so cold and so fair.'

I tried, but he had lost whatever force it was that had made him virile; and, some short while later, I left the prince's room, his curses and tears still resounding in my ears.

He left early the next morning, with all his men, and they rode off into the forest.

I imagine his loins, now, as he rode, a knot of frustration at the base of his manhood. I imagine his pale lips pressed so tightly together. Then I imagine his little troupe riding through the forest, finally coming upon the glass-and-crystal cairn of my stepdaughter. So pale. So cold. Naked beneath the glass, and little more than a girl, and dead.

In my fancy, I can almost feel the sudden hardness of his manhood inside his britches, envision the lust that took him then, the prayers he muttered beneath his breath in thanks for his good fortune. I imagine him negotiating with the little hairy men – offering them gold and spices for the lovely corpse under the crystal mound.

Did they take his gold willingly? Or did they look up to see his men on their horses, with their sharp swords and their spears, and realise they had no alternative?

I do not know. I was not there; I was not scrying. I can only imagine . . .

Hands, pulling off the lumps of glass and quartz from her cold body. Hands, gently caressing her cold cheek, moving her cold arm, rejoicing to find the corpse still fresh and pliable.

Did he take her there, in front of them all? Or did he have her carried to a secluded nook before he mounted her?

I cannot say.

Did he shake the apple from her throat? Or did her eyes slowly open as he pounded into her cold body; did her mouth open, those red lips part, those sharp yellow teeth close on his swarthy neck, as the blood, which is the life, trickled down her throat, washing down and away the lump of apple, my own, my poison?

I imagine; I do not know.

This I do know: I was woken in the night by her heart pulsing and beating once more. Salt blood dripped onto my face from above. I sat up. My hand burned and pounded as if I had hit the base of my thumb with a rock.

There was a hammering on the door. I felt afraid, but I am a queen, and I would not show fear. I opened the door.

First his men walked into my chamber and stood around me, with their sharp swords, and their long spears.

Then he came in; and he spat in my face.

Finally, she walked into my chamber, as she had when I was first a queen and she was a child of six. She had not changed. Not really.

She pulled down the twine on which her heart was hanging. She pulled off the rowan berries, one by one; pulled off the garlic bulb – now a dried thing, after all these years; then she took up her own, her pumping heart – a small thing, no larger than that of a nanny goat or a she-bear – as it brimmed and pumped its blood into her hand.

Her fingernails must have been as sharp as glass:

she opened her breast with them, running them over the purple scar. Her chest gaped, suddenly, open and bloodless. She licked her heart, once, as the blood ran over her hands, and she pushed the heart deep into her breast.

I saw her do it. I saw her close the flesh of her breast once more. I saw the purple scar begin to fade.

Her prince looked briefly concerned, but he put his arm around her nonetheless, and they stood, side by side, and they waited.

And she stayed cold, and the bloom of death remained on her lips, and his lust was not diminished in any way.

They told me they would marry, and the kingdoms would indeed be joined. They told me that I would be with them on their wedding day.

It is starting to get hot in here.

They have told the people bad things about me; a little truth to add savour to the dish, but mixed with many lies.

I was bound and kept in a tiny stone cell beneath the palace, and I remained there through the autumn. Today they fetched me out of the cell; they stripped the rags from me, and washed the filth from me, and then they shaved my head and my loins, and they rubbed my skin with goose-grease.

The snow was falling as they carried me – two men at each hand, two men at each leg – utterly exposed, and spread-eagled and cold, through the midwinter crowds, and brought me to this kiln.

My stepdaughter stood there with her prince. She watched me, in my indignity, but she said nothing.

As they thrust me inside, jeering and chaffing as they did so, I saw one snowflake land upon her white cheek, and remain there without melting.

They closed the kiln door behind me. It is getting hotter in here, and outside they are singing and cheering and banging on the sides of the kiln.

She was not laughing, or jeering, or talking. She did not sneer at me or turn away. She looked at me, though; and for a moment I saw myself reflected in her eyes.

I will not scream. I will not give them that satisfaction. They will have my body, but my soul and my story are my own, and will die with me.

The goose-grease begins to melt and glisten upon my skin. I shall make no sound at all. I shall think no more on this.

I shall think instead of the snowflake on her cheek.

I think of her hair as black as coal, her lips, redder than blood, her skin, snow-white.

The Trench

Steve Alten

The ocean will never be safe again . . .

They thought it was over. Meg, the prehistoric, sixty-foot great white shark, is dead, and her female *Megalodon* pup is safely imprisoned within the Tanaka Lagoon.

But outside hundreds of male great whites are gathering – drawn by the scent of a mature female. And the pup is now grown to seventy-two foot. And she's ready breed.

'It's definitely entertainment – and it's going to make one Meg of a movie' *Publishers Weekly*

'Jurassic shark' *Los Angeles Times*

0 7472 6303 5

Cat and Mouse

James Patterson

Psychopath Gary Soneji is back – filled with hatred and obsessed with gaining revenge on detective Alex Cross. Soneji seems determined to go down in a blaze of glory and he wants Alex Cross to be there. Will this be the final showdown?

Two powerful and exciting thrillers packed into one, with the electrifying page-turning quality that is the hallmark of James Patterson's writing, CAT AND MOUSE is the most original and audacious of the internationally bestselling Alex Cross novels.

'Patterson's action-packed story keeps the pages flicking by' *The Sunday Times*

'Patterson, among the best novelists of crime stories ever, has reached his pinnacle' *USA Today*

'Packed with white-knuckle twists' *Daily Mail*

'Patterson has a way with plot twists that freshens the material and keeps the adrenalin level high' *Publishing News*

0 7472 5788 4

HEADLINE
FEATURE

Dead Headers

James H. Jackson

Officially the British Intelligence organisation known as Executive Support doesn't exist. But for its far-from-innocent victims it is all too real. Its aim: to terrorize the terrorists, to eliminate them before they can act. Its nickname: the Dead Headers.

When a sadistic mortar attack turns the streets of Paris into a charnel house, no group claims responsibility and there are no clues to the killers' motives. But the attack is only the first piece of a terrifying jigsaw that leads the Dead Headers from a secretive German pharmaceuticals company to an Iraqi biological weapons base in the Libyan desert, from a gruesome sex-murder in London's Hammersmith to a power struggle at the heart of the Iranian revolutionary regime. And by the time the final piece is in place, the fate of millions will have been decided . . .

'Tense, well researched, fast-paced and hard-nosed'
Frederick Forsyth

'Hair-raising' *Guardian*

0 7472 5771 X

Seize The Night

Dean Koontz

One by one, the children of Moonlight Bay are disappearing. No one knows if they are dead or alive. Christopher Snow, suffering from the rare disorder xeroderma pigmentosum, has glimpsed the dark and torrid secrets of the small-town community where he has spent his entire life. And only he has the key to the truth – a truth that could only exist in the genetic chaos of Moonlight Bay.

'Not just a master of our dreams but also a literary juggler' *The Times*

'Plausibly chilling . . . Koontz at his best' *Express on Sunday*

'Fast and furious . . . like a hospital trolley on a taboggan run' *Mail on Sunday*

0 7472 5833 3

The Midnight Tour

Richard Laymon

'The Beast House – legendary site of ghastly murder! See with your own eyes where the bloody butchery took place!'

The sales pitch hasn't changed much over the years – except now you can listen to it on earphones. But the audio tour of the house only gives a sanitized version of the horrific events that made the Beast House infamous. If you want the full story, you'll have to take the Midnight Tour. Saturday nights only. Limited to thirteen courageous tourists. It begins on the stroke of midnight.

You'll be lucky to get out alive . . .

'If you've missed Laymon, you've missed a treat' Stephen King

'No one writes like Laymon and you're going to have a good time with anything he writes' Dean Koontz

'In Laymon's books, blood doesn't so much drip drip as explode, splatter and coagulate' *Independent*

'A gut-crunching writer' *Time Out*

0 7472 5827 9

The Night Crew

John Sandford

Anna Batory is a scavenger. Roaming the streets of LA by night, her video news crew hunt for sensational stories to sell to the TV networks. And Anna knows just where to dig to find the stories people want to see.

When they film an attack on the UCLA Medical Center by animal rights activists, Anna's not convinced the networks will go for it. Later the same night, however, they get the scoop they've been hoping for – a teenager jumps from a five-storey hotel window to his death and all of it's on tape.

For Anna it's the beginning of a dizzying freefall into madness, obsession and murder. Soon, disturbing connections between herself and the dead teenager start coming to light. And then she finds she is being stalked by someone who claims to know her better than she knows herself . . .

'John Sandford is a brilliant writer' *Guardian*

'In a crowded market, Sandford shines at the quality end' *Daily Telegraph*

0 7472 5621 7

If you enjoyed this book here is a selection of other bestselling titles from Headline

THE TRENCH	Steve Alten	£5.99 ☐
SION	Philip Boast	£5.99 ☐
THE HIDING GAME	Jane Brindle	£5.99 ☐
WILDWOOD	Louise Cooper	£5.99 ☐
CHANGELING	Frances Gordon	£5.99 ☐
AMONG THE MISSING	Richard Laymon	£5.99 ☐
TATHEA	Anne Perry	£5.99 ☐
VESPERS	Jeff Rovin	£5.99 ☐
CADDORAN	Roger Taylor	£5.99 ☐

Headline books are available at your local bookshop or newsagent. Alternatively, books can be ordered direct from the publisher. Just tick the titles you want and fill in the form below. Prices and availability subject to change without notice.

Buy four books from the selection above and get free postage and packaging and delivery within 48 hours. Just send a cheque or postal order made payable to Bookpoint Ltd to the value of the total cover price of the four books. Alternatively, if you wish to buy fewer than four books the following postage and packaging applies:

UK and BFPO £4.30 for one book; £6.30 for two books; £8.30 for three books.

Overseas and Eire: £4.80 for one book; £7.10 for 2 or 3 books (surface mail).

Please enclose a cheque or postal order made payable to *Bookpoint Limited*, and send to: Headline Publishing Ltd, 39 Milton Park, Abingdon, OXON OX14 4TD, UK.
Email Address: orders@bookpoint.co.uk

If you would prefer to pay by credit card, our call team would be delighted to take your order by telephone. Our direct line is 01235 400 414 (lines open 9.00 am–6.00 pm Monday to Saturday 24 hour message answering service). Alternatively you can send a fax on 01235 400 454.

Name ....

Address ....

....

....

If you would prefer to pay by credit card, please complete:
Please debit my Visa/Access/Diner's Card/American Express (delete as applicable) card number:

Signature .... Expiry Date ....